apocrypha

T. S. FERGUSON

D0922445

TATE PUBLISHING, LLC

DEDICATION

*To the One God who created all men and women
to be brothers and sisters to each other. The One
God who is calling all men unto himself.*

This work could not have been created without my constant helpmate and lifelong companion, Christina. Her immeasurable help and constant support have sustained me in more ways than I am able to express.

I also wish to thank Christopher, Scott and Alex for their support and love, and most of all for putting up with me. Thanks and help also must go to G. Walter Hansen, D. Hensley and James Ferguson who have encouraged me to tell the tale.

CHAPTER 1
HASID'S BUSINESS

Relegated to a dingy and decrepit area of Cairo, the warehouse, built around 1910, had been used for everything and anything, including use as a storage dump by the Allies during World War II. Falling into disrepair year after year, it had taken on the patina of disuse that fitted their purposes. Surrounded by a rusted chain-link fence with barbed wire strung along the top, it was land locked amidst crumbling tenement buildings inhabited by even shabbier tenants. It was perfect for their purposes; no one cared to watch the comings and goings of the men using the place.

Walking through the side door after parking his Mercedes, Hasid stared at the two men, each with a noose tied around his neck, standing stretched on their toes. For six hours they had been tied that way and as they tired the noose tightened. He knew they would eventually strangle as their weakened leg muscles quivered and gave out. A feeling of satisfaction stole over him as he looked at the Mosad agents. Catching them had taken a lot of his time during the last few weeks and he did not want them dead, yet; no, not just yet.

Savoring the time, he wanted to extract everything he could out of them, stretch this out until their fear was a palatable thing—something he could almost taste.

"Lower them, Abdullah. This is barbaric. You will kill them. I cannot imagine the pain you have been causing them. Is this any way to treat them? Next time I find you doing something like this, I will have no choice but to report you. Praise Allah, I arrived before any harm was done."

The tall Palestinian quickly lowered the rope around their necks, turning and giving Hasid a look of fear.

Looking at them gasping for air where they lay collapsed on the floor, he had to suppress a smile. "Untie them. Then give them something to eat. When they have eaten, bring them to my office. I wish to have a civilized talk with them."

Following his orders, Abdullah escorted the men to a table, setting a bowl of greasy vegetables, fruit, and glass of water in front of the two men.

"You think he is soft. Perhaps you are right, but if you do not cooperate with him—I get you back," he said. "Once back with me, time will stretch out along with your necks until you beg me ... yes, you will beg me to end it. Now eat."

Two of Abdullah's men stood to one side of the dusty warehouse holding their Uzi submachine guns at ready. Despite their weakened condition and with their ankles tied, Abdullah was taking no chances. When they finished eating, he led the older of the two down a hallway covered with dusty footprints and into an old office.

Seated behind an old oak desk, Hasid offered the man a seat. "All right, Aaron, tell me what is going on in Egypt? Why were you and your men scouring the southern Sinai?"

He was afraid that the young man knew the game, probably knew in his heart that his life was forfeit. The Mosad trained its agents well, preparing them for this type of scenario. He was trying to work on his emotions—playing the role of the good guy, while Abdullah was the bad guy. Prisoners under stress often started trusting their captors when they showed them sympathy, and he wanted to build this trust. *Would it work though?* Hasid thought.

"I know what you are doing, and we won't talk, Hasid, if that is what he called you. Aren't you the tough one who works for Quati, the one who pays the Palestinians blood money to blow up our school buses? You won't get cooperation out of me."

Hasid suppressed a smile. "Now, Aaron, I had you lowered from the rope—that is an awful way to die. We are not savages here. We are compassionate and only want peace."

"If you really wanted peace, you would stop supporting those monsters who think nothing of killing innocent children. You blow up our buses and buildings, kill our children and all in the name of what—peace?"

This was going better than he expected, the man was tough and well trained, his end would be something to savor; yes, something to savor for a long time. "I am a reasonable man. I have the power to let you go. Just think of being home with your family or being free to go wherever you want. You could even go to America or any place else you like. You don't have to go back, you know. I can arrange it all if you cooperate with me."

Hasid could see the strength return to the young man after the food and feeling the blood circulate again.

"I spit on your power. You have no power. You're just a puppet for Quati and his demonic dreams."

"I tire of this. I am able to help." Hasid took a deep breath. "But my patience is not infinite. I am going to give you one chance to help your friend and yourself. Tell us what you were doing in Sinai. I will be most generous."

Aaron just sat there and stared at him.

"I will let you and your friend go if you tell me about Sinai."

"You speak in lies—that is the only language you know. You hide behind your religion, which you have twisted into some dark thing, and then speak lies to us. All I see is a dark hand—a claw stretching out to take our peace away. Peace you say? Well, then, let me go."

Even though he prided himself on being patient, he felt his anger rise. "I will let you go, as soon as you tell me what you were doing in Sinai."

"Sinai, Sinai . . . in your worst dreams you could not imagine. I will go to heaven knowing of your fear, Hasid. I will know that in Sinai lies a secret that will crumble your world, crumble it in such a way that it will never rise again as you know it."

Hasid's anger rose in him like a burst dam. Stuffing it down with an effort, he said, "I am truly sorry it has to be this way, but I have given you your chance."

Pushing a button, he called Abdullah back to the office. "Take him to the back room, then bring the other one—I am done with this one."

A few minutes later, Abdullah led the younger man into the office. Hasid motioned for him to take the chair.

The arms of the chair were still sweaty from Aaron's palms. The younger man sat in the chair and glared up at Hasid, but said nothing.

"Your friend Aaron was very helpful, Moshe. He told me of the work you were doing in the Sinai area and I just need you to collaborate his story," Hasid said, while doodling with a pencil and pad on the desk. "I can then set you both free."

"Aaron told you nothing."

"He told me what you were doing in Sinai and what you were looking for."

"I don't know what you are talking about. What does Sinai have to do with anything?"

"Come, come. We caught you sneaking around in Sinai—you have been sending agents into the southern Sinai to disrupt our work. We know you think something is going on there that will help your cause. Now, tell me what you found—if it collaborates with what Aaron told us, you can go free."

"When you say free, you mean death, don't you? Whenever you say freedom, don't you mean bombs? Aaron told you nothing. He is far stronger than I am."

Hasid couldn't suppress a smile as he smelled the sweat of fear on the man. He savored these moments. "I am talking about your freedom here. Isn't that important to you?"

Moshe knew he and Aaron were lost when he saw Hasid smile. He couldn't help his anger from rising. "Even I know the game you are playing."

"Aaron told us everything. He even told us how old Benjamin gave your orders to you. Trust me in this, Moshe, and all will be well."

"The last time we trusted Quati, he paid the Palestinians to blow up a hotel in downtown Jerusalem. You are doing a poor job of convincing me to trust you. Set us free and we'll meet in the lobby of the Palms hotel in downtown Cairo. We can then discuss things and work on our mutual trust."

"You know I can't do that. I do not have the authority. You must collaborate Aaron's tale, and after that I will get permission to release you."

"First, you're the big man who's in charge, but now you don't have the authority? What is this, some kind of lie?"

Berating himself for the slip, he needed them to think he could do anything and had the authority to work out a deal, but now everything was falling apart. Well, it wasn't likely to succeed anyway, he told himself. He could use drugs, of course—force them to talk, but he doubted they knew anything anyway. They had been in Sinai doing surveillance, and when caught, they had taken out two of his agents. What to do with them now? Let Abdullah have them? Shoot them out in the desert—leave them for the jackals? There was a slim chance he might still get them to talk. A sly smile stole over his face. He could put them back on the rope and see how long they lasted. Abdullah would take bets on it and it might be fun to see.

❉   ❉   ❉   ❉   ❉   ❉   ❉   ❉

Four hours later Hasid came back into the warehouse. Each of their necks was stretched taunt. At first, he thought they were dead, but when he moved across the room, Moshe raised his head, his blue lips in a snarl.

"Feel like talking yet?"

Moshe could only look at him. He was too weak from standing on his toes. His legs quivered—every time he tried to relax them. The rope tightened around his neck, choking him.

Aaron turned his head and tried to spit at Hasid, but the saliva only dribbled down his chin.

"Give them some water, Abdullah. They are thirsty," Hasid commanded.

He brought a water jug over to Hasid, who poured some in a glass, drank from it, and then walked up to the pair.

"Just tell us about Sinai," he said, offering the glass.

Moshe twisted his neck to stare at Aaron, who tried to nod, giving him a brief smile. They turned to Hasid, then slumped as far as the nooses would allow, almost crushing their windpipes and strangling themselves. They bent their knees and jumped as high as their strength would allow—pulling their legs up—they fell to their deaths.

Hasid stood transfixed as defeat washed over him. How could they be so strong? If only his men were like these, how Islam would advance. He could not help but admire them—they were perfect soldiers, these Israelis. What glorious enemies Allah had given him.

CHAPTER 2
OUTSIDE CAIRO

Scott Chad and his partner Samuel Rogowski struggled up the dusty trail. Scott and Samuel had taken on a freelance project to help the people of Afghanistan chart the mineral deposits in the northern portion of the country. Staying in a village with the Mujadeen freedom fighters, they were now helping them flee a Soviet battalion that was raping and pillaging the countryside as they withdrew back home to Russia.

Scott had become fast friends with the Afghani villagers as he and Samuel worked and lived amongst them during the last few months. His preconceptions of the villagers had changed as he lived with them and he was enchanted to find them always full of laughter, lovers of chess and all other games even during the Soviet occupation.

One of the local leaders, a strong young man with a thick black beard named Sayed, stopped along the side of the rocky trail and helped Scott setup two Claymore mines to cover their escape route back into the mountains. They set the mines up on each side of the trail so they pointed down the hill to cover a spot the Russians would have to traverse to make it through the narrow pass. Scott armed the mines so they would be set off by a trip wire when the Soviet's passed. The claymores would then plaster the area with steel ball bearings moving at twice the speed of sound.

Sayed stationed his scouts at the top of the pass and gave them orders to signal Scott when the Soviets approached. The scouts signaled that they had about a half hour before the soviets entered the narrow defile. The plan was that once the mines went off, Sayed and his men that were stationed amongst the boulders along the trail would jump out to finish off any survivors.

Crouching behind a boulder, Scott was hot and nervous as he waited. He looked back up once more and saw one of the scouts waving from the top of the pass. Thinking the attack was about to commence, he climbed to the top of the boulder to better see down the trail. His heart froze as he saw Al-Bakara and his little sister Jezrella running up the rocky trail. Jumping down, he dashed out screaming and waving for them to stop but Al-Bakara and his little sister only increased their pace when they saw him.

All they saw was the tall friendly American waving to them as they ran.

Time slowed to a crawl as Al-Bakara felt his foot pull on the trip wire. He and Jezrella froze as they looked down at the wire he'd pulled loose. They knew what it meant. Their wide eyes stared at Scott as if imploring him to help them. They had seen enough children with blown off limbs from the mines left by the Soviets to know their peril. The mines exploded with a thunderous clap, covering the area with their deadly shrapnel and leaving a haze of red-mist and dust that was forever branded into Scott's mind.

Shaking himself out of his daydream, a feeling of dread and anxiety coursed through his veins. Every time he relived the experience he wondered why it had happened—*how could he have saved them, what could he have done differently?* His black moods would cycle with his stress levels and he couldn't seem to forgive himself. Feeling cold and not able to sleep, he would wake in the middle of the night with fear clutching at his heart and a feeling of dread in his veins. *What was the purpose in this? Why did this have to happen? Would he ever feel whole and happy again?*

Getting up from his chair, he went outside and stood beside the wall of the tent his interns had set up on the outskirts of Cairo, which he was using as a field office. He looked down at the Nile River and the green strip of land alongside it then turned back and stared at the pyramids being baked by the noon sun. His reverie was interrupted when his green eyes noticed the blue Chevy sedan bounce up the sandy trail in a cloud of dust to the site he was working on. A tall dark Egyptian man, dressed in an immaculate suit, climbed out of the car as he walked down to greet him.

Extending his hand, Scott said, "Rusta, come out of this sun. I've almost finished the project and I think your idea of pumping water out of the deep aquifers for irrigation will actually work."

Leading him into the tent and what passed for an office, he showed him over to a large table strewn with charts, computers and papers. "You'll find it all in our reports, of course, and I think you'll be surprised as to the low initial costs."

Rusta held up his hand, looked sternly and him and said, "That can wait. I've another survey project that I want you to start right away. I've brought the paperwork and parameters for the job with me."

Scott sighed as he sat down in an old worn camp chair. His craggy face, rumpled red hair and tired green eyes showed some of the stress he was feeling, but his inner strength hid his fatigue well. "What's the big hurry? It's not like you to come all the way out here to discuss a new project." Scott's lanky six-foot-four-inch frame appeared deflated as he slouched in the chair.

Rusta leaned forward looking him in the eye. "The President's pushing me to get this done. He wants you. Wants you because of your reputation and because you went to school at the Colorado School of Mines. He wants an excellent geologist and surveyor, not someone who will rape our country. He likes the ecological aspects of your reports and the way you design your projects."

"There are plenty of other surveyors. As I said, why the rush?"

"Someone's pushing the President to have this completed quickly for reasons I don't understand yet."

Scott held up his hand, but Rusta went on. "It's a survey for the whole blooming southern Sinai Peninsula! We thought about hiring Arkady the Russian, but you know how much I detest working with him. I'm getting pushed to have this completed quickly. The pressure's immense if they're thinking about using Arkady instead of you. If you decide to take it, watch your back though!"

The last comment caught his attention and he looked at Rusta in the eye. "What do you mean, watch my back? It's not like you to talk like that?"

"We've worked on a number of jobs together for a long time now. We've sat in long meetings and I've a feeling about this project that I've never had before. I've heard rumors about something going on that I can't quite put my finger on. When I try to find out, all I get is silence and strange whispers in the halls."

"Your warning to watch my back . . . may . . . I don't know. I need to talk with Samuel first. We're just about finished here and the only thing I have lined up is a project in the Yucatan working on a meteor impact site. As I recall, the British did the last decent survey of the Sinai in 1896, and before that Napoleon. It's tempting . . . but. Give me some time and come see me in the morning and we'll talk about it."

"Think it over and talk with Samuel tonight if you need to. I'll bring the papers by in the morning and see what you think."

As Scott sat down to breakfast the next morning, he saw Rusta driving back up the bumpy trail to the work site. He walked up the slope to the command tent and said, "Good morning, did you decide yet?"

"Do you have the details?" Scott asked.

Rusta was dressed in a white linen tropical suit that looked expensive and blended well with his dark complexion. Nodding to Scott, he got up and looked quickly out the door. "The president called again to discuss the project we talked about. The Sinai's mostly untapped, with a wealth of mineral resources. We need a comprehensive geological survey, just like the one you did for the Saudi's on the Empty Quarter. We'll pay your usual fee plus a standard bonus for any minerals or oil-bearing formations you find. We want you to take the job, but you have to start right away. I know your assistants can wrap up this current project."

"You said this was a rush job and didn't understand why. What's going on? You then told me to watch my back."

Rusta looked Scott in the eye. "There are strong political forces at work. More than I see in a whole year working for the Ministry. It's rare when the president takes a personal interest in any survey, let alone one in the Sinai. I've heard rumors, but don't have any facts to substantiate them. Rumors that some of the Islamic extremists are interested in something. The scuttlebutt says they're agitated for some reason."

"Where do you want us to start?"

"I think a good place to set up your base camp would be in the area near St. Catherine's monastery, but you can set up wherever you wish. We are hoping you may find some oil fields and other minerals that will help our country grow."

His curiosity was piqued, but also his anxiety over the cryptic warnings pushed at him, "What's all this rumor stuff about the Islamic extremists?"

"I haven't made the connection yet. They are interested in this area and I'm worried. Quati's name has been whispered and that alone is reason enough to keep your eyes open. This project's important. It may do more for my country than the deep wells. I cannot stress how much it could help us if you found oil or other minerals!"

Scott felt an odd tug at his conscience. *Something . . . a feeling about Afghanistan perhaps,* he thought, *a mixture of dread and hope.* Without really knowing why, he held up his hand. "My mind's made up . . . it's as if . . . as if I should take the job . . . it's just something I have to do! Am I making any sense?"

Rusta smiled. "Are you sure?"

"More than ever. It feels like something I have to do. Sounds silly, but I feel as if I should do the project. After what you said last night I slept on it and know it's something I need to do. Did you bring the paperwork and parameters of the project?"

Opening his briefcase, he took out a sheath of papers. "I've drawn up the contract outlining the boundaries of the area to be surveyed. Take your time, but not too much. I've told you this is a rush job and we have to get going on it. The contracts are all the standard stuff that we've used before. The only difference is an escalation of the bonus clause to ten percent, instead of the usual three."

Scott lifted an eyebrow. "That's a seven percent difference. What's the reason?"

"Hazard pay! Call it that, if you want, but I think the president's anxious to get you on this job, providing you do it quickly. Remember what I told you earlier about the Islamic extremists? I think the president's being pressured from all sides to have this done before June."

"Before June? I don't think that's possible. I have to assemble a team, get equipment, arrange the financing and all the other details I need for this type of job."

Rusta smiled as he pulled more documents from his briefcase and handed them over. "Financing is not a problem. Here's a letter of credit for $750,000 drawn on Banc One. You can assemble your team, procure your equipment, hire transportation and get the project under way. You may draw on it as long as you provide the proper accounting, contractor's sworn statements and affidavits as the job progresses. Should you need further funds you'll have to show progress reports and provide detailed information regarding your findings and status of the project."

The last vestiges of doubt left him and he laughed. "It appears you've done all your homework, I guess I'll start right away."

"Good. Assemble your team and we'll meet at St. Catherine's in a couple of days."

They stood and shook hands. Watching as Rusta left, Scott wondered what he'd walked into. Outside, the day appeared to take on new meaning as he watched the sun rising over the Nile and feluccas beating upstream to the sounds of humanity in the morning air. The smell of cooking and firewood wafted gently to his nose, giving him a sense that things hadn't changed much in 2,000 years.

Rusta's cryptic warnings gave rise to a sense of foreboding that was hard to shake, but also a sense of excitement and purpose. It was a feeling that he was meant to do this job, for reasons he could not fathom. Pausing under a fig tree as he walked through the garden, he listened to the cries of the merchants in the Souks. Looking at the sun, he noticed a halo of dust and smog around it. Be good to be out in the field again, he thought, as a shiver ran through him, but a sense of peace and purpose crept in after.

Shaking off his feelings, he walked over to the phone and asked the operator to get his assistant back in the states, hoping his right-hand man was in. The operator called back a moment later connecting him.

CHAPTER 3
FUNDAMENTAL THOUGHTS

The shiny black Mercedes 600 raced through the outskirts of town scattering dust and pedestrians as it made its way toward the Palace Hotel. Small children, old men and women dressed in Chadors, hurried to get out of the way of the speeding car. The dark tinted windows kept any bystanders from seeing inside, and the poverty of the people on the street kept them from bothering anyway. The car entered the plaza of the hotel, circling through the drive and pulled into a side entrance at the rear where the occupants quickly got out of the car.

Two men in western clothes hurried into the rear entrance where a tough-looking man dressed in a threadbare uniform motioned for them to walk down a dingy hallway. They briskly walked down the corridor and up a flight of stairs, entering a spartan room, dimly lit by a single bare bulb dangling from the ceiling. The room was filthy. Small scraps of paper lay on the floor and cobwebs covered the walls. The greasy windows were covered with filth and grime. Only a weak light filtered through from the low November sun. Mustafa and Hasid stood waiting for the general to speak.

General Quati stood looking at the windows and slowly turned their way. Looking resplendent in his dress uniform with the gold braids and medals on his chest, he fished a cigarette from a pack, lit it, and watched the smoke rise through the pale sunlight coming through the dingy window before he spoke. "I tell you, Hasid, the infidels will rue the day they started this war. Holy Islam's place will be assured far into the future when Allah's plan unfolds!"

"The day long foretold is coming, my General," Hasid said.

Quati threw his cigarette on the floor, grinding it into the grime with the toe of his boot. "You are right, Hasid. We cannot let the enemy find the key before us, the key that is the sign that will bring about a new Jihad. We must keep our eyes open and be prepared to stop Chad and the Interior Minister from gaining any information before we get it ourselves. Do we have people in place in Sinai?"

Hasid's heart stopped and he caught himself at the general's words.

Chad? What did he mean by Chad. Did he mean Scott Chad? He controlled himself and quickly stammered. "Our top operatives are in Cairo right now and ready to move at a moments' notice. I have placed some of our men in Sinai. They are awaiting your orders." Hasid paused and looked at General Quati. "How did you know the Egyptians were going to hire Chad? Based on our people in the President's office, I thought they were going to hire Arkady, the Russian geologist."

"I have people in the office of the Interior Minster. They keep me informed. Is there something bothering you about this, Hasid? You do not look yourself. Did everything go all right with the Mosad agents?"

"Yes, but they would not talk and I didn't get anything of value from them. Sometimes I wish our men were trained as well." His mind spun over the new events; *Chad, why did it have to be Chad?*

"I trust you will handle this operation personally. Are you sure you are feeling all right?"

Composing himself, Hasid felt an unfamiliar twisting in his gut, a feeling he had not felt in a long time. He was proud that his peers considered him the man of ice when he was on a mission. The emotions he was now feeling felt so foreign. He hadn't felt anything but anger in more than sixteen years. Why did Scott Chad have to be the one?

"It is nothing, General Quati. It is my duty to carry out your orders. The infidels must not succeed in this. Chad is only a geological surveyor and amateur archeologist. He is nothing we cannot handle."

Mustafa turned to General Quati. "Do not underestimate him. Our people in Saudi Arabia say he is a tougher adversary than any of the other scientists sent over by the west to help rape the wealth of our soil. The others were weak and quickly folded whenever we had dealings with them. Chad is different apparently. They say he broke the neck of one of the Taliban with his bare hands when he was in Afghanistan. There is also a rumor he is working undercover for the CIA, but it has never been substantiated."

Fishing another cigarette out of the pack, Quati lit it and said, "He is tough, apparently. But we have dealt with many tough people before—I expect you to handle him. Do I make myself clear?"

"As I said, I do not think it wise to underestimate him," Mustafa said, as he shuffled his feet and looked at Hasid. "We have come long and far because we have been careful, not careless. Being the first to find the holy writings is our first concern. This is important to all of Islam and particularly the future of our country."

Quati took a long drag on his cigarette. "We cannot be timid, particularly when dealing with westerners. I don't like to show weakness, the time is coming and will soon come when Islam's banner will fly from the top of the tallest buildings and flagpoles in the West."

"Our operatives are in place," Mustafa said.

Quati leaned against a clean part of the wall, watching the smoke rise from the cigarette. The smoke slowly curled up and around the bare bulb. Pushing off the wall, he paced back and forth, finally turning to the two men. "Chad should be on his way to Sinai tonight. His partner is also on his way from the United States. See to it that Jared and his men take out Rogowski. I want to set an example. Let's see how tough they really are, see what they are made of. Make sure someone is watching Chad's every move and get someone inside his organization. I want one of our people working on his team. We need to know what is going on the moment it happens. This is important. Our future and all Islam may well depend on it. I will brook no failure on this. Make sure our men know that their very lives depend on success."

Bowing to the general, they left the room. Hasid let out a deep breath once back outside. He looked up at the darkening sky, which seemed to have taken on a streaked grey color as if scrubbed by a dirty rag once too many times. Shivering, he found it hard to shake the feeling of dread he was experiencing. Usually he felt exuberant when starting a mission. Chad! Why did it have to be Chad? His gut twisted as he wondered if he could truly follow his master's orders. He had not felt this way in years. Was this a portent of things to come? His mind drifted back sixteen years.

He and Scott ran through the backyard, as twilight descended on the little town, feeling as if the very wind was their ally. Running silently at Scott's side, they prowled the neighborhood. Their lungs took in great drafts of air scented with the smell of fresh cut grass and growing corn from the distant fields. The fresh air fueled their young and tireless muscles as they ran across their territory, heading to the home of Tommy Baker, where his mother was cooking a barbeque. They were the lead agents for the Backyard Marauders and could not be seen taking the sidewalks for the four-block trek.

The backyards were open to them in ways no adult could imagine. Stopping for a moment by some bushes, they looked at the lights shining out of Mrs. Buckhols's house. Hasid leaned over to Scott. "Should we check it out and make a report?"

"Nah, she's going to stay up late and watch TV. It doesn't look like she's having company tonight. We can check it out on the way back, see if anything's changed."

With a quick nod to Scott, they dashed through the bushes and onto Jefferson Street, where they met up with their friends. The party was wonderful, hamburgers and hot dogs with all the usual trimmings. Hasid never ate the hot dogs, and never told Scott why, but took full advantage of the hamburgers, chips and Coca Cola.

After the party, they flitted from dark shadow to shadow as they made their way back home. Stopping once again outside Mrs. Buckhols's house, they looked it over, as the ghoulish blue flicker from the television lit the curtains from the den.

He leaned over to Scott and whispered. "Let's sneak up and look in the window."

"You first."

"I went first last time. You go first."

"No, I went first last time. Your turn."

"You're chicken. I went first last time."

"Let's go together then."

Nodding, they crept up on the deck to the back of the home, stepping carefully lest the boards creak. Bending over and crab walking, they made their way to the window on the back of the home and slowly lifted their heads to peer inside.

It took a moment for their eyes to adjust. The television was facing away from them, lighting the back wall of the room. Slowly looking around the room, they finally made out Mrs. Buckholz sitting on the couch.

"Run!" he yelled to Scott.

Needing no urging, they quickly dashed off the deck as fast as their legs could carry them. Dodging the large pines in the center of the block, they crossed the street without breaking stride, running three blocks without stopping.

"What was it?" Scott asked him.

"I don't know. I've never seen anything like it. Maybe she's one of the clay people, like in that movie."

"Come on, she's not one of the clay people."

"You never know. Maybe she sheds her skin at night and soaks up the moisture in the air to regenerate or something." He could remember the fear he felt even now, sixteen years later.

"It's probably just one of those makeup things women do. I saw my mom with a bunch of cold cream on one night. It scared the heck out of me."

He heard his mother's bell ring. "Night games later, in Tim's back yard."

"Yeah, and you're going to lose again."

"What makes you think that, Scott?"

"You always do. You pick the wrong team."

"I get to pick first this time, and we'll see who loses."

Meeting up later with their friends, they divided into teams in Tim Stevens's backyard. He and Scott acted as captains, chose their teams and staked out their offensive and defensive strategies. They all wore black clothing and smeared their faces with shoe polish to blend into the shadows. They headed off to defend their flags at opposite ends of the block.

The homes in the area were set on about an acre and a small creek ran through the neighborhood, overgrown with bushes and trees. Scott set his team up and posted his defensemen. The rules were simple: capture the other guy's flag, don't get tagged. Simple but tough for you had to crawl through the bushes, creeping silently up on the other team.

Hasid set up his defense and then went to capture Scott's flag. He knew Scott would hang back and defend the flag so he sent out two of his players, one to the right the other to the left of Scott's flag. Staying back, he could still remember the tense feeling of the night, the smell in the air—his senses and ears were hyper tuned to the night noises, as he waited.

His team crept through the bushes near Scott's flag. Pausing to listen, he sent another of his players off to the right hand side of the flag to create a diversion. Their job was to pull Scott and his boys away from defending the flag while Hasid ran in and captured it. It was a brilliant plan, and if fairly executed, he had faith that it would work this time. Creeping through the bushes to his left, he waited until he heard the commotion of Scott's team chasing off his team. He then dashed toward Scott's flag.

Somehow Scott hadn't fallen for the diversion and had hung back, sensing when he ran up and calmly stepping out from behind a bush and tagging him on the shoulder as he rushed up.

The feeling of defeat washed over him. "How did you know I was there?"

"You always go to the left when you send your team right. Try a new tactic next time," was all he said as they heard bell ring again.

"Time to go," Scott said.

"Race you back," he said with a smile as the game was forgotten.

Running toward home, they never could have guessed what the bonding of their shared experiences would mean.

Two years later, they celebrated their fifteenth birthdays the same month. The July day was perfect as they lay around the pool. It was one of those days when they would get out of the water, dry off, get hot, and then dive back in to cool off. Hasid was feeling wonderful after beating Tim Steven's team at water polo. They lounged in the chairs, watching the summer cumulus clouds float by. He felt alive and immortal, as only a fifteen-year-old can.

Samantha Eggers climbed out of the pool and smiled at Scott and Hasid. Her blonde hair tied in a ponytail, bounced along on the back of her head.

His black hair contrasted with Scott's red as they watched her walk up.

"Why don't you guys quit lazing around—show me one of those famous dives?"

Hasid perked up, as she looked at him. "Which one do you want to see?"

"The full gainer, with the half twist."

"Your wish is my command, my lady."

Scott got up and whispered. "What's the matter with you. You can't swim—you play water polo in the shallow end. What are you trying to prove?"

"I can do it. I've seen you do it a hundred times." He remembered his fear of the water, but also the larger fear of not being accepted by this beautiful girl.

"Yeah, but you can't swim worth a darn."

"All I have to do is push off the bottom."

He smiled when he saw Scott expel a breath. "I'll stand on the side and watch. Be careful."

Getting up from the lounge, he walked over to the high dive, smiling at Samantha.

Tim Stevens carefully watched as he climbed the ladder. Stevens had created on and off trouble for him during the last few years, and it had lately become worse as Stevens had put on weight. He liked to bully them, but his size was turning to fat like his father.

Walking out on the end of the high dive, Hasid placed his toes on the board as he had seen Scott do. It looked awfully high up from up there, but he wasn't going to chicken out now. He started flexing his knees and said a silent prayer. Just as he launched, Stevens snapped a towel at him, but his leap was effortless as his fifteen-year-old body carried him into the air. He twisted and turned and it felt as if it were going to be a perfect dive. Setting himself up and over he headed back down when his forehead caught the end of the diving board. All he remembered later was a thud, no pain. He still made the dive.

Scott told him later what happened next.

Scott was instantly on his feet, running at Stevens.

"What the heck is the matter with you, Stevens? Have you lost all your senses?"

"What a baby you are, Chad. Want to do something about it?"

Scott turned and looked at where Hasid entered the water, but he couldn't see him moving. He should have been coming up by now, but appeared to be hanging lifeless and still deep in the pool. Scott and Samantha stood a moment transfixed at the sight then Scott sprang into action, diving into the pool going deep. Grabbing Hasid around the neck, he pushed off on the bottom. Hasid was limp and lifeless in his Scott's arms and there was a red smear in the water coming from the top of his head. Breaking the surface, Scott kicked toward the side, pulling him out on the deck. A large gash across his forehead was oozing blood into his eyes and he didn't appear to be breathing. Taking his pulse, Scott felt a thready heartbeat. Quickly turning Hasid's head, Scott tiled it back, took a deep breath, held the nose and blew into Hasid's mouth, inflating his chest.

A deep cough and gush of water came out of his mouth.

Two weeks later, Hasid's father was transferred back to Iran. He and Scott kept in touch on and off over the years as he moved to different countries across Europe and the Middle East.

His father was killed four years later when he was on a business trip to Haifa, as he was caught in the cross fire of an Israeli operation against some Palestinians who had blown up a bus full of tourists and children.

❋ ❋ ❋ ❋ ❋ ❋ ❋ ❋

His feelings died the day his father was shot, so why was he feeling anything now? He shook himself then looked over at Mustafa. "Quati will be a rage if we don't find them first. I hope it is what we are looking for. I would hate to go to all this trouble when it would be best if the writings were never found. Get Talbin in place. He should know our goals. Fisal and Abdullah should watch over things and keep an eye on Chad's camp while they are working with Dr. Abu. We must be careful. We have no way of knowing if this information should be just left to lie for all time. I am afraid that we may need Chad to find the writings, and if he does—then we have to decide what to do with them."

Mustafa looked perplexed. "I do not know either. You may be right and they should be left alone. How are we to know though? I think the general is correct to keep an eye on Chad. We cannot let that American infidel find the holy writings first."

Inwardly Hasid cringed. "Chad's good. I am sure he is better than Abu. At least he is far tougher. I have met Abu. Competent, yes, but not a free thinker. I still think we have to give Chad free rein—it is people like Abu who worry me in the end. They are too rigid."

"Are you sure we can trust Abu?"

"I don't know. One thing I do know is that Quati said to use him and I do not wish to argue with him on this point. Quati has something over Abu."

"That concerns me, too. I do not think we can trust this Dr. Abu. He likes money too much."

"It is as Allah wills. We will soon find out. Until then we shall do as ordered. The other thing I do not understand is why Quati wants to take out Rogowski. It is hard to trust Jared. He is strong, but he is a brute. He is all muscle and no brains. He likes to kill for the sport, not for our ideals. Do you think he will succeed?"

"No. I think Rogowski will prove far tougher than Quati thinks. I have heard of his exploits in Afghanistan and do not think he is to be trifled with. When Jared fails, it will tip our hat to Chad, and then Quati will be in another rage. Who knows what Chad will do then. We must obey Quati and see this through, as Allah wills . . . yes. As you said, we may need Chad before the end. Abu may not be able to find the writings, and odd as it may seem—an infidel may be Allah's instrument."

"You know the price of failure?"

"Yes, I know the price. We must not fail, no matter what!"

"I need better intelligence about Chad and his companions. There may also be others who might have knowledge of these things. I do not want the Iranians or Iraqis showing up out there in the desert, and what if the hated Mosad knows something? They are not to be dismissed. This is like a big battle which is slowly unfolding; where it goes we do not know, but must be ready. We do not know if we are making the right moves with our men. There may be other forces at work that we know nothing about."

"The price of failure will be great, indeed. It is a slender reed we are relying on. One that can break."

"Remember that a reed can bend with the times," Hasid quietly replied as they drove off in the car.

A small man wrapped in rags made his way down the alley behind the hotel after the car left. Glancing over his left shoulder, he bent down and retrieved a small electronic object from under the window, then quickly rounded the corner of the street.

CHAPTER 4

SINAI

A deep baritone voice sang through the lines, "Rogowski here!"

"We have a new job, Samuel. I want you to book a flight to Cairo on the next plane. Bring the Geodimeter, G.P.S. equipment, two laptops and the seismic sounding equipment. Call Jim Buhl over at NSA and get the most recent aerial photographs, maps, satellite imagery—including infrared of the Southern Sinai, and anything else you can get your hands on, then call Jenny Larson with the Geological Survey and get all the standard stuff."

He felt good to be talking with his partner and assistant. They'd worked together for many years, traveling across the globe on surveys in Saudi Arabia, Afghanistan and anywhere else interesting work would take them.

Samuel Rogowski, son of an English mother and Polish Russian father, was a short-swarthy fireplug of a man, who never knew when to quit. The word 'no' wasn't in his vocabulary. Carrying his stocky frame with aplomb, he usually had bed-head of one sort or another, rarely having his sandy-blond hair styled or even combed. Piercing blue eyes that sparkled with intelligence belied a mind that was both quick and full of wit, which led to an even larger laugh. A large bushy mustache, hairy arms and torso, gave him a dwarfish look. It was a mistake to categorize him until you knew of his kindly demeanor and quick intelligence.

Rogowski's strongest skills were computer programming, fixing any-thing mechanical, and being an incredible marksman. Spending a couple of years in the Marines after graduating from college, he earned a marksmanship badge along with other honors in a Special Forces unit, but this came nowhere near describing his talents. Not one to love the military life, he never looked back once receiving his discharge papers.

Able to close down bars, get out of scrapes and fights, he and Scott contrasted each other. Scott's six-foot-four-inch frame of sinewy muscle and Samuel's stevedore arms and short stature belied their hearty fun loving nature. Always willing to help each other, they were inseparable.

Whenever Scott needed someone to watch his back, Samuel was who he wanted.

"Whoever you're with, gently say goodbye. We need to get on this job now. They've raised our usual bonus clause to ten percent instead of the usual three. They want this project completed right away."

"Ten percent? We'll be lucky if we collect anything! What's the job?"

"A survey of the southern Sinai area. We're going to need trucks, workmen, equipment, and all the usual stuff. A small plane for aerial work would come in handy; we'll charter one if we have to. Water will be a problem and you should send the small desalinization plant over. It's going to be cold, hot, dusty and probably a whole lot of fun. We'll have terrorists breathing down our necks and there won't be any women for miles around except some nuns at the monastery. So get your butt in gear and get over here. You're missing all the fun!"

After getting off the phone, he made a list of other personals he'd need. Rusta should be able to supply some of the local workmen, but the tough spot would be finding a botanist who'd be capable of writing the ecological report. Writing a brief job description for the position, he posted it on his web site, requesting resumes and references.

E-mailing the Coast and Geodetic Survey, he requested any information they might have on potential oil or mineral formations in the Sinai and contacted the Smithsonian Institute and National Geographic Society for information on any archeological sites or finds in the area. Finally, he sent Sadat a request for clarification about the exact boundaries of the survey area and requested a list of any archeological sites from the Egyptian government.

The last time he'd been offered such a large project was when he surveyed part of the Empty Quarter for the Saudis. The project took a year and half and he had a lot of help. Finding the new oil field had raised his reputation to a new level but the black moods remained. There was something about this project that gave him hope. He didn't understand it, but felt that he had to follow it until the end, wherever that was.

❄ ❄ ❄ ❄ ❄ ❄ ❄ ❄

The cerulean blue sky arched overhead on the early November day, the desert still hot. Trudging up the slope, Scott entered the command tent, his mind full of doubts about hiring a woman for the botanist position. Feeling ill at ease, he easily came up with excuse after excuse on why he shouldn't hire her. She was certainly well qualified. It wasn't like him to discriminate, even against a woman, he reminded himself, but he was working in an Islamic area, which could bring out many problems when western women were around.

He tried to shake off the black mood that threatened to fill him with anxiety. He knew that if he continued, he'd beat up on himself and then not be able to sleep at night. Even if he did, he'd wake up a couple hours later filled with foreboding. Whenever the black dogs attacked, they awakened the painful, unforgiving memories that seemed to rob his life of all joy. When the moods came, they sapped his energy and it took tremendous work to dispel the melancholy.

Walking over to the chart table, he slammed his hand down. "Hillard's out, I think I'm going to have to contact that woman botanist from Illinois."

His new intern, Luke, looked over to where his boss was standing and didn't dare say a word when he saw Scott angry.

Taking a deep breath, Scott plopped into a chair. "She has a good resume, but I think it's going to be difficult for an American woman around here."

He played with his breakfast—his appetite gone, partly from the black mood and partly because of the decision he had to make on the Botanist issue. Something someone once said nagged at his thoughts. What was it? Something about a plan laid out for his life.

Shrugging at his thought, he decided. Since it's right in front of me, I'll do it—who knows, maybe that's the plan. He felt instantly better once he'd made up his mind.

Back at his computer, he composed an e-mail and sent off an offer and contract for the botanist position to the woman in Illinois. She replied an hour later, agreeing to take the job immediately, saying she would fly to London and then on to Cairo. Later that morning he received confirmation that she would be on the next day's flight.

The dawn was bright and clear the following morning, his mood matching the sky. Ali, one of Scott's hired workmen, had driven earlier to Cairo to pick up the new botanist. Her flight was due at 11:00.

With the November sun still about a hand above the horizon, Ali arrived with the new botanist. Stepping out of the truck, she walked up the slope to where Scott was waiting.

Standing outside his tent, he felt nervous and like a schoolboy as she walked up. The email picture didn't do her justice. Twenty-eight, five-foot-ten and weighing a hundred and twenty five pounds, she was, to Scott's eyes at any rate, perfect. Dressed for travel, she was wearing a long khaki skirt, long sleeved shirt and running shoes. Covered by a scarf to keep off the dust, her long red hair glowed with golden highlights in the remaining light.

Scott extended his hand. "Welcome, you must be Julia Apostoli."

"You must be the great Scott Chad," she said with a smile that showed her white teeth, while shaking his hand. "You don't know how much I've wanted to meet you. I've heard so much about you over the years."

Blushing at her praise, he answered. "Welcome aboard, but please don't be condescending, I'm not great or anything else for that matter, just a humble scientist trying to get a job done. Let me show you around. I'll introduce you to some of the workers. We have a fair-sized team here, a lot of equipment and a tight schedule to keep if we're going to get this project done in seven months. Hope you're up to the task."

Walking toward the main command tent, Scott couldn't help but notice that she wasn't like some of the other women he'd worked with over the years. He was having difficulty taking his eyes off her and there seemed to be some indefinable tension that she held and threw back at him. He didn't know what to make of it and knew even less how to figure it out.

"Over to your right's the mess tent and straight ahead is the command tent. That's where we meet and plan the survey for each day and wrap up at night. If you leave camp, you have to sign out on the board and take someone with you. The board is set up at the end of the tent, note where you're going and when you'll be back. The data tent is off to the side, over to your left above the little valley," Scott said sweeping his arm toward another tent as they walked. "Our sleeping tents are up there on top of that ridge. We might move those later, depending on the wind that comes up during the winter. They should be okay, since we have heaters installed in them. Your tent's the one on the right, mine is next to it. Ali will put your bags in while I show you the rest of the camp."

"Quite a good setup, having only been here a few weeks," she said.

"Yes, but we've done this before."

"I don't see a latrine?"

Scott pointed down the valley. "Shower tent's down there, off to the far left. It has a couple of private thrones that are plumbed to a small anaerobic treatment system that we've installed. Don't need an outhouse or have to put up with the smell. We need to set an example for the environmentalists when we turn in our report. The only problem may be the amount of water it takes to run it."

She smiled and said, "It's great to set an example and not pollute the environment. It's more important to teach the local inhabitants about pollution and safe drinking water."

As they entered the command tent, Samuel, Alex and Luke stood up. Walking up with a big grin on his face, Samuel extended his hand. "You must be Julia. Of course you are; we've been expecting you. Come on, sit down and take a load off. Have some chow, you must be famished by now eating airplane food." Samuel had a completely disarming effect on women. It could be that he was only five-six or the huge grin he always wore. Whatever it was, it instantly worked on Julia and they were soon fast friends.

Alex and Luke followed the group to the main table where they sat around discussing the survey, what had been completed so far and their plans for the coming week. Good hot food was served all around and as night was closing in, they soon started drifting off to their own tents.

"Well, I'm glad you made it safely," Scott said.

For some reason he felt like a schoolboy, nervous and tongue-tied around her and didn't quite know what to say. Whenever he had been nervous as a teenager, he'd been able to come up with some sort of inane remark or another, trying to put the other person off-balance, not knowing what he really wanted to say. Now that he was older, he tended not to say anything when he felt nervous.

Walking up to the tent she turned to him. "I want to thank you again for offering me the job," she said, extending her hand. "Good night, Scott. I have a feeling this is all going to work out well."

Tension erupted immediately the next morning.

Julia came to the mess tent wearing a long Egyptian style skirt with a long sleeved blouse, her long red-hair tied up in a ponytail that swayed back and forth across her back as she walked. The Muslim work force was in an uproar because she wasn't wearing the traditional scarf or veil.

"Hijab, hijab, does the woman have no decency!" Achmed, the Arab foreman yelled, while pointing his finger at Julia. Scott had long ago given up trying to figure out the Middle Eastern frame of mind, at least as far as it related to their women. He'd never understood their vehemence in this regard, knowing it had to do with their religion, and because they were just so hot headed and conservative.

"What's the trouble here, Achmed?"

"Hijab, Mr. Chad . . . that woman, she is trying to dress like an Egyptian woman, then leaves her head uncovered. That is an insult to our way of life."

"Don't take that tone with me, Achmed. She's a western woman. You know western women don't dress like Muslim ones and that hasn't bothered you before. They don't practice the wearing of the hijab. Why's it bothering you now?"

Achmed snapped. "She is a western woman and is trying to dress as an Egyptian without the hijab. My new men are upset and don't want to work with her. She must dress correctly, as a woman should. This is an insult to us. The men will not tolerate it. Without the hijab, she looks like a whore! That is how we see this and feel about it. She must dress properly!"

"I said calm your tone, Achmed! Which men are complaining, who are they?"

"That doesn't matter, Mr. Chad. I'm sorry for yelling, but we've always felt uncomfortable when western women work on these projects. We know westerners are different—they dress differently—but this is a Muslim country. It would just be better if she dressed properly, as a woman should."

Julia snapped at the foreman, "This is the twenty first century, not the dark ages. We're all scientists here. What did you expect?"

Scott interceded when he saw Achmed cringe at being sternly addressed by a woman in front of his men. "Julia, you're going to have to conform to their customs and wear the hijab, veil or whatever you want to call it. The way I understand it, they'll not tolerate it for you to dress this way. It upsets the whole work force and disrupts what we're trying to accomplish. You must dress to please them, dress completely like an Egyptian woman or dress as a westerner. Do you understand?" Scott stated, the anger rising in his voice.

He really disliked confronting women, and he responded even worse whenever someone yelled at him. The whole scene was threatening to bring on the black shroud of his melancholy. He could feel his nervous tension rising as the day's routine was disrupted. Whenever his anxiety rose, he tended to focus the tension inward and then had trouble keeping his anger in check. He wasn't really angry with Julia. She was actually trying to show respect by wearing the long Egyptian skirt and blouse but didn't understand the Muslim mindset. He was just frustrated with the whole thing and wanted to get on with the survey. He couldn't afford to go into a black mood when things were about to really get underway.

Julia's eyes flashed at Scott and Achmed. "What do you mean dress like a Muslim woman or dress like a western one?"

Achmed looked to Scott for help. "Mr. Chad, please, I just want my workmen to get on with their work."

"Julia, I know you're trying to do the right thing by dressing in the Egyptian manner, but I'm asking you, please, to respect the workers' wishes," Scott said, as his anger slowly dissipated.

His eyes flashed at Achmed, then looked at Julia with a questioning hope that she'd follow through with what he was asking, but it was too late, his earlier outburst had done its work.

"You can be sure I'll dress to please everyone here. You can bet it, Mister," she said as she stalked out, walking up the hill to her tent.

An hour later, she called out from her tent, "Scott, would you come up here, please?"

He'd sent the crews out to get their work done and finally been able to shake off the morning's black mood. Work usually dispelled the black fog that threatened whenever he felt stressed. Looking up the hill toward the sound of her voice, he walked up to her tent, pulled back the flap and stood there speechless.

She was wearing a blue jean mini skirt, tall boots with high heels and a knit top that seemed a size or so too small, which only accentuated her figure. Her hair was still up in a ponytail and she had put on big gold hoop earrings and red lipstick.

"Now do I look like a western woman? Have I dressed to please?" she said with a pouty smile.

"Well, I must say . . . I like . . . but I don't think that's really your style. You know if you go out like that I'm going to have a revolution with the workmen and probably our American interns who won't be able to keep their minds on their work, let alone me," he said with a hearty laugh. "I'm sorry, but Achmed's outburst and mind-set have disrupted my morning enough, I shouldn't have lost my temper, I'm sorry! My temper gets the better of me once again. We need to go over the charts of the survey area, so you're brought up to speed and I need to get you grounded and trained on the equipment we're going to be use."

"Well, Mr. Chad, what charts do you want to go over?" she said, leaning over a table, staring up at Scott. She didn't want to waste the hour of work she'd put in or the fun of the moment. To see him contrite and fumbling over himself was probably not something she'd see again and she relished his apology and humility.

"These are men of extreme faith. Their faith motivates their whole lives. It's not that I agree with their methods or extremism, I don't. But I do admire the depth of their belief. What do you believe in, Julia?"

His question and candor shocked her. "The only thing I believe in is myself! My parents died when I was young and I've seen and heard a lot of religious mumbo-jumbo over the years. I believe in myself and everything else seems like just dumb luck. I believe in the strength I have, my intelligence and ability to learn, hard work and a good plan. That's what I believe in."

A short look of sadness crossed his face. He didn't have any particular belief either, and could relate. It just seemed shallow and that something was missing. That was his credo, too, wasn't it? Believe in yourself, you can do it if you only put your mind to it. But something was creeping in to his thoughts, something bigger . . . what was it? His problem was his intelligence and he habitually and logically tried to sort out all the evidence before making a decision. His mind quickly ran over some of the decisions and beliefs he'd made over the years. What was it about the faith of these Muslims? Was there a God who cared for man? Every culture had a religion that believed in some type of god. Some were weird and primitive, others ornate and full of mysticism. Where was truth? But he couldn't dwell on it too much; he had a job to do.

"Look we need to go over the charts of the southern area by the two gulfs, the aerial photos, too, and maybe the gulf between the male and female mind. That's the one I really want to understand." He said, as he laughed and turned toward the tent flap to leave.

She chuckled. "I think we should look at the charts, too, but I'd also like to go over your software and data base programming," she said, moving toward the entry.

They were unconsciously brought close together by the crates and boxes stacked around, Scott had to turn sideways to move closely past Julia as he pulled open the flap.

The scent of her perfume only increased his nervous feeling.

Each felt an awkward tension at the closeness of the encounter, a closeness that would either get them at each other's throat or . . . ?

Pausing at the entrance, he turned. "Oh, come on, I think you look great and believe me you've made your point. I couldn't agree with you more, but we're not in America. We're in Egypt, almost Saudi Arabia. I am also sorry I lost most temper. Believe me, I really do agree with you, but if you keep it up I'm not the one who's not going to get any work done, and not because of Achmed wasting my time with his attitude."

Once again, he became aware of her scent as they stood face to face and he looked down into her bright blue eyes.

She responded with a tilt of her head that made her ponytail swing and bounce. "Agreed. I'll find something that should make them all happy, even you, even though I think you're even a little bit stuffy and a chauvinist yourself."

Twenty minutes later, she came back to the command tent wearing the long black skirt with a traditional Egyptian scarf over her head. She didn't wear a veil, but Scott was able to smooth things over and the workers began to accept her. The next day one of the workers was brought in with a bad rash from contact with one of the local plants and she concocted a salve made from honeysuckle, witch hazel and some secret ointment of hers that quickly healed him. This went a long way toward raising her prestige in the little community.

The survey continued over the coming weeks and months, with Julia working more and more with Scott, Samuel and the crews. One Saturday morning she walked up to Scott. "I need to go to Cairo for some supplies. I'll probably be gone a couple of days. Do you need anything?"

Scott thought a moment. "No. I'll send Achmed up with you; he can keep an eye on you while you pick up the stuff you need."

"I won't need him. I think I can handle myself."

"Suit yourself, but I would feel better if he went with you."

"I would like to do some shopping while I'm in town and would feel more comfortable if I was alone."

"Please be careful, Julia. You can take one of the Hummers. Fill it up in Suez on your way back."

Taking her pack, she walked down to the vehicle compound and drove off in the black Hummer.

CHAPTER 5
SURVEY PROGRESSIONS

As they descended the mountain after setting the survey marks, Scott turned to Samuel and said, "Another good day at the office, huh?" He was feeling much better after the exercise and getting the work done.

"I didn't think you were going to make it all the way up, old man!"

"Just a little out of shape . . . a little out of shape. It's all that paperwork and hanging out in the Nile River valley."

"I was working near the Mississippi, if my memory serves me right."

"Yeah, but you were busy chasing the local women. You got plenty of exercise while I had to work all day inputting data into the computers."

Samuel gave him a more serious look. "It's good to be out again together. I don't know what I'd do with a regular job. You should delegate more and get out in the field more often."

"You're right, of course. Let's get back and see how Julia and the boys are doing."

The afternoon sun was low, thin and weak as they approached the camp, bringing extremely large appetites from the day's hike. As they walked down the last grade, they found Rusta Sadat waiting for them at the mess tent.

Throwing down his backpack, Scott said, "Rusta, I thought you were in Cairo. What brings you out here?"

Turning to Samuel, he said, "I see Scott's got you out working with him again. That's good, very good. How much did he tell you about this job?"

"Not much, he did tell me about your warning to watch our backs though," Samuel said, while reaching in his pack and pulling out a Beretta 9mm with a 15 shot magazine. "I thought I'd carry a little backside protection. That is, if the Interior Minister doesn't mind."

"I shouldn't ask how you got that into country, I don't want to know. Just be smart on this job, okay. Do you like being out in the real field again?"

"It's great, saved me from a life of domestic bliss. Just think of it, I can be out here in the dust with Scott and a bunch of your workmen. Who could ask for more?"

Rusta nodded at Scott. "Let's go up to your tent. I want to share some information I've found out."

Once in the tent, Scott and Samuel sat down then Rusta turned toward them. "Quati's onto this project somehow. I don't know how for sure, but I'm afraid he may have an agent in your camp, probably one of the new workmen. It's imperative you keep a low profile and watch out."

"Rusta, you keep saying watch out, keep a low profile. What's Quati after?" Scott asked.

"I don't really know . . . I'm just not sure, but think it has something to do with some old Islamic religious stuff that may be buried out here somewhere."

Samuel laughed. "What, a treasure hunt? Is Quati out of his mind?"

"No, Samuel, at least not in the usual sense, not in the way you're thinking. Quati's been advised by a number of the Mullahs and Ayatollahs who think Mohammad buried something, what or where they're not sure. But their best guess is somewhere near St. Catherine's."

Scott looked up. "Why not in the monastery itself?"

"Could be, but I don't think so. It was a Christian monastery back when Mohammad was here in 622, and even though he could have left something there, it doesn't make sense. He had followers and a large commitment to follow through on. If he left something there, the monks would know about it and no one would ever find it. Some of our old Muslim legends tell a tale that his scribe, a man named Zayd ibn Thabit, made a confession on his deathbed, a story that Mohammad left some writings or a final revelation of some sort buried in a secret chamber somewhere. Some legends say in Cush, some in Saudi Arabia, others in Greece or Europe, but the best authorities say here in Sinai. Al Sud's name is tied to one of the old legends. He was a famous Caliph in the area back then. His tomb is just to the south of us. It's not hard to find. Maybe it's in his tomb, though I doubt it. Dr. Abu is working on the tomb and if it is in the tomb, then that's probably the end of it. But don't trust anyone, especially Dr. Abu."

"What are these old legends, are they in the Koran?" Samuel asked.

"No, most are oral traditions from Bedouin tribes in the area. Others are apocryphal writings found in mosques here and there around the world and some are secular writings from the period. Who can say which are true? Doesn't Christianity have old writings and legends, too? You have your Bible, but what about the Apocrypha and other writings from St. Augustine and elsewhere? What about Prester John? Don't they all have some truth in them?"

"No one has a monopoly on truth, Rusta," Scott said as he stared out the tent flap. "If you asked a Christian, he would tell you he had the truth about the Son of God, and maybe the Chinese have the truth about meditation. I don't know. I've always thought that real truth is what's found in a man's head and heart. How he believes in himself. I used to believe that real truth was found in what I would call humanism today, but now . . . I'm not so sure."

"Enough of that. How's the survey going so far? My country needs all of your help, my friends!"

"Your government sent a request that we map and identify any archeological sites on the peninsula. It might have something to do with what you were saying before, maybe not. It's a good idea anyway and would be good to make sure they aren't spoiled during any mineral exploration or mining that may happen." Scott said. "What more can you tell us about this Dr. Abu?"

"He works for the Egyptian Department of Antiquities, supposedly knows his stuff pretty well. I don't know him personally, but he has a wife and family. Don't trust him though. My sources say he has met with Quati, and that can only lead to trouble. I will try to find out more if I can and pass it on to you. How is the survey coming, find anything interesting yet?"

"Most of it's the usual stuff: looking for oil and minerals, charting the ecological areas and figuring out the costs required to extract anything. The other parts are more difficult. We're not far enough to document anything yet, but I'll let you know. My interns Luke and Alex are actually doing most of the work."

"Make sure your final report shows a buffer area along the coast to protect the diving sites, reefs and hotels," Rusta said. "Oh, by the way, how's the new botanist working out?"

"Great. Really knows her stuff. A little trouble the first day, but the men seem to have taken to her now."

"From the look in your eyes, Scott, it's not just the men who have taken to her. She must be really something."

Chapter 6

Benjamin's orders

Julia sat across the desk from her boss Eli in the antiseptic government office while old Benjamin looked on. She stiffly delivered her report about what Chad had found so far and how the survey was progressing—finally concluding with her opinion of the safety of the team.

Eli looked over his spectacles and asked, "What do you think of this Chad character? Is he honest and trustworthy? Do you think we could bring him around to our cause?"

A faint red flush came to her cheeks which she tried to dispel, hoping Eli and Benjamin didn't notice. "I think he is an extremely honest man. He has friends that are Arab and Muslim and is unprejudiced.

"He has fought with the Afghanis and Saudis against fundamentalist warlords and has friends in high places across the world, but doesn't hold to any dogma or creed. He's not a religious man but has very strong convictions and ethics, an odd combination in today's world."

"You're not telling me about the man though. What do you think of him?"

The flush to her cheeks increased slightly as he spoke. She wondered why. "I think he's arrogant, intelligent and witty. He has a kind of stupid male sense of humor that he and that sidekick of his Samuel seem to enjoy. Well, he's sometimes funny and makes me laugh, but he's so American and male. Do you know what I mean? Do I think he would turn against Israel for the Muslims? No, if that's what you want to know. I think he would stand for the truth no matter what it was or where it came from. He would never fabricate something or stand up for any falsehood, even if it furthered his career. He doesn't need money; he's made more than he would ever need. He works solely for the pleasure of his work, the finding of things, helping people, and the truth. His real passion is to bring economic benefits to the people. We should consider hiring him to do a survey of Israel."

"You've given me something of the man and his methods but I'm sure there's more. I don't want you to lose sight of the big picture. Your job is to keep him safe. Don't get lost in the process. I need you to keep focused," Eli said.

A flash of anger now lit up her cheeks and she tried to keep herself in check as she answered. "I would appreciate an explanation of that comment. It was a little cryptic for me and I'm not sure I like the tone of it."

"I just want you to be careful and stay focused on this mission. Your first task is to report anything you find out or if you see any other parties snooping around and your second is to see to the safety of Scott Chad and his party. You can count on us for any support you may need. This is important. There are forces moving that could spell the end of our tiny country or something possibly wonderful may happen, if our intelligence is correct. Even the orthodox element is behind us on this."

"I have spoken with Marshall who hangs out with those orthodox rabbis and even they think something of portent may come about that could spell out a horrible or wonderful future for us," Benjamin added.

Eli continued, "I usually don't go in for their mumbo jumbo, but Mohammed did stay at St. Catherine's, and who knows what he did there. I just can't have you losing your focus and getting emotionally involved on this mission."

"Emotionally involved! I don't think you know me very well, and you should by now after all the years we have worked together. You can remove me if that's what you think, or you can keep to your own business!"

"That's enough now, Your booked on an El Al flight to Geneva and then a Lufthansa flight back to Cairo which should get you back tonight. Pity you can't just drive back, but we need to cover your bases and not let anyone think you're working for us. Off you go," Eli said with a motion of his hand.

After she'd left, Eli sat lost in thought for a moment. He knew Benjamin was still in the room but also knew when to let his boss think. He wondered if he should keep Julia on the case or not.

Turning to Benjamin he said. "She's getting emotionally involved with Chad. That much is obvious and that's not a good idea. Yes, she's young but she doesn't really have to become like us, does she? Nonetheless, an agent shouldn't get involved with whom they're working with. The trouble is it's probably too late to put someone else in who could work his or her way into Chad's organization. She's probably falling in love with him. I don't think she even knows it herself but you can't fool me."

He then said in Hebrew. "What did you think? Do you have any thoughts on letting her continue?"

"Oh, Eli, I'm even older than you and understand what you're saying. I think she's compromised her judgment on this, but you and I are old men and romance may well be dead in our hearts, but not in the young. I say we keep her on. It may be a mistake, but could also be the correct thing. Who can fathom the wisdom of fate?" He then used an old Hebrew phrase that when translated went something like: "It's not like she's falling in love with the competition."

Eli turned to him. "If that were the case I'd be the first to say pull her out. But no, I don't think she knows it herself, and only time will tell, but maybe there is part of the old romantic in me somewhere still, and I say keep her on. She's very good at what she does and we don't have the time or the talent to come up with someone new. Hasid being in her past scares me more. Can she do the right thing with that emotional tie? And don't forget Hasid knew Chad when they were kids, which may complicate things even more."

"Agreed, but we had better be careful."

Benjamin's words died off in the air of the small room. Eli paused a moment, then answered. "All very well and good, but are we sure what Quati is really after? Do you think he is really after the writings, as our sources would have us believe? What is so important about them that Quati should get in such an uproar over them? I know what the rabbis have said, but I don't believe in that stuff."

"Our mole in Quati's camp isn't sure. Quati rants and raves about the glorious banner of Islam flying over the whole world and that he will not be denied. He raves about kicking the Americans out of Afghanistan and Iraq and how Al Queda has been run to ground by the great Satan, the United States, and then brings up some stuff about how Mohammed's glorious prophecies will usher in a new age for Islam and all mankind."

Eli nodded. "The funny thing is one of our agents in the Sinai and another in Greece who work with some of the Orthodox monks say much the same thing, just the other side of the coin. Seems that while we, old friend, have much forsaken religion it has not forsaken us, for this all seems wrapped up in some sort of religious thing that I have trouble believing in. That's not stopping me from the practical aspect of the whole thing however. If Quati's moving, I know it's my job to stop him, no matter what the ramifications or where they come from. I don't care if it is religious, cultural, or just their old hate crap. I just wish they'd learn how to forgive, grow up and live in peace."

"I learned how to hate after what my parents went through in World War II. Learning how to forgive was much harder. How my parents could forgive always astounded me. I was never able to understand it until my mother sat me down one day. She told me, 'It's not religion, even though the Torah said we must forgive, it is a human necessity, and I must forgive. It would ruin my life if I didn't. Life is too short and I have better things to do and think about than being filled with hate and anger and then more hating.' I think the hate has gone on long enough, Eli, but we must still protect this country from whatever madness and hate that gets stirred up and from wherever it is being stirring from. We are a small country and cannot afford to let our guard down."

"Well put, but I find it harder to let go of the hate than you do. After losing a daughter to a bus explosion and a nephew to a suicide bomber in a grocery store, I find it harder to forgive myself. My wife has gone on now but losing our daughter Sari just broke her heart. The doctors say she died of a heart attack but sometimes when I lay awake at night, I think it was a broken heart that killed her."

"Well, old friend, we all have our mountains to climb, and what I care about is our little country and keeping it safe. My willingness to forgive has not nor will ever stop me or keep me from doing my duty. Now back to Julia. We need some agents near her in case she needs backup, but not too close where they will cause a problem or be visible. Do you have any ideas on whom we should send?"

Hasid paced back and forth across the cream carpet in the Palm's Hotel, his thoughts in a turmoil—*Scott Chad, why did it have to be Chad? Quati's orders are specific, I must follow them. Why Chad? Why am I feeling this way? So, what if it's Chad. What difference does it make? He used to be my friend but we were children then. My father's death and the great Jihad have changed all that. I haven't felt anything but hate in so long, it's as if I don't even know myself anymore or how to keep the true faith alive.*

A knock at his door startled him. Crossing the cream carpet he opened the door and Abdullah walked in. "What do you want, you are supposed to be with Talbin watching Chad?"

"You told me to let you know when Dr. Abu was in place and working on that tomb south of Chad's camp. We have a plan to get a worker inside Chad's camp."

He paused a moment before answering, his thoughts still on Chad. *I must get a grip on this. The great Satan must come down and all the enemies of Islam must perish. That is the way, yes. Allah in his infinite wisdom has defined the way for me. No running, I must face it and pull through. Quati must be pleased and Allah's will done. Chad does not matter at all.*

"Tell me about it," Hasid said, putting aside his turmoil of emotions.

CHAPTER 7
THE CHAMBER

Julia worked with Scott to help set traverse stations after she got back from Cairo. They slowly filled the database and the geological map started to take shape with the information they collected. Once they had completed the triangulation and spatial measurements, they began plotting the botanical and other geological information.

Scott and Julia were setting a survey station position above Al Sud's tomb one bright morning so the tomb could be accurately located. The Egyptian government was swarming all over the tomb area, wasting their time and asking questions as they tried to set up their equipment.

Finally, the man who appeared to be in charge slowly climbed the rocky hill to where they were working. He was tall and rail-thin, looking and walking almost like a pigeon. He was dressed in a rumpled tropical white suit with balding hair. "You must be Mr. Chad. My name is Dr. Abu. I am the head archeologist on this project. I was told by our Department of the Interior that you were working in the area."

Scott listened to the man, taking an immediate dislike. He said, "They didn't originally tell me that you would be working in the area. I've located every archeological site on the list they sent me. My final map should be helpful to you since all the archeological sites will be added to our final database and map."

"You must contact me personally before working on or near any site."

"That might be difficult. As I said, we've located most of them already and some of them are in very out of the way areas."

"Excuse me, Mr. Chad, I mean any sites you come across that are not on the list. I insist that you contact me personally and immediately with anything you find!"

"Dr. Abu, we're on a tight schedule. Your people wasted about an hour of our time this morning asking questions and generally just getting in the way."

"We place great value on our heritage in this country. You are going to have to abide by my rules, no matter how much time it costs. This is not Jamaica, you know."

Scott stared at his eye, wondering what he was getting at.

"Yes, I have heard how you helped them. I have also heard about your work in Saudi Arabia and Afghanistan. I do not need any loose cannons around here. I have some of the same problems as you do, except I am short of workers and funds."

"I'm short of workers, too, and your people getting in our way doesn't help me get my job done."

"I am sorry, but those are the rules. You must honor my request. Report to me immediately on any new site you find. Failure to do this will result in severe penalties."

"Now you threaten me. Have you discussed this with the Department of the Interior?"

"I work for the Department of Antiquities. As I said we have a very rich heritage in this country. I do not mean to threaten you; I need your cooperation. Please excuse me, I am under much pressure, too. I also need to borrow one of your workmen for a day. Two of my men have come down sick and we are clearing an important portion of the tomb. Will you help me out on this?"

"Dr. Abu, you come to me and waste my morning, then set restrictions on me and now you want to borrow one of my workmen?"

"I am asking you to cooperate with me on this, Mr. Chad, and I am asking politely. Do you understand me?"

"Yes, Dr. Abu, I understand you." He paused and sighed. "You may borrow one of my men for an afternoon, but I expect you to reciprocate if the need arises."

"Thank you, Mr. Chad, I knew you would see reason. Please send him over this afternoon so we can get our work completed."

The next day Scott and Julia sat eating lunch in the warmth and sunshine while sitting on a small boulder after finishing locating the tomb. They faced south toward the tip of the peninsula. The worker Scott had lent Abu had suffered a freak accident yesterday and broken his ankle while helping clear the rubble from the tomb entrance. Abu had assured Scott that he would get them another worker, even promising to find them one by this afternoon.

"I'm concerned how Ali broke his ankle," Scott said.

"Seems suspicious to me, too. Ali's always so careful. He was born in these mountains and it's hard to imagine him slipping and breaking his ankle walking down that slope."

"That's what gets me. Ali's a Bedouin, knows the mountains, and no Bedouin could fall and break his ankle just walking out of that tomb!"

Julia put her hand on his shoulder. "What are you going to do?"

Looking at her hand, she quickly pulled it back.

"That fellow Abu's sending is supposed to be good with rock. Apparently he's worked with hard rock mining before. He doesn't have any survey experience, but we need him to run the rock drill. It just . . ."

"That's not what I mean . . . I'm concerned! Don't you see? Remember how Rusta warned you that someone might be interested in what we're doing. He also warned you about Abu. This project's gone smoothly so far. This is our first injury, but . . . I've just got one of those feelings!"

"I know, Julia, I know. I'm concerned too, but I don't know what to do about it and I need to keep this survey on time and on schedule. Let's see how this guy works out, okay?" He paused and looked at her sitting next to him. "I've learned that it's probably a good idea to trust one of your feelings, but I don't know what to do about it. We have to keep this project going."

He felt the anxiety welling up inside, giving him a feeling of dread and fear roiling in his gut. Seeing Julia, her red hair shining like gold in the sun, should have lifted his sprits, but not now. Staring at his feet, he kept dwelling on the accident. *How did Ali break his ankle? Is something odd going on? Is there more to this than meets the eye?* When he'd interviewed the Egyptian workers at the tomb, they'd acted dumb and didn't know how it happened. Ali wasn't of much help either. Since Abu had given him a sedative to help with the pain, he was out of it by the time Scott came to talk with him. They'd then taken him to a doctor in Suez. Scott had set bones before but didn't have an x-ray machine to look at the ankle, which certainly looked badly broken. Hopefully, he'd regain full use of his leg, which was important to a Bedouin.

There was silence between them for a while and he watched as the wind curled her hair around her face. After finishing lunch, Julia started down the hill while he packed up the basket and trash.

A large flat-topped boulder caught his attention as he was starting after Julia. Wandering left about half way down, he paused to look at it, struggling over a few larger rocks, before hoisting himself to the top. The large solid granite slab rested horizontally on the side of the mountain while a double row of flat boulders led down the hill to the southwest, looking like the plates of a stegosaurus. *What made me look at the rock,* he thought afterwards. It certainly wasn't anything peculiar about the rock itself, for that's all there was in the area, large rocks, small rocks, round rocks, and every other type and shape of rock imaginable. Most of the rock was sandstone but the basement formations were granite and metamorphic.

No, it was something else. He tried to describe it afterwards to Julia and

Samuel. It was as if he was almost meant to find it . . . but that made no sense, so he tried to rationalize it, as if the color was different, which wasn't true.

"Julia, stop! Come back up here, right away!" he yelled from the top of the slab.

Quickly turning when she heard his shout, she climbed back up the rocky slope. Coming to the base of the boulder, she looked up at him. "What is it? What have you found?"

"I'm not sure, something strange. This slab of rock appears to have been worked on. There's a small hole bored or drilled into the slab. Could be some old surveyors mark, but I don't think so. I think it's much older. It appears hollow underneath, but there's not enough light to see. Maybe it's another tomb. I don't know!"

She smoothly negotiated around the boulders lying about the base of the slab and walked out on the flat surface. "Show me."

"Look here." He pointed toward a one-inch diameter hole drilled in the center of the slab. "There are also some marks over here," he said, pointing to three notches carved in the surface. They were spaced around the hole, one pointing to the northwest, one northeast and the other southeast. "They've been worn by the wind and weather over the years but look like they were originally cut deep into the rock."

Their shoulders were touching as they bent over the hole. She peered in, then noticed his touch and quickly moved back. "I think you've actually found something not on any of the lists the Egyptian government provided us."

He looked at her, forgetting the slab of rock. The spot on his shoulder felt odd, almost hot. He was afraid to approach the feelings he was having. Her hair was blowing in the wind, her blue eyes clear, and the smile on her face seemed to light up the day for him.

She looked up at him for a second, then quickly grabbed his hand and shook it. "Good job boss. People could stumble around here for years and not find this!" Her hand felt soft and smooth and for a second he just held it and looked almost staring at her, when they suddenly realized they were holding hands. Quickly withdrawing her hand, she turned and looked at the rock.

"Let's look around and see if we can find anything else," Scott said. "There might be something more. No telling how large it is, but those rows of rocks over there . . ." he pointed at the double row of boulders with a gesture, "seem out of place, not natural. They could be, but look as if they were placed there for some reason. Maybe it's another tomb, but why the hole on top? Do you have a flashlight in your pack?"

"I think so. Give me a moment." She tossed her backpack onto the slab and started rummaging through it, pulling out items and laying them out. "Here it is," she said as she handed him a black flashlight made of anodized aluminum. "Shine it in. Maybe you can see the bottom. I have some string I use for tying up plants. We might want to lower it down and see how deep it is."

Taking the flashlight, he bent over the hole trying to shine the light in. It was difficult since the hole was only an inch in diameter and he had to get his eye and the flashlight up to the hole at the same time.

"I can't see much of anything. The slab's about eighteen inches thick. I need a smaller light or a smaller head. I can't get my eye over the hole at the same time I put the light up to it. Do you have a mirror or anything else we could use?"

Sorting through the contents of her backpack again, she turned to him. "I have a small compact. Try it and see if it works," she said, tossing him the mirror.

Holding the compact up with his left hand so it caught the afternoon sunlight, he directed the bright light down the hole. Kneeling down on the rock, he tried to peer inside.

Shaking his head, he said. "Here, hold this," and handed the compact back to her. "Reflect the light down the hole while I try and get my head to the side so I can see in."

Kneeling down, she held the compact while he held his head to the side of the hole. She turned the mirror back and forth to reflect the sunlight, but they couldn't quite seem to get the angle right.

"Here, let me try," she said as she handed him the compact. She knelt on the rock with her eye to the hole while he held the compact up and reflected the sunlight. It was tricky but if he got it just right, the reflected beam of sunlight went down the hole and illuminated the interior.

"Well, you're right. There's a chamber of some sort here," she said with her face flattened against the rock. "Let's measure it. I'll get that string. I can just see the bottom but, because of the angle, it's hard to see anything else. I wish we had a fiber optic camera we could lower down, but we'd have to send away for one I suppose."

Reaching into her backpack, she came out with a small bundle of string, which she tied a small washer to.

She tossed it to Scott who looked up with surprise. "What, are you fixing cars now, too?"

"I don't know the first thing about cars. I carry an assortment of washers to give away to children whenever I'm out in the field. They like to string them together and make necklaces and things."

Taking the string, he lowered it through the hole, then looked up at her. "The hole's at a slight angle, even though it looks fairly straight from here." When the string went slack, he marked the position with a small knot and pulled it back. "We need a tape measure, but I'd estimate about twelve feet."

Julia asked, "Well, what do you think is inside?"

"I'm not sure. That double row of rocks over there appears to be some sort of entry. Looks like someone placed the rocks there, whoever created this place. I don't know if the slab's natural and the chamber carved out. Someone may have placed the slab here. We'll have to excavate some of the gravel and debris from that area, then we can see."

Looking up at him, she asked, "Why don't we just use the rock drill and saws and cut a hole in the top?"

"I don't think so. We might destroy something and if this is an archeological site, the good Dr. Abu wouldn't be too happy if we started cutting holes into things. I don't want to see any more of Abu than I have to. I don't need his type of problem. We should probably just locate the thing and tell him about it, but for some reason . . . some reason I can't put my finger on, I don't feel like it. I don't like Abu's attitude either."

Hopping off the slab between the two rows of rocks, they tried to figure out how much gravel and debris they'd have to remove. "From the top of the slab to the bottom of the chamber measures about twelve feet," Scott said.

"From the top of the slab to the gravel debris measures about four," Julia added.

Scott shrugged. "We have to remove about eight feet of gravel and rock debris. We may not have to go all the way down, but . . ."

"But what?"

"We need help. It's getting late, too. Let's go back and find Samuel and see what he thinks."

It was dark as they made their way back to camp and Scott cautioned Julia as they were walking up. "Don't tell anyone but Samuel about this."

"Why not? Seems like it could be quite an exciting find to me."

"Remember Rusta's warnings. What did he say? Watch our backs. I never give out information until I know what we have. I don't want Abu slowing us up any more than necessary. The guy gives me the creeps. He would have the government swarming all over the place and that would slow down the rest of the project. We'd be filling out forms, entertaining the bureaucracy, and wouldn't get anything done. Then all kinds of curiosity seekers would be swarming all over the place. It's probably just a small rock chamber where the workers building the tomb went to cool off during the day. Let's just keep this to ourselves to be on the safe side until we know more."

"Whatever you say. You're the boss."

He was somewhat surprised. He wasn't used to her being so cooperative. She was usually so prim, proper and professional, but always somewhat aggravating. He never knew quite what to expect out of her. She always seemed to keep him off balance. She was just so distracting.

❋ ❋ ❋ ❋ ❋ ❋ ❋ ❋

Hasid leaned back in his chair, his fear mounting as he tried to figure out how to implement Quati's orders. His emotions, other than hate, were usually non-existent, but sending Jared and his cohorts to get rid of Chad's friend Samuel was bothering him. Why was he feeling so tense?

He used to be Chad's friend, his best friend. What if Quati ordered him killed some day? Why did they always have to resort to violence? Was there not another way? Maybe they should just scare Rogowski off. No, the sword was the way and path to the new future. They could never let the Israelis win. The Israelis killed his father in cold blood. They stole a land from his people who had tried to live in peace with them, but never could. Wasn't Chad's friend an American, and America supported Israel?

Why was he thinking like this? Taking life in the cause was a swift reward into heaven. Isn't that what he believed?

He must follow the general's orders, but how? Was Jared the answer? Getting up from his chair, he stared out the window at a sky that was smeared orange and grey from all the pollution of Cairo. The very air was a burnt color that looked almost cancerous. The air-conditioner chugged away under the window expelling cool and hopefully cleaned air. He longed for the desert and open air again, even though Cairo was one of the most vibrant cities in the world.

Reaching for the phone, he quickly dialed a number. "Jared, get over to my room. I want to talk with you about tomorrow's operation."

Slamming the phone down on the desk, he turned back to look at the orange sky.

Jared's knock startled him out of his reverie.

Opening the door, the six-foot-six inch man waded into the room, opening his mouth to show his toothless grin. "Good to see you again, Hasid. I am always happy when we work together to do Allah's will. The general told me about the work you have for me and my men."

"Yes, but I am modifying the general's orders. I want you to shake Rogowski up, then bring him to our warehouse in Cairo. Do not kill him, not just yet. He may be important before this is all over."

"Do you really think it right to change the general's orders?"

"Do not question me, Jared. You have felt my wrath before. Just rough him up, then bring him to the warehouse. Do you understand?"

"I think you are getting soft, Hasid, but yes I understand you. My boys and I can take care of this one easily."

"Make sure they keep their mouths shut this time. Rogowski is to know nothing. Do you understand me?"

"Yes, Hasid, I understand you. No names, just take him down and bring him back to the warehouse. What if things go wrong? I still think it best to just take him out."

"See that they do not go wrong, but if they do, it shall be as Allah wills. Be careful. Rogowski is tougher than he seems from all the reports I have heard."

"The man is only five-six. How tough can he be? He cannot be tougher than Fasha, Fisal and me. Come off it."

"Just remember I warned you. My reports are that he is tough. Small but tough, so take care to do as you are told. Now tell me what your plans are."

"We are going to St. Catherine's tomorrow morning. We will wait and watch. First chance we get, and find him out of camp, we will do him."

"Just remember who you work for. The price of failure will be greater than you can imagine. I do not relish having to teach you or your friends another lesson."

A look of fear passed quickly over Jared's face, but with an effort he brought it under control. "I will be careful, and do as you say." He bowed and turned toward the door. "As Allah wills . . . yes, as Allah wills."

"Make sure you follow *my* will, Jared, or there will be trouble."

Hasid turned back to the burnt orange and grey sky that lay over the city outside his window. He felt his fear edge up in his veins. *Why am I feeling thing this?,* he thought as he walked over to the mini-bar and poured himself a drink.

Chapter 8
Fun at St. Catherine's

Samuel turned from working on the database in the main tent as Scott and Julia walked in. Julia let out a gasp as she noticed Samuel's face. Looking as if someone had used him for punching bag, he looked up and smiled. "Well, how'd your day go? Mine was rather odd."

Scott looked at him, and then around the tent to make sure no one was within earshot. "Better than yours, I'd imagine. Care to enlighten us."

"You first. Ever since I was a little boy, I've always been proud of a black eye."

"We found something interesting over near that old tomb site the Egyptians are working on. Might be another tomb, but it is more likely a small workman's shelter. It's odd though . . . there is something else about it . . . something that I can't quite put my finger on. I don't quite know what to make of it."

Julia blurted, "It's a chamber about twelve feet deep with a flat slab of rock on the top with a small hole drilled into it. There are three inscribed notches pointing in what I'd almost call directions, but they aren't points on the compass. They could point to something else. It's a mystery!"

Scott held up his hand. "I don't need to remind you two not to discuss this with any of the other crew members. We're the only ones who know about this right now. Let's keep it that way."

"I know when to keep my mouth shut. I don't want to be entrenched in bureaucracy up to my neck. Been there, done that and don't want a whole army of bureaucrats looking up my nose while I'm trying to get some work done!" Samuel said.

Pacing back and forth, Scott said, "Remember when we located Al Sud's Tomb the other day? When we were setting the survey marker on top of the entrance, we found a small inscribed stone with a simple seal. It looked like a dove in flight. There was a notch pointing to the north, as I recall, possibly pointing to the chamber we just found. I didn't think much of it at the time.

I just thought it was one of the masons' marks. But enough of all that, what happened to you?"

"Well your day sounds more interesting than mine. I went up to St. Catherine's to get some supplies. But I got more than I bargained for."

"What happened? Are you okay?" Julia asked.

Scott sat and listened to his tale, wondering if Abu's appearance had anything to do with what happened.

Samuel's trials had started after he found an open shop outside the monastery. Filled with icons, candles and incense, the shop had a small section that sold honey and the local wine, which the monks made. After buying a jar of honey, two candles and three bottles of the local red wine, he made his way back to the car as evening was closing in, taking a round about way back to the Hummer. He passed through an old section of the village filled with stucco-clad rock homes leaning in on each other. He then followed a narrow road lined with a steep concrete ditch on each side. Narrow alleys that would be a tight fit for a Yugo or even a Mini intersected the road as it twisted and turned.

Passing one of the alleys, three Arabic looking men dressed in dirty fatigues stepped out, blocking the street. The man on the left was short and thin, the man on the right tall and stocky. Looking like he had lost a prizefight, the third man was missing most of his front teeth. A foot taller than Samuel, he looked as if he weighed two hundred and eighty pounds and had a six-inch longer reach. The man looked up and down the empty street, nodded to his companions on each side who grabbed Samuel's arms, pulling him into the alley.

Samuel looked up and down the alley for any possible help but they had chosen it carefully and it was empty of anything but a few small rags of clothing fluttering on lines, strung between the upper floors to dry. The two men holding his arms backed him against the wall while the large toothless man advanced toward Samuel brandishing a large knife.

Feigning fear, Samuel went limp in the two men's arms, which required them to hold his weight with more of their strength, allowing him to keep his knees bent without their noticing.

"Be quick, Jared. Quati said we would receive a big reward for taking this one out."

"Be still," the toothless man with the knife said. Directing his toothless grin at Samuel, he said, "An even bigger reward is promised to us if we take out your partner, little man." He said this as he twisted the knife so it glinted in the dim light from the end of the alley.

"Please, my friends will pay a great deal if you let me go!"

"We do not want your money, little man. We have already been paid, and you do not have enough to protect us if we do not do as we are ordered."

"What do you want from me? I haven't done anything to you?"

"You have upset General Quati, that is why! My stupid friend should not have told you his name, but now that he has, you can die knowing who sent you to Allah!"

"We've more than money to give you, how about cars and trucks or guns and ammunition for your cause?"

"Stupid man, just die in peace," the big man said as he advanced with the knife.

Samuel was waiting for just this moment. He grimaced, opening his eyes wide as if afraid, then dug in his heels, straightened his knees and threw back his arms knocking the two men holding him into the wall, cracking their skulls against the concrete and knocking them out cold. Lashing out with his foot at toothless Jared, he knocked the knife out of his hand then lowered his head and charged, butting him in his stomach.

The shock was tremendous and his head felt as if he ran into the concrete wall of the alley, instead of human flesh.

Shaking off the shock, he stepped back just in time to slip a lightning fast blow that glanced off his forehead. A flash of pain crossed his eyes.

Backing down the alley, he held up his hands as the man pummeled at his defenses. For the first time in his life, he thought he might lose a fight. He'd fought in the Marine Corps and won his weight class in every fight, but had never beaten an adversary as large and tough as Jared.

He knew he would have to be fast and lucky.

Jared waded in again and shot a left jab at Samuel, hitting him square in the forehead.

It was quick, a hard punch, a punch with muscle behind it, the left jab of a man who had worked out on bags in a gym for a long time.

A trained punch that left Samuel seeing lights out his left eye.

The man was fast, even if he looked like some drug-crazed thug. Shaking off the punch, Samuel felt a foreign, cold wash of fear creep across his consciousness. Holding his fists up, Jared came at him with another left, then a right that he slipped only just in time.

Samuel threw a short jab to the man's chest, which felt like he'd hit a brick wall.

"That is the best you have, little man?" Jared taunted as he danced on the balls of his feet. "Taste one of mine." Faking left, he came around with a roundhouse right that Samuel ducked by only a fraction of an inch. It still grazed his shoulder and slid along his face, bringing a hot flush of heat to his skin.

"You are a quick little man. Stand still and Jared will make it painless for you!"

"I'm going to send you back to the dentist so that your wife doesn't even know you, you pitiful excuse for a pig," Samuel taunted.

"Oh, he wants to play now." Another left came out of nowhere and rocked into Samuel's arm.

Samuel saw a small opening and quick as a viper launched a right jab only to come up with empty air.

Jared turned and spun on his feet, launching a blow at Samuel's midsection.

It was a hard fast punch.

A punch that would have knocked most men to their knees. It flew through his defenses and hit him in the sternum, a quick snapping blow with power behind it. Samuel felt his heart flutter as a blackness crept over him. He staggered back wondering, *Is this what it feels like to lose?*

Jared saw the effect of his blow and waded in again. Closing on Samuel like a mad dog, raining blows to his head and body, each felt to Samuel like he was being hit with a hammer. Samuel kept his defenses up and tucked in his head, taking the punishing pain hoping for the right opportunity.

None came.

He tried to bring up his strength, but his legs felt like jelly. His will wavered. The man was indomitable and no opportunity seemed to present itself. The man's six-inch extra reach made Samuel's blows, which would have flattened any ordinary man, seem puny in comparison.

Jared kept raining blows.

Samuel thought he saw an opening. Was it real, or was the pain deluding him? There it was again. When the man came around with a right, he dropped his chin and left shoulder, only for a fraction of a second as he tucked his left arm in to help him turn his right. It gave his right more power and if Samuel caught one, he knew the fight would be over.

Samuel jumped back.

Jared waded in again.

Samuel threw a left jab hitting Jared square in the right shoulder, bruising his hand but feeling a satisfying connection with the man's flesh.

Jared waded in again and faked a left then cocked back to throw his right when he saw an opening in Samuel's defenses.

Samuel lifted his head. Sensing his only opportunity, he threw a powerful right uppercut as Jared dropped his shoulder. Having everything Samuel could put into it, the blow slipped through the man's defenses, coming up under his jaw, and snapping his head back with a resounding smack.

Jared's knees turned to jelly, and a dazed look came over his eyes as he fell back against the wall, sliding slowly down.

Searching the alley for the package he'd been carrying, he found it fallen to the pavement where the two men had grabbed him. Dashing over he quickly picked it up pulling two of the bottles out, holding one in each hand.

"It's not nice to call other people names," Samuel said as he advanced.

One of the assailants was still out cold against the wall. Getting shakily to his feet, the tall thin one pulled out his knife, coming at Samuel with a look of fear and astonishment that he'd felled his companion.

Meeting his advance, Samuel ducked the knife then brought the bottle crashing down on the man's head.

Glancing over, he noticed Jared pulling himself up from the wall. "Hey, Jared, you're next. I see you need to visit the dentist!"

Still recovering from Samuel's blow, he grabbed his knife and charged, swinging the knife fast.

Samuel jumped back. Astonished at his speed.

Lashing again with the knife, Samuel jumped forward instead of back, to get inside his defenses, bringing the bottle round at the same time, square into his mouth, where he felt a satisfying crunch as the broken glass mixed with what was left of his dentures.

"Complete waste of a good wine!" Samuel said to no one in particular. "Being teetotalers, I wonder what you're going to say to whoever sent you when you go back smelling like a brewery."

Making his way back down the street, he noticed the little shops shuttered for the night. The sun had set and the streets were dark as he came back to his truck. No one had bothered the Hummer, but he checked it over carefully, just in case. Slowly making his way through the streets of the village, he rounded the base of the mountain toward the camp. . . .

CHAPTER 9
BASIL'S PHILOSOPHY

Scott shook his head after hearing Samuel's story, "I still think you look like you're wearing a grapefruit on your head. Let's have a look at that."

"I'll be all right. It doesn't hurt, at least not too bad, at least not my head," he said while holding up the bottle of wine. "This is all that's left. I hope it was worth it."

"Do you think this had anything to do with Rusta's warnings?" Scott asked.

"They said Quati sent them to kill me."

"You didn't kill them did you? We don't need that kind of trouble."

"Nah, just roughed 'em up a little. One of them will need another trip to the dentist and the other two will probably have a bad headache for a couple of days."

"Well, I know you can take care of yourself Samuel, but I think it best that we travel in pairs wherever we go. Rusta warned us to watch our backs and he was right, it seems."

"When don't we take care?" Samuel said with a laugh.

"I want us to take more than normal care. We haven't lost anyone out here yet and I don't want to start now. These extremists seem interested in us for some reason and you've just had a taste of how interested they are."

"We've dealt with militants before and we always watch our backs but, you're right, we'll travel in pairs. Want to try the vino?"

Scott laughed. "Not tonight. I have work to do. Find Luke and Alex. They'll be happy to give you their opinion on the vintage. I want you to check out that chamber with us first thing in the morning. We're going to need your help so don't stay up too late."

❋ ❋ ❋ ❋ ❋ ❋ ❋ ❋

Scott tried to sleep, but it wouldn't come. Something kept bugging him. Father Basil, Abbot of St. Catherine's Monastery, had said something the afternoon he'd first come and visited with Rusta. What was it? He tried to remember what he had said that day.

He'd been directing his interns and workmen as they set up camp. Looking up he noticed a trail of dust descending the slope, a shiny red jeep emerging from the cloud of dust. When it stopped, he was surprised to see Rusta Sadat hop out.

"Come on, Scott!" Rusta said, motioning toward the jeep, "we're off to meet the abbot."

"I just got my men here. I need to get them organized."

"Time enough for that later. The monastery's part of this for some reason. Come on, it won't take long."

"Okay, give me a moment." Walking over to where the crews were working, he said, "Luke, I'm going up to the village. I'll be back in a couple of hours. Keep the men working."

Luke nodded. "No problem, Mr. Chad."

They took the Jeep up the dusty trail to the little village and then turned south to climb the steep trail to the monastery. The monastery was set on the slopes of the tall mountain and when they pulled into the little parking area, Scott just sat and stared at it for a moment. Getting out, he stood in amazement as he looked at the beautiful structure.

From before the time of the Crusades, Latin pilgrims, Crusaders and others were attracted to the monastery of St. Catherine, which gradually formed a brotherhood, the members of which acted like knights to protect the monastery.

Impressed by the setting, Scott looked at the exterior walls. The fortress was formed as quadrangle resting on the solid rock. The structure was beautiful and ancient.

Coming out of the thick wall into a sunlit courtyard, Scott asked, "What do you know of this place?"

"Here comes Father Basil. Why don't you ask him?"

A balding man of medium height with a full grey beard, dressed in the traditional garb of a Greek priest came forward to greet them. Wearing a face deeply creased by smile lines with blue eyes that sparkled in the sun, Scott immediately took a liking to him.

"Rusta, good of you to come. Who have you brought with you?" His voice was a deep baritone and he tended to laugh and chuckle as he talked.

"This is the old friend of mine I told you about, the American geological surveyor who is working south of the mountain for my government. Scott Chad, meet Father Basil."

"Pleased to meet you, Father," Scott said as they shook hands.

"Any friend of Rusta's is a friend of mine," he said as he looked Scott directly in the eye.

He led them through a deeply carved arched doorway into the cool interior. They walked through a labyrinth of passageways and corridors, past old Byzantine mosaics and artwork, with statues in little niches along the wall. "So, Mr. Chad, Rusta's told me of your proposed work in the Sinai. Please let me provide you with a blessing on your project."

"I would appreciate that," Scott said.

Continuing their walk, they worked their way deeper into the interior. The walls were old, the stairs steep and ancient, and the monks kept it clean and spotless.

"What was the monastery originally founded for, Father?" Scott asked.

"We are on the slopes of Mt. Sinai, which is holy to the Jews, Muslims and Christians. We believe this is the actual site where Moses received the Ten Commandments and talked with God in the burning bush."

"The actual Ten Commandments?" Scott said.

"Yes, the actual Ten Commandments! Would you like to see the site, the actual place where we believe Moses talked with God?"

"Very much so." His interest was immediately kindled. The archeologist inside him stirred whenever ancient things were around. The monastery was so old, it was as if he was being fed as he walked through it.

Basil led them through a long passageway then down a staircase toward the back of the monastery. They exited the main structure then walked through a small gate in a courtyard. A small stone oratory stood against the main wall of the monastery soaking up the afternoon sunlight.

"You'll have to take your shoes off because this is considered sanctified or holy ground. We always keep a candle burning in readiness for the great I Am."

Placing their shoes in a row by two pairs of sandals, they entered as a shaft of sunlight from a skylight was shining on a small patch of ground, which held a lovingly tended bush near the rear of the stone structure. The bush was the same type they'd seen growing along the slopes of the mountain.

Basil stood next to Scott and Rusta. "We believe this site is where Moses spoke with God on the mountain. God appeared here in the form of a burning bush giving Moses and mankind his Ten Commandments and the Law. See those steps over there, behind the oratory?" Father Basil pointed past the wall to a small cleft between two large cypress trees. "There are 3,750 of them and they lead to the summit of the mountain. You may climb to the top using those, instead of scrambling over the rocks as Moses did."

"That's a lot of steps, Father." Scott said.

"There is also a gentle path east of the monastery. Both ways lead to an amphitheater known as The Seven Elders of Israel, after which a person must climb the remaining seven hundred and fifty steps in order to reach the summit. There's a small chapel on top called The Holy Trinity, which was built earlier this century. The view is impressive. Many tourists make the climb to watch the sunrise. You can see both gulfs on a clear day. I would think you would have good lines of sight for your work. The steps also pass the shrine of The Virgin, and then climb through The Fountain of Moses, and finally, The Gate of The Law. We have the highest esteem for The Law."

Scott noticed the slight emphasis he had placed on his words when he said, "The Law". He turned his head and said, "I never knew such a place existed." Looking around at the beautiful sight, he added, "I want to thank you for taking the time to show me this. I've never considered myself a religious man, even though I did go to Sunday school as a child and learned about Moses and his flight from Egypt. I never really believed the stories in the Bible and would like to thank you for letting me see this . . . for it seems to stir something . . . stir something. I don't know what!"

"Not religion, of that I am sure, for that is for zealots, but maybe God's power is at work in your heart, calling you to his purpose. Yes . . . yes, perhaps you are being called, to what purpose, I do not know."

"What do you mean by 'called', Father?"

"Called by God of course," Basil replied. "The book of Romans calls them the elect, called by God from before the beginning of time to his purposes. Every priest, monk and missionary has a calling from God or we do not believe they are truly suited to their profession."

"Why would he be calling me? I'm not a priest or missionary."

"Who is to fathom His purposes, Mr. Chad. People tend to put Him in a neat little box when, in fact, he is probably the most wild and untamed thing we could imagine. Satan could never figure him out, so how could any man be so bold as to think he had all the answers. Many a philosopher or theologian thought he had the answers, but they have ended up disagreeing with each other. God is much bigger than all of us, that is for sure."

Smiling, Scott said. "It seems to me that you're speaking in riddles, Father?"

"I am sorry, I digress. I believe God is calling all the people, all the time, but do they listen? It does not mean he is calling them to be a priest like me, no. What I mean is, I believe he is always calling us. Sometimes the call is stronger for some purpose only he knows. Or let me put it this way, who could figure out a better plan for my life, God or me?"

"Well, I suppose God could," Scott said.

"Well, then who could figure out a better plan for your life, you or God?"

"I know the answer's supposed to be God. I guess I'm not ready to give that up to him. I've always known or felt I had the answers and direction for my own life. Maybe that's what kept me from . . . oh, I don't know."

"A good answer, but since he is God, I would have to say he could come up with a better and far more wonderful plan for you than you could imagine. We have to respond, and that is what is in our power. Not everyone responds and since God is not bound to time or the earth, the way we are, he can see past all that and make use of it in his infinite wisdom."

"So, you think he's calling everyone?"

"Yes, I do. Many would disagree with me and say he only calls the chosen ones or the elect. I think he does both, calls all men, calls the elect. Since He is not bound by time as we are, he knows who will respond. They are the elect. Do you see? I also think he has special plans that are outside of our philosophy and theology and that he calls other shots and flocks as well."

"Thank you, Father, now I'm even more confused, perhaps on a higher level and feel . . . like . . . feel like, I'll have to think on your words. I'd like to talk with you some more if we could sometime?"

"Of course, come anytime and ask for me. You would be most welcome."

Exiting the oratory, they put their shoes on and walked out a side exit that took them onto a gravel path that wound past the western wall and through vegetable gardens, vineyards and orchards.

"Come back and see our library. It is one of the high points of our order," Basil chuckled and said as they walked through the orchards and gardens. The afternoon was advanced and the day was taking on that golden hue as the late sun struck the mountainsides and gave a soft surreal color to everything it touched.

"I'd like to come again. We plan to be here for about six months, but I'll be very busy," Scott said as they neared the little parking area.

"It has been wonderful to meet you," Basil said as he extended his hand. "I pray that God blesses both you and all your endeavors. Please feel free to sample our hospitality and come back whenever you wish."

"Thank you, Father, and may your God bless you also," Rusta said as they shook hands with the priest.

Scott looked up at the monastery as they got to the car and said, "Basil's amazing. He seems to be a man of peace with a passion and love for people that I haven't seen before. Do you think the place is as old as some people say?"

"You should have asked him. I'm sure he knows more than he says. Did you see the plaque at the entrance? Mohammad took refuge here in the year

622 when the Quraysh warlords and pagan Caliph's were trying to kill him for bringing the tribes together and starting Islam."

"No, I didn't notice."

"The monastery was old even then. The plaque gives thanks to the monastery for providing him sanctuary and swears protection to the monastery. When wars have swept through the region, the Muslims have always left it alone to show their respect for harboring Mohammad."

Sleep finally came as he thought of those times fourteen hundred years ago.

CHAPTER 10

CHAMBER

Scott found Samuel and Julia eating breakfast in the mess tent, discussing the data they'd obtained during the last week.

Julia turned to him. "What are you smiling about this morning?"

"Nothing much, just remembering that first morning you were on the job."

"Well, forget it! Let's get to work."

Scott laughed when he saw a small smile appear on her face at the memory. "It's not something I want to forget. It was fun."

"Well, I said forget it. Load up the truck and let's get going. Come on, Samuel, time to go."

Scott shrugged and looked over at Samuel, who only grinned and said nothing, following her out the tent.

Taking one of the trucks loaded with equipment, they drove out to the site. The early April sky was clear, which added to their sense of expectation.

Scott turned his head while they bounced up the track. "No one's working on the tomb. Looks as if Abu's busy elsewhere today. We might have the whole area to ourselves and actually get some work done without being noticed."

Samuel pointed to the right. "I see the tomb. Where's this slab of rock you keep talking about?"

Julia pointed out the window. "It's up over there on that little hill off to your left. See that spire of rock?" She leaned forward and pointed. "Just to the left of it are two rows of rocks that run up the slope toward the slab we found. Do you see them?"

"I see them." He nodded then turned to Scott. "I know what you mean. It looks like a perfect place for a rest area or shelter for the tomb workers."

"We'll park over there," Scott said as he pointed with his finger off to the left, "away from the tomb and behind that little hill. Hopefully we won't attract attention if someone comes along."

"Do you think we really ought to do this?" Julia asked.

"I thought long and hard about it last night . . . and something about the way Abu confronted us. If he had been polite . . . who knows. It's as if he was trying to set us up."

"That's not what I mean. What if he comes out while we're here?"

"We're going to set a survey marker on the slab and locate it as they requested. I wouldn't ever take anything from a site. That's not my style, but it's also not my style to discover something then turn it over to him."

"I know what you mean. I understand. I was just raising the question."

"That's fine. Keep going ahead and raising questions. Two heads or even three are better than one."

They parked behind a boulder at the base of the hill and hopped out, distributing shovels and some block and tackle equipment. It was a difficult climb hauling the load up the hill between the boulders and rocks.

When they reached the two rows of rock, Scott pointed out, "I could be wrong, but it appears there may have been an old trail here. Look down the hill. Do you see what could be the remains of an old switch back that winds its way back and forth across the hill to this spot?"

"Maybe, but it's filled with rocks and boulders now," Samuel said.

Clambering onto the rock slab, they laid their equipment out. Samuel looked down. "So this is the hole. Doesn't look too impressive to me," he said as he walked around the slab. "But look here. Did you notice this?" He pointed to an area near the southeast corner of the slab mostly covered by a layer of thin topsoil and sand. "There are some large scratches and gouges in the granite."

Scott knelt down where he was pointing. Taking a small brush from his pack, he started brushing away the accumulated sand and dirt. Samuel and Julia stood over his shoulder as he worked. His work soon revealed a small picture with some Arabic letters.

"Mohammad's name and a picture or drawing of a scroll," Scott said as he stood up.

"If it wasn't written in Arabic, I'd have thought it looked like old Celtic runes or something! Mohammad . . . didn't Rusta say he stayed at the monastery?" Samuel asked.

"Mohammad stayed there in the year 622. He was taking refuge from the Quraysh warlords out of Mecca and Medina who were out to kill him for his preaching. The Muslims have revered St. Catherine's ever since. They even have a legend that Mohammad's horse, Boraq, ascended to heaven from the top of the mountain behind the monastery!"

"His horse went up to heaven?" Samuel asked with a laugh.

Scott chuckled. "He must have loved his horse a lot!"

"But what's the significance of the picture or whatever it is? Is it a picture of the Koran or something else?" Julia asked.

"The Muslims call themselves people of the book. They also consider the Jews and Christians people of the book and respect them for it. Just because I read and speak Arabic doesn't mean I understand everything there is to know about Islam. In many of their ancient traditions, it was considered holy to just look at the Koran or Bible. This may have been a place where Mohammad came to read or study when he was staying at St. Catherine's. That's what we are here to find out. Isn't it?"

Samuel grabbed a pick, jumping down between the two rows of rocks. "I'll start clearing some of the debris. You two work at widening the area behind me and hauling it off. We may need to go back to camp and get the large tripod. We could then set up the block and tackle if we need to move anything large. We should try and get as much as we can done before it gets too hot," he said as he hefted the pick and started working like a dervish, loosening the rock and filling buckets.

They went to work with a will. It was a beautiful morning and the early spring air wasn't too hot, but soon would be. Samuel quickly worked up a sweat, trying to loosen the rocks and gravel from between the larger boulders. Scott filled buckets with the gravel loosened by Samuel's pick, handing them up to Julia, who dragged them across the slab and dumped them over the side. She then tossed the empty one to Scott and repeated the process over again. It took some time but they could soon see some actual progress. In the middle of the afternoon Samuel cried out. "Hold . . . hold it! There seems to be an old door or some sort of slab that used to be an opening or something here. It's also getting hot." He paused and shook the sweat off his head.

Scott clambered into the trench to see what he was talking about. "Good job, Samuel. I think we're close, but I also think we ought to close up for now and come back first thing in the morning. We have a problem with this large boulder," Scott said as he pointed at a large rock wedged between the walls. "I don't want to be here too late tonight. The interns and men may miss us and who knows where the good Dr. Abu is."

"The boulder's wedged tight against the walls," Samuel said. "We'll have to haul it up with the block and tackle."

"You mean you really want to stop now. We're almost there," Julia said hopefully.

"We don't want to rush it, Julia. I want to document it correctly. It's the right thing to do, and I want to do it just in case Abu comes by. It is still going to take a lot to move that boulder."

"Oh all right, and it is hot. It will go better first thing in the morning."

❊   ❊   ❊   ❊   ❊   ❊   ❊   ❊

Talbin walked up to where Hasid was standing in the shade of a large rock in the desert.

"I want you close to Chad, but no killing," Talbin said.

Hasid turned to him and said, "Do not look at me that way. I know what Quati said, but Chad must be kept free to keep working. Abu thinks Chad may have found something but doesn't know what. Something tells me that Abu cannot figure this out. We may still need Chad before all this is over."

"Are you getting weak on us, Hasid? Quati warned me to keep an eye on you."

Hasid stepped up to him. "Do not ever take that tone with me, or you will be in paradise with your virgins long before you planned it."

Talbin stepped back. "It is just not like you to go soft on us. We have done many operations together, and you have never blanched from knife work."

"I am not blanching now. I must think of the higher cause. Killing is not always the answer. Things are bigger than we imagine, and it is not often one gets to see the unfolding of Allah's will in things. We do not know for sure what Chad is up to. Abu says he has an eye on him and he thinks he is working somewhere near Al Sud's tomb. The ancient writings are what we are after, and Abu does not think Chad has found anything yet. We need to be patient and see where this leads if we are to find the prophet's work. We do not know what the writings say and do not know if they should be made public. Abu is not stupid, but he is not as committed to the cause as we are. Chad may be useful. Keep an eye on him. We need to know where he keeps his data. Should he find something we want all of it. Any notes, film or negatives he may have. We do not want anything getting out to others."

"Quati will be in a rage if anything goes wrong. You know that, Hasid."

"You let me handle Quati and just make sure you are accepted into Chad's camp. You and your men must be ready to follow my exact orders at a moment's notice, or you will have more than Quati to worry about."

They made their way around the boulder, looking up at the darkening sky. The sun had set, leaving the desert sky a pale blue streaked with gold behind them.

"How will I contact you if Chad finds anything?"

"Lower the Egyptian flag to half staff at sunset, and we will meet here at midnight."

"I will do as you say until Quati counteracts your orders."

"For the last time, Talbin, watch yourself. You are working for me on this not Quati. I know he is our leader, but leaders fall and others take their place."

"You would do well to remember that also, Hasid."

Hasid walked down the sandy path to his waiting car, his feelings once again in a turmoil. He felt like killing Talbin for his insolence, but that would only cause more problems in the long run. Maybe it would be better to just kill Chad.

CHAPTER 11
THE LOST MARKER

After sending the crews out the next morning, Scott, Samuel and Julia packed up one of the Hummers and drove south to the site to the north of Al Sud's tomb. Abu's men weren't working yet and Scott skirted the site, parking behind the little hill.

Julia stood on top of the slab and said. "Well, let's get at it."

The morning wore on and the temperature rose as they continued clearing the debris and rubble so they could get at the large boulder. Scott stretched then slapped Samuel on the back. "Let's take a rest and eat something before we go any further."

Julia moaned and arched her back while taking a deep breath. "Sounds good to me. You guys know how to work a girl to death!" she said, wiping her brow with a small handkerchief. "It's getting hot, too!" She reached down and rolled up her long skirt. "There aren't any extremists around. I hope you two don't mind!" she said with a flash of her eyes and tone of defiance that said don't push it.

Scott looked over. "Just fine, don't mind at all. I'll go down and bring our lunch up. Relax for a moment and take a breather." He hopped down and descended the hill to the Hummer. Peering around the hill, he looked around to make sure no one had come to work on Al Sud's tomb. Retrieving the lunch box and a jug of water, he climbed back up to where Samuel and Julia waited.

The sun reached its zenith while they were eating and the temperature continued to rise. The noon sun painted the land in an incredible richness of color that was usually only apparent in the mountains or desert. After finishing lunch, they started hauling the last of the gravel and debris away, exposing the large boulder at the base of the wall.

A couple of hours later, Julia paused and looked at Scott. "You're a hard taskmaster. Seems you like to work a lady to death! A lady's not supposed to sweat, only perspire," Julia said as she hauled another bucket of gravel over to the edge.

Samuel moaned, "I agree, you are a hard taskmaster. You must want to work this man to death, too! This sun's starting to feel like a hammer striking an anvil on my back."

"Come on, you two, let's try and wrap this up. It's getting late and it will be dark soon! I'd like to get this cleared as soon as we can. I'm anxious to see what's inside, too. I know it's hot, and I'm hot, too. But, Samuel, quit clowning. You could work ten horses to death and you know it. Stop ingratiating yourself in front of the lady! Keep working while I set up the tripod. We want to get this done before the good Dr. Abu shows up and sees it sitting up here!"

Julia and Scott finished setting up the tripod while Samuel cleaned out the remaining small rocks that were wedged around the boulder between the wall and the double row of rocks. After he cleared it all away, he went down to the truck and brought back a large steel pry-bar and cable to attach to the block and tackle. Reaching around the boulder with a metal cable, he hooked the end and attached it to the block and tackle.

"Julia, stand here and help me with the rope. Samuel, stay down there and decide where to wedge the pry-bar, then lean on it when I say. Everyone pull when I count three. Understand?" He looked at Julia and Samuel.

"Wouldn't I be more help down there with Samuel on the pry-bar?" Julia asked.

"Who's the leader? I'm sorry . . . I must be getting hot. If the rock comes loose, I don't want you down there. Samuel might have to get out of the way fast and he needs all the room he can get. We don't know which way the rock will swing when it comes loose. I need your help and your weight up here pulling on the rope."

"I was just trying to help, not get in the way."

He reached out his hand to give her a lift up but she brushed it out of the way as she climbed up.

He just shrugged. "Here, hold onto the rope. When I say three, we'll pull. Are you ready, Samuel?"

He looked up and bent his thick back as he pulled on the bar. "Yeah, I'm ready, but I think that with the fire between you two, you could probably crack this thing instead of going to all this trouble!"

"Can it, would you, Samuel? Okay, one, two three, pull!"

Everybody pulled, the rope grew taut, and the veins stood out on Samuel's neck and arms, but nothing happened.

The boulder remained firmly wedged in place.

"Okay, let's try again. Ready, one, two, three, pull!"

This time the end of the boulder moved just a hair.

"Okay, once more, on three! Samuel, move the bar to that crack, a little bit to the left, near where the boulder moved." Scott said as he pointed.

"Looks like a good place," Samuel said as he moved the bar.

"Ready, one, two, three, pull!" This time the boulder came up with a groan and swung back and forth on the end of the tackle.

"Samuel, quick. Get up here and help us pull on this thing. Hurry, it's heavy!" Scott said with a strain in his voice.

The two of them were having difficulty holding the boulder, and even with the advantage of the block and tackle, the weight threatened to pull them off the ground. It was a miracle they were able to dislodge it at all and not bend the tripod.

Samuel quickly climbed out of the hole and scrambled over. Grabbing a hold on the rope up near the pulley on top, he just sat down.

His mass, even though he wasn't tall, was considerable. All muscle and years of hard work made it no contest. The addition of his weight caused the boulder to rise a foot.

Samuel reached up, getting another good purchase and sat down again.

The boulder rose another foot. After a couple more pulls, the boulder was high enough to swing it out over the side.

This was the dangerous part.

If they let go too soon, the rock would fall back in the hole they'd just worked so hard to clear or the tripod could collapse and crush them.

Scott looked at the tripod, then nodded to Samuel. Glancing at each other, they didn't need words to express their mutual understanding and danger of the situation.

Scott turned his head to Julia. "I think you and I can hold it, but Samuel will have to swing it. Are you okay with that, Julia?"

"Yes, so far I am. Let's get this over with!"

Samuel let go of the rope and moved to the side of the boulder, which left Scott and Julia straining to hold the full weight.

Samuel placed his hands on the rock. "Ready when you are."

All Scott could do was groan and nod.

Samuel gave the large rock a shove, and it started swinging back and forth on the end of the line. The centrifugal force started to lift Scott and Julia off their feet.

The rock swung back and forth between the double rows of rocks on both sides.

Samuel waited, then pushed once more and yelled.

"Now!"

Scott and Julia immediately let go of the rope as Samuel gave one last gigantic shove. The boulder went crashing over the edge, tumbling down the slope to its ruin. Scott and Samuel stood on the edge watching its fall, but Julia looked down to where the boulder had come from.

"There's an opening at the bottom!" She turned and hugged Samuel then Scott. "You were right, Scott. You were right all the time! I'm impressed. I don't know how you do it!" She noticed her arms around him and stepped back to the edge of the slab, leaving an odd expression on Scott's face, but a smile on Samuel's.

CHAPTER 12
ABU AT MARKER #1

Scott turned to Samuel. "Would you go down and get the rope out of the truck? I think we need to rope up before going in."

Julia raised her eyebrows. "What do you mean? Why don't we just go in now?"

"I'll be right back with the rope. Why don't you explain what happened to that archeologist in Egypt when he entered the tomb!"

"What archeologist? What tomb?"

"Sir Bernard Shaw, the eminent archeologist once opened a tomb in the Valley of Kings and entered it right away with two of his helpers. The next day, his wife came looking for him and found them all dead about twenty feet inside the tomb. The autopsy report said they'd died from some sort of poison in the air."

"Poison in the air?"

"This was in the early part of the twentieth century and we now know they probably suffocated from lack of oxygen. Certain grains and dead materials stored in tombs can also poison the air and take all the oxygen out of it as they decompose. The lack of oxygen can make you pass out and suffocate. Sewer workers always use a ventilation system before going down a manhole and wear a harness so their partner on top can pull them out. Samuel and I have worked together for a long time and he has the strength to pull me out, if the air's bad. Never go in alone! I doubt the air's poisoned but there may not be any oxygen. Who knows? It's not worth taking the chance."

"I guess I just don't like this waiting."

Smiling, Scott said. "Like Christmas, knowing the day will come but not being able to wait till it comes, right?"

She just shrugged. "I don't know about Christmas. It feels like waiting for your birthday or something, though."

Scott thought this rather odd. No one he'd ever met had been able to wait for Christmas. The thought fled his mind when Samuel came up and tossed the rope and harness to him.

Putting on his harness as Samuel fed the rope through the pulley at the top of the tripod, he rapelled down the slope, then stood at the bottom of the excavation.

Samuel tossed him a large flashlight, then Scott knelt down and peered into the chamber. Sniffing the air a couple times, he said. "Smells okay. I think it's probably fine." Standing back up, he asked Julia. "Would you hand me the video camera?"

Kneeling back down with the camera, he turned on the flashlight and wedged his way under the rock overhang where the boulder had broken the side of the wall as they lifted it out.

Samuel and Julia could hear his voice as he filmed and narrated. "The chamber's about what we thought. It's a twelve-foot cube, unadorned except for the small round hole in the ceiling that's drilled in the rock at an angle. There are some rather strange markings on the far wall. I don't think I was right when I said I thought it was a sheltering place for the tomb workers. Seems to be made for some other purpose. I just don't know right now." He popped his head out and looked up. "The air seems fine I think it's okay if you two want to come down. Bring the Nikon with the flash so we can document the room."

Julia and Samuel made their way over the edge and scrambled under the broken rock and into the small room. They each carried a flashlight and the additional light brought more details out on the walls. All the walls were bare except the north wall. Adorning the north wall was a strange Arabic script.

"Julia, use the Nikon and take pictures of the walls, floor and ceiling. Samuel, do the same with the video camera. The state of preservation's remarkable, the floor is almost spotless, just a little sand and debris that looks like rust and some broken glass under the hole in the ceiling. It doesn't look like a lot of water's got in over the years," Scott said.

He turned back to Julia. "After you've finished, switch to the infrared film and do it all over again. Concentrate on where the writings and markings are. Use a whole roll if you have to. I'm going to make sketches. Let's get to work, people!"

They worked swiftly, each of them a professional. Having used various types of camera equipment before, they knew the settings and their relationship to f/stop and shutter speed. The markings on the wall appeared at first glance to be in an ancient Arabic style script. They were fuzzy and weren't well defined. This wasn't typical for Arabic writing from that period. Most of the older murals Scott had seen used a bold positive clear stroke. This one was different from anything he'd ever seen. In one corner was a painting of a dove, in the other a scroll. Filling the rest of the wall was a large fuzzy Arabic script that he couldn't read and didn't appear to make much sense.

Scott wrinkled his forehead as he finished his sketch. "It's really weird. It is not your normal Arabic writing. It translates like this; 'Mohammad left this: The time will soon come, the time of the brethren.' It says the same thing repeatedly all the way down. In the lower right-hand corner, it says: 'Follow your heart of grace to the four markers. The first of which is this, and woe to the person who brings out the light before the appointed time!' "

"That's all it says?" Julia asked.

"I thought we were on to something big," Samuel said.

"Things aren't always what they seem."

Julia switched to the infrared film and started taking pictures of the back wall when Scott stopped her. "Did you bring your compact, the one we used yesterday?"

"Well, I think so . . . yes. Here it is," she said as she fished it out of her pack.

"Keep going with the infrared. I just want to check out an idea."

"Forgot to freshen up your face, pretty boy?" Samuel asked.

"No, I could say something about your maturity level though, Samuel! I was wondering why the hole in the ceiling's angled. I was thinking of Stonehenge and thought that . . . maybe they wanted the sun to shine in at certain times of the year. Did you notice the sunbeam on the floor? Maybe if I angle the mirror correctly, it will tell us something else . . . I don't know, I'm just trying anything. See the little pile of rust and glass under the hole? Could be an old mirror they used when they built the place or painted the mural. It's really just a long shot, but I thought we should try it. It doesn't seem to show anything that the flashlights don't show," he said as he kept reflecting the sunbeam around the room and looking intently where it fell.

Julia kept snapping away with the Nikon then stood up. "It's a lot cooler in here. I should have brought my sweater."

Scott turned. "I was just getting used to your new style."

"I liked the new style, too," Samuel chimed in.

"I don't know how I got mixed up with the two of you. Part of me likes all this attention and the other part wants to smack you both upside the head."

Scott chuckled. "Let's finish up, okay. I don't know if we'll be able to come back, so collect all we can now. I'll probably have to tell Abu about the place."

They were busy working and filming when they heard the scraping sound of someone's footsteps and a rain of soft gravel fall into the entryway.

Their heads snapped around at the noise.

A high thin voice from outside called, "Mr. Chad, what have you found, another tomb? Why didn't you report this to me?"

Scott stepped to the entrance and called up, "Oh, Dr. Abu, no, it's not another tomb, just a small workman's shelter. I think they must have used it when they were building the tomb." In a quiet whisper, he said to Samuel and Julia, "I wish we'd taken down the tripod. He must have seen it when he came to check on the tomb. Pack the cameras."

Sticking his head out the opening he saw the Egyptian leaning over the edge. "Dr. Chad, please come up and tell me what you've found!"

"It's really nothing, Doctor. Probably just a workman's shelter where they went to cool off. It's empty," Scott said as he struggled out under the entrance. "How are you? I looked for you at your tomb earlier but didn't see you or your men."

"My men took the day off. The new man I promised you has arrived and I left him at your camp. He should be of enormous help."

Scott clambered up to the slab and stretched out his hand. "Good of you to come see us, Doctor. We found a small chamber that's probably from the same time period as the tomb you're working on, but it is empty."

Julia and Samuel climbed up while Scott was talking. Julia walked over to her pack, slowly pulling out her long sleeved sweater and put it back on, then bent over and slowly rolled her skirt down. Abu kept his eyes glued on her as she made herself more presentable. Samuel used the opportunity to stash the cameras in his pack.

"Would you like to see the interior of the chamber?" Scott asked.

"I'm extremely upset with you, Mr. Chad. You have a lot of nerve to explore this area and open an Egyptian archeological site without notifying me. Didn't I tell you the rules and what the Archeological Institute has charged me with. They've entrusted me to protect the antiquities of this country. Should I find that any artifacts or antiquities have been tampered with, I will make it my life's mission to make your life miserable. The penalties are most severe and punishment is unusually swift in this country, so I'm warning you. Opening this site without notifying me is a grave infraction of Egyptian law! I specifically warned you to report to me anything . . . anything at all that you found."

"Dr. Abu, you know my reputation and know that I've never dealt in stolen artifacts. I've been a worthy and prime benefactor for your country and a proponent for protecting your sites and artifacts while keeping them in their natural setting. I've supported your institute for years and will continue to do so for years to come." He smiled and changed his tone. "So don't lecture me when I've done nothing wrong, other than let my curiosity get the better me. We just found the place and I was going to notify you after locating it."

"Mr. Chad, I'm sorry, but I am not my own man in this. I have a supervisor to report to and many responsibilities. Oftentimes, just filling out all the paperwork for a new site keeps me from doing any valuable work for weeks and weeks at a time. I must constantly work for funding, which is never enough to hire an assistant so I can work in the field. My family is underfed and our government is very stingy about granting funds for new research. It is very difficult in this country to protect the sites we have already found and even more difficult to restore them and make them available to the public. So you must understand my reluctance to let this pass!"

"Dr. Abu, I'm working for your government, too, under contract, yes, but also directly for your country. Please look inside the site and you will notice that nothing's missing, nor was there ever anything there. I've set a control point on the slab and have marked this location, which will be dutifully noted on my survey. Please, feel free to take over this site. You may have all the credit for finding it, if you wish, and we'll each get on with our own work. My company will make a donation to your cause that may help expedite your work in the future. Any delays in finishing our contract will upset Mr. Sadat from your Department of the Interior!"

Abu's face turned into a stony grin. "I guess we can let it go this time, Mr. Chad. I knew you would be professional and reasonable. I will get a team up here right away and I look forward to your donation to our cause. I am sure you will be most generous and see that we are able to continue our work throughout the summer." He stopped and looked Scott directly in the eye. "Please remove your equipment, and make sure and notify me directly before entering into any other site!"

Abu and Scott shook hands while Julia made her way down to the truck with her backpack, shovel and pick. Samuel took the tripod, threw it over his shoulder, and grabbed another one of their packs before proceeding down to where Julia was waiting.

"Dr. Abu, I've heard you're an excellent scientist. Please keep up the good work," Scott said as he picked up the remaining shovels and pry bar, then made his way down to join his companions.

Scott finished stacking the equipment in the back of the truck, then looked up the hill to where Dr. Abu was pacing back and forth looking at the slab. "Let's get out of here. Everybody agree?"

"I couldn't have come up with a better suggestion myself," Samuel said.

Julia laughed. "What do you guys do for fun?"

Scott looked at her. "Whose idea was it to stash the cameras while you were putting your sweater back on?"

"That was her idea. She knew Abu would keep his eyes on her. She suggested I grab the cameras and hide them when Abu was distracted," Samuel said.

"Well, he couldn't take his eyes off you when he saw you with your skirt rolled up."

Chapter 13
Hasid's Chat

Hasid reached for the phone, dreading the conversation. "Yes?"

"You had better make sure you get all of Chad's data, Hasid. I will not tolerate failure. You went well beyond your bounds with Jared, and any disobedience to my orders will be severely punished."

"I understand, General. Talbin and I will take the camp and bring back all of Chad's data. I want you to reconsider having them killed. We may need Chad in the future, and I do not think Abu has been able to decipher the writing on the wall of the chamber. What if Abu fails to figure out what this is all about and we kill Chad?"

"You may have something, but I do not like you second guessing my orders."

"I am only trying to offer my council, General."

"It is written that a wise man has many counselors. I will listen to you and take this under consideration, this one time. Put the plan into motion, but make absolutely sure you get all the data Chad has, all his notes, his computers, his photographs, everything. Do you understand me!"

"I understand, General, and it will be done as you command."

"I am disappointed. You should have told me you knew Chad."

Hasid's gut churned, but he quickly answered. "You never asked and I didn't think it important." He wondered who told Quati. *How did he know? Was he becoming that transparent?*

"I will be the judge of what is important. Remember that. I hope this does not affect your judgment. I am tempted to take you off this little endeavor of ours. Your behavior in dealing with Rogowski and pulling Jared off, knowing my express orders, makes me doubt your judgment and commitment."

Hasid quickly pushed down the anxiety he was feeling and said, "Rest assured, Chad means nothing to me. I knew him when we were children, nothing more."

"Word is Chad has hired a Jewess to work as his botanist. You may have to take her out, if it comes to that. You have not become soft on me have you?"

"You know me. I will do as you command. My only desire is to see the Great Jihad spread, as do you. Our desires are the same."

"Well, be sure to tell me if something comes up and changes your mind. I want to know how my soldiers are doing. Now get together with Talbin and keep me posted."

Hasid stood there holding the dead receiver in his hand. "Yes, General, as you command."

Samuel bounced the Hummer over the rough trail toward their camp while Scott brooded over the whole experience. He kept ruminating about the look on Abu's face when they'd come up out of the chamber. There are thousands of old workers caves throughout Egypt. It wasn't as if it was a big deal and they both knew it. Something else seemed to be flickering across Abu's eyes when he'd confronted them.

"That was close. I should have left one of us on watch. Should-a, would-a, could-a. Hindsight's twenty-twenty. Next time we're involved in something like that let's try to be more prepared. I could kick myself for not taking down the tripod."

Julia was more afraid of Abu than Scott was. She just didn't know how to formulate her words and what she could safely tell. "I know what you mean but, for some reason, I don't think we've seen the last of Abu. The way he was looking at me makes me think we're going to see more of him! Remember, he hired the workmen that were around when Ali broke his ankle and now he's brought us that new one. We'd better keep an eye on him!"

"I think you're right. His eyes were glued on you. Quick thinking on your part, by the way," Scott said.

Samuel turned toward Scott. "Very quick in doling out the company's money, aren't you? It was interesting the way he asked, don't you think? I thought he was going to stick to his guns and actually turn us over to the authorities. I like the way you soothed his ego and suggested you could help support his ongoing operations. Did you catch the way he said his family didn't have enough money?"

"Yeah, I caught it. That's what gave me the idea to talk about my donations to the Egyptian Archeological Institute in the past. I hate to do it, but bribery's a way of life in this corner of the world. Call it squeeze or bakeesh or whatever you want. The way I offered it, he could keep his pride . . . save him face! It's a system as old as time, and even though I don't like it, it's been going on for centuries. Get used to it if you want to do business around here.

It's actually going to cost us a very small part of what we stand to make. The preliminary results are in and it looks like a large oilfield could extend under the Gulf of Suez! If this bears out, Egypt stands to do very well and we'll make enough to help pay the good doctor. We have to make sure and keep the ecology intact. Tourism's the largest growing business and keeping all those dive sites and hotels along the coasts running depends on keeping the area clean and natural. No one's exploited the area up until now, for they thought nothing was here. Then came the rich tourists who wanted to see what's below the surface and, viola, hotels, dive operators and the rest. It's still primitive, but we passed a couple of nice hotels in those villages along the way down here. You've seen some of the others scattered along the coast but particularly down by the tip at Rash Mohammad."

Evening was closing in and some high thin cirrus clouds were blowing their way in from the west, the sun lighting them into streaks of red, gold and a pale violent shade, which gave the camp a golden look. Luke and Alex stood outside the main tent as they pulled up. Julia and Scott hopped down out of the truck and made their way over to the mess tent while Samuel parked the Hummer with the other vehicles. Scott still felt nervous from the encounter with Abu, but it was impossible not to enjoy the beautiful sunset and evening.

"Hey, Luke, Alex, how did your day go? Did you get your stuff done?" Scott said as he walked up.

"Sure did. The preliminary results are more promising then we believed. The field could be as big as the one we discovered in Saudi Arabia last year. I won't know till we get more seismic information and finish the computer graphing and modeling for the report, though," Alex said.

Luke's face beamed. "I've some better news, if possible!"

"What could be better than a major oilfield?" Alex asked.

"Come on out with it, Luke. What've you found?" Scott asked.

Luke stood up and faced the group. "Well the preliminary results indicate a large deposit of gold ore near the Gulf of Aqaba. Remember, this is a very preliminary finding and the other cores might show something different, but the results are promising. The ore might assay ten ounces per ton. That's high-grade ore, isn't it, Scott?"

"Very high-grade. I think we're going to make a geologist out of you yet! You need to take Julia over and see if there are any ecological difficulties with mining the site. She also needs to go over to the western side to help Alex finish the botanical portion of the survey. It's important to see what ecological damage might happen should they exploit the area for oil. Gold mining can be very dangerous to the ecology also. The process used for extracting the ore can easily damage the environment if handled incorrectly."

"Where were you three off to today? We didn't see or hear from you all day. Anything interesting or was this just a day off for sightseeing?" Alex asked.

"We were over by Al Sud's tomb and ran into the good Doctor Abu! He said the new worker was here to replace Ali. Has he arrived yet?" Scott asked.

Luke gave Scott an odd look. "Yeah, he's here. His name's Talbin and he came right after you left this morning. He seems to know rock drilling but only speaks Arabic so directions were a little rough. He's in the workers tent, I think, setting up his kit. Want to meet him? I'll have one of the guys go over and get him, if you want?"

"No, not right now. I need something to eat first and then I want to work on the reports and go over the seismic charts you made. I'd like to see Alex's preliminary results on the gold ore. We should take a larger sample of cores in the area. It's weird, I never thought we'd find gold out here."

They walked over to the command tent where they found the new man, Talbin, standing by the computer and plotter looking at their maps on the table. He was tall with long dark hair, a full beard, and wearing a grey robe.

Stopping at the entrance, they stared at him and he just looked back with a blank expression on his face. Scott stepped forward extending his hand and said in Arabic, "You must be Talbin? Abu said you were familiar with rock drilling. Luke told me you handled yourself pretty well out on the west slope today. I am Scott Chad. You will be working for me."

"Yes, I worked with Mr. Luke today over by the Gulf of Suez. We used the wonderful new drill to take samples, the one you brought over from America. I have worked with rock drills before in the Sahara and in Afghanistan where I worked for the Russians, but never worked with a drill like that."

The general workmen never came into the command tent. To have this newcomer looking over their equipment, computers and maps was disturbing to Julia in a way she couldn't explain.

"Well, Talbin, welcome aboard." Scott pointed at the tent door and explained, "I need you to get a good night's rest. You'll be working with Luke first thing in the morning. We have some reports to go over so if you'd excuse us please."

Talbin stood there for a moment looking Scott in the eye then tilted his head, and walked briskly out of the tent.

Julia shook herself. "Well that was strange to say the least. I don't feel I can trust that guy. He gives me the creeps."

"I didn't like the way he looked at me when he left, but we need to get the drilling done and keep it on schedule. We can leave the detailed stuff to Luke and Alex, but we need to keep on top of this phase and get it organized for the final results."

"Well, what do you want us to do with the film and other information we've collected?"

"I need you to develop it right away, the regular and infrared film. Samuel, I want you to make a copy of the videotape and then download it onto a disc so we have a digital copy. Do it now and see if we can meet back here in an hour or so."

"Yes, sir, right away, boss man sir!" Julia saluted and turned about with a snap and left for the darkroom attached to the back of the mess tent.

Scott smiled, shook his head and looked at Samuel. "After you've finished making copies of the tape and downloading the digital information, would you go over and keep an eye on Julia?"

"What, don't you trust her? She's been working with us for months now and everything she's done seems up and above board."

Scott paced the tent lost in thought for a moment as he tried to compose his thoughts. "No, that's not it. I trust her, but I don't trust the others in camp or Abu. Maybe the stuff Rusta said! Just keep and eye on her. It'll probably be a waste of time but I'd feel better if you did."

The darkroom was fully furnished and they used it constantly for documenting their survey sites. They could develop anything from black and white, infrared, to 35 mm film in color. They could also make prints, slides and digitally scan the photographs for storage on their computers. Julia pulled the tent flap closed and tied it, turning the sign outside so that it said, 'Do not enter.' She went through a second flap made from a dark fabric, dug into the ground then tied that door closed. She turned on the safelight and turned off the main light then took out her materials and tanks. It didn't take long to develop the film and make the prints. She dried some of the more promising shots with a hair dryer, made a second set of negatives and put them in an envelope to take to Scott.

While she was working on developing the film, Scott downloaded the digital camera to his laptop and reviewed the images from the wall of the chamber. He knew he should go over Luke's assay report on the ore, but Luke was competent and it could wait until they assembled more information.

The chamber and its secret seemed to pique his interest more than the gold, partly because of the way Abu had shown up. Or was it something Father Basil said? It was strange, but he wanted to get to the bottom of it. A mystery always challenged him and the writing on the chamber wall was like nothing he'd ever seen before.

Julia came to the tent with an envelope full of pictures, followed a minute later by Samuel. "Well, that didn't take long. Let's see what you two have." Scott said.

"The pictures don't show much more than what we saw in the chamber.

Just the fuzzy-looking Arabic script on the wall," she said as she handed the envelope to Scott. "The infrared doesn't seem to show anything either, except for something . . . almost geometric, that seems to have blurred the film. It's most predominant on the shots where you reflected the sun with the mirror. The sunlight may have overexposed the film or something, but I'd swear the light meter reading was correct."

"Here, let me see."

She handed the pictures to Scott, pulling out the infrared exposures to show him. She leaned over his shoulder where he sat in the chair, her long hair brushing against his face, and pointed. "See here? This is where you were reflecting the sunlight with the mirror and shined it on the wall. I was still using the flash so we may have overexposed the film, even though it almost looks like a double exposure. See that geometric pattern on the mural. Kind of weird, huh?"

He shook his head. "I see what you mean. Did you find anything different on your videos, Samuel?"

He handed Scott the disk. "It looks the same as when we were there. I didn't notice anything like these pictures show. Well . . . maybe when you moved the light around. I thought it was just the shadows though!"

"I know it's getting late, but I have to help Luke get started tomorrow, so if you both could look at them one more time, I'd appreciate it. I need you both over near Aqaba tomorrow where Luke's working. We need to put some finishing touches on the report." Scott rubbed his head with both hands. "Julia, when you're done, would you mind leaving the prints with me? I want to run them into the scanner and save the images on my hard drive?"

"Sure, Scott, go ahead. I don't read Arabic anyway, and I've no idea what I'd be looking for."

After Julia and Samuel left, Scott started feeding the photos into the scanner and downloading them onto his laptop. When he was done, he made a backup disk that he put in his backpack and then started looking at the shots again.

He kept thinking about the small pile of debris and broken glass on the floor of the chamber. He thought he had been on the right track when he reflected the sunlight on the wall, hoping to find some hidden message, but there was nothing there except the fuzzy writing and geometric patterns.

An hour later, he was still staring at one of the photos on his laptop without any insight. Setting the pile of eight by ten infrared enlargements in front of him, he closed the program.

The blue light from the liquid crystal display was dimly illuminating the top photo, as he looked at it cross-eyed with fatigue.

He just sat staring at it and at first thought he'd fallen asleep, when the picture snapped into focus and wasn't fuzzy any longer.

Shaking his head, he jerked the photo off the pile, staring at it and moving it closer to his eyes, then suddenly he smiled.

It was finally clear how advanced the people who made the chamber were and what it meant. He knew what the message was! He shot out of his chair to get Julia and Samuel then stopped dead in his tracks staring at Talbin holding a Kalashnikov assault rifle with another man standing behind him in the dim light, holding Julia with a knife to her throat.

CHAPTER 14
LOST DATA

Hasid and Talbin stood in the shadows outside the camp. Hasid turned to Talbin. "You know what to do. Take everything, every photo, every negative, any evidence they took from the holy chamber."

"My men and I will do our work. Where will you be?"

"I will be the first into the command tent. Send your men to round up all the others, but wait for my command. I want the camp asleep. We will go at three, when everyone is most sluggish."

The moon shone weakly through the high thin clouds as Hasid stood to the side of the tent holding his Uzi.

Talbin struggled up the slope, dragging the woman toward the tent, pausing at the entrance as he pulled Julia close.

Achmed crept up the slope then stood by Talbin, who then shoved Julia into his grasp. He took a large knife out of his robe and held it to her throat, then shook her like a small doll. "What have you done with the photos? I want them now," he screamed as he pushed her through the tent flap, followed quickly by Talbin.

Hasid quietly moved around the backside of the tent to listen and provide any backup if needed.

Scott shot up from his chair as Julia stumbled through the flap. "What is the meaning of this, Talbin? What photos are you talking about? What do you mean by coming in here holding a knife to her throat?"

"I will ask the questions! Do not play the fool with me, Chad. You know very well what photos I am talking about! Abu saw your camera equipment. You were taking pictures and despoiling our holy place, a place that is sacred to Islam, a place where the Prophet Mohammed spent time in prayer and contemplation. It is a desecration for one of the infidel to have been in the chamber without a Mullah's permission."

"Okay, Talbin, give me a minute. Don't let Achmed hurt the lady!"

"I want the pictures now! Get them!" Talbin screamed, pointing his rifle at Scott.

Scott carefully stood. "Let her go first, then I'll give you the pictures."

"You are in no position to bargain. Achmed, cut off her finger. Do it now!"

Achmed grabbed her arm, looked once at Talbin, then brought the knife down to her hand.

Julia looked at Talbin and screamed, "Please don't let him cut me!" But Scott saw something else in her eyes, something he had never seen before: a look of determination, a sense of strength and hardness that welled to the surface, a look not of fear but of anger.

Her screams unfroze Hasid's heart. He knew that voice. It awoke emotions in him that had lain buried and dormant for years. Rushing around the side of the tent, he dashed through the flap, seeing Scott standing by his desk with Talbin pointing his rifle at him and Achmed holding a knife to Julia's hand.

"Hold, Achmed, change of plans." He motioned for Scott to move over by the desk with his Uzi. "Achmed, stand by the entrance and make sure we are not disturbed. Scott, I want you to gather all your computers, disks and notes and give them to Talbin. Do it now, before someone gets hurt."

Scott could only shake his head as he took in the sight of Hasid pointing his Uzi at him. With his best boyhood friend threatening him with a gun, his system went into shock as he took in the situation. "Hasid, what are you doing? Why are you doing this to us?"

"Not another word, Scott. I mean it. We work for different causes now. I prayed that our paths would not cross this way, but it is Allah's will, in his wisdom. Maybe you will see the truth in what we are doing, who knows."

"Hasid, how can you do this to us?" Julia stammered. "Why are you doing this?"

Suddenly Hasid's emotions were boiling inside of him, roiling around and twisting in his mind in ways he had not experienced in years. He tried to quench them and bring back the hate and anger but the wave kept on. With a supreme effort and force of will he snapped, "You have despoiled one of Islam's holy places. You, a Jew, you dare ask me why I am doing this. Answer Talbin. What have you done with the negatives?"

"They're in the tent at the top of the hill. There's a darkroom inside and they're hanging up to dry."

"Talbin, call Fisal and go get them, do it quickly. Leave Achmed with me to help me cover these two, remember Rogowski is still around here somewhere. Remember what he did to Jared."

"Why not just shoot them and be done with it, we have our orders?" Talbin said.

"Yes, we do and yours are to obey me, now move!"

Talbin nodded and rushed out of the tent while the four remained, Scott staring at Hasid, while Achmed held a knife on Julia by the entrance to the tent.

"I want all your notes and information, Scott, and I want all of it," Hasid said as he pointed the Uzi at him.

Scott quickly reached down to his desk, "Hold on. Hold on, here take them, you win! Here's the folder, I don't want anyone hurt!"

"You should have thought of that before breaking into things you were not supposed to." Hasid leafed through the folder, "Where are the disks? I'm sure you made a copy for your computer."

Scott was desperately trying to gain more time. He didn't know where Samuel was and was counting on his showing up.

"What has happened to you Hasid, I thought we used to be friends. I'm just a simple surveyor and geologist and love archeology. It's my life's work to discover lost things. I didn't spoil or desecrate the place. I believe sites like that are for the benefit of everyone, especially the people in the area where they're found."

"That chamber is one of Islam's sacred sites; it is not for an infidel dog to tell me what to do with it, especially when I am the one holding the gun." Hasid pointed the barrel at Scott's chest, "enough, give me your computer, disks and all your notes too."

Scott sighed, leaned over and turned off his laptop, closed it and unplugged the cords. He collected the laptop, disks and a small notebook he'd jotted some of his notes down in and carried the armload over to Hasid. While he was handing them over, he heard a muffled grunt by the entrance to the tent and dropped the laptop on the floor at Hasid's feet. Achmed, who was holding a knife to Julia's throat, turned at the sound and was hit in the side of the head by Samuel's right hook.

The punch was delivered with all Samuel's force and dropped him to the ground like a bag of flour.

Samuel strode into the tent and shoved Julia behind him. Hasid jumped back from Scott, ignoring the laptop and immediately fired the Uzi into the ground at Samuel's feet. Samuel leapt back, raising his arms, "Okay, enough. Take what you need. Just don't shoot anyone!"

"Achmed, did he hurt you?" Hasid asked, as the man rose to his feet, rubbing his jaw where Samuel had hit him. The third man that was outside was moaning and also rising to his feet. "Are you all right Abdullah?"

"I am fine, Hasid, let us get out of here," he said, shaking his head.

"Grab the disks and computer, take them down to truck and start it up, get Talbin and Fisal then wait for us. Achmed and I will be down, as soon as we have finished here!"

a p o c r y p h a

Abdullah picked up the computer and notes then paused at the entrance, "remember, our orders we were to leave no witnesses."

"Your orders are to do what I say and do them now!" Hasid said.

Abdullah took the computer and notes, shrugged, and left, while Achmed stood at the entrance and brandished his knife at Scott.

Hasid walked backwards to the entrance and pointed the Uzi, directly at Scott. He waved the barrel at Samuel and Julia, motioning them to get behind the main desk.

Hasid smiled, "I did promise Abu, but he's a fool. He's been working for the Egyptians in their Archeological Institute for far too long and he has no idea what this is really all about. He plays the role set out for him very well and it's sad to disappoint him. I wish there was another way, but you've seen our faces and unfortunately heard everyone's names now!"

Scott and Samuel were furiously trying to come up with a plan. As they edged up against the desk, Samuel reached behind and palmed a rock pick that was sitting on a low file cabinet.

Scott looked at Hasid. "Since we gave you everything, why don't you just take the stuff and we'll figure we never saw you! You can leave before anyone gets hurt."

A cold smile lit Hasid's face. "Maybe I can make some sport out of this."

"What's happened to you Hasid," Scott said. "We used to be friends?"

Suddenly, Hasid's mind was thrown back to when they were teenagers together. He pulled himself together with a force of will and straightened his shoulders. "Allah's will is what has happened. That was in another life. Forget it, you never knew me."

Achmed spoke up, with a look of nervousness on his face. "Come on, Hasid, we do not need this, get on with it, or leave them alone. I could tie them up. We really need to get going, and need to get across the border and to Medina by morning."

"Do not talk about our business in front of them. I will get going when it is time, as Allah wills. The woman might bring a lot of money. She may even get to like being a slave."

Samuel edged slightly away from the desk as the two talked. "Oh, as Allah wills, is it? First we talk of killing and now you bring religion and God into it, I don't understand you people, first you call us infidel's, when in fact you're the infidels or is it Kaffirs? You talk about trying to kill us when in fact we've been trying to help your people for years."

"Enough . . . enough of this useless talk! Achmed take the girl to the truck, go now!" He then pointed the gun at Scott.

Achmed grabbed Julia's arm and started dragging her toward the entrance to the tent when two things happened at once. Hasid took his eyes off them as he ordered Achmed. Samuel nodded once at Scott, who dove to the floor and rolled at Hasid's ankles, while Samuel spun around and threw the rock pick, planting the point deep in Achmed's butt. Achmed screamed and Hasid spun at the sound, spinning on the balls of his feet and leveling the Uzi at Samuel. Scott rolled and grabbed Hasid's ankle, lifting and twisting it, knocking him to the floor. As Hasid fell, his head hit the sharp corner of a file cabinet, gouging the base of his skull.

Abdullah ran back into the tent, after hearing Achmed's scream, carrying a 9-mm Beretta rifle which he pointed at Julia's head. "Enough of this!" He looked around at his companions. "Are you all right Achmed?"

Achmed pulled out the rock pick with a groan and nodded with a grimace. The wound was messy and painful, but not serious.

Abdullah motioned to Achmed. "Pick up Hasid and put him in the truck." He then looked at Scott and Samuel. "If anyone moves, a 9-mm slug will end this conversation. I have had enough. Move Achmed, quick, I know you are injured but we have to move now."

Achmed held one hand on his butt, grabbed Hasid's limp body and threw him over his shoulder. He made his way out and a moment later they heard the door shut on one of the Hummers and the engine start.

"Do not get any ideas, Mr. Chad. I will use this thing, I am not like Hasid who likes to talk and play games. He has his orders, as we all do, but I do not want to kill you, but will have no hesitation should the need arise. Nor will I draw this out with useless discussions, like Hasid would."

Achmed limped back into the tent a few minutes later. "Talbin and Fisal found all the negatives. There were two bundles, one set was hanging to dry and the other appears to have been dried with a hair dryer."

"Go to the truck and wait there," Abdullah snapped.

He slowly backed away and raised his rifle and fired the high-powered slugs at the equipment in the corner. The impact of the high-velocity shells blew apart the computer, plotter and monitors, which disintegrated into pieces and flew about the room. Scott and his companions automatically ducked as the rifle fired. Abdullah ejected the spent clip and expertly inserted a fresh one, cocking the bolt in one smooth motion.

"If you try to follow, bigger trouble will come to you than this, I guarantee it. You should be grateful I have spared your lives, next time you will not be so lucky. I know you are itching to follow us, but if you try, we will not spare you a second time. Stay in the tent till we are gone," Abdullah said as he backed out of the tent and ran out to the waiting truck.

The moment Abdullah left, Scott turned to Samuel, "Grab the knife in the desk and open the back of the tent!"

Samuel leapt over the desk in a flash, grabbing the knife, and quickly slicing the fabric. They dashed through the opening, leaving Julia standing there flabbergasted. She looked around the tent, and quickly made her way to the main door where she stopped and listened, peering out into the dark night. She waited until she heard the truck's door close, then dashed out, pulling a small 25-caliber automatic out of an ankle holster and ran to the bottom of the hill.

The Hummer started up and instead of going up the hill toward the monastery, Abdullah drove around to the area where the trucks were parked. Julia heard the clatter as they opened up with their Kalashnikov's, firing a staccato burst at each truck, shredding their tires and punching holes in the sheet metal.

They then spun the truck around, kicking up clouds of gravel and dust as they raced around the west edge of camp toward the gravel track that led back to St. Catherine's.

Julia took up a stance on top of a boulder as the Hummer came around the bend and emptied the 25-caliber automatic at the fleeing vehicle, using up all six shots as she took aim at the tires. The shots didn't seem to slow it or make any difference as the truck continued off into the distance.

"Whoa, what was that?" Scott said as he came running up to where she was standing.

"Just something my mother told me to carry, whenever I was out in the country with strange men." Julia said.

Samuel came running up too, "Sounded like you knew what you were doing, but I don't think it did much good. That thing's a peashooter. I don't think it would even go through the side of the Hummer from this distance. There's more to you than meets the eye, I'd say. Thanks for trying anyway. Where'd you have that thing hidden, by the way?"

"In a little ankle holster. I always carry it when I'm out in the bush, just in case of trouble. I wasn't trying to shoot them, just take out a tire or two. Do you realize we've lost everything! All the computers are smashed, the plotters ruined, the film and the disk from your computer and everything else is lost! Everything we did or found is for nothing, what are we going to do now?"

Samuel looked at her, "We haven't lost everything. We still have all our survey data and everything from Luke and Alex's work. It's on a backup disc. The only thing they took of value was Scott's computer with the chamber pictures. They weren't interested in the survey data, just the information on that chamber we opened this morning. It's a set back, I agree, but we can replace the trucks, equipment and other stuff, pretty quickly. The problem is we're probably stuck waiting around here for a couple of weeks, with nothing much to do."

Scott joined in after thinking a moment, "No, they obviously didn't care a bit about the survey data. They're concerned about what we found this morning. Good old Dr. Abu and now these three. You know, Samuel, it's probably got something to do with those three who tried to rough you up. Talbin was only interested in that chamber and what's inside of it. You heard him, he was outraged we'd been in there."

Samuel turned to Scott, "'One thing at a time' my mother used to say. Let's see how much damage they did to the trucks. I'd really like to go after them . . . but." Samuel's arms were taut as he pounded his fist into his palm, "I don't think letting them get away is a good idea, but by the time we get organized here, I'm sure they'll be half way to Suez!"

"You're right, Samuel. Let's see what we have left to work with," Scott said as they made their way down the hill. The workers were milling around their tents, woken by the sharp shots from the rifles. Luke and Alex came running up full of questions, but Scott raised his hand, "Some of the local brotherhood just having fun with us. They haven't disrupted the survey thankfully. It was a close call and they seem to have shot up our vehicles. I want you to help Samuel and see what you can do to get the trucks running again. We have to stay in business. Thankfully no one was hurt."

Hasid stood outside the truck they had taken from Chad's camp. He was shaking inside and wondering if it showed to Talbin and his companions. Her scream had paralyzed him, were all his old ghosts coming back to haunt him?

Talbin looked over at Hasid, "We should get moving and report back to General Quati as soon as possible. Those were his orders."

Hasid glared at him, "Since when are you in the habit of telling me what to do? Did not Quati put me in charge of this operation?"

"You seemed to freeze in there, that wasn't like you. I have worked with you before. What happened Hasid?"

"Nothing, that lady reminded me of someone I knew once, they are dead now and it only brought up old feelings. It is over now. Yes you are right, Talbin, you did well back there, but do not quote orders to me ever again. I need to think about the next step. Chad did not find the lost writings, that much is clear, and Dr. Abu does not know what any of it means."

Her scream had frozen him. Dredging up emotions he had not felt in years. Chad was bad enough, but Julia.

His mind went back to when he had first met Julia in Paris.

Hasid stood outside the little Parisian café watching the redhead walk up to the counter and order her lunch. He'd grown into a talk, dark and handsome man and was spending a couple of weeks in Paris before starting College at Oxford in the fall. The tall redhead grabbed her tray and looked around for a place to sit, catching Hasid's eye, who nodded to the empty seat beside him. She looked around once more, lifted her chin and walked over nodding to Hasid. He spoke in his halting French and she answered back in French equally as bad. He then tried what little German he knew, switched to English and the conversation was off.

"So tell me what are you doing in Paris this August?"

"Spending a couple of weeks with a group of students, studying the art and architecture. What about you?" between mouthfuls of her sandwich.

"Same as you, a couple of weeks then off to England to College."

"Oh, really. Which college?"

"Oxford I'm afraid, family thinks I need polishing up or something."

They went to a party above a little restaurant that evening. Julia was wearing a black leather mini-skirt, black heels and a lavender silk blouse that set off her complexion and red hair.

Hasid was wearing a cream linen suit with black tie, his thick black hair combed back.

A number of local students attended and all different languages seem to be spoken at once, but mostly French and English. A small acoustic band was set up in the corner playing a succession of hot jazz tunes from the thirties and forties. Hasid and Julia danced some, which Julia was good at and Hasid rather stiff, talked with the other students and finally took their leave.

Stopping at a little outdoor café, they ordered espresso and sat at a sidewalk table. The evening was pleasant and for a moment, they just watched the couples strolling.

Julia finally turned to Hasid, "Well, how do you like Paris nightlife?"

"It's okay, but I must say the only thing worthwhile I've seen so far is you."

"Did you practice that line or is that how you really feel?"

"You've got me there. I thought about what to say to you all afternoon and rejected most of the thoughts off hand. It's just that I'm rather shy and have never really been with girls too much."

"Well you did a good job there; did anyone ever tell you that you're handsome?"

"No one who looks as beautiful as you do."

"So how long are you going to be in Paris?"

"Long enough to get to know you I hope."

She crossed her legs as she sat in the chair, distracting Hasid from what he was going to say next.

The next few months were a whirlwind of joy. He had never felt this way about someone else and the only time he had felt such peace was when living in Illinois with his parents.

When the news of his father's death came, his world came crashing in like a black cloud of despair.

He slowly walked to the café where he was going to meet Julia, not noticing the pedestrians and almost hit by a Paris cabby as he crossed the street.

Julia immediately knew something was wrong as she saw him walk up. "What happened, Hasid?"

"My father is dead, gunned down in Tel-a-viv, by the Israelis."

Julia froze. They had never talked about religion and being brought up in France and Belgium, Hasid had naturally assumed she was just another girl, maybe Catholic or something. His Islam was not practiced all that much and his mother and father had not instilled anything deep into him as he had grown up. It was cultural. The fact that she had not told Hasid that her parents were Jewish seemed to come rushing to the front of her consciousness.

"Why, what do you know about it?"

"He was innocent, just crossing the street when the police opened up and started shooting. They say that some Palestinians bombed a bus and the police were trying to retaliate against the bombers, but my father was just crossing the street . . . I am going to miss him terribly."

She put her arms around, him holding his head while he sobbed.

When he finally lifted his head up the look in his eyes stabbed her heart. It was if the light had gone out, replaced by something cold and feral.

"What are you going to do Hasid?"

"I am going home, my mother will need me and we will put my father in his grave. After that I do not know."

"Please call, do you want me to come with you, I have classes, but will skip them if you want?"

"No, this is a family matter, I will call if I can."

That was the last time he had seen Julia and the ten years had only intensified his hatred.

Walking down to the parking area, they stood in horror as they looked at the damage. Antifreeze and oil flowed over the ground and puddle here and there, while the trucks were leaning crazily on their flattened and shredded tires. Scott looked disgusted as he stood there with his hands on his hips, his blue eyes staring to the northwest at the gravel track Abdullah had taken when he'd left. "See what you can do with this mess, Samuel."

Samuel, dressed in blue jeans and a T-shirt that left his huge hairy arms hanging out like some stevedore, said, "Okay, Luke, you and Alex follow me, let's see what we can to do to straighten out this mess."

They started taking an inventory of what they had available to get the vehicles going again. "It's important to get at least two of the six wheelers going so that you can work on the survey and one of the Hummers so we can go for supplies. I don't think we're going to chase after these guys, though I wish we could. They're long gone by now anyway. So, let's get to work."

Scott walked up to the tent with Julia, "Look at this mess, we have to try and straighten it up." The plotter, computers and stereo optics were shattered where they were hit by the high-powered slugs. Equipment lay in pieces and the shattered pieces were scattered all over the floor of the tent.

Scott and Julia set to organizing it and trying to clean it up. A couple hours later Samuel came up, "Well, I think we can get one of the Hummers going again and two of the six-wheelers. I was able to salvage the radiator from one of the Hummers, where a slug went right into the manifold. That one's out till we can get it to a shop or get the parts sent over."

Scott collapsed into a camp chair with his head in his hands, "I don't know Samuel, it's not like me but I almost feel defeated on this. Why would they come and take all that stuff. They can take all the pictures they want at any time. I think we're missing something. What are they up to?"

"It's not like you to just give up Scott. You can do it, I've never seen you give up. Figure out how to beat them at their own game, that's what we do best anyway. Get off it and get your chin up, there's still more to this than meets the eye. Rusta warned us, they don't want us nosing around for some reason. You heard Talbin. I'm going to go finish working on the trucks, should be done by dawn."

Scott sat there after he left. All of a sudden a spark of intuition came to him as Samuel's words said sank into his thoughts. He sat up and an odd look came to his eyes as a small smile appeared. He turned to Julia, "More than meets the eye. I wanted to head out and chase this thing down anyway, but was worried about finishing the survey. Certain things Father Basil said about choices and being chosen. Now I have to make the choice. More than meets the eye, ha!"

Julia just stood there, "What are you talking about?"

He smiled at her stubbornness, "Who ever built the chamber and left the markers was way ahead of their time. They knew science and things that have been lost till recently. Go get the other laptop."

She felt depressed looking at the mess but responded, "What are you talking about again? I feel hopeless. Look at this mess. We've lost everything, all our notes, the computers, all the equipments smashed . . . everything do you hear me!"

"We still have ourselves and we can't quit now! We can't quit, we'd never know what's waiting for us if we did, and we may never have another chance at something like this. We have a choice to figure this all out, or we can go to authorities who won't do anything. We have to choose to go on or not. Only I feel . . . well, feel's not the right word, I . . . something's been stirred up inside of me. I think I'm meant to see this through till the very end. They could have just shot us, remember their orders, Talbin wasn't going to follow them and Abdullah was upset." He noticed the look she was giving him, "No, that doesn't mean we don't do anything. It means just what I said; think about it for a minute, would you?"

"What you're saying is they could have shot us and that would have stopped this whole thing. They then smashed our camp and took all our data? I feel so useless they took everything we worked so hard for. All the data on the chamber's gone."

Samuel walked into the tent, looking at the shattered laptop, file cabinets and mess. Scott turned and grabbed his backpack while they looked on. When he stood back up, he was holding the disc he'd burned as a backup. "No, we haven't lost everything, I burned a backup before they came. I put all your photos on it, Julia, and your video, Samuel. The only thing really gone, is my notebook and the photos taken with the regular film. I only backed up the shots taken with the infrared film. We won't be bored. As soon as we get Luke and Alex back and the trucks sorted out, we can take a little vacation, I know just the spot."

Julia beamed, "You're a wonder, Scott. I've been so tired. I would have waited till morning before remembering to backup the data."

Samuel added, "Backup soon and backup often. Isn't that what I taught you Scott?"

"And I thank you, Samuel, your little lectures over the years have kept us out of more trouble."

"Well here's the scoop, I have one Hummer running and two of the trucks can be used. Ali will be able to keep some of the crews working while we're gone."

"Where do you think we should go, Samuel?" Scott asked.

"To where this all leads us of course."

"I feel anxious, nervous and lousy about all this but also like I need to see this through. Keep working on the trucks, do the best you can to get them going as soon as possible," Scott said.

Samuel looked at him and laughed, "Okay, where do I sign up? Where we going? I've never been a quitter and you know it. I for one want to get the guys who destroyed our camp and have been hounding us from the beginning."

"It's not for revenge, but I agree with you. It's for something else that I want to find these men. Talbin's not the one in charge, did you hear him? No, there are bigger fish than him."

Samuel nodded and went out of the tent and back to work on the trucks, while Scott and Julia continued their discussion in the tent.

"Scott, now you're talking in riddles, can't you make yourself a little clearer?"

"Fine, bring me the other laptop from your tent and I'll show you."

CHAPTER 15
MAGIC EYE

Scott loaded up the disk and burned another copy as a precaution. "Now look, this is where it gets interesting, see anything?"

"No, looks the same way it did in the chamber to me, just that fuzzy pattern and old Arabic writing on the wall."

"Now look closely, here try this," Scott switched the program to show the streaming video Samuel had taken. "See, this is where I reflected the sunlight on the wall with your compact, see anything different?"

"The writing looks fuzzier . . . maybe . . . oh, I see some sort of geometric design or something, but it seems out of focus."

"You're actually seeing it. Now look at the infrared shots you took when I reflected the sunlight on the wall."

"I see the same thing, maybe the geometric pattern's clearer. It almost looks like a design of some sort now."

Scott punched the print button on the computer and sent a copy to the only remaining printer, "What we really need is a photo printer to get better resolution." He grabbed the print and said, "Hold it up by the screen and look at it kind of cross-eyed, move the picture in and out toward your nose and the design will become clear."

She looked up at him as if he was nuts, "What do you mean cross-eyed?"

He just smiled, "Just try it . . . it's hard to explain, just give it a try."

She stared at the picture and moved it in and out while thinking, *if someone sees me they're going to think I'm nuts.* She was a little nervous therefore. "I don't see anything different, what am I supposed to see?"

He just smiled at her, "The answer to the riddle, of course!"

"What riddle?"

"The riddle of Mohammed's apocrypha writings of course, that's what this is all about!"

"What do you mean, Mohammed's Apocryphal writings?"

"Just look at the picture, it's like one of those magic eye books or posters where objects appear in three dimensional relief that are hidden in the design. Didn't you ever look at one of those when you were a kid?"

"No, I don't' know what you mean, I've never heard of such a thing."

He frowned at her answer, "Where did you say you grew up?"

She snapped, "Illinois, I told you that in my application, what does that have to do with anything?"

Scott raised an eyebrow, "Well, there's more to you than meets the eye, but these books and posters were all the rage back when I was a kid, and I'm surprised you've never seen or heard of one. Try this, take your two index fingers and hold them end to end. What do you see?"

"Why my fingers touching each other, of course."

"Now defocus your eyes and look at the far wall of the tent, but concentrate on how your fingers look. What do you see now?"

"Same thing, of course, my two fingers touching together. What am I supposed to see?" She said with a tone of exasperation in her voice.

"Be calm, forcing it doesn't help."

"Don't tell me how to feel, okay! Now tell me what I'm supposed to see? I'm tired of playing this stupid game of yours?"

He patiently explained, "You're supposed to see a . . . kind of little sausage of your fingers. You're really focused on the far wall, and you have stereo vision. Your eyes will be converging in the distance, now try it again."

She held her hands up and looked at the far wall and glanced down at her fingers and shook her head.

"No . . . no, don't look at them, try to do it out of the corner of your eye or use your peripheral vision, it's more a matter of not concentrating on it, than seeing it with your eyes, your brain does it for you. Come on, trust me," he said.

She looked once again then dropped her hands, a look of dejection crossing her face. Scott gently grabbed her hands and held them about eight inches from her nose and said. "Now look over at the plotter, focus on that, look at what a mess it is. See it? Now without changing your focus, think about your fingers . . . no . . . no, don't move your head or eyes, look with your peripheral vision."

All of sudden a look of understanding crossed across her face. "I see it! A little sausage between my two finger tips, I thought you were just playing with me." They were both suddenly conscious they were holding hands, and Julia quickly pulled her hands down to her lap, looked up at Scott and thought. *It's too bad I have to be professional all the time. I could almost fall in love with a man like him, but duty comes first and mixing work with pleasure's not a good idea. But where do you ever find love? Don't you find it where it happens? Doesn't it just come to you when it's time?*

She forced down the thoughts, "I understand, but what does this have to do with the photos?"

"Now hold up the infrared picture you took of the wall."

"I don't see it. I'm still not sure I know what you're talking about. Oh . . . oh . . . I see something, no, it's gone."

"Relax, your mind will do it. Try it again."

"No . . . okay, yes I see it now. I see how it snaps into focus if you look at it just right. Amazing, it looks like the letters are carved out of the wall, really deep from the wall, in a three dimensional relief. This is amazing, what do the letters say?"

"They say that this chamber is the first marker for Mohammed's Scroll. A revelation to bring the brothers together under Gods will. A light for all the people. It says there are three markers, this is the first. The second and third, when found, will provide new insight and understanding to the words of the Prophet. They are for the people of the book and all the people of the world who will believe. The second marker's in Greece, if I understand this right. It's a poem you see. The poem says to follow the reflection of the lady to the holy place that Georges held dear." He stopped and looked up at her, "Maybe in Meteora, where you went as a child. When we find the second marker, it will tell us where the third is. It doesn't exactly say it, but I think when we find the second one it will make it clear."

"What's the poem actually say?"

"Well it's hard to translate into English, but I'll try my best."

'This is the chamber where vision decried,
Mohammad's scroll will one day arise
The law was put into affect
For sin to be known and a time to reflect

Follow the marker, to Hellas and near
To the holy place, that Georges held dear
The need for Grace, will wipe away fear
The lady's reflection, will soon make it clear

Long hair was this woman's glory, tis said
I said that she should then, cover her head
She longed for the day, when she would be free
To worship the Lord, on her bended knee

The reflection's the key, to marker number two
The woman amongst you, should know what to do
They are not chattel, but wisdom so wise

The look in their eyes, as they look to the skies
The brothers and nations will come under his will
Grace so abundant, till they've all had their fill
The law is the pointer, to the sin that entraps
But grace so wonderful, that it springs all the snaps

Georges agreed, about this new light
A light so bright, the nations have sight
A light that existed, from so long ago
I am so sad, that I missed it so

I call him Allah, and they call him Lord
The brothers and nations come and adored
They all come together, for the grand plan of his
rejoicing and singing, for the new grace that tis.

You will then need to find, Marker number three
All will be clear and then you will see
The finder and bringer of wisdom will then
Have the choice of making real strong men

Men who will worship, the Lord not ask why
The maker of universe, earth, sea and sky
The bringer of rain, sunshine and hope
To a mankind downtrodden by its own long rope.'

That's about the best I can do with the translation," Scott said.

"So, that's what you meant, we were going on a little trip? You knew all along? When did you find out?"

"I knew some that night, right before Hasid and Talbin broke into our camp. It came to me while I was staring at the photos in front of the light from my laptop. I was about to go to bed, had turned off the lights, was tired and it just came to me. I can't believe you've never heard or seen the magic eye books, they were everywhere when I was a kid."

"Well, maybe I led a sheltered life."

Samuel walked in about eleven thirty and noticed Scott and Julia had packed. "Well, where we headed this time? Did you go over the data with Julia, what did it say?"

"It says we're going to Greece, to look for the second part of the riddle. Off we go to the land of Saganaki, Retsina, Dolmades and the taverna, sound good to you?"

Samuel stood up and smiled, "I love Greece, ah, the Golden Age, the

Age of Enlightenment, I can't wait. I hear the Greek women are the most beautiful in the world."

Scott cautioned, "this may be dangerous, Samuel, we're not going there to find a Greek Goddess for you. I don't think Abdullah or Talbin and their friends will be able to decipher it the way we did. It was an accident, but you never know. Abu could swoop down on our camp and take the boys while we're gone. You said there was more to this than meets the eye and you're right. Abu's not as dull as Abdullah or Talbin, so pack with care!"

"Sure Scott, you know me, I'm always careful."

"I do know you, and that's what worries me, Samuel."

"Do you two always carry on like this? You're like a couple of school boys off on a field trip sometimes," Julia asked.

"We act lighthearted and jest when we're really serious because we don't know what to say, don't take us wrong. Samuel really has a big heart and is careful all the time. I'd trust my life in his hands, and have numerous times in the past, and would do so again in an instant. Did you see the way he handled that guy with the hammer, he thinks quick on his feet. You acted quickly on your feet too with that little 25-auto. I want to stop and see Father Basil again, before we go. I've a feeling he knows more than he says . . . just a feeling that he can somehow bring some wisdom to all this."

CHAPTER 16
FATHER BASILS WISDOM

Scott went over some things with Luke and Alex when morning came around, then walked over to where Samuel was working on the trucks. "Julia and I are going up to see Father Basil, we should be back by late afternoon. Do you need anything?"

"Not right now, unless you want to stop at that shop and get some vino."

"Maybe, Samuel, we'll see. Keep the boys working while we're gone."

He looked at the mountain rearing its head into the blue sky as they drove the Hummer north along the dusty track. His thoughts took on a new direction as he looked up at the mountain; so much religion had sprung from this red granite mass. Moses, who was he? The Jews and Christians revered him, and the Muslims respected him. *I guess I have to start reading my Bible,* he thought.

When they pulled up to the gate, they were welcomed by one of the monks.

Father Basil walked out in the courtyard and welcomed them. "Have you come to see our famous library or come to worship with us on this Lord's Day?"

"We'd love to see the library, Father. Something else has also come up and I'd love to have a talk with you, if you have the time. I want you to meet my new assistant, Julia Apostoli. She's the botanist working with our team."

Julia reached out her hand. "Father Basil, a pleasure to meet you. Scott's told me so much about you already."

"Thank you for your kindness and welcome to St. Catherine's, I hope I'll be able to guide you on your quest for information and enlightenment." He showed them into the main part of the complex, pointing out features and nodding and greeting monks as they passed.

Scott paused near a winding staircase and asked, "Father, could you tell us about the founding of the monastery and about when Mohammad took refuge here? I'm concerned. Our camp was attacked yesterday after we found an old chamber, apparently built by Mohammad. We've come across some information that has me confused. Rusta told me Mohammad was being chased by the Arabs or something."

Basil looked at him with concern. "I'll tell you what I know. Our order was founded about eighteen hundred years ago, in the year two hundred. There's some evidence that there was a small altar here from ancient times, about 1000 B. C. or so, that a sect of Jewish aesthetics set up on the mountain to honor Moses and the Law. Mohammad stayed here in about the year 622. Did you notice the plaque and letter by the main entrance?"

"No, we didn't," Scott said.

"It's a letter from Mohammad that offers protection to Christians and gives them his blessing. It's called a Charter of Privileges, and he sent it when he came into power in 628, after leaving here. It goes something like this:

'I Mohammad ibn Abdullah, give this covenant to those who adopt Christianity. To all who adopt it far and near, I give my blessing. We are with them.

'I pledge myself, my helpers, servants and followers to defend them. Christians are my citizens and, with Allah as my witness, I pledge to protect them.

'No one is to compel them.

'Their judges and monks are not to be taken from their work or monasteries.

'No one is to destroy a home or house of religion, they shall not harm it or take anything from it to a Muslim's home.

'I am God's Prophet. If someone takes anything or anyone, he will spoil the covenant. Christians are my allies and have my blessing and charter. What they hate we hate.

'They shall not be forced to travel or made to fight.

'Muslims are to fight for them.

'If a Muslim is married to a female Christian, it must take place with her approval. She may not be forced into marriage. She must be allowed to visit her own church to pray.

'Respect their churches. The Christians shall be allowed to repair them, and their covenants are sacred.

'This covenant shall last till the end of time, till the last day and no one shall disobey it.'

"Father Georges was head abbot at that time and left accounts of his talks with him. Georges stayed on here for many years afterwards, retiring to the Great Meteoran Monastery. He was also affiliated with the monasteries on Mount Athos, where he studied as a young man. They're in the northern part of Greece on one of the peninsulas. He went back to Athos one more time before he died to see it one last time. It's a beautiful area. I'm sorry, but women aren't allowed there, ever!" he said looking at Julia.

"Early male chauvinists, huh?" Julia said with a small smile.

"I guess you could call them that," he said with a chuckle.

They walked further through the rock walls. "Although the monastery has thick walls and looks like a castle, it has never been attacked. Wars have swept over the area over the centuries, but they've always respected St. Catherine's and left the monastery and monks alone.

"During the time Mohammad stayed here a number of rich Persians built homes in the surrounding area. The elevation was higher, the climate a little cooler, and we're near the major crossroads of numerous old caravan routes."

"Father, you told me before about your library. What's in it?"

Before he could answer, Julia chimed in, "Yes, I've heard your library is famous and you have manuscripts no one else has."

"This way, I'd be happy to show you. St. Catherine's is famous for its library and research materials. We have many manuscripts dating back to the time of the Apostles. The one that we're most famous for is now in the British Museum. It's the Codex Sinaiticus from the year 400 A.D. We're trying to get it back but these things take time. Translation scholars from around the world come here or ask for copies of our manuscripts for their research," Basil said, as they followed him through the winding passageways and up a small staircase.

The library wasn't at all what they expected. Books lined the shelves in a haphazard fashion and there was an old wood cabinet with two doors. The doors were covered with deeply carved figures and inlaid with stones and ivory. Basil opened the cabinet, which was filled with small square shelves, each stuffed with a rolled scroll.

He pulled out a scroll and turned around, "This is one of our manuscripts, written about the end of the first century." It was wrapped in plastic and he carefully removed the wrapping and lovingly carried it over to a table that was set under one of the windows. Slowly and very carefully he unrolled the scroll so they could see.

"Obviously written in ancient Greek, this is a copy of the book of John, some say it might possibly be the original manuscript, Basil said."

Scott with his passion for anything ancient stuttered, "this is just . . . just amazing Father, I could spend hours pouring over all this and trying to learn what went on during that period."

"What does it say here?" Julia asked as she pointed at the scroll, where a marking set off a portion of text.

Father Basil and Scott bent over the manuscript. It translates like this, Basil said, "the wind blows wherever it pleases, you hear it's sound, but you cannot tell where it comes from or where it is going, so it is with everyone born of the spirit."

"What does it mean?" she asked.

Basil laughed, "That's a good one. I think Christ's teaching us that we are all blind until we have the spirit and his sight. It's a good question. Most people skip right over this because of the other part of the passage. It's about being born again. Jesus is talking to Nicodimus and telling him we must be born again. Being born of the spirit is like being with the wind and willing to go Gods way . . . to trust in him."

"Do you have a tabulation or reference of the documents the library contains?" Julia asked.

"'Yes . . . yes, of course. It's in the telephone room."

"The what?" Julia said.

"The telephone room, follow me. I'll get you a copy," Father Basil replied.

They followed him down the hallway to what he called the telephone room. They were astonished when they entered.

"This is what we call our telephone room. We can connect with the outside world, receive instructions from our order and carry on business like any other organization."

"For some reason, I expected an old crank telephone, after seeing the rest of the monastery," Julia said.

Basil laughed slowly in response, "I know . . . I know, I've heard it all before. Most people after seeing the monastery think we're still living in the dark ages. But you know, all pleasure's from the Lord. Most of the monks got together and watched the NBA championship on this TV last year. It is one of the small pleasures that we don't deny ourselves."

He walked across the room, opened a cabinet and took out a file folder and extracted a stapled sheath of papers. Handing them to Julia, he said "This is a tabulation of what's in our library and the books and objects we have on reference. Only the Vatican has a larger collection."

"Thank you father. This means a lot to us that you've taken the time to show us around. Can you tell us more of when Mohammad stayed here?" Scott asked.

"Our records say Father Georges became head abbot right after Mohammad left. Apparently, Mohammad asked for refuge here when he was being chased by the Quraysh out of what we would call Saudi Arabia. The Quraysh warlords didn't like his preaching which was bringing the tribes together under a common law. Prior to Mohammad, there was little law and each tribe was a law unto itself. Some of the local warlords still act that way. Well . . . when Mohammad started his preaching, a number of what we'd call pagan warlords took it upon themselves to rid the world of Mohammad and what he represented. They didn't like his message and were afraid how of big his following was becoming and that he might unite the tribes. They threw him out of Mecca and Medina, then chased him here, to St. Catherine's where he asked for sanctuary. He stayed for a while, conversing with Father Georges about the Koran, his visions and Christianity. George's letters say he tried to convert Mohammad and that something happened on the last night he was here. The letters don't say what, only that Gabriel knows, and we're to look to two places to get the answer of where to find his final revelation. Almost reminds me of the winds, in the third Chapter of John we were reading about earlier."

"How long did he stay, Father?" Julia asked.

"Georges' letters don't say. They only say that he and Mohammad had long talks, which gives me the idea that it was for some time, months perhaps. The writings are interesting and cryptic about when he left the monastery. The letters say that Mohammad's eyes were opened to grace."

"What do you mean by grace?" Scott asked.

"Grace is . . . grace, don't you know? It's to give thanks, to be forgiven, to have the favor of God on you. Don't you have a song, Amazing Grace?"

"Well, I guess, but I don't really understand," Scott said.

Basil looked at Scott with his amazing grey eyes and asked, "Are you a Christian?"

"I never gave it much thought. I believe in God, I guess, and went to Sunday school, but have always been uncomfortable with religious stuff, if you know what I mean. I considered myself a scientist first and all this, made the world in seven days, moved mountains with a mustard seed of faith, has never made a whole lot of sense to me," Scott said.

"Well I don't like to call being a Christian religious stuff, but spiritual stuff, if you know what I mean," Basil said.

"What about the Jews, Father, what did Mohammad say about them?" Julia asked.

"I've no idea. I know what the Koran says. I know what the Bible says. Basically Christians are Jews in a way. They revere Moses, Abraham and the law. They just go a step farther and believe the Messiah has come, while the Jews are still looking for him. I've found that some of the most deeply spiritual Christians are converted Jews. In Israel you have to be a Jew to be a citizen, I recall. You can be a citizen if you're an atheist Jew, Orthodox Jew, or merely secular, but the moment you become a Christian Jew, you can't be a citizen, you're not Jewish anymore." Basil spit, "Pah, so much of religion's become cultural. The question was, are you a Christian? That's where the light is. I'll tell both of you. You've a long journey ahead of you. You're wrapped up in something that's beyond all of us! I can't tell you how, even if I knew, it wouldn't do you any good, for it's something that must be played out till the end, for good or evil. I believe you will prevail, if you stay in His will. That's why we pray, 'Thy will be done.' It's a turning over of my will to the will of the almighty."

"Did Georges' writings say what those two places were, Father?" Scott asked.

"Not in so many words. There was a saying from Friar Nikita, a young monk at the time, that goes something like this:

> 'I call my Daughter from Cush, and then
> To Meteoran three and two, go instead
> Then Cush and caves, to find the last
> To go where the daughter is called first and fast'

"There's more, and I'm not sure if I have it right. Nikita used to make up poems and sing a lot, and it might be just some old rhyme of his. I've translated it from the Greek, maybe it would translate differently, I don't know."

They walked into the sunshine and heat of the day. The bell in the monastery was calling the monks to their midday meal. Basil walked them out to the truck and leaned on the door after they'd gotten in. He paused and weighed his words carefully before he spoke, "I don't like to push, but there seem to be forces at work you probably don't understand. It would ease my heart if I knew you were Christians. I don't know how else to put it. It will illuminate your lives and path for you, I do know that, for sure."

Scott smiled, "Father, you've no idea, something's been tugging at me. I've always prided myself on being my own boss, though. I always believed that my own strength was enough and didn't believe in anything else. I wanted to find my own job, women, car and everything else on my own. I felt Christianity was full of don't do this, don't touch that, don't say this and don't drink that. When I meet people like you, I find that it's much more positive; do this, say that, let your light shine. It's more about doing than not doing."

"How right you are. It's about not doing evil that's for sure, and when a Christian does something evil it gives the whole church a bad name. Christians should have the spirit working inside, guiding them and coaching them to keep them from doing evil. But temptation comes and God meets us where we're at."

"Thank you Father. Your words are a comfort to me," Julia said and smiled, sticking her hand out the window. "I'll look over your list. May we come back if we need too?"

"Please do, and welcome. We pride ourselves on hospitality," Basil said as he turned back to his duties.

"Nice man, Father Basil," she said as they drove through the little hamlet.

"Hard to find a nicer one, kind of makes you feel important when you meet him. He makes me feel like I'm the only person in existence when he's talking with me. I've never felt that before."

When they pulled up to their tents and hopped out of the truck the heat pressed in on them.

Samuel walked into the tent, carrying a tray piled with eggs, steak, potatoes and tomatoes. "You'll have to find your own juice, I couldn't carry anymore," He said as he cleared off the desk and set the tray down. "Here, dig in, I already ate."

"What kind of shape are the trucks in?" Scott asked.

"Well, I could only get the one Hummer running, the one you used. The other two are trashed. They'll have to wait till we get parts. Luke and Alex will be able to use the two trucks. One had two shredded tires and a small hole in the radiator hose. I've taken the hose off the damaged one and Luke is putting it on the good one. We should be ready in an hour or two."

❋ ❋ ❋ ❋ ❋ ❋ ❋ ❋

The meeting with Quati was held in a room at the Palms in Cairo. Hasid, not normally one to fear a meeting with the general, did not feel well prepared when walking into Quati's room.

He caught a quick glimpse of the girl as he walked through the door, but the door was quickly shut and Quati strutted over to stand in front of the window.

"So you blew it Hasid, care to tell me why?"

"I saw no reason to kill them, General. The preliminary report on the chamber indicates that there is more to this. We may still need Chad if we are to find the Prophet's writings before anyone else does."

"I thought my orders were clear. Twice now you have violated my orders. First with Chad's companion Rogowski, and now with Chad himself. My orders are to be obeyed, do you understand me Hasid. You are lucky this time, and in fact are probably right that we may need Chad, but it disturbs me that you so glibly defy my direct orders."

"General, please excuse me, but you put me in charge since you know that no operation goes according to plan. You need intelligence in the field to make a decision. I made that decision and I believe it was a good one. Chad will follow the trail now and we will follow Chad. I am afraid we cannot use Talbin again on this, at least right now, but perhaps we can put someone else on his trail."

"You are excused, at least this time. Next time you want to take matters into your own hands you will contact me first, I do not care what I am doing, you will contact me first. Do I make myself clear, Hasid?"

"Yes, my General, very clear. Chad is on his way north. We do not know where, but we should be able to follow him from Suez. I suggest we get someone on his tail and keep them there. We also need all our electronic people to be keeping watch for any money transactions he may make, that will help us to keep a watch on him."

"That part is already done and I have taken steps to bring in some outside people to keep an eye on Chad. That Jewess he is traveling with upsets me though, you could have at least killed her."

Quati's words hit him like a slap in the face, what did he mean by Jewess? I am sorry, General, what do you mean by that Jewess he is traveling with?"

"That botanist, Apostoli, she was raised in France by her Jewish mother and father, and we suspect she may be working for the Mosad."

Hasid's mind turned at Quati's words. Julia working for the Mosad? How could it be? He quickly put it aside, a mixture of hate and adoration twisting around inside.

"Who did you have in mind to tail them, General Quati?"

"The most unlikely people of all, you do not have the need to know. I want you to keep a loose tail on them, not too close, and report their movements to me. Do not get to close. We want Chad to have a free rein for awhile. The people I send in will get closer, just to check up on the information we have and see if Chad has been able to gain any knowledge that we have not been able to find out. Abu seems to be the fool you said he was. He cannot make anything out of Chad's notes, the writing in the chamber or anything else."

"Abu is not a fool General, you misunderstand me. He is puffed up with pride and that makes him do foolish things. He is a good scientist, but until he gets his pride out of the way, he will not be effective."

"I will keep him working, now go and do your part and keep me informed."

❋　❋　❋　❋　❋　❋　❋　❋

After Hasid left, Quati picked up the phone and dialed a number stored in his memory.

The phone was answered on the third ring. "Bestin, how nice of you to answer right away. I have something I want you to do for me."

"General Quati, what a pleasant surprise. How can we assist you?"

"I have a little problem, and I need someone discreet to lend me a hand and take care of it. Your Italian friends can help. How soon can you bring some of them down to Suez?"

CHAPTER 17

SUEZ AND BEYOND

The next morning Scott met with his interns, Luke and Alex, to go over the final phase of the survey. Scott left them instructions and told them he would be going north and that Julia and Samuel would be coming with him. "After last night, I don't need to warn you to keep your eyes open and watch out for anything strange, do I?"

Julia and Samuel were waiting for Scott in the Hummer Samuel had been able to get running. Samuel got in back and Julia sat in front while waiting for Scott. He came down the hill at a brisk walk and Julia leaned out and said, "Well, is everything set?"

"Yes, M'am," he answered. "It will be nice to go somewhere where they have decent food for a change. I love it out in the field and wouldn't ever be happy in an office, but my stomach yearns for civilization sometimes."

"What I yearn for is not having to wear a Hijab every where I go without causing a stir. I like civilization because it's civilized and I like places where they don't subjugate women."

"I think we've a woman's liberation expert here, don't you, Samuel?" Scott said as he negotiated the track up and past St. Catherine's.

"I don't think I want to touch that! Some of the best people I've ever worked with are women. They say they have bigger brains than men, but I really don't agree with the Muslim way of treating them myself. You'd have to ask a Muslim woman what she thinks, though, if you wanted to really know."

"I can't wait to get to a hotel, take a bath, and sleep in a bed for the first time since I can't remember when," Julia said as they made their way toward Suez. The journey from their camp was long and hot since the air conditioner was literally shot. The heat kept building as the day wore on.

Scott was concentrating on the roadway and hoping to get to Suez before nightfall. He loved the heat and dryness of the air. As he drove along, his mind was on the message in the chamber. He was almost oblivious to the temperature and sun. He kept thinking over and over why Hasid had shown up and the words Talbin had said and wondered what they'd gotten themselves into. He was hoping that whoever was behind this would be satisfied with smashing up their equipment and taking the negatives and computer and would assume that since they now had all the data, that he wouldn't look any further into the matter. *If that's what they think . . . they don't know me very well.*

When they got into Suez, they skirted the port area and made their way to the center where they found a local hotel. Scott made his way to the front counter where he rang the bell and booked them into three rooms on the top floor.

"I don't know about you two, but before anything else, I'm going to take a long bubble bath, get a sandwich from room service, then take a nap!" Julia said with a tone of dismissal as she turned the key in the door of her room.

She opened the door and Scott followed immediately behind her, placing his bag in the center of the room.

"What do you think you're doing?" she asked.

"I just want to check the layout of the rooms first," Scott said.

He opened the adjoining door to his room and checked the layout to hers. He turned to her and said, "I'm going to see how Samuel's doing."

He went out in the hallway and knocked on Samuel's door but got no answer. He pounded louder and still got no answer. He was about to knock again when one of the chambermaids came around the corner pushing her cart. "I left my key in the room. Could you please open the door for me?" he asked in his fractured Egyptian.

"Surely, sir, just one moment. Your name please?"

"Scott Chad. I have rooms 312, 314 and 316 under my name."

The chambermaid consulted a printout attached to her cart, and said, "Yes sir, no problem, sir, it's right here." She opened the door to room 316, letting him in the room and shutting the door behind him.

He wasn't too surprised at what he found. Samuel was sprawled out on the bed, sound asleep, with a pillow over his head. Scott made his way to the connecting door, opened it and gently knocked on the second door, which Julia opened from the other side. She walked in the room and laughed when she saw Samuel asleep on the bed.

"How long do you think Samuel will sleep? I'm starved."

"He's probably down for the count, but I'll leave him a note and he can order room service or something. Let's be careful, don't use the phone. I'll knock twice on your door when I'm ready. I need to grab a hot shower and change before we go out. Will you be okay?"

"Sure, I'll be fine. I'd love a hot shower, too."

He went back to his room, closed the door, quickly stripped and turned the shower on hot. Once it was steaming, he adjusted the temperature and stepped under the warm spray, luxuriating in the feeling of washing off the dust and grime. The warm water and lack of sleep over the previous 48 hours were catching up to him. He got out, rummaged through his clothes, picked out an aloha shirt, khaki slacks and loafers that he quickly donned. Feeling much better after the shower and a change of clothes, he walked across the room and gently knocked on Julia's door.

"Come in, it's not locked. I'm just about ready."

She was wearing a medium-length khaki skirt, blue knit short-sleeved top and calf-high boots. The most amazing transformation was she was wearing makeup and had let her hair down, which Scott hadn't seen since that first day she showed up at the campsite and had the problems with the Arabs yelling hijab. She'd worn the headscarf constantly since that day and Scott had forgotten how beautiful her red hair was with the golden highlights.

He grinned when he saw her. "Well, this is a great pleasure. I must say I am astounded."

Julia looked up at him and teasingly said, "What are you so astounded about?"

"Uh . . . well, you know, I haven't seen your hair in months and I guess . . . I've just kind of become used to being around you and had forgotten what you looked like without the scarf."

The way he was tongue tied caused her to smile. She held out her arm for him to escort her. "Well, come on. I'm starved. Let's get something to eat. Camp food's okay. I can't say I'm complaining, and your cook is wonderful with what he has to work with. But, well, you know you can't beat a nice restaurant with a steak instead of soup or lasagna and when someone cooks for thirty it's just not the same."

"I forgot. I was going to leave Samuel a note. I'll be right with you," he said as he went through the adjoining doorway and quickly left a note on Samuel's table by the bed, where he was still happily snoring away. He gave her his arm and they walked down the hallway.

They took the elevator down to the lobby where Scott went to the front desk and left his key. The clerk returned their passports, which he'd required when checking in.

The evening was balmy as they walked down the street, the smell of cooking wafting on the spring air. They walked a few blocks toward the center of town and Scott noticed that, for some reason, neither of them was talking which often left him feeling awkward, but not this time. As if she could read his thoughts, Julia said, "My father once said, 'Only families don't need to talk, because they're comfortable with each other and silence says more.' I don't know what it is, but I feel that type of comfort with you. I guess I feel safe and secure, too."

"I don't really know what to say, but I mean . . . well, I guess I was feeling much the same thing. I hadn't realized we were so quiet at first, and I was just content to be with you and was enjoying the walk when I noticed we hadn't said a thing in blocks. Well . . . I thought maybe I should say something, but it seemed better for some reason to just keep quiet. You know what I mean?"

She smiled and put her arm through his, saying nothing but giving his arm a little squeeze as they rounded the corner and came upon a street with restaurants on both sides. The street was brightly lit and the wonderful aroma was carried on the gentle breeze, mixing and stirring so it was difficult to tell which establishment it was coming from.

Scott asked, "What do you feel like, French, Italian, Egyptian, Moroccan or what? Seems we can choose whichever we like on this street."

"Definitely French. Their sauces can't be beat."

"A girl with expensive tastes," he teasingly answered. "It's going to be hard to keep you fed and in style. Don't you know that all those sauces go to my waistline?"

"You look like you can eat whatever you want and not gain a pound. In Italy they say you look poor if you don't have big belly. It's a sign of prosperity on a man. Didn't you know? It's *my* waistline I'm worried about, but not tonight!"

They spotted Les Tres Gros, a small French bistro with a blue awning by a brick paved alleyway. The maitre d' welcomed them and showed them to a small round table against the back wall and tucked into a corner. It made Scott happy to have his back against the wall after the last few days' events.

The waiter showed up and asked for their drink orders in English. How he knew they spoke English, Scott didn't know.

"I'd like a glass of ginger ale on ice," Julia said.

Scott was somewhat taken aback, coming to a French restaurant and ordering a soft drink and not wine. He really didn't drink all that much himself and had given up smoking years back, which was one of the hardest things he'd ever done, but still, no wine in a French restaurant? "I'd like a Coke please," Scott said.

The waiter looked at them and raised his nose a little, but being a Muslim country he was used to teetotalers, but usually not Americans. He left menus and went off to fetch their drink orders.

Julia let out a deep sigh as she perused the menu, and a feeling of relaxation encompassed both of them. "It all looks so wonderful, Couton Savage, what's that?"

Scott looked at the menu. "A savage pig. I think it means a wild boar of some kind in a blueberry sauce with a red wine base. Sounds good. I think I might go for the tenderloin with the béarnaise sauce. The venison looks good, too, which in a French restaurant is usually cooked medium rare."

"Foie gras, I've never tried it. Is it really duck liver?"

"No, it's goose liver. They fatten the goose and force feed it corn and stuff and its liver grows huge. When they harvest the goose they separate the liver, clean it and de-vein it. It's just wonderful. The last time I tried it, it was tender as butter, not what you'd think. Let's try one. What do you want for an entree?"

"I'd like the venison in the Madeira wine sauce with the wild huckleberry finish and saffron."

Scott smiled and hummed. "I'm just mad about saffron, she's just mad about me. They call me mellow yellow! Every time I hear that word, I think of that old song. Don't you?"

Julia looked at him quizzically. "I've no idea what you're talking about, but I hear the French are really creative with their sauces."

Scott looked at her for a moment wondering who hadn't heard of that song, but the waiter approached the table with their drinks and a loaf of hot bread.

"The lady will have the venison. I'll have the tenderloin, done medium, and we'd like a foie gras as an appetizer."

Scott opened the bread tray, took a piece of the piping hot bread, put one on Julia's plate and another on his. "Do you want butter, or want to wait for the foie gras? The foie gras is excellent spread on bread!"

"I'm starved. It's been awhile since I've had fresh bread with butter."

As they were waiting for the waiter to bring the appetizer, he asked Julia about some of her travels. "You must have had an interesting life, studying botany and traveling around the world in search of different plants. What's the most interesting place you've ever been?"

"Oh, I don't know. If I had to mention one place it would probably be the Dead Sea. Something about being more than a thousand feet below sea level, the air pressure, humidity and history of the place really appealed to me. What about you? What's the most interesting place you've been?"

"Well, that's tough, I guess the most interesting place I've ever been is Afghanistan: something about the mountains, the Hindu Kush and all the tribal leaders. The country doesn't have many natural resources, but I think if they could bring themselves out of the Middle Ages and take careful stock of their environment, they could probably develop more of a modern economy. Their problem is the state is strictly governed by how they interpret Islamic law and all the different factions. They wouldn't let men shave their beards when I was there, and they made all women wear a burqa, which covers them from head to toe and has a mesh opening for the eyes.

Julia frowned. "I'm sorry about that first day on the job, Scott. It seems you've had more experience working with these people than I have. I was brought up to be independent and in a place where women took their side right by their men. I always believed a woman could grow up to be Prime Minister or President and think it must be awful for a woman growing up in an extremely fundamentalist environment. I don't like what these extremists are doing to the state of Israel either. Jews should have a chance to live in their own country and be at peace with their neighbors."

For some reason her words made him think of the Magic Eye Book and wonder why she'd never heard of the song "Mellow Yellow." Why had she brought up Israel? "Kind of like a powder keg waiting for a fuse to be lit, isn't it?" he said.

"Yes, it's explosive, from what I hear! Maybe it'll be fine if they can keep those right-wing ministers out of power and get on with some sort of peace process. I don't know!"

He looked at her blue eyes. "Yes, but also a very dangerous country to tangle with. I don't think the Palestinians really understand what it's like to tangle with a country that can scramble F-14s to strafe their cities. It's not the same thing as sending suicide bombers in to blow up buses, police stations or schools, as when an actual war starts. Tanks rumbling through the streets with F-14s strafing you overhead is not a battle I'd choose to fight! The funny thing is, why didn't they ever learn from Gandhi or Martin Luther King? They tried to change things in peaceful ways. They would have a hunger strike, a peaceful sit in. That way they'd grab the world's media attention and win the people over by political means. It's a long struggle, but the real way of change is through peace, not paying some boy's family twenty-five thousand dollars to blow himself up on a bus!"

The waiter brought their foie gras, which was superbly prepared and presented on a small round dish, garnished with cloves of garlic in a brown sauce and surrounded by small pieces of toast tucked into a napkin.

"Umm, looks good to me," Scott said as he took two of the pieces of toast and divided the foie gras. "Just take a small piece and spread it on the toast or eat it however you like."

She took a small bite. "Oh, wow, it's even better than I expected. I guess for the price you'd expect it to be wonderful, but I never believed it would taste this good!"

"Try it with the garlic, too. It's even better. I once knew a girl who was a sauce addict. She'd try every sauce the restaurant made and try to weasel the recipes out of the chef. She was also a fantastic cook, somehow had a taste for it."

"A woman after my own heart. My father used to call me the condiment queen when he was in the teasing mood. I'd also try every sauce on the menu and even invented my own sometimes while cooking at home. I usually made a big mess of things, though. I did learn to love cooking, but never really got to practice much since finishing school."

The waiter appeared with Julia's venison which was prepared with little round medallions from the tenderloin arranged in a semicircular pattern, and was garnished with carrots, scallions and sweet potatoes. Scott's filet was served on top of a crunchy grated potato and garnished with wild mushrooms, carrots and scallions, with a brown sauce all-around and a béarnaise sauce on top of the filet.

"Wow, looks good enough to eat, if I do say so myself. Something this good makes me almost want to say grace," Scott said, while chewing on a mouthful of his steak. "I wonder where they get the venison and beef?"

She ignored his question. "Are you religious, Scott? I thought you were a scientist."

"What does that have to do with it? But, no, I'm not particularly religious, but I was raised in what you'd call a religious household. My father would say a spiritual household, because he was kind of down on religion himself. We did say grace before meals as I was growing up, and the better the meal, the longer the grace."

"I know what you mean, I was raised by religious parents also, and they had their quirks and idiosyncrasies about religion, just as I assume your parents did. I didn't mean to pry. But I guess I know what you mean. This venison is out of this world delicious. I don't know where they get venison or beef here in the Middle East. I guess they'd get it from Africa. I don't know, but it's wonderful."

CHAPTER 18
THE TRIAD MOVES

Henderson stood, slamming the phone down on the cradle. "Damn it! Why does he have to run off half-cocked all the time? We agreed we'd talk about this and not act independently. I'll tell you, Farrell, if Bestin doesn't stop, I'm going to pull out my support. The chips can fall where they may!"

"Listen, Frank, Bestin's only trying to do what he thinks best. Chad's found something. We know that now. Bestin's man talked with their head a guy, Dr. Abu, who works for the Archeological Institute. He was in the chamber that Chad found. They've taken pictures of it, and Bestin's man sent them to us. I have them on e-mail. We'll get better copies by morning. There's nothing there, I tell you. Why Chad's left and gone up to Suez is a mystery. We need to trust Bestin on this. His people are following Chad and know how to operate smoothly. Calm down and we'll let things play out. Nothing can be traced to us anyway."

"Well, Farrell, you just sit there and now we have Bestin's mafia buddies chasing my niece's fiancé all over the desert, and who knows what they'll do when they find him. Shoot him up into little pieces with their Tommy guns, I suppose."

"Oh, don't be melodramatic, Frank. Nothing of the sort will happen. They'll just put him on ice for a while till we can figure things out."

"You don't know Chad very well, do you? Did you hear what he did in Afghanistan?"

"You've said he got out of a couple of rough spots. So what!"

He paced the room. "Rough to say the least. He and his sidekick were back in the mountains when the Russians strafed the village they were in with a helicopter. A number of the Mujadeen fighters were killed in the attack and when the Russian's landed, he and Rogowski stormed the helicopter carrying nothing more than pistols. They took out fifteen men and stole the chopper. He then ferried the wounded from the village up and over the mountains, fueled it up and came back and strafed a Russian military base. Pretending he was Russian, they let him right in. He's resourceful, clever and smart. He'll eat

Bestin's boys up and be long gone before we know what happened. I'm warning you."

"Time will tell, Frank. Sit down and take it easy. We have other problems. I agree your idea was best and we may still try it, if Bestin fails. We'll have to see. Let's take one thing at a time."

"We need to plan for all contingencies, Farrell. I don't agree with you about taking one thing at a time. We have to put this other plan into action and get our people in place if we're going to head this off before it blows up in our faces. Do you want Quati for a neighbor? I don't, I tell you! We're going to have people in our churches and kids in our schools wearing funny clothes and who knows what else. We must move on this, now! Call Bestin and get him to see the light!"

"I've a conference call scheduled with him tomorrow afternoon, Frank. We should know how his people did in Suez by then. I'll also have the pictures from the chamber. Maybe we can figure out what Chad's up to and what he found. Here, look at the e-mail pictures. Do you see anything?" he said as he threw a folder on his desk.

Henderson walked over and picked up the pictures and stared at them for a minute while Farrell continued to sit in the chair. Finally he shook his head and said, "I don't see a thing. Just looks like some stupid writing out of the *Arabian Nights* and some sort of design, like in one of my kid's books."

Farrell leaned forward. "What did you say? Like one of your kid's books? What do you mean, what book?"

"Just one of those stupid kid books where you see funny pictures in the design. I don't know. We're going to have to get someone over there if we're going to find out anything."

"I vote for you, Frank. You can get away for awhile. It's much harder for us to," Farrell said.

"Why me though? What good am I going to do?"

"Because if you find Chad, it would be a lot easier for you to talk with him. You knew him once didn't you say."

"I never knew him very well and that was in passing when he was in College. You may have a point, but I don't think it will be easy," Henderson said.

"Well think about it, it may be our only chance to get a handle on this thing."

"I don't know. I'll let you know in the morning. You work on watching to see if they use their credit cards and I'll see about getting a flight out, but you'd better get Bestin to get a handle on those boys of his. I don't want them close to me if they go off half-cocked again."

"I'll be really specific with him. There shouldn't be any trouble. Frank, try to remember and find one of those kid's books you were talking about and bring it with you. Maybe it would help, who knows?" Farrell said.

"What is it about you, Farrell? Kid's books?" He looked at his friend's face and decided not to press the issue. "Okay, I'll look for one of them."

CHAPTER 19
FUN IN SUEZ

Scott and Julia finished their dinner and she took his arm once again, strolling slowly toward their hotel. He had that stuffed and satisfied feeling with a pretty girl on his arm and a balmy spring evening about him. He noticed two men he'd seen earlier following about a half block behind them on the other side of the street. He pulled Julia to a stop pretending to look in a shop while he watched their reflection in the window. The men stopped and quickly turned in the opposite direction, which was all the confirmation he needed to know they were being followed. Scott's question was, were they just being tailed or was something more dangerous afoot?

He pulled Julia closer and whispered, "Don't look now but we're being shadowed by two men across the street." She started to look up, but he squeezed her arm and whispered, "Don't look. I don't want them to know we spotted them. Act naturally."

She squeezed his arm and pointed to the window. "Oh, look, Scott, aren't these beautiful carpets, and that samovar," she paused and pointed, "wouldn't that make a nice gift for your parents?"

He bent down to her ear. "Let's work our way up to the corner, turn left and see if they follow." He grabbed her hand, hooking her arm through his and set off toward the corner. When they reached the intersection, they turned left and quickly walked up the little hill. They stopped after a block and a half at a little jewelry shop that was still open, looking in the window and pretending to browse. The owner, a short Egyptian wearing a red fez, waved and called them in and they stepped into the shop and around a glass counter where they could look outside. The store was small and the counter filled with diamond wedding rings with the other cases filled with pearls, bracelets and earrings.

Scott glanced out the window then looked down and asked. "Which one would you like, darling?" He pointed at the wedding rings with a sly smile on his face.

"Oh, I don't know, can we afford that one, honey?" she said, as she pointed to one with a big diamond near the front of the case.

"I think you're worth it. Nothing's too good for you! I'm sure we can make up the money somewhere."

The owner's smile grew when he heard this exchange, and he quickly unlocked the cabinet and pulled out the ring she'd pointed at.

"This very nice merchandise, sir," he said as he looked at the tag. "VS quality, F color, 1.75 carats, and I'll give you special deal of only $6,000 American dollars if you pay cash, 5% more if you pay by credit card. I take Visa and American Express. Do you like?" he said as he handed her the ring.

She looked back at the shopkeeper. "I like it very much, only that seems a lot for a diamond that size, doesn't it, honey?" she said turning toward Scott.

Scott was watching the men who had crossed the street and were approaching the shop. "Yes, it's very nice. We'll take it. Please wrap it up."

Julia looked up at him astounded, figuring they'd just walk out. "Oh, darling, are you sure? It's lovely and all, but can we really afford it?"

He caught her eye and motioned outside the window with his eyes. "I told you, nothing's too good for you. Now is this the one you'd like? I know you've looked all over the place. What do you say?"

"Oh, yes. Thank you so much, sweetheart." She threw her arms around him and gave him a kiss full on the lips. It caught him by surprise but he responded by wrapping his arms tightly around her and returning the affection. They were still entwined when the shopkeeper interrupted.

"How do you want to pay for the ring?"

Scott untangled himself and pulled out his American Express card, which he threw on the counter. "Please wrap it up."

With a sly smile, Julia asked, "Now, where were we?"

"I think about right here!" he responded with a slightly husky tone and put his arms back around her and pulled her to him once again. He could see out the window and the two men were slowly working their way down the street, stopping now and then and casually looking into the shop at Scott and Julia. She responded by pulling him tighter and kissing him once again on his lips. This had the effect of taking his mind off the two men and the shopkeeper, who was trying to signal him to sign the receipt.

"Please . . . please, sign here." Scott disengaged from Julia and signed the slip. The man in the fez placed the ring in a small box and handed it to Scott. "Lucky couple, you have man with excellent taste, young lady. Do you want a man's wedding band, too? I'll give you an excellent deal on one?"

"No thank you, sir. I'll use my father's," Scott said. "Thank you very much for your time. It's been a pleasure working with you." He then turned to Julia, and asked, "Now, what were you saying darling?" as he peered out the window and noticed the men standing at the far corner.

In a husky voice she answered, "You know very well what I was saying. Let's go outside and talk about it if you want to hear more."

Once outside the shop they quickly turned back the way they had come. They headed the opposite way and Scott flagged down a taxi. They hopped in and he told the cabby what hotel they were at. Once back at the hotel, they lingered in the lobby by the elevator a moment watching the patrons come and go.

"Would you like a night cap?" Scott asked.

"Maybe something light, but I'm wondering why you bought that ring?"

"I bought it to see if you would be properly grateful, of course, and you passed the test with flying colors," he said with a conspiratorial air.

"Passed the test . . . what test? With those two following us, what was I supposed to do but act naturally?"

"If that's the way you act naturally, I'm a happy man. I knew I didn't choose wrong."

She stepped back, placing her hands on her hips, with her voice rising. "What are you talking about?"

A sly smile lit his face, "I'm sorry, I was just teasing you and really enjoyed the hug and kiss! I needed to see what those men were doing, I bought the ring because we can always sell it, and I wanted to act naturally in the shop. The $6,000 was a lot, but . . . I can afford it and," his smile grew bigger, "you'll never know when it might come in handy."

A look of pain crossed her face. "You probably bought it to give to some old girlfriend of yours, or something?"

His smile vanished. "Oh, Julia, I'm sorry if you think so. In my work I don't have much time for all that romance stuff, and there aren't any other women in my life. I've been too busy trying to get you to do your work!"

A small smile came back to her eyes and she shrugged. "I'm sorry. We women can be like that sometimes. I shouldn't have said anything anyway. I'm your employee. As you said, you need to get more work out of me!"

He looked at her for a moment totally in a quandary about what to say. "How about that drink?"

They made their way to the small bar where they each ordered a soft drink. They sat at a corner table behind a large potted palm which partially screened them from the lobby. They sat sipping their drinks for a while when Scott noticed the men who'd been following them come into the lobby. The taller of the two went over to the front desk, asking a question of the manager. Scott noticed what he thought was a palmed handshake pass between them and the manager consulted his computer, came back, shook his hand and quickly whispered something to him. The man walked over to his partner and then out of Scott's field of vision.

Julia frowned and asked, "What do you think he asked? What do you think the manager said?"

"Bakeesh—I think he bribed him. It's not safe here anymore, if it ever was in the first place. As soon as they leave, let's get up to our rooms, check on Samuel and get out of here!"

They sipped their drinks for a moment more, got up and made their way to the lobby. There was no sign of the men but the manager quickly looked away when Scott approached with his passport in hand and asked for their keys. The manager handed them their keys but didn't take the passports. Scott thought this odd as they made their way to the elevator.

When they got off the lift, Scott opened Julia's door and they walked into the room.

"Look out, Scott, right behind you," Samuel screamed, as the tall man moved toward Scott with a knife in his hand. The short man was holding Samuel with a small caliber revolver pointed at his head.

The short man shouted at Samuel, "If you say another word or even quiver, I'll blow your brains all over the carpet."

Scott came further into the room and raised his hands. "All right . . . all right. Don't hurt him."

"Stop right there, stay where you are and don't move a muscle," the tall man said, brandishing his knife. "You," he said, pointing at Julia with the tip of his knife, "get over against the wall with Chad and keep your hands in the air. We're going to have a little talk and if you tell me the truth, maybe you can all go back to Sinai unhurt."

Scott looked the tall man in the eyes. "You know my name, so you're not common burglars. What do you want to know?" When he spoke he shuffled a half a step closer to the man with the knife.

"I'll ask the questions, let's make that clear. Stay back and don't move!" Scott froze, but didn't move back.

"I want to know what you found in the chamber. If you don't tell me the truth, you'll all die."

Scott frowned. "Aren't Talbin, Hasid and Dr. Abu on your side? They shot up our camp and took all our data and a truck," he said, as he inched another half step forward. Samuel noticed Scott's movement and saw that every time the taller one spoke, the man holding the gun turned to face his companion. He knew it was dangerous to take your eyes off your adversary, but these two seemed like hired thugs.

"Talbin and Hasid? Who are you talking about and who's Dr. Abu? We don't know what you're talking about and want answers to what you've found in the chamber."

"Why is it everybody's interested in my work all of a sudden? We found a chamber across the valley from Al Sud's tomb. It had some writings on the wall which are still there, and we took photographs of the place but they were all stolen from us. What else do you want to know? We don't know anything else. Who do you work for?" he asked as he took another half step.

"You're lying! You found something or we wouldn't have been sent to follow you and ask questions. What did the writing say?"

"Nothing, other than Mohammad was here. It's kind of like modern graffiti. That would be a good translation." He took another half step.

"I said stay back!" the man screamed at Scott and brandished the knife once again. Scott stopped and moved his foot back for better balance. Samuel had managed to slowly move his foot against the wall and nodded to Scott.

"Well, since they stole our truck, film, cameras, and computers, we were trying to get them back. We didn't find anything in the chamber that you couldn't see with your own eyes if you bothered to go look." Scott nodded at Samuel and two things happened at once.

Samuel pushed up off the wall with his foot. The man holding him came down at his head with the gun.

It was a quick downward blow that the man thought couldn't be blocked. He knew that to turn and fire would waste time and he wanted to disable Samuel not kill him. It had the full force of his body behind it. The man was strong and his reflexes fast.

The blow came down in a flash.

He knew Samuel should be out cold on the floor, for he was trained by the mob, by the best.

He put his hate and fury into the blow and came up with nothing.

It was like striking at smoke.

Samuel's head just vanished from where he'd struck and at the same time it felt like a jackhammer went off in his chest, and a feeling came over him as if his heart exploded. He'd been in any number of fights, could stand pain and usually fought it with raw fury and rage, to no avail this time.

Samuel had pushed off the wall, turned like oil and, faster than the eye could follow, blocked his blow and threw a cocked elbow into his captor's chest, cracking two ribs like a lightning strike. He then spun and grabbed the man's wrist that held the gun and twisted with his dock loader arms.

The snap and crack of the bone was unmistakable in the small room. The man cried out and dropped to the floor hitting his head against the table.

Scott launched himself at the thin man who had turned at the noise. The man became aware of Scott's movements. Ignoring his companion, he came down in the classic knife riposte. He had earned many a cut and scar and knew he was one of the best with a knife. Hearing his friend's bone snap and the sound echo across the room increased his rage as he flicked out at Scott with all his hate and fury.

Scott kept to the side that held the knife, ducked his thrust and, faster than the eye, threw a powerful chop to his throat. The man's knife clattered to the floor and his knees buckled as he clutched his throat, staring at Scott.

Julia blew out the breath she'd been holding. "I'm starting to think it's probably safe to hang around you two! But, oh boy, does trouble ever follow you."

"Come on! Let's tie these two up and get out of here. It's not safe in Suez any more, at least not in this hotel. What happened, Samuel? We went out to eat."

"I ordered room service when I woke up and saw your note. I thought about walking in town, but was still tired. I was going to take a shower when these two showed up. They caught me off guard, opened the door without a sound." He shook and lowered his head as he finished.

"I think the manager gave them my key and I left all the connecting doors open. It's my fault, forget it."

"I think you hit this tall one a little too hard," Julia said, as she used a lamp cord to tie his hands.

Scott looked over at her. "Just make sure you tie him good and tight or he might still be coming after us with that knife of his."

Samuel added, "The little guy's out cold. The way he his head hit the floor, I think he'll be out for a while. Tie em up duck fashion with his hands and feet behind his back and then pull them together with the lamp cord. That should hold them until morning. Check his wallet, Julia. Let's see who these guys are."

She pulled a passport and wallet out of his jacket and handed them to Scott. She then found a gag for his mouth. Samuel found a wallet on the little guy, which he tossed to Scott.

Scott looked at the wallets, then threw them on the table after taking the money. "Looks like they're Italian. I thought at first that they were working for Abu. I was wrong. We'll try to figure this out some more later, but it's obvious that someone else is interested in that chamber other than Abu and whoever he's working for."

Julia looked over at him. "Why did you take the money?"

"Because we're out of cash and we need to get out of town. I don't think it's a good idea to start using our credit cards. We have to disappear and we would leave a trail if we do. Let's get moving. Come on and pack your bags. Samuel, give yours to me and go downstairs and turn in your key to the manager and get your passport back. If he asks any questions, tell him you're going out to find some entertainment or something. Then meet us two blocks west down the street."

"Got it. Two blocks west. Be careful you two."

Scott and Julia made their way down the back stairs to the main level and walked out a maintenance door that led to a back alley. They walked around the hotel and threw their packs in the truck, then drove two blocks west and picked up Samuel.

Chapter 20
Hasid's report

Hasid walked into the dusty room, looking at the fat stomach and stretched gold braids decorating Quati's uniform. The smoke from his cigarette circled into the air above his head, creating a surreal look.

Quati turned from the window as Hasid entered. "Well, what have you found out?"

"I told you that Bestin's men would foul it up. They were no match for Chad and Rogowski. They took them out as quick as can be."

"When did you hear about this?"

"I have my sources, same as you. Suez is not so big that news does not get out."

"Where did Chad go? We cannot afford to lose him now."

"We are trying to put a tail on him, but for now he appears to have disappeared."

"Track everything. All electronic data. Get our men out into the surrounding area. I bet they go up to Israel, and if they do, it will make things tougher."

"General, I do not think they will be heading to Israel. I just have this feeling. Chad is the type who once he gets something into his head, he will not let go. Going to Israel leads nowhere on this. He will follow his nose. Our task is to follow Chad."

"Oh, yes, you knew him when you were younger. Why did you not remind me of that? Are you sure that you can remain objective on this?"

"General, I have worked on many operations with you over the years and your Great Jihad is my life's dream."

"Make sure you know where your loyalty lies, Hasid. I will not tolerate failure."

"I will do as you command. You may wish to ask your western friends for help on this also. They have better electronic gathering ability than we do, and if Chad uses his credit card or the airlines, they may be of help."

"I will make the call. You get on it on your end."

Hasid walked out of the old hotel to where his car was waiting. Getting behind the wheel, he laughed as he thought of the Italians Bestin had sent over to track Chad. *What imbeciles!* To think they could just muscle in and trap Chad and Samuel. He blew out a breath he hadn't realized he was holding and found himself feeling thankful that Scott and Julia were safe and away. *Did he really want to catch them? Follow them? What would Quati eventually ask him to do and could he do it?*

CHAPTER 21
SEA OF REEDS

They took the road north along the eastern side of the canal. The night was balmy and the breeze wonderful after the heat of the day. The large meal they'd eaten and the warm breeze assuaged their anxiety as they drove along the road.

"I know we all need some sleep, except Samuel, but we should try and get to Isma Iliya, and if not there, Port Sa'id. But that's probably too far to go tonight without some rest. What do you say?"

"Port Sa'id kind of has a romantic tone, but you're right. I'm bushed," Julia said.

Samuel shook his head and answered, "I got about two hours of sleep, but right now it feels almost worse than getting none at all. My head feels stuffed and woozy. I say let's look for a place in that first town, what did you call it, Isma Iliya?"

"Yeah, it's on an old caravan route which was used before the canal was made. We should be able to find somewhere safe to stay for the night. I don't think we can get a flight out of there though. We need to go to Port Sa'id or Alexandria to get a flight. All I have is about a hundred and seventy-five bucks, the money I took from those two back there and some credit cards. Do either of you have any cash?"

Samuel dug through his wallet. "I have about two hundred and fifty."

Scott pulled out the bills he'd taken from the men and handed them to Julia. "See how much is there. How much cash do you have?"

She dug through her pack and pulled out some cash. "I have about three hundred dollars and we have about three hundred Euros from those two, or about six hundred total."

"Let's see then. That's about a thousand total, not enough to get a flight for where we want to go."

Julia pulled her credit card out. "What about getting a cash advance on our credit cards?"

"We could try but they can probably track us if we use them. What do you think, Samuel?"

"Whoever's following us is probably upset now that we've given them the slip. They probably have the power to track us in any number of ways. It's not that hard to track credit card purchases. You just tie into the banking network—easy pickens for a computer geek. They'll also know when we've booked an airline flight and can track us that way, too. Maybe we should drive to Greece. What do you two think?"

"I think it's a long way through a number of countries before we get to Greece. They'd be able to track us through passport control, if they're that good, and it would be expensive, unless we can find someway to generate some cash."

"Let's look for a small airport. Maybe we can find a pilot who will fly us for the cash we have. You never know if we find the right guy. Maybe he'd even do a visa transaction and wait to put it through," Julia said.

Scott thought a moment and then replied, "A cash advance would just delay things and might get the pilot in trouble with who knows what kind of people coming up and asking him questions. Ask a guy a favor and then bring trouble to him. No, I'd rather find another way. The small airport's a good idea though."

"Why don't we trade the Hummer for the pilot's services?" Julia asked.

"Do you have any idea what one of these costs? About $70,000, I think that would raise a red flag in and of itself. No, I'll have to call Luke or Alex to come and pick it up when they get sorted out down there, I don't have the title anyway."

Julia quietly asked, "Do you think they really use titles for trucks out here?"

"That's not the point. The truck will raise a flag if we leave it with someone. These aren't just found everywhere, and if someone's closely following us, they'd then interrogate the pilot. I don't want to leave a trail of any kind if it's at all possible."

They were traveling along the shore of the Great Bitter Lake which was formed when the French dug the canal in 1882. They could see the lights of ships traveling north and south as the commerce of the world coursed through the canal. The canal wasn't big enough for the large bulk oil tankers, but smaller tankers and cargo ships used it all the time.

"I see the boats' lights off in the distance. Didn't they call this the Sea of Reeds at one time?" Julia asked.

Scott chuckled at an old memory. "It's called the Great Bitter Lake now. I'm not sure about the Sea of Reeds. I seem to remember something about

Moses from a Sunday school class or something. I had a Sunday school teacher who said that Moses probably went through the Sea of Reeds and that it wasn't any great miracle parting the water since it was only about twelve inches deep back then. He was always trying to use science to explain things in the Bible, like the wind blew all the water to one side or something, as I recall." Scott laughed again at the memory. "At any rate there was this smart kid in my class who said, 'That wasn't the miracle. The real miracle was the drowning of all Pharaoh's army in twelve inches of water.' The whole class roared with laughter and the teacher just stood there and didn't know what to say."

Samuel was snoring in the back as they cruised along the roadway. The salt smell and scent of the sea was in the air. The ships' lights twinkled off in the distance and Julia was about to fall asleep when they pulled into the outskirts of Isma Iliya, which was mostly situated along the western side of the canal at the north end of the lake. The city had spread out over the years, and buildings and homes were now scattered here and there along with some small hotels on the eastern side of the canal.

Scott started looking for a place to spend the night and catch up on some needed sleep. There weren't many hotels on this side of the canal, but there were a few. Passing up the first one which looked rather shabby, he pulled into the second, a place named the Flamingo that looked somewhat decently maintained at any rate.

Scott left his companions in the car and walked into the lobby, which was situated back off the road and surrounded by palms. Painted in a pastel pink, the lobby was probably beautiful at one time, but over the years had taken on the look of an old pale flamingo. The manager on duty was very happy to rent two rooms, especially when Scott paid cash in advance. The man was so happy he didn't even ask for Scott's passport. The rooms were in back, had connecting doors and faced a small garden area between the two rear wings. The best thing about it was there was a rear parking area where he could park the Hummer out of sight and walk into the rear courtyard without being seen from the front. Uninvited guests could also enter this way but hopefully they'd be thrown off pursuit, at least for a while.

Scott walked back to the Hummer, where he found Julia and Samuel asleep. They slowly stirred when he hopped in. "They only had two rooms, but they're adjoining. At least ours has two beds so I don't have to sleep with Samuel. There's a small parking lot behind the building. We can park the Hummer out of sight. I think we're probably clear for the night, which is good since I'm beat."

The rooms were furnished with rattan furniture, ceiling fans and two double beds. The walls were covered with a stucco finish and painted the same faded pink color as the rest of the hotel. Two old paintings were on the wall, one showing the pyramids, the other showing the making of the canal. A small potted palm stood in the corner by a glass topped rattan table.

Scott and Samuel quickly cased the rooms for bugs and came up empty. They didn't have a phone or television and when he was done he nodded. "I think we're clear."

"Well, I'm going to bed. I'm absolutely whipped. You two can argue or flip for which bed you want all night long for all I care, but I'm saying good night now," Julia said as she started to close the connecting door.

"Hold on a minute!" Scott walked past her, through her room and over to the main door. He locked the door, put the chain through the chain holder, and grabbed a small chair that he placed under the doorknob. "There, at least if someone tries to get in, we'll hear him. Keep the connecting door unlocked, okay? I want you to feel safe and get a good night's sleep. I hope Samuel's snoring doesn't keep you awake." Scott turned and started to leave the room when he stopped and turned back. "Remember the jewelry store in Suez? Don't you want to say goodnight?"

"Get out of here right now and go to bed. This girl's had enough excitement for one day and doesn't need anymore." Her tone was harsh but a conspiratorial wink came from her eye and a small smile lit her face as she showed him to the door. "Now, good night, both of you."

The next morning Scott rushed to Samuel's bed. "Get up, now!"

"What is it? What's got into you now?" he asked, shaking his head to clear the cobwebs.

"Julia's gone, her room's empty. I don't see a sign of a struggle, but she's gone! The door's unlocked and the chair's been moved over to the side."

Samuel grunted. "Maybe she went to get something to eat. Did you think of that?"

Scott scowled. "You might be right, but I'd think she'd have had enough sense to stay and wait for us, or at least wake us before leaving. She could have left a note. I'm going to walk down to the lobby and see if I can find her. You stay here and wait, in case she comes back."

As he walked out of the room, the early morning sunshine blinded him. It was so clear and bright it was almost painful, and it brought on the old black shroud of his anxiety, churning his nerves and making him feel like he was descending into a pit. The day was beautiful, but his fear over Julia threatened to upset his emotions like a wobbly cart. He didn't notice the beautiful courtyard, with its interplay of light as the breeze fluttered the palm fronds. Walking into the hotel, he saw Julia in a little niche screened by some palms, hanging up a wall phone. She quickly turned and started walking toward him when she noticed him, her expression changing from concern to joy.

"Oh, I'm glad you're awake. I found a small airport near El Kantara where we can hopefully hire a small plane."

"You scared the wits out of me. What do you mean by leaving the room and not letting us know where you were going? Don't you ever . . . ever do that again! Do you hear me?"

"Don't you talk to me that way. Two can play at this game!" she said, tossing the words at him like a rock.

He felt like he'd been hit. "I've half a mind to leave you right here. I don't need this arguing, nor the stress of being scared to death every time you get something into your head to do something on your own. You have to learn to keep us informed or I'm going to let you off at the first available stop. Do you understand?"

"Oh, yes, Mr. Boss man, I have that clear. Next time I'll leave you a note. You can be sure of that."

After breakfast they started on their way back north, hoping to find some way to get to Greece without being followed. Julia turned to Scott as he drove. "Listen, I'm sorry and you're right, I should have thought how you'd feel if you found the room empty. I just wasn't thinking." She gave him one of her little girl smiles. "But I was trying to help."

He was still angry, but it was better than the feeling of anxiety and despair he'd swallowed when he woke and found her gone. He was finding it hard to hold this against her when she was actually trying to help. He had wondered who she called, though. She said she'd found an airport near El Kantara, but he was learning not to push at her. He looked over at her and said, "Okay, you're forgiven, but don't let it happen again. I'm just glad you're safe. Tell me about the airport?"

She sat up straight. "I found a small airport a few miles up the road where we might be able to hire a pilot. It's near a small town they call El Kantara on the east side of the canal. I'm sorry I scared you. I want to apologize again."

"Forget it, okay! A private airport sounds like it may be a good idea. Let's check it out."

The highway broadened after leaving town, being the main highway from Cairo and Alexandria to points east. They kept their speed down as they followed along the canal to the little town of El Kantara, about twenty miles up the road. They couldn't find a sign for the airport when they reached the town, so they kept driving and finally noticed an old weather-beaten sign hanging off a wooden post with a small airplane painted on it.

"Well, this must be it. I haven't seen any other signs and you said it was near El Kantara, didn't you?" Scott said.

"Yes, and I called but wasn't sure if he said it was north or south of town."

They turned off and followed the gravel track which wound its way up a small switch back over a dune, bisected by a single line of power poles. As they crested the dune, they noticed a small airport below with a lone rusted Quonset hut which must have been a hanger of some sort. A bedraggled and forlorn windsock hung limp in what was left of the late morning breeze. The sun and heat shimmered off the hut and the gravel runway, creating heat mirages in the distance.

CHAPTER 22
IF IT ISN'T SCOTTISH?

When they pulled up in front of the hanger Scott got out, leaving all the windows down. "Wait here. I don't think we should surprise them with a western woman. I don't know what we'll find or how they'll react. I'm glad you wore the scarf this morning; that was good thinking on your part, but these may be Muslim extremists and it pays to be careful and respectful." He walked up to the hanger and entered through the door that was slightly ajar.

The interior of the Quonset hut was dim, and a single desk, coffee pot and small refrigerator stood off to one side. There was a door in the rear that led to the hanger area that also stood ajar. Scott walked through and found a twin engine Bonanza marked ZB 222, which looked to be lovingly maintained. The engine cowl was open, and a large man wearing grey coveralls with grease smeared forearms was deep at work on the engine.

"Hello, good morning," Scott said.

The brown haired man working on the plane slowly turned around and Scott was surprised to see a craggy face framed by a full red beard and obviously Caucasian features. "How do you do? Name's Eric Mc Dougal, from Glasgow. Dinna seen you around here before. How may I help you?" he said with a thick Scottish brogue.

Scott walked forward and extended his hand, "I'd like to hire you for a trip to Greece, if that's possible?"

He shook his head and showed him a grease-covered hand, but offered a large smile. "Nae problem, if you've got the cash for the gas and the proper documents to get into Greece. I'd say about two thousand dollars would do the trick. I have to finish changing the oil on this engine first." He gave him with a sideways glance. "Just you? When you want to go?"

"Well, no, there are three of us and we'd like to go as soon as possible. Cash is a problem, unless you know of a cash machine around. I don't suppose you take Visa?"

"Nae, I don't take nae plastic, and I don't think there's a cash machine that works between here and Cairo. There might be one in Suez, or maybe you could get an advance at a bank. You said you had two more. Bring em in and your luggage so's I can see how much weight we have and how much gas we need."

Scott walked out to the truck leaving Mc Dougal to work on the plane and told Julia and Samuel what he'd found. "Good and bad news. Got us a plane to Greece, but he doesn't take plastic. We have to figure out how to pay."

"And how to stash the truck without causing suspicion," Julia added.

"We'll work it out somehow. Grab your backpacks and we'll talk to this guy. He's Scottish, so you don't have to worry about the hijab anymore. How a Scottish guy ended up here ought to make a good story."

They unloaded the Hummer and Samuel locked it and pocketed the key. The big Scot was wiping his hands on a towel and let out a low whistle at Julia when they entered the hanger. Somehow she'd found time to add some makeup, and her transformation from the sedate woman wearing the hijab to the western woman with the flaming red hair caught Mc Dougal's attention.

"Well, I haven't seen a real woman in this old hanger in all the years I've been in Egypt. Now, with you and the two gentlemen and, if that's all your luggage, I guess our takeoff weight would be about 415 kilos or about 950 pounds." He smiled and pointed to his pride and joy. "Nae problem, she'll easily make it to Greece and then some. Where do you want to go? Athens?"

"We'd like to go to Corfu, or Ioannina in the northwestern part of the country. It's probably a couple hundred kilometers farther. Can we make it that far?" Scott asked.

"Little more gas, say twenty five hundred dollars to northern Greece. Why don't you take a scheduled airliner?" he said as he looked at the trio. "Nae, I guess I don't need to ask. Nae one hardly ever flies with me who wants other people to know where they're going. Keep it to yourselves."

"Well, that parts the rub. The problem is we've only got a thousand dollars in cash, and I also need you to deliver a truck for me. They could pay you when you deliver it?"

"What guarantee can you give me that I'll get paid? This little baby sucks up gas and I nae see a refinery out there, did you?"

"I'll tell you what, if you call my associates, they'll either pick up the truck and pay you or you can deliver it and they'll pay you. Look at it, you can use it for collateral," Scott said as he and the big Scot walked outside.

When Mc Dougal saw the Hummer, he stopped and whistled. "What a beauty. I wish I could keep it."

"You can, if my boys don't pay you what you ask. They'll give you a certified check or get you cash, whatever you desire. I'll write them a letter and you can give it to them."

He shook his head. "I nae believe in the bird in the bush. I need cash and this won't do. What do you think the Egyptian police would think if they caught me driving this beauty around? Me and the Egyptian gendarmes go way back in this neck of the woods. Nae, I don't think so. You can leave it here, but using it for collateral won't do me nae good. What else do you have?"

The only other thing he could think of was the diamond ring he'd bought in Suez, but for some reason he felt strange parting with it. Maybe it was the kiss, but it wasn't real! She was just acting. "The only other thing I have is this ring," he said as he pulled the box out of his pocket. "I bought it in Suez and it's worth about six grand." It glittered in the sunlight radiating its colors. "Here's the jeweler's appraisal."

Eric looked at the stone in the ring. "Looks good to me, but what am I going to do with a diamond?"

"Keep it for collateral. Give it to my associates and they'll pay you for your time and for bringing the truck back. Here, let me write out our agreement and I'll give you directions. They're working in the Sinai, down near St. Catharine's on a survey for me." Scott got out his business card and handed it to the big Scotsman who perused it with a puzzled expression on his face, but took it. Scott pulled a notebook from the Hummer and quickly wrote an agreement for the plane and delivery of the truck to the Sinai base camp. He signed it and handed it to the pilot.

Eric looked the paper over. "That's nae right. I said twenty-five hundred dollars for the trip. You've made it for six thousand."

Scott nodded at him and smiled. "I added some to deliver the truck and for your silence." He cocked his eye at the Scot.

"I don't know, gas costs a lot and I nae want to be stuck with the truck or have to pawn the ring. You know these jewelers. They sell you something for five thousand and you know they pay half that, and when you go to sell it, they'll only give you a thousand for it. I still say a bird in the hand's better."

Julia walked out from around the back of the hanger and heard the last part of the exchange, "How about if I said please? We really need to get to Greece and we can't fly on the airlines. I can't explain why, but I can say, Please!"

The big Scot's demeanor seemed to crumble. He smiled. "The lady knows the way to a Scotsman's heart. She's gone and done it. Okay, pack it up. Let's go."

"I don't know how to thank you Mr. Mc Dougal. I know you probably don't trust us, but believe me, when you deliver the truck and this note, my men will see that you're paid. Thank you so much again," Scott said.

They made their way back into the hanger and the big Scotsman quickly closed up the engine cowling, hooked a small trolley to the nose wheel, and then pulled the plane out of the hanger with a small all terrain vehicle. The plane had looked forlorn in the hanger but gleamed in the sunshine.

"Any of you ever fly in a small plane before?" he asked.

"I have about 125 hours in Piper Cubs," Scott replied.

"I've had some time in helicopters when I was in 'Nam," Samuel said, "but never a prop plane."

"The only plane I've ever been in was a 727 and rode in coach class," Julia chimed in and laughed.

"Okay, then Mr. Chad, you sit in front with me and the two of you sit in back. There's a small fridge box back there if you get thirsty, some sausage, chips and dip in the lower cabinet if you get hungry. Never pays to fly on an empty stomach, just nae booze on the plane. Always have to fly straight. Nae sense rotting around here dying of boredom and booze, I say."

They stowed their bags under the cargo net in the rear and climbed aboard after he closed and locked up his shop.

When he got in, he checked the local weather forecast for the Mediterranean and cranked over the engines.

They taxied out onto the strip. The wind sock was still limp. With a roar of the engines the plane fairly jumped off the runway and into the air. The view was spectacular as they banked north and followed the canal. They could see the Mediterranean off in the distance as they gained altitude, and the verdant green of the Nile Delta off to the west was stunning in contrast to the brown and red colors of the sand all around them. Port Sa'id quickly came up on their left side as they gained altitude and started to bank the plane to the northwest toward Greece.

"Beautiful spring day for flying. Forecast's good all the way. Now all we have to worry about is figuring out where to land this baby without causing too big a stir for you folks. You did say Corfu, didn't you?"

"Corfu or somewhere near there would do. We're really trying to get into north-central Greece but aren't that particular about where we start. I have a feeling you know the best places to go," Scott answered.

"Greece is a funny country. Sometimes they're very strict and at other times it's wide open and they couldn't care less who came in or out." He half turned toward the back as he spoke. "Yes, I know two or three where we can set down, gas up and not cause too big a stir. I forgot to mention, I could use some cash to gas the plane up and get back home. You can deduct it from the final payment."

Scott looked over at him. "We'll give you all we can spare. Just leave us enough to rent a car and get a meal and a couple of rooms for a few nights. We'll help out anyway we can but we don't want to use a credit card in Greece. I don't want to leave an electronic trail, if you know what I mean."

"I know . . . I know, everything's all on computers these days. You probably didn't notice, but I'm online in my office and talk to people all over the world. Most of my flights are pre-booked on line and I have e-mail and understand computers and know what you mean by an electronic trail."

The African coast had disappeared into the haze behind them and there was a hint of land off to the northeast that Eric said was Cyprus but he was turning further west to avoid Turkey's airspace. The deep blue sea was quiescent as they traveled, and the skies mostly clear except for a few cumulus clouds building over the sea below. Now and then they could make out the wake of a large ship as it crossed the Mediterranean. Aside from that they felt absolutely alone, cruising along at 12,000 feet.

❈ ❈ ❈ ❈ ❈ ❈ ❈ ❈

The island of Corfu soon appeared as a green smudge on the horizon.

Eric gently pointed the nose down and left the throttles set and they quickly accelerated until they were going about 290 knots. About when Scott thought they were going to crash into the sea, Eric gently pulled back on the yoke and the plane smoothly leveled off about 150 feet above the waves. The coastline of the island was quickly coming up. They could make out the golden rays of the setting sun on the mountains to the north and on the Albanian coastline to the northeast.

"I need to pass over the strip first to see if it's clear. If it's nae clear, we go to plan number two."

"What's plan number two?" Julia questioned.

"Maybe a mainland strip I know about. The problem is, it's getting dark and I'd rather land in daylight. Just pray this strip is clear, okay?"

They quickly came up on the island. Tall thin evergreen trees were growing all over the mountainsides, the greenery spilling down into the valleys which were interspersed with olive groves and fruit orchards. Kavos was a little beach town on the southeast corner of the island and the small gravel strip was located between it and Panagia where an old monastery sat at the very southern tip of the island.

They came roaring over the monastery and Eric set the flaps and reduced the throttles. Banking the plane over a hillside, he leveled out over the grass airstrip and found it full of goats out for an evening meal.

His Scottish accent was hard to decipher. "Dumb buggers, eat the tires off your plane and chew up the ropes if you tie it down. I nae know what they really think they're good for. Hold on for I'm gonna buzz them off the field."

Quickly banking the plane, he circled out over the sea and then back toward the strip. When he was lined up again, he came in lower this time, extending his landing gear and descending to about ten feet above the runway where the goats were feeding. He extended his flaps to full and added power to the engines while feathering the prop, so that the engines would be louder. He headed right toward a large billy that seemed to have taken up station in the middle of the runway and acted like he wanted to butt the plane. At the last moment Eric bobbled the plane down, touching the wheels down in front of the goat and then gently lifted it off again. The effect was astonishing. The old billy goat took off at a run and the rest of the herd followed him. At the same time a young boy came running out of an old stucco building at the end of the runway with a rod in his hand and started shooing the remaining goats out of the way.

A smile lit Eric's face. "I think it worked. That boy's probably the shepherd and will keep them off the runway at least long enough for us to land. Gas is what the problem's going to be, but I have enough to get part way back and fill up somewhere. Nae to worry's my motto. If I worried all the time, I'd have used up all my luck."

He turned the plane in the same wide arc and came in again, this time reducing the throttles, leaving the gear down and coming in for a smooth landing. "Welcome to Greece," he said.

"We thank you, kind sir. You're a gentleman and a scholar," Scott said with a smile.

"I'm nae thing of the sort. I'm a Scotsman pure and simple, all of whom are of noble of birth, but probably not gentlemen or scholars. We like our scotch too much, except when we're flying. I'm glad I could help. I don't know how you talked me into this, with only a diamond as collateral, but here we are. Let's see if this shepherd boy knows where I can get some gas around here."

They piled out of the plane and approached the shepherd boy who was standing at the end of the runway by the little stucco building. Scott walked up and asked, "Evening. What's your name? Do you know where the field master is? My pilot needs to fuel his plane."

The young boy answered in fractured English, "My name is Laki. We all have to take English in school here. There is no one here but me and I don't think there is any fuel. When the planes that are big come they bring out a truck to fill them up."

Scott turned to the big Scot. "Sorry, Eric, I think you're going to have to wait for us to go into town and send a truck out or take your chances farther south on one of the other islands you mentioned. It's getting dark now. Want to come into town with us?"

"Nae, I may as well just get going. I can fly this thing in the dark as well as the light. I'll stop at a bigger field with lights. How about some of that cash, though, for the pump?"

"Almost forgot. How about two hundred? I'd like to give you more, but

I don't know when we can get any more and I've given you everything else I had of value."

Julia walked over and pulled Scott aside. "I heard you gave him the ring you bought, for a moment there . . . I almost thought . . . wasn't there something else you could have given him?"

Eric listened and smiled. "You know, for some reason I'm about to break all my principles." He reached in his pocket and took out the box and tossed it to Scott. "Here, use it well. I hope I get a hold of those two friends of yours. What did you say their names were?"

Scott neatly caught the box and gave him an odd smile before tucking it into his pocket. "Luke and Alex, they're my interns on the survey project in Sinai. They'll treat you right if you show them that letter. If something goes wrong, call the number on the card I gave you and I'll work it out for you somehow. You're a blessing, Mr. Mc Dougal, that's a fact. Well, since we have the ring, I suppose we could spare another hundred or two. We just need enough for tonight."

"Nae, two hundred's enough. It will get me enough gas to get home, if I fly her high and slow. Nae to worry's my motto. Good luck to you all. Take care," he said as he waved and climbed back into his plane, started it and turned around to roar off into the darkness.

CHAPTER 23
QUATI, WHERE ART THOU?

Quati strode toward the window looking out on the desert. "I do not care Mustafa. Do you hear me? Find them before I really lose my temper."

"My General, I cannot tell you what I do not know. After Chad left Sinai he went north and has disappeared. We have no indication that he went to Israel and he has not been seen in Egypt or anywhere else. We have checked the airlines, we are tapped into the computers and are checking to see if he or any of his companions used their credit cards. Nothing has come of it, so far!"

Quati strode across the dirty floor. "Dig farther. I will brook no excuse on this. It is Allah's will that Islam's and my banner fly everywhere, even in the land of the Great Satan, the Shitan, America. I am tired of your excuses, Mustafa. Get to work on this now."

"I have told you, my General, Chad has slipped our grasp. I am going to put his picture out to our network and will see what comes up. There are many ways to slip out of Egypt. We have used them many times ourselves when moving our operatives in and out. The teams we have sent to America have slipped in many times without being caught. How hard do you think it is to get out of Egypt? Al Queda has trained our operatives and we can slip in and out of any country without a problem. I am sure Chad can do the same."

The general looked at him, turned and stared out the window. Outside it was the Middle East. The desert sun beat down, and even the scrubby plants would have complained if they could have out of orneriness. "Listen well Mustafa, if you do not find Chad by the end of the week, you will be taking a look at that wall out there. Do you understand me?"

Mustafa bowed, and quickly walked out into the heat. He made his way over to where a truck was waiting and drove away.

Back inside the old building, Hasid looked over at Quati. "My General, we may wish to look further for help on this. I hate to do it, but maybe you should call your acquaintances across the sea?"

Quati banged his hand against the wall. "Those pious religious dogs! All they care about is feathering their own nest." He walked over to the desk that sat in the corner gathering dust. "You may be right, even though I do not trust them . . . what can it hurt?"

"I have thought about it and you are right. They only care about keeping their nest feathered, but that works to our advantage, yes? You see, General, if they find Chad first, they will stop him and his information from getting out. They do not want anything at all to happen that will upset their carts. We only need to keep an eye on them. Contact these men and I will call one of my operatives to keep an eye on them. What can it hurt?"

"Allah does not want us in bed with the heathen, but you may be right. He also tells us to be sly as foxes. The great Shitan is about to come down. Al Queda has promised their demise and has trained for this for many years. Our friends over there have given much money to our cause. We may be able to use this as an excuse to get some more out of them, too. Let us keep that in mind, also. First and foremost you must keep and eye on Mustafa. See that he does what he says. He is not the most competent technically and he needs your guidance. Chad will use some sort of electronic data or some type of transfer, then we will have him. Get on it, Hasid. Get on it now."

Hasid bowed and backed out of the door into the hot desert air which parched his throat. He thought of how this had been a testing ground for many of God's people over the years. Walking over to his Mercedes limousine, he told his driver to take him to the airport.

※　※　※　※　※　※　※　※

Scott turned to the young Greek. "Well . . . well, young man, do you know where can we get a meal, hotel and rent a car around here, in that order?"

"Well, the meal is easy. My uncle's taverna is down the road in Kavos. There are a number of hotels on the island, too. I would be happy to show you as soon as I pasture my goats for the night. You would probably have to go to Kerkyra to rent a car though." He stopped and looked at them. "At the big airport, I guess, but I am not sure."

"How far is it to Kavos?" Julia asked.

"Not far. I walk it every evening after school when I put the goats in their nighttime pasture. It is not more than half hour. You will see."

They sat on the edge of a concrete wall beside the old stucco building. It had once served as the airport's terminal during the war. The boy shooed the goats down the hillside and through a gate which he wired closed. He came bounding back up the hill with that exuberance that adults wish they had and that seemed wasted on the youth. "Come with me, this way," he said as he skipped up the narrow gravel road.

They walked and listened to Laki's chatter about his life on the island, his school and how he'd learned English. He then started questioning them about where they'd been and what they thought of his island. "Do you like Corfu? I know the rest of the world calls it that, for I learned this in my English class, but we call it Kerkyra. I have heard that our island is very green compared to some of the other islands which are dry and full of sticker bushes. Have you ever been to Igougomitsa? I was there last year buying parts for my uncle's car and supplies for his taverna. Where did you fly in from, Athens, Italy, Africa?" he asked as he looked around as if seeing those distant places. "I would like to go to Athens someday when I am older and have a chance. Herding goats is fun, but I have heard that there are movie theaters in Athens with ten different movies showing at the same time. The theater in Corfu town shows one at a time. I like your spy movies best, like James Bond secret agent. Sometimes they are shown in Greek without having to read the words. But reading the words helps me to learn the English, do not you think?"

He rambled on so fast and asked so many questions that Scott didn't know where to begin and just nodded saying, "yes," now and then.

Julia looked at Scott's befuddlement, smiled and tried to answer Laki's string of rapid-fire questions. "We enjoy movies with subtitles, too. I'm sure they help you with your English. The big movie theaters with ten or more screens are really cool. They have some near Chicago that have thirty screens, but they usually don't show thirty different movies at the same time. We came in from a place called Sinai."

"You must be very rich to live near Chicago. Is not that in Illinois?"

She laughed. "No, most people aren't rich who live in Illinois. They're rich or poor just like here. A lot of Greeks live in Illinois, too. They own restaurants, work in the factories, are managers and lawyers just like everywhere else. But that doesn't make them rich. They went there and were willing to work hard. That's what helps them succeed."

They crested a little rise in the road which was lined by those tall cypress trees they'd seen flying in. Interspersed between the cypresses were large rhododendrons with white blossoms that stirred in the breeze and scented the path as they walked. At the top of the rise, the little village of Kavos came into view. The stars were bright overhead and twinkled in the darkness. The village was nestled between the hillside and the sea and its lights beckoned to them in the darkness, filling their senses with the sounds of life and song that was filling the air.

"There's my uncle's taverna." He pointed. "It's called The Lazy Pelican in English. I'll run ahead and tell him to expect company," he shouted as he ran down the roadway.

Distant strains of a lilting Greek song came to their ears as they strode down the pleasant lane into the village. The old inn had seen more prosperous times in years gone by, but still attracted a large local clientele for it was the main place for the local inhabitants to pick up gossip in the little hamlet.

Making their way down the small lane, they stopped when they came to the taverna. Laki came bounding off the porch, pulling an elderly gentleman by the arm. "This is my Uncle Georgio. He is setting up a table for you. Come on in, please!"

Scott nodded at the bearded gentleman and extending his hand said, "Hello, sir. Your nephew's been most helpful. We'd appreciate your hospitality, a hot meal and maybe some local advice."

The red cheeks of the older gentleman seemed to swell up in a smile, his large mid-section seemed to rattle as he laughed and said, "Come on in. Cannot leave you standing out here. Hey, Laki, where is Nick? Tell em we have some special guests and to get a load off and get busy. Now where was I . . . oh, yes. Please come in and enjoy our hospitality. You and your friends are most welcome." He quickly strode through the double doors of the inn and they could hear him calling for his helpers over the music and conversation.

They followed Laki up the steps and entered the inn. Their noses followed the tantalizing scent of Greek cooking that was filling the air. Chickens were being roasted over an open fire in a brick hearth, bottles of wine passed between the tables and the patrons were singing an old Greek song. The inn was a large open room with a bar in one corner and a small band playing in another. The patrons sat around at small tables while the waiters balanced trays of food and drinks as they negotiated their way through the throng. Laki showed them to a table where they sat in wonder in the big room. He soon came back with a menu and took their orders.

"I'd like the dolmades," said Julia, "and a glass of seven-up, please."

"Spanikopita, saganaki, some octopodi and a glass of the house wine to drink for me," Samuel said.

Scott nodded at Laki. "I'd like a saganaki for myself, a few pieces of spanikopita and some tomatoes and cucumbers, along with some fresh bread, Greek potatoes and a large Coke, please."

Laki handed their orders to his uncle who bustled into the kitchen shouting at the cooks, who quickly started putting things together.

Scott was sitting in thought, trying to relax after the long flight, thinking about the beautiful sites they'd seen along the way. He knew it was a blessing to have had a cloudless day in which to fly across the Mediterranean and get away without being found. But for some reason a melancholy mood descended over him like a shroud, his fingers and toes went cold and he shivered, trying to shake it off.

"Penny for your thoughts?" Julia asked.

"Oh, nothing. It wasn't a pretty thought and I'm kind of ashamed to have been thinking it in this kind of atmosphere," Scott dryly said.

"Well, I agree with Scott. This is not the type place to be thinking morbid thoughts. It seems as if we've jumped out of the frying pan and landed in Paradise. So I say, we should enjoy this place while we're here. I could go for finding a Penelope, too," Samuel said as he nodded to one of the waitresses. "So let's think happy thoughts, Scott," and he lifted his wine glass in a toast.

"Oh, I don't know," Julia said. "I admire a man who can feel things and isn't always running around bragging. It's not about how many toys you have or how much money you make or . . . but I also agree with Samuel and think there's a time and place for everything. Ecclesiastes says that there's a time for everything and for every season. Right now seems to be the time to eat, enjoy and relax." She paused and smiled at them. "So there, I agree with both of you. At least we're safe for awhile and have thrown off pursuit."

Laki and a waiter appeared bringing dishes and laying out bread, oil and butter on the checkered oilskin tablecloth. Georgio somehow seemed to be everywhere: bustling out with a big smile, throwing a shot of brandy in the sizzling tray, yelling "Opa," as he struck a match and flamed the cheese. Julia laughed, quickly backing away from the flame as Georgio, Laki and the waiter created a whirlwind around them as they laid out plates, platters and food all over the table in a twinkle. Georgio's attitude was infectious as he bustled breathlessly about, laughing with a huge grin as he went about his work, stopping at each table. He moved ubiquitously through the room, but mostly they could hear him jovially yelling at the cooks in the kitchen or telling stories and laughing with the patrons.

Georgio came up as they finished. "Would like anything else?"

Scott pushed his chair back. "No, this was just wonderful."

"Well did you like?"

"It was just wonderful, Georgio. I can't thank you enough," Scott said.

"That flaming cheese, what did you call it, saganaki? That was wonderful," Julia said. "I never knew they had such things in Greece. I knew about dolmades; my mother used to make something like them, but she just called them stuffed green peppers." She then looked over at Scott. "It's as good as the French restaurant the other night. You're going to spoil me."

Scott looked over at Georgio. "We'd also like to find a place to stay for the night and need to find somewhere to rent a car or get a ride up to the airport in the morning. Could you recommend a place and give us some ideas?"

"You have the look of Traumata, and I would like to help. I feel you need our help. Not many people come into that airstrip unless they are in trouble."

"Georgio, your hospitality has been enough."

"Let me finish. I can sense the spirit on you and strong things are moving. I do not know what, but know when to give a helping hand. I want you to stay at my home tonight. Laki will show you the way. I will think on it and see what else I can do to help."

"No, you've helped us already. I don't want to put you to any trouble," Scott said.

"No problem. I will speak with Laki, then it is settled."

He bustled off, laughing and chuckling, yelling at the cooks in the kitchen, then went over and spoke with Laki a moment who bounded over to their table with a big smile on his face. "My uncle says you are staying with us tonight at our house. It is large and he often rents rooms to travelers during the summer season, ever since his wife passed away."

"Your uncle's hospitality, I think, is what we would call amazing!" Scott said.

"You would be putting us out if you refused. You would not be letting my uncle practice his hospitality. He would be most ashamed."

"How can we say no to that?" Scott said.

Julia smiled at him. "Lead the way, young man."

"We wouldn't want your uncle to feel ashamed. He's a man of great and jovial character which should never be spoiled," Samuel added.

"Well, you don't have to live with him all the time and do chores or herd his goats. He's a hard taskmaster, always something to do, but he is kind and I am happy with him and love him."

After paying the bill and thanking Georgio, they followed Laki out the door, listening to the strains of music and laughter slowly die away as they headed onto the village square. The evening was balmy, though not as warm as Sinai, but spring had come to this corner of the world and the trees were in blossom and their scent filled the air. They followed Laki up a short hill, past old village homes to Georgio's house, which was perched at the end of the street, backing up to the hillside and facing the sea. It was a beautiful home, much larger than they'd expected and they were surprised by the many modern conveniences.

Laki noticed their appraising looks. "My uncle has done a lot of investing over the years. Here, follow me. I will show you to your rooms."

They followed him down the hallway to the rear of the home where he opened a door and showed Samuel into a room with a small single bed and dresser. "This will be your room, Samuel. There is a washroom right across the hall that you can use if you need to."

Samuel, who could sleep on a rock, plopped himself down on the bed, smiling and said, "This will do just fine."

He looked at Scott and Julia. "This way, I will show you to your room."

They followed him up a short staircase which opened onto a veranda. He opened one of the glass doors saying, "This will be your room. It has a private bath and a small sitting area so, please, enjoy it. My uncle will not be home till very late after the taverna closes. But he has told me to lend you his car. You can use it to drive up to Kerkyra to see if you can rent a car. Please come and get me in the morning. I'll be downstairs in the kitchen by seven so I can get you set up before I go to school. I start school at 9:00 A.M., so we have to get going early. Good night," he said as he closed the door.

Julia stood there looking at Scott with an arched eyebrow. "Well, where's your room? I think he's made some sort of mistake thinking we're married or something."

He grinned and looked around the room. "It was probably just the way you were looking at me in the restaurant. Flip you for the bed."

"What do you mean, flip me for the bed?"

"Exactly what I said, flip a coin for it. Heads I win, tails you lose, that type of stuff. Sometimes you amaze me! The stuff you know and don't!"

"Well, get this right, heads or tails you loose, flip or no flip. You get the couch! Why don't you figure that one out and see how that amazes you!"

Scott mumbled under his breath, "No fury like a woman scorned."

"What did you say? Are you talking to me or just yourself?"

"Just talking to myself. Good night!"

He went into the bathroom, brushed his teeth, washed his face and cleaned up. On his way out he grabbed a comforter and a pillow off the bed while Julia was sitting at the dressing table brushing her hair. She'd changed into a large white t-shirt and long socks and as soon as Scott left the bathroom and got on the couch, she went in.

When she came out, she hopped into the bed, pulled the sheets up and turned away from him toward the window and tried to fall asleep. He lay on the couch and pulled the cover up and turned away from her.

CHAPTER 24
HASID'S LAMENT

Hasid picked up the phone and dialed a number from memory. "Get me Quati, now."

"The general is not to be disturbed."

"Azhan, if you know what is good for you, you will get the general on the line *right now.*"

"Hasid, you overstep your bounds. The general gave me strict orders not to disturb him unless it was an emergency. Tell me what the emergency is and I will consider whether or not to disturb his peace."

"It is a wonder we ever get anything done, Azhan. Tell the general that we have a line on where Chad has gone."

"Who is this Chad, and what are you talking about Hasid?"

"Something you do not need to know. Just tell the general."

"Hasid, if the general is displeased, you will live to regret this."

He waited on the phone for a moment then Quati's voice came through the receiver. "Hasid, my good friend Azhan tells me you have a line on Chad. Tell me, what have you found out."

"We believe he went north. We have a line on a small plane that took off north of Suez and are checking its flight path."

"Good work Hasid. Find out where that plane went. Use everything you have to keep on it. I will be in touch. You know what to do."

"Yes, General, we will be ready to move in the moment we find anything."

"When you do, and I know you will, I think you should take out the Jewess. I don't like her being around the Prophet's work."

"We've talked about this, General, and I will do as you order, but please consider the consequences. Chad may quit and then we will have to bring in Abu or someone else to try and follow up on this."

"Find out where Chad has gone and then we will talk about it, make sure you keep me posted."

❉　❉　❉　❉　❉　❉　❉　❉

The early morning sunlight came filtering in through the curtains after Scott had tossed and turned most of the night. He couldn't remember when he'd finally fallen asleep. He shook his head when he woke, turned over and noticed that Julia was still sound asleep on the bed. He quietly got off the couch and made his way to the bathroom, where he brushed his teeth and splashed cold water on his face. When he came out Julia was up.

They followed their noses and found coffee perking and Samuel cutting up tomatoes and cucumbers for a morning breakfast. There were rolls and pastries laid out on the table, and Laki came buzzing in with a bouncing step and bright smile.

"It's 7:15. We have got to get going. Let me show you the car and draw you a map of where to leave it. My uncle wants you to leave it at his brother's house in Kerkyra, which is near the airport. You can rent a car at the airport or take the ferry across to Igougomitsa."

Scott looked at him. "What car?"

"My uncle is lending you his car. I told you that last night?"

"Why would he do that?"

"Because he trusts you and he's a man of deep principles that are hard for me to understand."

"Well, that's too much. We can't do that," Scott said.

"Well, I don't know how you are going to get to the ferry dock then. You should not turn this down. He wants you to take it to his brother's house, who may be able to help you more than we can. He said he was going to speak with him last night."

"Well, I don't . . . think we can take it. It's too much. I can't believe we've met people like you and your uncle."

"My uncle will be unhappy if you don't. He would say that you are ungrateful and that you're not giving him a chance to show grace."

"What can I say? Okay, let's get going."

They followed him out to the garage and, to their surprise, a brand new silver Mercedes AMG was in the garage. Laki handed Scott the key and said, "My uncle really trusts you and likes you to lend you this car. He will not let me drive it even though I have a license. Please take care of it," he finished with a wincing smile.

Scott shook his hand. "I can't stress enough how impressed I am by your uncle's and your hospitality. You and your family have given the word a whole new meaning to me."

"My uncle told me your name means to wander. We have a patron saint that wanders the world looking for the lost, and my uncle thinks that is your calling. He said he saw it in your eyes and heart. Here is a map to my other uncle's house. He is expecting you. Good luck, Mr. Chad, and God speed."

They got into the car and made their way up the coast toward Lefkimmi, where they caught the main highway, if that's what you'd call it. The highway followed the center of the island for a while then bent east toward the coast where they followed it to Perama. They made their way around the lake and airport until they saw a small Eurocar agency where they pulled off the road.

Scott looked around at the agency. "I'm not sure about renting a car. I don't think we can rent one without a credit card. Maybe we should just take the ferry over to the mainland and try our luck there."

"What about buying a car or just using this one?" Samuel asked.

"We might be able to buy a car but, remember, we don't have a lot of money and don't want to leave a plastic trail. As far as using this one, I wouldn't dream of it. Georgio was far too gracious for me to think of doing something like that."

Julia stretched and said, "Well, let's drive on and see if we can find some old cheap car we could buy to get us over the mountains. It's still early, maybe something will turn up. I'm sure you could probably trade that diamond for a car if you found the right place."

"I thought you were upset when I gave it to Eric for the plane ride?" Scott answered.

"Oh, just do what you want. We have to get over to the mainland and we don't have enough cash. I was just being pigheaded."

They drove along and came upon one of those newsstand kiosks known throughout Greece, where Scott noticed international calling cards for sale.

"I have an idea. I'll buy one of those calling cards and have my office wire some money to us. Any other ideas?"

Samuel lectured, "You have to go to a bank to have money wired. Then you have to cash the check, and for that you need identification of some sort or they won't give you the money. That seems to defeat the whole purpose of staying incognito."

"I agree, if it's in my name or yours, but maybe if we had it wired to Julia they wouldn't trace it back to us. It's just a thought. Any other bright ideas?" Scott asked.

Samuel thought a moment. "The other problem is they'd trace a transfer from our company offices to Greece, to anyone, even Laki or his uncle. That would get them in trouble."

Julia shook her head, her red hair flying about. "If you call your company and have the funds transferred to a supplier, and then transferred to Laki's uncle, that might work."

"I just don't like the thought of leaving a trail or getting these people involved. They took us into their home and lent us their car. If the wrong people start looking down the money trail, that could bring them a lot of trouble later on. It's just not worth the risk."

Julia asked, "Does your company do any business with Greek suppliers?"

"Not that I can think of."

"Does your company do any charitable giving to anyone or any organizations?"

"We give to a couple of organizations, but none in Greece. As my mother used to say, 'You're not a success, Scotty, unless you can give some of it away.' So the company gives to orphanages, to some medical groups in Africa and India and some others. We support students who take up surveying and mining and offer scholarships to them if they intern and work with us. They have to agree to work in their own countries after graduation."

Samuel said, "We don't know how much of cyberspace these people have access to either. Maybe using the calling card, they wouldn't know it's you but they might know your company got a call from Corfu in Greece and that might be enough to start them looking. No, I think we got clean away so far. Let's try and keep it that way. I'll sleep better at night knowing we're safe and they're not on our trail."

Scott thought about it for a moment while the traffic and motorbikes whizzed by. "Let's take stock. How much money do we have left? And what do we have to sell? We have the ring. We have about five hundred bucks left. We could probably take the ferry across, have a taxi to take us inland, and get a room and some meals for a couple of nights with the money we have. That way we could save the diamond ring for an emergency. No telling how much we'd get for it either, probably only about a thousand or two, knowing jewelers and the way they jack up prices."

Julia shrugged. "Let's go to Georgio's brothers, drop off the car and see what comes up."

"We should probably check out the ferry schedule too, while we're at it," Samuel added.

They drove around the airport as scooters whizzed by like little gnats on the wing. The road passed the bay and they turned north toward the old castle and fort next to the ferry dock. The old port was a backdrop for the beautiful old Venetian city built into the side of the hill facing the sea. The old fort protected the entrance to the harbor and was perched on a hill next to the town. Driving into the main part of town, Scott pulled over, consulting the map Laki had drawn, and proceeded north to Voulgareos Street. He turned left into the old Venetian quarter and up a hill to Montsenigou Street, pulling up to #12. They all got out and proceeded up to the door of the residence.

Scott knocked on the blue door and a little old lady with a babushka wrapped around her head answered, "Kaleemera!"

"Ya sas, Ti kanete, Kaleemera, Parakalo, Laki's Theos, parakalo?" Scott answered using his fractured Greek.

She raised her finger, turned and shouted off a rapid-fire stream of Greek into the home. Soon a huge bear of a man with hairy arms the size of oak limbs appeared and came to the door.

He smiled and offered his large hand. "You must be Laki's and my brother's American friends who landed last night at the old air strip. I'm Stephanos which is Stephen in English. If you travel around much on the island, you will see a beach up north named after me, Agios Stephanos, which means Saint Stephen." He paused and laughed. "You don't look like smugglers, but I sense you are in trouble. I have talked with my brother who has a good eye for people who need help. How can I help you?"

Scott pondered how much to say to this giant of a man, who seemed a copy of his brother at least in laughter and spirit, if not looks. He decided on the spur of the moment he could or must trust him for some reason. "We need to get into central Greece and we can't use our credit cards or create an electronic trail, and we only have about five hundred dollars to get there. We need a car for what we have to do, and all we have is a watch and a diamond ring. If you know somewhere where we could sell them, that would help."

Stephanos laughed. "A watch I do not need, nor a diamond ring, but let us see. My brother and Laki spoke highly of you." He paused and laughed again. "You seemed to remind him of his days in the resistance for some reason, though Lord knows why."

Scott reached into his pocket, pulled out the box with the diamond ring in it and tossed it to Stephanos. "I bought it in Suez the other day, and it's all we have of any real value. It's 1.25 carats, VS quality and E color. Cost me six thousand in Suez."

"Well, from the look on the young lady's face, I don't think you want to part with it. When's the happy day?" he said and handed the ring back to Scott.

"This is all we have right now and it's a long story!" Julia said while giving Scott a quick glance. "It's not what you think. It's important that we get to Meteora . . . just a feeling, that's all!"

His eyebrows narrowed as his grey eyes looked at her. "Young lady, I've been around Greek women all my life and their feelings are not something you just brush off. No, I will not buy the ring, but I will tell you what I can do." He paused and smiled at them. "How about I lend you five thousand and when you get things straightened out, you send me a check? Will that work out okay?"

Scott walked up and extended his hand. "That's most kind of you! That will work just fine. Here's the key to your brother's car and since we didn't get to see him this morning, I'd appreciate it if you could tell him thanks for us."

Stephanos took the key and laughed. "The problem is he works late and sleeps late. We live on what's called Greek time. I will get you the money." He turned and waved for them to follow him into his study. "I know a place in town where you can get a car without a lot of questions being asked."

"Greek hospitality once again. I would have never believed it," Scott said.

They followed Stephanos to his study. There was a glass table with two ancient columns supporting it and antiques scattered throughout the room. He went to his desk and opened a drawer with a key from his pocket. Pulling out a stack of bills, he counted them and handed it to Scott, who tossed him the box with the ring. They followed his huge form out to his brother's car and took the main road north, past the bay, turning off on a small gravel road around the back of a garage and then up a steep driveway where they found a small gravel lot filled with old cars in various states of repair or disrepair. A young man was hunched over one of the cars tinkering with the engine. He looked up and waved as they drove into the lot.

"Kalimera, Janni. These are friends from America and they need a car. Can you help them?"

The mechanic wiped his hands on a rag from his pocket. "Kalimera, Stephanos. Anything for you and your friends. What kind of car would you like and how much do you want to spend?"

Scott looked around, a little disappointed at the choices. "About a thousand dollars, what would that get us? We need to drive across Greece and need something reliable."

"I'll show you." He beckoned with a wave of his hand. They followed him around the back of a little shop and he showed them two cars: one a green Fiat 500 and the other a newer black Audi with four doors. "The Fiat, even though she is small, is very reliable, I just rebuilt her engine and she purrs like a kitten. The Audi is a newer and bigger car but has many miles on it. The Fiat may be too small for you but should not break down, and she runs very well."

Samuel and Julia looked at both the cars, and she laughed when she sat in the Fiat. "I've always wanted one of these. They're cute!"

"I think it's cute, too," Samuel said.

Scott smiled as he listened to them sitting in the Fiat. "What's the world coming to! You want to buy a car because it's cute! Come on, you two, we've a long way to go."

The mechanic leaned into the little Fiat and twisted the key. The motor spun and started right-away. "See, she starts right up and purrs like a kitten.

Thirty-six horsepower is what she has on tap. When I rebuilt the engine, I took special care and milled the cylinder head and valves, polishing everything. I bet she actually puts out more like forty or forty-five horsepower now," he said with a look of pride on his face.

"How much for the Fiat and how much for the Audi?" Scott asked.

"A thousand American dollars for either one and I'll throw in the license plates too, so you don't have to register the car." He looked at Stephanos and winked. "My friend and I have done business together in the past."

"Let's see this one, too," Scott said as he sat in the Audi. "Do you have the key?"

"No, she doesn't need a key. Just put a screwdriver in the lock and turn it. All the tumblers have been filed off."

Scott took a nail file that was lying on the floor, inserted it in the lock, gave it a turn and the motor rumbled to life, letting out a cloud of white smoke and then settling down to idle a little rough and leaving a small cloud of bluish white smoke puffing out the tail pipe. He could see a little light coming through the floor where the pan had rusted out but the brown leather seats were in magnificent shape. He pressed on the accelerator and turned the wheel which had a lot of play in it. The odometer read 320,000 kilometers. He looked over at the mechanic. "How many kilometers does it really have on it?"

"I don't know; the speedometer is broken. Stopped recording before I got the car. I have not had it off the island so maybe not too many more than it shows." He shrugged. "But I do not know when it broke."

Scott went over to the Fiat which still sat there idling happily away. He sat in the seat, felt the wheel play and firmness of the brakes. "Can I take it for a spin?"

"Sure," Janni said.

He drove the car up the hill and around the lot, feeling the transmission, steering and brakes which all felt tight. It seemed someone had also replaced the shocks not too long ago. He pulled back in the gravel lot where the group was waiting and said, "I know it seems funny but, if no one has any objection, we'll take the Fiat."

Scott looked at Julia and Samuel who nodded. "Okay, deal. Can you get it ready Janni?" Scott asked.

"Just give me a few minutes to change the plates and she is all yours."

Scott and Stephanos walked away from the group while Julia and Samuel transferred their bags into the back of the little car. Samuel handed Julia their backpacks through the cloth sunroof.

"I don't know how to thank you. I'll have my company send you a check as soon as things settle down a little. Here's my card with my address in the states and phone number. If you ever need anything please don't hesitate to ask," Scott said.

"My brother called last night and he was right about you, I know. Keep on with this work you're on and I think maybe you'll find friends. We have a name for it which is hard to translate." He struck his chest with his hand. "Friends in unlikely places. May you go with God!"

"I'm once again lost for words and don't know how to thank you. May God guide your steps also," Scott said shaking his hand. He pulled back his hand and stared at the box in it. "No, Stephanos, that's not fair. What if something happens to us, then you'll be out five thousand dollars? We had a deal."

"I know we had a deal and I'm the one who has set the terms, since I am the one who has the money. If I want to be free with my money, what is that to you? Remember the worker's in the vineyard? It is grace! So do not argue with me; you would lose. At least that's what my brother would say. I saw the look in the lady's eye when she said sell it. You never know, it may come in handy. I don't know why, maybe there is a little of my brother in me after all. Now go, before I change my mind."

Scott smiled, shook his hand again then hopped in the Fiat.

CHAPTER 25
HENDERSON'S MOVE

Henderson walked out of his office, crossing the parking lot to where his Jaguar was parked. His cell phone chirped in his pocket. "I think we have a line on where Chad went."

"You're amazing, Bestin. Tell me, what have you found?"

"A small plane took left the north coast of Africa. I think they submitted a false flight plan. It headed toward Athens and we think it landed on Corfu. We're checking now, but the plane has left and our people will talk with the pilot when he touches down. He is headed south toward Africa again."

"Well, if Chad's in Greece, can't you get some of your Italian friends over there to find him?"

"Greece is a backwater. Normally in Europe you need to deposit your passport whenever you book a room, and the hotel faxes the numbers to immigration or the local police department every night. In Greece they do it once a week, if they even bother to get around to it."

"We have more information than we had ten minutes ago, we can probably focus more of our electronic gathering on Greece and that will give us a better chance of catching him. Get Farrell's technical weenies to focus on Greece, every credit card, every passport, car rental, email, anything."

"Already done, Frank, I want you to think about going over there."

"Fine. Keep me posted, Bestin."

He loved the smell of the leather in the Jaguar. Too bad the car was in the shop about once a month. Well, you couldn't have everything, could you?

❋ ❋ ❋ ❋ ❋ ❋ ❋ ❋

Shifting the little Fiat into gear, Julia pulled up the hill as they all waved goodbye.

Stephanos raised his hand, signaling them to stop. Walking over to the car he bent down by Scott's window. "If you have the time, I would drive around to the north side of the island and maybe visit the castle. It is up near Palaeokayastritsa. You can stop and rest then take the main road back to the ferry. It is a beautiful drive and if you have never been to Kerkyra it is worth the trip. You will still be able to get lunch and catch the evening ferry to Igougomitsa. If you went to the dock right now, you'd just have to wait about three hours for it to come. But suit yourselves, you are almost halfway there anyway."

They took his advice and followed the coast road along the eastern side of the island. The views from the hillside overlooking the Ionian Sea were magnificent. Near Agia Pelagia, they drove up a grade to find homes perched precariously on top of the cliffs a thousand feet above the sea. One moment they were looking at spectacular views of the cliffs and the sea, the next they were plunging into a little hidden valley filled with ancient hoary olive trees growing up the hillsides. Interspersed throughout the area were tall green cypress trees whose lushness and greenery delighted their senses.

The vista constantly changed from expansive views of small islands in the distance to beaches and valleys as the road twisted up the switchbacks before taking them back down to the water's edge. After cresting one rise, they came upon an azure blue bay set between steep cliffs and the little village of Agios Georgios. The village sat at the end of a pebbly bay gently washed by the sea.

Julia smiled and pointed at the sign. "Agios Georgios must mean St. George."

"Everything around here seems to be named for one saint or another," Samuel answered. "It's beautiful though. I'd like a small piece of property back there up on the hillside where I could just sit and grow some olives in my older age."

As they crested a rise Julia shouted and pointed, "Look at that!" A tall medieval castle was perched on top of a steep bluff overlooking the sea. It seemed to defy gravity, the ramparts and main battlements standing fully five hundred feet above the glinting waves below.

When Scott looked up, it awoke a long held memory of castles and crags and reminded him of castles in children's books he'd read. At one time the castle was stupendous, but now it sat forlorn and forgotten. They parked the car near the bottom of the slope and walked up the stone-paved switch back to the main gate which was lying in shambles on rusty hinges. Once inside the gate they stared in awe at the ancient stonework.

Scott caught his breath. "Stephanos said it was a worthwhile trip, and I agree!"

Julia gasped. "It must have taken a thousand men years and years to build all this. Did you see the size of the one in Corfu? Why would they need two of them on the island?"

Scott looked at her. "Maybe it was for a knight or some Venetian merchant. All the old buildings in town are Venetian and they held the island for centuries I'm told, or maybe it was for some long forgotten Crusader king who stayed here, holding out the infidel from the area."

Samuel was walking near one of the walls looking at the stonework and crenellated battlements. He looked up at the arrow slits and could picture-boiling oil pouring on the heads of any attackers or pirates trying to take the heights. "Maybe this was more than just a Venetian place. Look at this."

They hurried over to where he was bent down scratching in the dirt. "What did you find?" Scott asked.

Samuel pulled a strange shaped object out of the dirt by the base of the wall, turning it over in the light. "It's some sort of strange shaped old amulet. It might have belonged to a knight, but the inscription's in Greek, not Latin." He brushed it off with his hand and held it up to the sun. "It appears to be made of silver with gold lettering, shaped almost in the form of a cross but with a strange base. What do you make of it?"

He handed the amulet to Scott who looked at it after brushing off some more of the dirt and crud that had encrusted it over the years. "Seems to be a medal of bravery for one of the Crusaders. The only thing it says is, 'Yes, even in the darkness my heart instructs me.' It may have been for some order of their knights at one time." He handed it back to Samuel. "I don't know enough about their hierarchy to say for sure."

"At any rate, doesn't it fall under finder's keepers?"

"Probably not. Leave it and let's go."

"If I leave it, the first kid who comes by is going to take it. At least I have to rebury it!"

"I know how you feel. I have a passion for antiquities just like you. That's part of what got us here at any rate. It's not that big a deal, Samuel. Take it or leave it, I don't care, but we ought to get some lunch and be on our way if we're going to catch that ferry."

They followed the twisting road up and over the rise to one of the most beautiful views they'd ever seen. The road clung to the face of the cliff and laid out below them was the area of Paleostraki, which was a little village and resort set between two bays at the bottom of the cliff. The road switched back and forth as they descended, depositing them at the bay. Tavernas and shops lined the waterfront. They entered one of the restaurants where they sat on the veranda overlooking the beach on the bay. There were a few brave souls tempting the cold water, and the beach was full of sunbathers soaking up rays.

The waiter came up and took their order, bringing the local bread and olives which they all snatched at, dipping them in the wonderful olive oil and herbs. "I could get used to this," Julia said. "Definitely a place to spend some time."

"I couldn't agree more. I could die a happy man here," Samuel said.

"Samuel, it's not that much different here than in Spain or anywhere else we've been," Scott chimed in. "Personally, I think it's beautiful, too, but I think I'd get bored living on an island after awhile. Maybe a nice place to spend some time in the summer or winter though."

The waiter brought their lunch which they quickly finished with relish and Scott asked for the check in his fractured Greek. "Tologharyazmo parakalo?"

The ferry was more like a ship that carried cars on several levels and had room for passengers on the upper decks. They still had plenty of daylight when they landed and decided to try and make Ioannina before finding a room. The highway was good but twisting and they made good time even though the top speed of the car with the three of them in it wasn't great.

About nine they entered the town of Ioannina, which was surrounded by a medieval wall that had been added onto over the years by the Venetians, Serbs, Turks and Crusaders as each shared or changed power in the area.

Julia asked. "Look at those walls. Why did they fortify this place so?"

Scott turned to her. "Most of it was built by Ali Pasha, the despot of Epirus who held power and rose to prominence fighting for the Ottoman sultan in Constantinople, but he broke away and set up shop here, which became his capital city until he was beheaded."

They found a small hotel off Octobriou Street called the Hotel Palace, which was tucked into a quiet corner and backed up by a professional and courteous staff. They settled into their adjoining rooms, then went out for an evening meal and stroll through the old bazaar, where they could see jewelry makers, metal smiths, cobblers, tailors and others.

The next morning they enjoyed the fresh yogurt, fruit, nuts and dates. Scott turned to Samuel and Julia and said, "The Greeks make coffee differently from the rest of Europe, and Greek coffee is more like the Turkish kind, strong, thick and muddy, which you have to develop a taste for. They have what they call coffee Americano, which is weak, thin and almost tasteless."

"Apparently they haven't heard of Starbucks yet," Samuel said, after trying a cup of each.

"Oh, come on, let's get going. We have a fair amount of ground to cover still and we're probably going to want to stop and stretch, riding in that car," Scott said.

They checked out at the front desk and retrieved their passports. "Wasn't it dangerous to leave our passports over night with the clerk at the hotel?" Julia asked.

"I thought about that when we checked in. I hope it was safe and think it's probably okay. They give the numbers to the local police once a week or so, if they even get around to it, but I don't think the hotel enters them in a computer or over the Internet, so we should be safe, at least for a while."

Julia stretched her arms. "I just enjoyed relaxing and not being chased for a change of pace."

"Me too. It's nice not to have to watch my back," Samuel added.

"Well, it can't be undone now and I don't think anyone wanted to sleep in the Fiat." Scott said.

The road climbed till they reached the spine of the Pindos range and then descended following a rushing river in a steep valley. About an hour and half later, they came around a bend and could see tall spires of rock off to their left. A plain also stretched off into haze in the distance on their right.

"Behold the plains of Thessaly!" Scott gestured with his arm ahead. "The breadbasket of Greece, the largest plain in Greece. The country's mostly mountainous but this central area's flat and fertile. They can grow many crops down there while the mountains provide much needed water to help irrigate the crops during the long hot summers."

Samuel pointed. "What are those tall spires off to the left?"

"That's our destination, I bet."

They came to a branch in the highway with the left branch heading north to Kastoria and a sign indicating that Kalabaka was eight kilometers ahead.

"Well, that answers that. They must be the outlying spires of Meteora. I didn't really know what to expect."

The little Fiat went whizzing down the grade at its top speed of about a hundred kilometers an hour as she talked and they were soon entering the town of Kalabaka.

CHAPTER 26
METEORA

"Meteora means in midair," Scott said. "I looked at a guide book back in our hotel and the rocks rise almost a thousand feet off the plain. Some travelers compare them with the mountains of the Moon, but geologically they're not similar at all. It said that about 30 million years ago the plain of Thessaly was one vast inland sea. The land rose and the sea rushed out and the Pindos River was left to carve its slow and inexorable way through the rocks, which left these vast spires to be sculpted by the wind and water. The first inhabitants were ascetics about the year nine hundred or so, who scaled the cliffs and lived as hermits in the caves, spending their days in contemplation and prayer. Over time, more monks came who were seeking quiet and solitude and a way to live a pious life. About the year 1300, there were enough souls here for Saint Athanasios to found the great Meteoran monastery."

"Turn left up here and head for Kastraki," Scott directed to her at an intersection coming up. "We should find the main road up to the monasteries in the town."

She turned up the road and entered the town of Kastraki which was overshadowed by the beautiful mountains to the north. "I think we may have time to go up top and visit one of the sites before finding a room for the night. They close at six. What do you two think?"

"Sure," Julia said, "I'm doing fine."

"Lead on, young lady," Samuel added.

They headed up the main road out of Kastraki, climbing in sweeping turns and switch backs, and were soon out of town, past a campsite and small restaurant beside the road on the left. The large spires of rocks, which rose out of the plain, were on their right and filled their view up through the windshield of the car. They opened the cloth sunroof and were able to look up, as well as out, as the little car worked hard to climb the grade. They could see some old abandoned hermitages and small caves with broken wood ladders scaling the cliffs that were thrust out of the earth. The ladders were lying in haphazard fashion against the cliffs and were made of tree trunks with small log rungs tied with ropes. They passed the monastery of Pantokayrator, Saint Nicholas and Roussanou before coming to the end of the road by the monastery of Varlaam and the Great Meteoran, where a small parking lot and turnaround existed for travelers. There were a few small snack shops selling odds and ends and trinkets from Byzantine knives for boys to prayer books for the pious. A small ice cream and popsicle stand stood to one side which also sold Cokes and other soft drinks including Greek teas.

They stretched when they got out and looked out over the plain. Small clouds drifted below them, rising in the late afternoon as the sun heated the plain below. The clouds drifted slowly on the breeze to the head of the valley, only to be caught in the rock spires as they tried to break free and float off to the west. The plain was verdant with spring cultivation and the village of Kastraki lay below their feet. The red tile roofs glowed in the afternoon sun. They could see the larger town of Kalabaka off to their left in the plain proper, and Scott thought of how the quiet life of the monks up here compared to the hectic lives of the people in the towns below.

Walking to the top of the parking lot, they stopped in awe when they beheld the great Meteoran Monastery. Situated on top of one of the larger spires of rock, it hovered over a shear drop of 620 feet off the southern side. The northern side was sharply cleft by a 100 foot deep valley where a cable car was strung between the spire and the parking lot. The complex was tremendous. They descended the steep stone stairway to the valley and continued their climb up the steps. A monk requested a small donation from each of them when they arrived at the entrance. Luckily Julia had worn her long black skirt and tied a scarf over her head, for the monk had turned away a few women and men who'd worn shorts and women wearing tops with their shoulders exposed.

Coming to the tower and winch house, which was where they hauled up heavy supplies and building materials, they proceeded down a dim passageway to an intersection. Pausing a moment, they could hear the monks and cantors singing their prayers in a small chapel, their voices reverberating off the walls, the sound lending a beautiful air to their tour. A small passageway led off to the right with a sign in Greek and English that said, "Monks Cells - Charnel House."

Samuel nodded. "Let's look down there."

They followed the passage to their right and came upon a half door with the sign, "Charnel House." They looked over the door and gleaming skulls stood row upon row of shelves.

Samuel laughed. "Imagine a monastery doing this in America. Can you imagine the permits you'd have to get?"

They turned following the passageway toward the main church and museum and came upon an old bent monk in brown robes sweeping the hallway. He smiled a leathery smile as they approached and said, "How do you like our monastery?"

Scott bowed and answered, "We're truly impressed. None of us ever expected anything this wonderful or beautiful."

"Well, it's not changed much since when? I have been here forty years sweeping these halls and showing visitors around. My name's Father Nikita, I am head abbot here and I would be happy to show you around," he said as he leaned his broom in a little nook off the hallway and waved for them to follow. "Come with me. I will show you our church and would love to hear about your journey as well."

Father Nikita showed them through the museum where there were various drawings showing the original construction and some sketches from the 1700s of the original configuration. There was a layout of the church on the wall and various icons scattered around the room. "You may purchase an icon if you wish. Your donation will go to help support our order. It is not necessary, just something we do for the Orthodox to help keep up the buildings. The government, while officially sanctioning Orthodoxy, still requires certain codes to be met today, which is hard to do on a building this old." He paused, listening and glancing at his watch. "Follow me, the church is empty now and is the centerpiece of our monastery."

They followed his quick pace through an old arch and across a courtyard where he paused and pointed. "This is the Katholikon, a beautiful brick structure I think, shaped as a cruciform with a twelve sided dome. This building is the central church of the monastery and is dedicated to the transfiguration of Christ. It is 150 feet long and stands almost 90 feet high to the top of the central dome. Please follow me," he said as he led them into the church.

Scott noticed that a sign said, "No photography allowed." He hadn't seen any similar signs at other areas around the church. "Why don't they allow photography, Father?"

Nikita frowned. "They used to when I was young, but the tourists abused it and were using flash photography, which the experts said might damage the paintings and other old objects inside the church." He pointed to the walls. "Look for yourself. The church is painted in the Byzantine style and tells the history of creation as related in the Bible. We have at times allowed special exceptions for historical research, but that is getting harder. At one time we allowed non-flash photography, but it was difficult to control with the modern cameras with the built in flashes. Half the tourists don't even know how to turn the things off. I do not even know how to turn off the one my niece gave me last Christmas."

Father Nikita took a candle out of a rack, lit it and put it in a little sand-filled tray and kissed an icon on the right side of the entry. "This church is divided into the ante-narthex, narthex, nave and sanctuary and is a good example of Byzantine architecture. The murals you see on the walls and ceiling were painted about the year 1484."

As they walked Father Nikita explained, "The rest of the church was added in the year 1552 by the Abbot Symenon. Look here, below the cross. This is the screen of the Katholikon, which is carved wood and gilded with gold. It was carved in the year 1791 and depicts creation's plant and animal scenes. The two lecterns are decorated with mother of pearl and ivory. The Episcopal throne which is made of walnut was built and carved in 1620 and also employs the same theme and decoration of the animal and plant kingdoms."

Julia asked, "Can you tell us more about the murals and paintings, Father?"

Nikita smiled. "The murals and icons represent the doctrinal and liturgical cycle of the Orthodox faith. They remind us of the martyrdom of our saints and the uplifting of the spirit. It is hard to explain unless you know of the cycle of the church. Some of them were painted based on old works from the cave below. Some were painted over a long period of time," he explained as they walked through the church.

Julia turned to Nikita. "Do you ever make an exception to your rule on photography, Father? Part of our work was just completed at St. Catherine's monastery in the Sinai where we met Father Basil. He told us about your order and indicated that we could possibly complete some of our research here."

Father Nikita scratched his head and looked long and hard at Julia. "Exceptions have been made for scholars in the past. What credentials do you have? I would need something to show the elders in case someone made a stir. You know how it is." He shrugged and smiled. "Even though we are a small order, the church still has a bureaucracy."

"We've been working in the Sinai area of eastern Egypt the past few months, working on charting ancient archeological places, tombs and sites. Scott has an international reputation as a geological surveyor and archaeologist and has worked in many different parts of the world. His company's main business is in geological surveying and many governments and companies have hired him to assist in their research."

Father Nikita looked at Scott, wondering why Julia was the one answering. "I will take your request to our elders tonight and let you know. Come back tomorrow morning. Maybe I will have an answer for you then."

"We'd be happy to come back. I'd like to see more of this area, not just for the beauty, but for some reason . . . to learn more of the monks' lives and how they stay up here and, I guess, pray day after day." Julia said.

"Most people, young lady, do not understand the way of life of an ascetic. They come to Meteora and only see the natural beauty and do not understand the solitude and why we choose to live here, cut off from the world. It is beautiful, yes! But the way of our order is to eventually become one with the Almighty, to commune with his Spirit. I would be happy to tell you more but it is getting late and vespers start in a few minutes; I hear the bell now. Till tomorrow then," he said with a slight bow as he turned around and led them out of the church. The trio went back to the entrance where they exited down the stone steps and up to their car.

Scott was the first to speak when they reached the top and caught their breath again. "I think he likes you, Julia. You seemed to remind him of something, maybe long ago."

She was still breathing hard. "What does it matter whether he likes me or not?"

"Maybe he has a niece that looks like you, whatever. You're being awfully quiet, Samuel. Why the long face?" Scott said.

"When I was a kid, my mom used to take me to Sunday school at a Catholic church every week, confirmation and all that stuff. Well . . . at any rate, this place and Father Nikita reminded me of that for some reason. Believe it or not at one point when I was growing up, I thought about becoming a priest."

Scott laughed. "You, a priest, oh, come on! I find that hard to believe after all we've been through. You learn all there is to know about somebody and then, bam, they come up and surprise you with a whole new side. What's the world coming to?"

Julia watched the exchange between the two of them with growing mirth. The evening sun was still shining through the leaves on the trees, dappling the ground. "Okay you, two let's go to our rooms, get something to eat and get to bed early so we can come on back up here first thing tomorrow."

"You're right, Julia, let's go. Flip you for front seat, Samuel?"

"No, I had it on the way up. You take it now, I'll stretch out my legs sideways in back."

Chapter 27
Hasid finds the missing Chad

Hasid's Mercedes pulled up to the compound shrouded in a cloud of dust. Climbing out of the car wearing his grey suit and tan oxfords, he looked down with disdain at the dust ruining the shine. Straightening his tie while waiting impatiently for the elevator, he rushed down the corridor of the fourth floor of the large building. Two guards brought him to an abrupt stop as he strode down the hall.

"Halt!"

"Come on, Azhan, you know me. I have important information for the general."

"No one goes in without the general's approval. You know the rules. State your business!"

He blew out a breath. "Tell the general that I need to speak with him immediately on a matter of great importance."

"You are going to have to tell me more than that if you want me to disturb his important meeting."

"We both know the general and his important meeting has more to do with assuring his manhood is still intact than anything else of great significance."

The guard straightened his shoulders. "My orders are clear. The general is not to be disturbed. If you have something of importance to say, I will be the judge of whether of not it deserves interrupting his meeting."

"It is going to be a wonder if we ever advance beyond this little flea-bitten dump of a country. We spend too much time puffing ourselves up here with our own importance. Nevertheless, a king will be a king in his own home, it is said. Very well, Azhan, but you had better remember this."

"Do not speak to me as if I were one of his lackeys, he has put me in charge of his security and his sacred person."

"Now his person is sacred, too. Oh, come on, Azhan, he nursed at his mother's breast the same way you did, and I bet his mother changed him, too!"

"Now you speak insubordination against the general. We will see how he reacts to that. Now tell me your news that is so important or wait. It is your choice!"

"Okay, Azhan. You have heard about that business in the Sinai area?"

Azhan looked bewildered.

"Oh, I thought not. See you are not in on everything."

"Hasid, if you value your skin and do not want to spend sometime in the shade of the wall out there, out with it."

"Just tell the general that I think we know where Chad went."

"Chad who? What are you talking about, Hasid? What is a Chad?"

He'd lost most of his patience by now and usually considered himself a patient man, "Chad! You know. You watched the news about the American elections. It has to do with that . . . don't you remember? It is those little pieces of paper that hang on their ballots." He looked at him with a sly look. "We know where they went and how it was rigged. Just tell the general that."

Azhan thought for a moment. "Wait here, Hasid. Keep an eye on him," he said to the other guard at the door. He turned and let himself into the apartment, closing the door and walking softly across the thick carpet. Approaching the general's private quarters he winced and knocked softly on the door, his anxiety mounting.

Quati roared behind the door. "I told you I was not to be disturbed, Azhan. I will get a better door warden next time. This had better be good!"

Quati jerked open the door and Azhan could see the quick fleeting shape of the woman, with her hair in disarray, wrapped in a blue silk cloth heading off to the bathroom. "What is it, Azhan? You disturbed me at a time when a man does not want to be disturbed!"

Azhan bowed. "I am sorry my General, but Hasid has come, with what he says is important news. He says that we have found the Chad's from the American elections. I think it has something to do with how we rigged the vote on their last election."

"What are you talking about Azhan. What kind of brain are you working with? Now out with it, what did Hasid exactly say?"

He straightened and raised his shoulders. "Something about the Sinai and that he had found the Chad. When I questioned him more, he sneered at me and asked if I had watched the American elections and that was all the answer I needed, sir."

Quati laughed and even smiled. "You stupid dog. Hasid should not play with you so though. I will have a talk with him about that. Show him in and return to your post."

Azhan bowed and started to turn. "My General, what is this Chad business. Did we really rig the American elections?"

"No, Azhan . . . Hasid has tricked you into letting him in to see me. He is brilliant and you have been at his mercy, but come now, you have only been doing your job. Let him in."

"But, my General, it is my job to see to your security and I need to know if something is important enough to disturb you."

"You do not need to know about this right now though. Enough, let him in, that is an order, Azhan!"

Azhan backed away and went to the entrance, while Quati pulled his robe over his head.

When Azhan came back into the hallway, Hasid was leaning against the wall smoking a cigarette, the smoke being whisked into the ventilation ducts in the ceiling. "He will see you, Hasid. If you ever try to pull something like that on me again or make a fool out of me in front of the general, I will slit your gut and you will be screaming for someone to put your intestines back in for you, do you hear me?"

Hasid smiled and bowed to him. "Yes, Azhan, remember though that you work at the general's pleasure and if you keep me waiting while I am working on important matters that do not concern you, trouble undreamed of will come of it."

Azhan glared at him but opened the door to the apartment, closing it behind him and taking up his post again.

Hasid walked across the thick carpet and found Quati standing behind his desk. "Sorry to interrupt your important business, General, but I have news of Chad."

Quati smiled. "You should not play with Azhan so. It was funny, I admit, but he is a proud man and I like to keep him sharp to do his job. You play with him too much and trouble will come of it."

Hasid merely waved his hand. "Chad is in Greece. We received his passport number off the Greek government's Internet. The hotel he was staying at entered their passport numbers in their computer. Luckily this hotel sent them on Tuesday and did not wait until the end of the week. Possibly we can find Chad and put a tail on him if we start moving now. We are a lot closer than we were."

Quati slammed his hand down. "Greece? What in the name of Allah is he doing in Greece? We thought he would go to Arabia or even Israel, but Greece? Where in Greece?"

"Ioannina. At least that is where the hotel is that turned in his passport number. They have left by now. We called and he checked out of the hotel. I want your permission to send our agents in to find him. Time is important, General. We have to move fast on this."

"Yes, you are right Hasid, permission granted." Just then a door behind him opened and a young woman stuck her head out, looked at the general and smiled. Quati turned. "Not now, Fatima, wait for me."

She glanced at Hasid, a sly smile escaping, then closed the door and disappeared.

"Okay, Hasid, you may go to Greece, but do not kill Chad just yet. You were right. We may still need him, so go carefully. I am sending over Abdullah with Abin and Sa'd. They know our business and Abdullah knows how to be discreet. He had better."

Why is he sending Abdullah and his thugs? What has the general found out that he is not telling? A cold slice of fear swept through Hasid. *I wonder if he knows about Julia and me?* "Yes, General." Hasid smiled. "It was brilliant how you had the American election system rigged and created all those missing and hanging chads."

Quati laughed. "Watch yourself, Hasid. As I said, Azhan is a proud man! Go with Allah and may he watch over your endeavors."

Hasid walked out of the room, while Quati stood there a moment, smiled, then turned and opened his door. "Fatima, where were we?"

The old man sat hunched in his chair looking out at the smoke rising up in the eastern part of the city from the latest suicide attack. Outside it was Israel. A young Palestinian had blown himself up in a market, killing six and wounding many others. It was the promised land, the land fought over by the same people for four thousand years. It was a land where countless souls had lived and been brutally snuffed out in their quest for life, hope and love.

He turned when a knock came to his door. "Come in."

"Eli, we've news about Julia. I thought you'd like to hear."

"Yes, Aaron, thank you. My mind was elsewhere. What do you have?"

"She has left the Sinai with Chad and his friend after their camp was shot up by some men who we think are working for Quati."

"Quati, Quati, Quati. Why is it that when I hear his name, it raises my blood pressure? See that smoke out there?" he said, as he pointed out the window. "He's paid some young boy's family twenty-five thousand dollars for their son. To blow himself up!" He slammed his fist on the table. "How can I fight that? Young children blowing themselves up when they should be playing soccer or video games. Young children who should be in school learning how to make this a better world for their children to live in. Tell me that, will you? How can I fight it?"

Aaron stood silently, knowing there were no answers to Eli's questions. He shifted his weight from one foot to another and cleared his throat.

"I'm sorry, Aaron, just an old man rambling on about the times. You said you have news of Julia? You have no idea how important her mission might be. Come on, out with it, do you know where they've gone?"

"We think they've gone to Greece, sir. Our technical branch has intercepted transmissions from the Greek government that they used their passports in Ioannina and an email was sent to a Greek priest regarding Chad. We think they are connected and that they are on their way to Meteora."

Eli looked tired as he looked at his young agent. "See the Director of Operations and get a ticket for Greece. I want you out on the next flight. Find them and keep an eye on them and watch out. If we can get this information, you can bet that others will, too. I would have felt better if we couldn't have found them. Keep a good watch on them. Quati and others may be on their trail and we must keep them safe. I still don't know what this is all about, but it may be far more important to our country's future than we can imagine, so be sharp!"

Aaron bowed and left Eli as he turned back to the window and watched the smoke rise over the city.

CHAPTER 28

MID MOUNTAIN MORNING

Scott and his companions made their way back up the winding road to see Father Nikita after breakfast and found him still sweeping the halls and smiling.

"Good morning. Your reputation precedes you, Mr. Chad. Father Basil sent us a wonderful e-mail about you and recommended we let you do some research here. This has not been done in a long time for . . . for someone who is not orthodox. This is a bigger concession than you may imagine. There was some opposition to your being allowed to photograph the church and work in the library. Father Basil's recommendation was very persuasive. He thinks highly of you and your staff."

Nikita paused and stared at Scott for a moment. "Well, I don't really know what to say other than the perseverance of the saints has paid out."

"Do you mind if we start right away, Father?" Julia asked.

"It has been all arranged. I spoke with the elders about the urgency of your work when I met with them. These things normally take time and are not done quickly, but Father Basil's good word on your work in Sinai opened doors that would have been stiff and squeaky, even for the orthodox."

Scott looked over at Father Nikita. "Are there any special forms or paperwork we need to fill out?"

"No forms, but there are a few rules regarding photography in the church and research in the library. The first and foremost is do not remove anything without asking. When you need a certain book or scroll, ask the librarian in charge. Do not move anything in the church, and do not take anything! I am sorry, but I'm required to say that to everyone."

"Do you mind if we start this morning? We'd like to wrap up as soon as possible," Samuel said.

"No, as I said before it has all been arranged. You may start right now and may even come at different hours than the tourists do. Please do not interrupt the worship services, though, is all we ask. That is the only consideration on timing that we care about. I am going to assign a young monk, Friar Vasillus, to help you in the library. He is working in the museum now and I will take you to him and introduce you."

"Father, we don't know how to thank you and I'd like to express my appreciation with a donation to your order. There's also one thing I feel I must warn you about. When we left our camp in Sinai, we were attacked by some rough characters and . . . well, I don't know, but I'm worried they may still be looking for us. We've been careful as we traveled and haven't left any trails that we know of, but I'm . . . well. I just don't want to see anyone get hurt."

Father Nikita expression changed from a smile to concern for the trio standing before him. The birds were singing in the trees and wheeling about in the air as he paused. "Any donation is always welcome, but isn't necessary. I'm sorry to hear about your troubles, but that doesn't change our attitude or consideration for letting you work here."

Scott shifted his weight on his feet. "Father, I want you to understand, some terrorists shot up our camp with assault rifles before we left. Thank God no one was hurt, but that may not be true if we run into them again, but I hope we don't."

"I understood you the first time, Mr. Chad. Father Basil alluded to this in his greeting and prayer for you. We have a language and way of coding things that sometimes provides us with more information than readily meets the eye. Our deal stands. I will take your warning to heart and close the gate at night and pull up the bridge. If you have not noticed, this place would not be easy to assault."

"I wouldn't have felt right if I hadn't warned you about these people. I don't know what they want or why they want to stop us, but I had to be honest with you," Scott said.

The old priest looked up at the birds wheeling through the sky once again before answering. "You know, some things we must choose to do, even when we are called to do them. May the grace of the Lord be on your endeavor. I do not think evil will prevail in this, for our battle is not against these men or flesh and blood but is elsewhere. We will all pray for your success." He waved his arm. "Follow me, I will introduce you to Fr. Vasillus. He is young, but knows our library well. It is this way," he said as he showed them out the courtyard and down a passageway to the library.

The monastery's stonework shone in the morning sun giving them a warm feeling as they walked out of the courtyard then down a small stone hallway to a small room at the end of the hall.

They found a young monk dressed in black, but without the voluminous beard that the other's seemed to wear. "This is Fr. Vasillus. He speaks English very well for it is a required class in this country. He will help you with your research."

Scott extended his hand as he and his companions walked up to the young monk, "I'm Scott Chad." He pointed at his companions. "These are my associates, Julia Apostoli and Samuel Rogowski."

"I'm glad to meet you. Father Nikita explained some of your work to me this morning at vespers and I'm only too happy to help you. Where would you like to start? Is there anything in particular you're looking for?"

Father Nikita gave a short bow and said, "I think you are in good hands. Please feel free to call on me if you need anything. I would also like to hear more of your travels and your meeting with Friar Basil and would be most interested to know what you have found when you are done."

Scott turned toward the Nikita. "Thank you again, Father. Your help has been inestimable."

Father Nikita left the library after nodding to Vasillus to proceed.

"How may I help you? Where would you like to start?" the young monk asked.

Scott smiled back at him. "We're looking for any information about St. Catherine's Monastery, particularly during the time when Father Georges was abbot, about the year 620 to 630 or so. It's come to our attention that he provided sanctuary for the prophet Mohammad during that time. Some of our findings and research bear on some rather cryptic writings and archeological finds from that period."

"St. Catherine's . . . let me think, during the seventh century or thereabouts. I think I know of some old illuminated manuscripts from that time and some letters from the abbot to one of the Metropolitan's at Mount Athos. Come with me and we'll see what we can find." He got up and motioned for them to follow.

The library was in one of the older sections of the monastery and hung over the edge of the precipice. The rosy room was octagonally shaped and about ten meters across. At each wall was a rack of books or chest with small square cubicles with old scrolls tucked neatly into the slots. The room had one of those odd, but pleasant musty smells, the scents of old paper and dust. The light that filtered through the stained glass window gave every thing a rosy patina of elegance and age. Vasillus led them to one of the alcoves at the end of the octagon and pulled back on the bookcase. It revealed an old seldom-used staircase, which was carved into the gut of the mountain. He paused, lit a candle from a holder in the wall, and carried it down the staircase, which wound through the rock as they descended. He lit candles that were set in holders along the walls as they passed.

A little arched and latticed window was set in the wall at a turn in the passageway. Peering out, they could see nothing of the monastery, only the valley below and the birds sailing in the air.

Vasillus turned and nodded. "This way. It's not much farther." As he led them down another stair that ended at an old iron door with a large padlock secured around a dead bolt. Taking a key from a ring under his robes, he inserted it into the lock and turned it with a snap, which echoed ominously in the chamber. When he opened the door, the golden light from a rectangular window set in the carved rock spilled its light on the floor.

Pausing at entry, they stared at the large assortment of old books, scrolls, manuscripts and other items. Gold chalices, long gilded bishop staffs, gold plates, silver incense burners and other items were stacked here and there in a helter-skelter fashion. Filling one wall were large hand written and illustrated manuscripts bound in leather, while another was filled with magnificent scrolls hanging by beautiful woven strands, shot through with gold and silver or braided with leather.

Julia gasped. "I thought the library upstairs was amazing, but this is a treasure trove!"

Vasillus smiled with pride. "This collection's not kept in the library for a number of reasons. First being the insurance regulations and trying to get the bureaucracy of the insurance agencies to place a value on all this. The premiums are exorbitant and the order just can't afford it. Secondly, there are some items of . . . how shall I say, a sensitive nature and some of the old manuscripts and scrolls don't exactly fit in with the liturgical history of the church. They are from a time before 1022 when we were still part of the Catholic Church and . . . well, you know." He paused and shrugged. "There are different opinions on how things are to be done."

Samuel was looking at all the treasure lying about when he came across an old sword up against the wall. "Where's this from?"

Vasillus smiled. "We think it's a sword from one of the Crusader Knights who defended the monastery, from about the year 1100. Beautiful, isn't it? I used to love that when I first came here. I was thirteen when I first saw this room and the sword was the thing I liked the best!"

"Amazing workmanship," Samuel said. "Can I hold it?"

Vasillus nodded.

"The hilts interwoven with gold threads," he said as he examined it, turning it repeatedly in his hands. "I see some old Latin writing on the blade. Can you translate it?"

"I can't. I didn't take Latin in Seminary, just Hebrew and Greek," Vasillus said.

Scott nodded. "Let me see, maybe I can." Walking over to the window, letting the sunlight play on the blade, he turned it over in his hands then looked up in surprise. "I think it might be older than you thought. The language seems to be from the late Roman period, maybe six or seven hundred A.D. but I think it's from Gaul, for it talks of holding off the barbarian hordes from the north and was given to someone named Fredrick for his battles and bravery on the frontier. It seems more like a Crusader sword than a Roman one. We seem to have another mystery. This type of blade didn't really come into popular use until the time of the crusades and . . . well, maybe they just used old Latin to write on it, can't be sure. The other side says, 'Defend With Your Life-Key To The Kingdom-The Summit Of The Law- Kafina and Our Lord.' Do you know where or what the Summit of the Law is? Or what or where this Kafina is?" Scott asked as he handed the blade back to Samuel.

The young monk looked at him and paused. "The Summit of the Law is our Lord Jesus of course. Kafina's an old spot in the stone forest between here and the village of Kastraki. There are three caves that used to be monasteries and an old monastery called St. Nicholas Batovas perched on top of the stone spire Some have called it Kafina or Kofina. It's in ruins now and no one ever goes there anymore. We think it was founded about the year 1400 or so, but who knows. It's mentioned in one of our older texts called the Syngramma Historikon and in the register upstairs in the library. The Germans bombed the place in late 1943 trying to get the partisans out of the hills and the chapel on top was destroyed. The only thing left today are the ruins of the chapel and the old winch used for bringing up supplies."

Julia was only half-listening, being taken by the treasure piled around her. She looked at Vasillus for permission to examine a small hand-held mirror made from gold and silver and encrusted with emeralds that sparkled in the sunlight as she turned it in her hands. "Property of a lady, I'd presume?"

Vasillus smiled at her. "Tradition says it belonged to the wife of the Despote of Ioannina. She donated it to the monastery when she took a pilgrimage to Meteora. Beautiful, isn't it?"

"Very," she said as she turned it over in her hands looking at herself in the glass. "The glass is kind of warped and the slivering worn off, but I wonder what she was like. A very beautiful lady, I'd imagine."

"Somewhere around here is a poem she wrote when she came to the monastery. I remember reading it. It was an odd poem, a retelling of the scriptures, but also her hope for the future," he said rummaging through some old documents in a drawer.

Julia noticed a feeling of suspense steal over her as she watched him.

"Here it is." Vasillus said. "It's in Greek. I'll try to translate it. It's a poem so my translation may be a bit rough and not as good as the original. I'll do the best I can to render it."

Vassilius moved over by the window, holding up the manuscript and recited:

He came and sang a song of wonder
Of growing love and a wonderful hunger
He sang of trust and sang of power
Of strength that stands like a tower
Grew up strong in stature and wisdom
The day would come for his long kingdom
Eluding the sin that so easily entraps
Breaking the chains, and the snaps
The battle lines grew, and were drawn
His song would forever, go on and on
From age to age, his song would pass
Giving hope to the world, at last
That day on the mountain, tall he stood
Hunger was gnawing, but knowing what's good
The tempter did come, and made his offer
Gold and life, and some to proffer
I'm here to open men's heart's he'd say
Close the hearts the tempter did sway
The Lord's pure love is all that I need
Worship me now and I'll plant your seed
Never oh never, I'll bow no knee
If you bow to me now, I'll set you free
My father is life and love for all
Worship me now and you'll never fall
You're a liar and blindness awaits
The world will worship me, that's their fate
I've come to seal the door of time
You'll never, oh never for you are mine
I'll never, no never, sing your song
For my father is stronger and has memories long
Your father is weak he's given all to me
We laugh at your weakness, be gone from me
His song was stronger, the tempter did flee
His strength was like an old oak tree
The song he sang created a new plan
A plan from old that's why he ran
Withstanding the tempest and the angels did come
Nursing him from, the battle he'd won
Strengthening him, for days so near
Giving him strength to take-away fear

"Obviously it's a poem about the battle between our Lord and Satan when He was tempted in the wilderness during his forty days of fasting. The rest is rather cryptic and I never understood it. Maybe it's just nonsense, but here it is:"

The law of Moses, the law of God
never shall pass, and shall not be trod
It shall never ever pass away
It's been long fulfilled by his strong day
The real promise has already come
stretch the gates wider, let in the son
Scorn will pass like the wind on the plain
Grace will come like a warm summer rain
The law was given years long ago
given by Moses and others we know
But the prophets came and said here's the new law
Live by it and sin will not gnaw
The sin that traps and continues to grow
The law will point to it and all will soon know
That grace will come for him who believes
My prophets did leave the keys to succeed
Look in the cave, the third from the top
The altar is there and then tis not
Wash yourself clean and your way will be near
Listen now and it will all soon be clear

"I told you it didn't make a lot of sense. Third cave from the top, disappearing altars. We've talked about it every now and then. The writer's husband was a very cruel man. Let's see if we can find Father George's letters. They're here somewhere. Just let me look . . . I think they were in this old chest of drawers." Vassilius rummaged through another pile of manuscripts causing more dust to rise and be lit by sunrays slanting in from the lone window.

"Yes . . . here I think," he said as he pulled a bundle of withered old parchments out of the chest tied with a ribbon showing frayed edges. "Yes, I remember the ribbon and writing style."

"You say, you've read them before?" Scott asked.

"Just briefly and only to get to know the archives. I never studied them or translated them. They're written in Greek, of course, and some of it may even be in our political language . . . ah that's a way of writing a sort of code between priests. We used it a lot during the war. The Nazi's couldn't decipher it, but the Vatican and our order could."

Unwrapping the bundle, he laid the letters out on top of a small hutch standing by the window. Scott bent over the letters with Vassilius, who moved through the pile one by one.

"What exactly did you say you're looking for?" Vassilius asked.

"Anything about Mohammad Prophet and his stay at St. Catherine's. It would probably have been written about 622 or shortly thereafter, but it could have been written anytime after that."

"Well, the letter's are dated and someone thankfully organized them at one time, so let's see here . . . ," he said as he sorted through the stack of old parchments. "Here we are, January 622, letter to his mentor, Father Constantis, who was head abbot at the monastery on Mt. Athos where Georges studied. The next one's not until fall that year. It's another letter to Constantis," he said as he ran his finger down the page.

"The letter doesn't have anything to say about Mohammad, but it does talk about the pagan warlords of Medina and Mecca." He kept flipping through the pile of letters' going from the year 622 to 632. "This one says he's going to retire soon and move back to Mt. Athos, but doesn't say anything about Mohammad either." He came to the next to last letter. "These two are out of sequence. It appears someone took them out and didn't put them back."

He paused and looked at Scott. "As I said before, I never studied these, just opened the bundle once and quickly looked through them, but I did put them back in order. Let's see . . . the date's 623 and Father Georges is now head abbot. He's asking for money to rebuild the gate at the front of the monastery . . . here we go, 'Mohammad came and we offered him sanctuary from the Quraysh warlords, I told you about. I think his power in the region will grow stronger.'"

Vassilius continued as he ran his finger over the spidery writing. "'He stayed the summer and we talked at length about his visions. I tried to persuade him about our gracious Lord, how he was the final answer from God. Mohammad remained steadfast in his belief that his visions were real and how the angel Gabriel was giving him Allah's covenant and law for his people."

"I think you've found it, Vasillus. This must be near the time when the chamber we found was built," Scott said.

"Well, the letter goes on. ' It challenges my faith, Constantis, but I believe Mohammad is an honest and trustworthy man, and possibly his visions were real. I know you will find that hard to believe, but you have not met the man. He told me his people are stubborn and always fighting amongst themselves and Allah had given him a code of law to bring the tribes together to mold them into a great nation. We talked about Abraham and how our God made a promise to him that he would make him into a great nation from the time of Abraham, Isaac and Ishmael. It's interesting that God also made a promise to Hagar that he would make Ishmael into a great nation. Mohammad believes that Abraham was to sacrifice Ishmael not Isaac, but does agree that the Angel of the Lord came to Hagar at the well in the desert and made a promise to her.'"

"Is there anything about him making the chamber?" Julia asked.

"There's more in here about Mohammad and Georges but let's see . . . ," he said as he ran his finger down the page.

"This might have something to do with what you're looking for. Georges writes, 'Mohammad came to me on his last morning here saying that the angel Gabriel had visited him again last night after we had met and prayed. It was a strange night, the stonecutter was here who is working on the tomb for Al Sud, and then Mohammad came the next morning saying the angel visited him. Constantis, I tell you, this is important. I am sending you a part of Mohammad's plan. He said that the angel gave it to him and the plan will come to light when God's great nations are ready to hear the truth. 'Hide this well and keep it safe,' Mohammad said, 'we will know when the time is right.' I believe in my heart that Mohammad saw the light of true grace and not works. When he came to me that final morning, he was visually shaken and disturbed saying he was going to have Nawaldi, that's the stone cutter I told you about earlier, hide part of his plan in a chamber on the mountainside, to lie until Allah's time is right.' I really do not understand all of what he plans, but am sending on his notes as he wished. Please keep them safe."

Julia blurted out. "May we photograph the letter, and can you make a copy of it for us?"

"I suppose we could just as easily make a photocopy of it on the copy machine upstairs. Why don't we do both?" Vassilius said.

"I'd also like a copy of the lady's poem and a photograph of the mirror and sword, if that's okay?"

"That's not a problem. Go right ahead. I'll be right back, after I make the copies."

After Vassilius left with the letter and poem, Julia pulled out a cheap camera she'd purchased and started snapping away.

"Julia, take a picture of this last letter. I can't read the Greek as well as Vassilius, but I think the date's about the same as the other one," Scott said.

She snapped pictures of the letter, sword and mirror. Scott kept looking at the last letter and then put it with the others and went to look out the small window at the birds floating in the air.

Vassilius returned and handed the copies to Julia with a small bow and smile. She grabbed his hand in both of hers shaking it, thanking him for his efforts.

Scott watched and smiled when he saw the awkwardness of the monk in front of Julia.

Vassilius turned to Scott. "Can I help with anything else? I don't know how much help I've been."

"Do you know what monastery Constantis was from at Mt. Athos?"

"Vatopedion was the original name but it is now called Batopediou. It was founded in the 4th century, rebuilt about the year 970 or so. It's one of the older ones on the peninsula and some say the cross of Christ is kept there. I've never been there myself, so I can't say for sure. Someday I hope to go to Mt. Athos. There are about twenty monasteries on the mountain."

Scott nodded to him. "Thank you Vassilius, you've been so much help, I don't know what to say. We'll see you in the morning. Thank you again!"

CHAPTER 29
LATE NIGHT CALL

The phone rang, rousing Henderson. He fumbled to grab it from the nightstand.

"We have them. We intercepted an e-mail from that monastery in Sinai. It appears to have been sent to some place near a little town in Greece called Kalmampaka. There's some sort of monastery there, we think. It was addressed to a guy named Nikita. At least that's his screen name."

"Why are you calling me at this hour, Bestin? Don't you know what time it is over here? Do you ever sleep?" He shook his head to clear it. "Okay, what's the screen name?"

. Looks like some sort of school, church or maybe a college."

"Look in your directory, and get me anything else you can find on this. I'm tired of waiting, keeping Luigi and those Arabian thugs you sent over to keep us company. Do you understand? I want it now, right away!"

"I'll get right on it, Frank, and keep on it. I'll call you as soon as I get more specifics. Get over to Kalmambaka. Take Luigi with you."

"It's 2:35 in the morning, Bestin. I'm tired and crabby. You've done a good job on this, but I'm wiped out, I'll. . . ."

"I'm sorry for the hour, but you said you wanted to know right away if we found out anything and I . . . decided to call as soon as this e-mail thing came out of the filter with Chad's name on it."

"What did the e-mail say?"

"Two of them showed up. It appears that this Nikita guy was asking about Chad from someone named Basil at St. Catherine's monastery. At least we assume so, because the e-mail address is, and the body of the e-mail asked for references about Chad."

He let out a tired breath. "What do you mean by references?"

"Nikita's e-mail was filled with prayers and praying for all the saints and greetings and all that kind of stuff, then he asked if Basil knew Scott Chad and whether or not he'd give him a reference. Apparently, Chad is asking permission to photograph the Katholikon and look in some library. The rest of it just asks questions about his family, the weather and other stuff."

"What was his answer?"

"Well . . . Basil says Chad was very hospitable when he was at St. Catherine's and thinks Chad is close to some sort of awakening of the Lord's will . . . if I've translated it correctly."

"What do you mean translated it correctly? Speak plain English to me!"

"It was all in ancient Greek, is what I mean. It's not easy to get the wording and phrasing right. He mentions that Apostoli woman who is working with Chad and that's what caught in our filter. That's why we caught the message. Do you have any idea how many messages there are to run a filter through? It's a miracle we caught this one. If you hadn't followed that small plane flight up to Corfu, we'd never have found it. We were able to narrow our search to Internet addresses with a Greek IP. I directed our people to concentrate on the servers in Greece and that's why we caught it."

"Fax me copies to the hotel, and also your translation," he said as he hung up the phone.

Bishop Bestin handed the messages to one of the technicians who worked for Farrell's magazine and was left holding the phone, hearing nothing but static from the other end. "Jerk," he said as he put the phone back in its cradle.

Henderson glanced at the clock, deciding to go back to bed. No point in losing more sleep until he had the translation. He thought about waking Luigi and the men Quati had sent over, Abdullah, Jettur and Sa'd. They gave him the creeps, as if Luigi wasn't bad enough, but he saw no point until he had more information.

Sleep wouldn't come. He tossed and turned, finally getting up and rummaging in his suitcase for one of the sleeping pills the doctor had given him. He couldn't find where he'd put them, but found the Magic Eye Book he had brought over that his grandchildren had given him. Lying back in bed, he was trying to make the pictures appear like the kids had shown him. On the verge of falling back asleep, it finally came to him.

A look of wonder crossed his face and he quickly opened his briefcase and took out the pictures from the tomb his associates had given him. Sitting back on the bed he examined the pictures, one by one, under the lamp, a slow smile of comprehension settling across his face as he picked up the phone and dialed the hotel across town.

"Abdullah, I want you, Sa'd and Jettur to meet with Luigi and me in my room."

"Do you know what time it is, Mr. Henderson?"

"Yes, I know what time it is. This is important. I know where Chad is going. I want you to come now."

The next morning, Henderson met with Luigi and Quati's men in his room. Luigi was in a tropical linen suit standing in the corner of the room while the other three men lounged in the chairs and on the edge of the bed.

His voice was so cold, it threw Henderson off. It was like gravel and ice. "Mr. Henderson, I have been given my orders by Bestin and other men with whom I work with. I disagree with your assessment. Chad is dangerous. My orders were to take all his information and eliminate him and his companions."

"You are to appropriate his information, but are not to harm them. We may still need them. Bestin is wrong in this and I will be calling him to make sure your orders are clarified. Bestin sent me over here to be his eyes in the field. You are to take my orders in his absence."

"Don't you mean steal his information? Why are you afraid to say steal? That is not what Bestin has ordered, and I will not change my methods until I hear from him."

"Appropriate I said. We are not common thieves. We are on a mission to save the church and keep it safe from blasphemy."

Jettur looked over to Abdullah, the scar across his face livid in the light. "My orders are the same as Luigi's, but even more clear where the Jewess is concerned. She is to be eliminated. Quati does not want her any where near this."

"Hasid said that they should be watched, not eliminated," Henderson said.

"Hasid is a fool. He had better watch what he says or Quati will have him on a plate soon," Abdullah added.

Henderson shrugged. "Enough of this. We will discuss this later when we meet in Kalampaka and see the situation. Bestin has arranged for a small cottage for you outside of town. Assemble there and make your arrangements. Do not move until we have talked. Be discrete until then."

Chapter 30
Moon Light Serenade

"Well, if that's enough, let's get going," Vasillus said as they followed him out the door, locking it on the way. As they made their way, they could hear the monks singing afternoon vespers. The sound of their voices rising in harmony lent the air an effervescent feeling as they made their way out the entrance.

They stopped at a little taverna by the side of the road and had a nice meal. Once back at the hotel Samuel yawned, "I think, I'm going to take a nap. If you don't see me before nine, wake me up okay?"

Julia stretched and yawned, "I want to check out the town and watch the sunset, want to come Scott?"

"Sure, seems like a nice evening for a walk and I want to walk off some of that food before it goes to my waist."

"Exactly what I was thinking. Just give me a few minutes. I want to change and clean up first."

"I'm going to change too. Knock on my door when you're ready," Scott said.

He went to his room, cleaned up and changed into some pale-white linen slacks, blue knit pullover and sport coat, then turned on the television to look at the local programming. As he sat on the bed, his mind flipped back to when he and Samuel were in Afghanistan and the fighting he'd had to do. He hated it when that happened; it usually brought up feelings of worthlessness and pain, where he tended to berate himself for his actions while he'd been there. The black thoughts threatened to capture the evening and he quickly started flipping channels, trying to distract himself. He was just starting to think Julia had changed her mind when a gentle knock came at his door.

His mood quickly changed when he opened the door. He was surprised at her transformation as she entered. She was dressed in a tight white silk dress of conservative length. She was wearing a necklace made from some sort of blue stones and matching earrings that set off her blue eyes and matching shoes.

"Wow, when did you find time to put that in your suitcase?"

She walked into his room, pirouetted in a small circle and curtsied. "You like?"

"Ah . . . wow means, I like . . . of course, I like. But what does this mean?"

She turned her head smiling. "It means I'm going for an evening walk in a quaint little town in Greece with a handsome gentleman, is what it means."

Scott looked at her, deciding he'd never be able to figure out the female mind: at one moment ice cold and the next the polarity switched 180 degrees. He was wondering if his sport coat might be too hot.

"Well, young lady, let's go." *Beautiful,* he thought and wanted to say, but held his tongue as he offered his arm.

They walked down the cobbled street, past shops filled with Greek pottery, icons and jewelry. They talked with the merchants who were eager to sell their wares but polite enough not to push. Stopping at one shop that sold Greek pottery, icons and other items, they peered in the window. "Come in, come in, my name's George," said the owner as he extended his pudgy hand. He was short and rotund with a big smile on his face. "It is still early spring and I have good deals for you. Our prices are low. The Europeans will not start coming until June and it does not get busy until August."

Scott turned to him. "What's going on in town tonight?"

The shopkeeper smiled. "There is a dance in the square, and it should be starting soon. Take your young lady, listen to the music and dance in the Greek moonlight!"

Scott glanced over at Julia, trying to understand the expression in her eyes. "She might like that."

"I'd love to go to a dance!" she said.

Scott looked at her, not knowing what to think, and saw the expression she had worn when they were in the jewelry store in Suez, the fun loving troublemaker look. He turned to the shopkeeper. "Thank you, sir, I feel like we should purchase something but we're kind of strapped for cash on this trip. We are doing some research at the monastery."

"No need, no need at all. I just run the shop for something to do and to keep me out of the wife's way. She is the boss, runs a shipping company in Igougomitsa and I just get in her way if I hang around the house. You go and have some fun now," he said as he shooed them out the door.

"Thank you for your help," Scott said as he escorted Julia out the door and down the street, where they could hear the lively strains of music coming from the square.

The crowd grew thicker, until they were standing among a throng of people around a stage, where a six-piece Greek band was playing the theme song from "Zorba" as an old man was slowly pirouetting to the music and slapping his heel to the tempo. Circling around him was a line of people led by a large brown-haired man holding a towel. Electric lanterns were strung between the trees, romantically lighting the square; the lone dancer created a cynosure to the idyllic scene before them.

He reached for Julia's hand, but the dark feeling that threatened the evening earlier rose in his gut. He shoved the anxiety down by force of habit, looked into her eyes, and nodded toward the square where the dancers were circling around the lone figure. "Would like to join them?"

Her answer blew away the last tendrils of his foul mood. "I'd love to."

They walked out to the circle, holding hands. Julia grabbed a man's hand at the end of the queue, joining in the dance. The steps weren't too hard, Julia being much better at picking up the rhythm and pattern than Scott, but they soon got the hang of it. As the dance progressed, the old man started jumping from one foot to another as the ring grew tighter and tighter around him. The dancers twirled and spun to the music, going around and around, as the pace picked up. The song ended with a crescendo and they fell into each others arms laughing and gasping for air. They looked at each other, noticing their position, and quickly drew apart with an unsure feeling. The next song was a fast country hill number from the mountains; the steps were generally the same so they did better than with "Zorba." Halfway through the song the tempo slowed, the circle broke apart as each partner took the other and did a slow waltz, swirling and swaying to the quiet forlorn music. Julia rested her head on Scott's shoulder placing her arms about his neck. The feeling was so natural for both that he wondered where the normal tension between the two of them had gone. He breathed in the clean scent of her hair and the smell of her perfume as she rested her head on his shoulder. The feeling of his arms about her waist on the white silk of her dress made him pause and wonder when the song ended.

She pulled on his hand. "Let's take a walk. I'd like to talk with you for a minute about something that's been on my mind."

"Whatever you'd like," he said.

They walked away from the square, strolling along the path, still holding hands under the trees as the lanterns swayed in the branches. The path was of old stone cobbles, carefully set and meandered between groups of plantings, stone outcrops and the occasional bench or gazebo. The noise from the dance grew dim as they walked, just drinking in the night air. He wondered what she wanted to talk about but didn't want to spoil the moment. He'd developed an itch on his shoulder, but was afraid to take away his hand to scratch.

They stopped at a quiet spot and she turned and looked up at him. "I haven't been totally honest with you and think I've been unfair. You see, I came to work for you as a professional botanist and certain complications have come up . . . that make it hard to keep my real . . . well, my work, that is . . . what I mean to say is that my feelings are complicating things in an unprofessional way. This wasn't supposed to happen."

"What wasn't supposed to happen?" he said as he took her other hand, looking into her blue eyes. Her red hair framed her face, her lips looked full and the white dress fit her perfectly, to his eyes.

Shaking their hands up and down as they were clasped together, she said, "you know what I mean, this!"

"No, I don't. I want you to tell me. I have received mixed signals from you ever since the day we met."

"You're not making this any easier for me. I want you to know that I am work."

She never finished. Two men dressed all in black rushed out of the bushes, slamming into Scott, knocking him off the path and into the shrubbery on the other side of the path. Stepping quickly back, Julia reached into her purse, but a third man, unnoticed by her, came up behind and said with a sharp-silken voice, "I wouldn't do that, Miss Apostoli. Keep your hands at your sides, if you please."

She froze when she heard the voice. It had a slight Italian accent but that wasn't what disturbed her. It sounded as if it had come up from a grave and was deadly serious. She turned to face him. The man was in impressive shape, dressed in a grey suit, red tie and wearing a fedora on his head. His short blonde hair, what you could see under the hat, was shiny and well cut and he wore wire rim spectacles. His grey eyes were ice-cold and stared at her as if they could undress her and see not her nakedness, but her bare soul.

The two in black hauled Scott out of the bushes. Scott's eyes held a dangerous and haunted look. "Do not try anything stupid, Mr. Chad," the icy voice said. "I have a silenced 9mm automatic pointed at Miss Apostoli's lovely back. If you make one wrong move you are going to be looking at a red dress, not a lovely white one anymore. Do you understand?"

Scott glared at the man. "I understand. What do you want with us? Do you work for Dr. Abu? Obviously, you've been following us for some time and have set this up!"

His voice deadly cold, he answered, "I am the one who is going to be asking the questions, since I am holding the gun at your girlfriend's back."

"She just works for me. Let her go. You didn't answer me, what do you want?"

Julia looked at Scott and turned to the man in the suit. "He's right. I was hired to do research on his project. What do you want with us?"

The man in the suit smiled. "We have watched you for over an hour and if that is how you treat your hired help, more young women will be applying for the job. Enough! Tie his hands behind his back. Get them into the van!"

The larger of the two men in black, a man with large biceps and a long livid scar on his left cheek, pulled Scott's hands roughly behind him and tied them with a plastic zip cord, tight enough to cut off the circulation. The shorter of the two, a scrawny man in an ill-fitting black suit, pulled a silenced pistol out of his jacket and motioned Scott and Julia up the trail. They walked quietly out the back of the park, between two buildings, to a white van.

They opened the door and pushed Scott and Julia in, while the large man with the scar sat by the door. The short fellow drove and the suit settled into the passenger seat, holding his pistol on Julia. They drove through town and continued for about twenty minutes on a succession of twisty mountain roads to an old cottage, set well back off the road. Enormous trees shaded the white washed cottage, the darkness looking eerily dappled from the moonlight filtering through the leaves. The driveway cut into the steep hillside beside the little home. Large flat rocks stood out of the embankment, staggered up the side of the cut in the hillside, obviously used as a primitive staircase to access the pasturelands above. The suit got out, motioning with his gun for Scott and Julia to follow.

Scott whispered to Julia during the half second they were alone, "Wait, maybe they'll make a mistake."

She nodded her understanding, but whispered, "Now might be the only chance we get."

The man in the suit snapped, "No talking! You are going to have a chance to talk soon enough. Follow directions, if you don't want to get hurt."

Scarface opened the door and motioning them out. Julia stepped out and Scott stumbled and fell on the floor, half in and half out of the van and couldn't catch himself with his hands tied behind his back. He spun to sitting position with his feet on the ground, and then stood up.

Julia was clutching her purse when she got out and the suit immediately grabbed her, forcefully taking her arm and steering her toward the small home. He spun around when he heard Scott stumble, violently shoved Julia to the ground and, quick as lightening, fired a shot from his silenced pistol into the dirt at Scott's feet. Scott fell back, landed on his butt in the van and went still. "Be careful, Mr. Chad." He smiled as he talked, "next time you pull a stunt like that I will dye Miss Apostoli's dress red for you. Do you understand?" he said, as he shifted the aim of the gun to Julia's back, where she lay on the stony ground.

Scott nodded, "I understand, but what do you want with us?"

His voice was raspy and smooth. "Time enough for questions when we get inside. Hold your tongue, or I will have it gagged. If that does not work, maybe we will cut it off for you. How would you like that?"

Scott glared at him as Julia pushed herself off the ground and got to her feet, still clutching her purse.

Once inside, the suit pushed Julia into a chair, grabbed her purse, went through it then threw it aside on a table. The two others shoved Scott onto a couch. The leader lit a cigarette, watching the smoke curl up, and looked at his captives. "Now, Mr. Chad, what have you found in Greece? Where is the second marker?"

"What do you mean the second marker? What are you talking about?" Scott asked.

"You look surprised, Mr. Chad. Maybe this will surprise you." He looked over at Scarface, "Jettur, take your knife and cut out her tongue. Let us see how much they like to talk on those moonlit strolls!"

The man pulled out a large knife from behind his back and advanced toward Julia. "My pleasure, Mr. Luigi."

Scott looked from one to another. "Okay, listen, Luigi, if that's your name. I'll tell you all we know, but leave her alone."

"Don't tell them a thing. They're terrorists hired by Al-Queda to get information and as soon as you tell them, we're dead. Don't say a thing."

"She has spirit, this one. I'm going to have fun with her later, Mr. Chad, yes, lots of fun and, when I'm done, my associates will, too. Jettur, first her tongue then her fingers," Luigi said with a hint of pleasure in his voice.

"I'll tell you, just have your Jettur or whatever his name is back off."

A cold smile lit his face and an edge came to his vaporous voice, "I will not agree to anything until I hear what you have to say. You are the one tied up on the couch. Do you not understand? I am the one with the gun. You are in no position to bargain."

Scott looked at Julia then shrugged. "We think the second marker could be at Mt. Athos, in the northeastern part of Greece. I am not sure, but the abbot sent a letter from St. Catherine's back in the year 623. We don't know what it says. That's all I know, so far."

"How do you know that? Tell me about your research so far."

Scott shook his head then looked at Jettur who was holding the knife near Julia's hand. "We found a letter from Father Georges addressed to the head of the Meteoran order. In the letter, he indicated he was sending information about the second marker's location. It's in a kind of code of some sort. Until we find it, I won't know what to make of it. We were planning to go to Mt. Athos next to try and find the letter."

Death was in the voice. "How do I know you are telling the truth?" Luigi asked.

"Because I've nothing to lose. I've told you all I know. How did you find out what the markers were?"

Luigi looked at Scott and laughed. If a laugh could be called evil, this was. "Someone figured the puzzle out from some children's books with funny pictures. You are not the only smart one, Mr. Chad. My employer is far smarter than most people realize. We now know that Mohammad left a message of some sort and that others will pay greatly to get it. Many forces are at work, some of whom believe this message is very valuable. That is why they have hired the best to get it."

Julia looked at him. "What do you need us for then?"

"You are right, Ms. Apostoli. We do not need you anymore." He looked at the man with the scar. Take them up to the pasture, Jettur. You know what to do. We will then head into town and take care of Rogowski."

Scott looked at Julia and then back at Luigi. "You'll never find it without us. You need permission to go onto the mountain and you'll never get it."

He chuckled, his chill laugh saying more than words. "Out with them, Jettur. I have had enough of this talk."

Jettur jerked Julia roughly out of her chair while the small man pulled Scott up by the shoulders. Luigi covered them with the silenced pistol as they were dragged out the door. Jettur dragged Julia toward the van while the small man in the baggy black suit shoved Scott because he wasn't moving fast enough. Jerking on his wrists caused the shorter man to stumble on the threshold.

Scott was waiting for just such a moment and didn't waste it. He rolled forward as the man jerked on his cuffs, fell out the door and down to the ground headfirst. Julia was faster still, much faster.

She used the moment to pull her 25-caliber automatic from out of nowhere. She'd slipped it out of her purse and stashed it in her dress when Scott stumbled getting out of the van.

Spinning out of Jettur's grasp, she turned and fired at the shorter man, a small round hole appearing in the center of his forehead.

Scott's ears rang from the shot as he rolled and tucked, pulling his hands under his feet. He jumped up bringing both fists together, swinging them down on the Luigi's head like a sledgehammer. His blow knocked Luigi to the ground, the gun clattering on the paving stones in front of the little cottage. Scott quickly kicked the gun out of the man's reach.

Jettur spun like a cat charging Julia. She spun on the balls of her feet, firing from three feet away. The small caliber round didn't even phase his momentum. He landed on top of her, crushing her to the ground, her skull smacking into the flagstones with a loud crack. They lay on the walkway unmoving.

Scott glanced at the pair, turning toward Luigi. Taking one-step and raising his foot, he stomped on his wrist, hearing with some satisfaction as the bone snapped. He reached down grabbing the automatic from where he had kicked it then bent down to the man's ear. "If she's hurt, you're going to feel something a lot worse than my foot on your wrist." Raising his arm, he brought the automatic down on the back of Luigi's head, hard enough to stun but not kill. Running over to check on Julia, he noticed she was trying to push the huge man off.

"Are you okay?" he asked, heaving the man off and rolling him onto his back, who lay there staring up at nothing. Scott noticed a small round hole just to the left of his breastbone, exactly where his heart was.

She rubbed her head where it hit the pavement. "I feel like I was hit by a truck."

He glanced over at the two men she had shot, with a look of fear and respect. "Where'd you learn to shoot like that? I wouldn't want to mess with you when you're angry."

She was rubbing the bump on her head. "Girl Scouts, I guess. That was one of the things I wanted to talk to you about when we went for our walk."

He shook his head. "Girl Scouts? Well, going for a moonlit stroll with you isn't all it's cracked up to be."

She walked over to him keeping an eye on the guy in the suit lying on the ground. "A girl's got to be able to protect herself, doesn't she? I think they wanted you and not me anyway. That's why they threatened to dye my dress, to get you to talk."

He looked at the bump on her head. "Are you sure you're okay? You're probably right. Let's tie him up and pull these other two inside. We'll put them all in the cottage and get out of here. Sound like a plan to you?"

"We should check out the cottage first, see if there's anything that might tell us what they were really up to."

Scott walked up, turned Luigi over, bent down and rummaged through his pockets, pulling out his wallet, a knife, a wad of Euros and some Egyptian money. Opening the knife, he cut the zip cord holding his wrists.

Dragging the men into a back room in the cottage, Scott then tied and gagged the leader. Scott searched through the cottage and van while Julia combed through their belongings, looking for any evidence that would explain why they were following them and who may have hired them.

When Scott was done with the van, he came back inside and asked. "Find anything of value, anything that might tell us what they wanted?"

"Nothing but this." She turned and handed him a slip of paper. "The guy they called Luigi had this phone number in his pocket; it's got the name Abdullah on it. Ever hear of him? There's a scrawl on the back that looks like Bestin, Farrell and Henderson, probably some sort of code names."

Scott turned the slip of paper over with a puzzled expression. "I know a Frank Henderson: he's a magazine publisher. Lives in California but travels all over the country. It doesn't make sense. What could he have to do with this and who is Abdullah? What do you think of this phone number?"

She stopped what she was looking through and looked down at the paper. "It's a foreign number, not one from the states, so I'd have to look at the country code to figure out where it's from, but my guess would be Switzerland."

"I can't believe you kept your nerve and you're that good with that little gun. You didn't really answer me when I asked where you learned to handle yourself like that. Most women and many men I know would be upset after an evening like this. Why did they let you keep your purse at the start, I wonder?"

"I was taught if a woman acts scared and clutches her purse, people will usually leave her alone, thinking she's harmless and frozen with fear. These men were amateurs, not professionals, dangerous of course, but amateurs nonetheless. Let's get out of here before someone comes. I think we've been here long enough."

Scott thought. *Taught by whom?* Nevertheless he said, "I couldn't agree more. Let's go."

They took the van and carefully made their way back to town. Scott turned to Julia when they got back near the square. "Do you think we should notify the police?"

She frowned. "Probably not a good idea. I wiped the place down before we left so we didn't leave any finger prints, but it will delay us here for I don't know how long and probably get us deported." She looked over at him for his concurrence. "I say we meet Father Nikita in the morning and then decide what to do."

"I was thinking about the same thing but also thinking it might make international headlines if I was accused of shooting one of these guys." He stopped at a light and looked at her. "Oh, I suppose it might turn out all right if we came to them. But if we take off and don't report it there is no telling what they will do when someone finds them. Who knows what kind of story Luigi will cook up?"

The adrenaline was starting to drain from both of them and the after effects of the ordeal were leaving both a bit shaky. Scott pulled the van into a parking lot where used cars were stored. He parked and came around, opening Julia's door, who he found busy wiping down the wheel, dashboard and the backseat.

"You seem to know your way around a police kit," Scott said as he waited for her to finish.

"No sense in taking any chances," she answered as she got out and wiped down the outside doors.

They locked the van, put the key above the left front tire, and made their way back into town where the dance was still going on. He looked down at his watch, noting that only an hour had passed. It seemed that more than a night had gone by with his emotions strung so tight.

As they came under the trees on the outskirts of the park, Julia put her arm through his again. Walking up to the dancer's on the square she looked up at him. "One more dance?"

"Why not, might help to burn off some of the adrenaline," Scott said with a smile.

A number of dancers were still on the platform and the song ended just as they walked up, the dancers turning and clapping for the band, which immediately started up another number. A female singer came out, singing a slow sonorous number in a wonderful soprano voice, put to a Greek folk melody. He opened his arms and Julia laid her head on his shoulder as they slowly moved to the rhythm of the music and the voice of the singer. The song wasn't long and the band packed up after the solo. Scott and Julia walked back through the park staying with the rest of the crowd as it dispersed.

As they walked down the hallway after getting off the elevator, Scott gently touched her shoulder. "I guess this is goodnight. We never did have that talk you wanted to have. Be sure and double lock your door tonight."

She paused and looked at him, long and hard, for a moment. "No, we didn't and maybe it's for the best. Good night, Scott," she said as she extended her hand.

Scott stood in the hallway a moment after she entered her room, turned and opened his door. He walked across the room and sat on his bed staring at the door.

When Julia shut her door, she leaned back on it and just waited. She wanted to open the door and call to him, but knew it would cause complications far larger than the lonely feeling she was experiencing. She took a deep breath, looked through the peephole, then crossed to her bed and sat on the end of it.

Two people sat on the ends of their beds on a spring night in Greece as the moon slowly set. They eventually went to bed but very little sleep came to either. Scott stirred when he heard Samuel enter a couple of hours later. This gave him a feeling of comfort that finally allowed him to doze off and get a few hours sleep.

They all met for breakfast at the terrace restaurant of the hotel, which overlooked the valley and up at the stone forest of Meteora. The morning sun was playing on the rocks and the birds were singing as they busied themselves with finding food and building nests.

Scott looked over at Samuel who looked a little bleary eyed but alert. "Have a nice evening?"

"You said you'd wake me at nine. Where were you two?"

"Out to a dance," Scott said as he winked at Julia. "Where did you go?"

"Went down to the local taverna and met a wonderful barkeep named Demetria. She has long black hair and is shaped like one of those statues you see in the museums. Not one of the modern statues, mind you, but one of the old Greek ones that show real women. You two were back early. I saw the light on in both your rooms. What were you up to?"

"We weren't as successful as we thought at getting rid of our tail and there may be other people interested in us. We ran into a little trouble last night and probably shouldn't talk about it here. As a matter of fact, I think we should get going as soon as possible and get out of here before anyone else shows up."

Samuel looked at them and asked, "What happened? Are both of you okay?"

Scott looked over at him. "We'll tell you after we meet with Father Nikita or on the way. Let's pack your bags. Meet us at the car."

As they got out of the car at the monastery, a phalanx of storks flew overhead squawking in the morning light. This brought a smile to their faces and hearts as they ascended the ancient staircase into the monastery.

Friar Vasillus met them at the entry and escorted them into the library where Father Nikita waited.

"We had some trouble last night . Early in the evening, someone tried to break into the library and two of our monks were hurt. I do not think they were expecting any resistance or even an alarm on the library, but the insurance company made us install it a few years back in order to keep the premium low. They found the door to the lower crypt and blew the door to the archives; they took some old letters and the mirror left by the Despote's wife to the monastery. I do not know why they would break into the archives just for an old mirror. It is quite valuable, but it just does not seem logical."

Scott asked, "What letters or manuscripts did they take, Father?"

"Interestingly enough, they took Father Georges' letters, the ones you looked at yesterday with Vasillus." Nikita paused and looked at Scott. "I know . . . you warned me . . . fair enough, but still, I did not think they would dare to break into the monastery and use explosives on the door. They must have entered earlier in the afternoon and hidden until after we closed. We do not keep a head count and maybe we should, but this type of thing has never happened before." He paused and shook his head. "I doubt it will again, but who knows."

Scott looked at his companions before answering. "I'm really sorry, Father, if we brought this on you. Were the monks hurt badly?"

"No, not badly. One has a broken arm and the other is just banged up some with a loose tooth and a black eye or two. They are young and will soon recover except for their pride maybe, which could be a good thing, as too much pride does not become a monk. Yes, maybe there is a blessing here somewhere that we have yet to see."

Julia asked, "How many men were here and what did they look like?"

"There were three in the monastery and one waiting in a van. The three were . . . ," he looked over at the young monk. "You tell them, Vasillus. You saw them better than I."

Vasillus looked hesitatingly at the group. "One was small and unkempt, another was large and muscular with brown hair, and the last one had blonde hair and was neatly dressed in a grey suit wearing a hat. We didn't see the one waiting in the van, but know someone was waiting; the monks chased them up to the lot and the van was rolling and picked them up on the run. They got away."

Julia looked at the friar. "What time were they here?"

Vasillus scrunched his face in thought. "About six thirty or so."

Scott looked over at her. "Julia, tell them about what happened to us."

She took a deep breath. "We were in the park watching the dance and decided to take a walk. Some men came out of the bushes, tackled Scott and pulled guns on us."

Scott added when Julia finished. "They must have come here first. We were at the dance at eight and you said they were here at six-thirty. We didn't find the letters or mirror on them and looked carefully. We could have missed it, but I don't think so. The fourth guy, whoever that is, probably has it. We thought of calling the police but that would probably get us deported. We were hoping that you would call the police after we left. I'll draw a map of where we left them and they could check it out. The fourth man is what troubles me; if he's still around, there's no point in calling the police. He's probably cleaned things up by now or done something with the bodies. I am sure he's long gone by now, or he could be on his way here again with Luigi, even as we speak!"

"The laws about guns are strict here, Ms. Apostoli, I can understand why you did not call the police last night and you are right, it is probably too late. I am not comfortable with a death like this even if it was in self defense." Nikita paused and looked at Scott. "Draw us the map to the cottage and we will see if we can find it. We will not lie for you, but can say we were trying to follow up on these men after they left here. I think you are right and they will find nothing. Your worries are useless then. It was in self-defense anyway. I do not think they will come back here. They have what they want."

Scott looked at him. "Thank you, Father, we don't deserve your trust."

Nikita raised his hand. "Enough, draw a map to this cottage and let us get this mess cleaned up."

Julia went over to a table and with Scott's help drew a map to the cottage to the best of their recollection along with a description of the building. "You should be able to find it from this," Scott said.

Vasillus took the sketch and smiled. "This is very good. I already know right where this is. I used to play near here as a child. There's a peg stone stairway by the side of the cottage to reach the fields above, right?"

"Exactly, unless all little white cottages have stairways like that."

"No, it's one of a kind, I can tell, since your map's so accurate. You're a surveyor right, that explains it." Vasillus said.

Chapter 31
Geneva

The rain doused the city as Hasid stepped off the plane in Geneva. Quati wanted to meet in Geneva since he had been at meetings in Paris all week discussing trade agreements he was hoping the European Trade Union would approve.

As the large black Mercedes pulled up to the old bank, the doorman expertly ran to the curb holding a large umbrella over Hasid as he got out. Wearing a three-piece grey suit and carrying a briefcase, he had shaved close that morning, but his thick beard still threatened a shadow.

His anxiety over Chad and Julia, still new to him, rose like acid in his gorge. He thought he knew why Quati called this urgent meeting, knowing he was probably working up a rage over what happened in Greece

Quati didn't scare him after working together all these years, but there was really no way of telling how he would react. Hasid's real anxiety was what Quati would ask him to do about Scott and Julia. Quati acted irrationally and you never knew quite what to expect.

His thoughts turned again to Julia and Scott. Would Quati change his mind and order him to kill them? Could he do it, he asked himself. "God was great, God was good and there is no God but Allah and Mohammed was his prophet," he quickly said to himself as he walked into the old bank. Expelling a deep breath, he knew he had to keep the whole operation going and it would be nice to keep his numbered accounts intact.

Ushering him to the elevator, the receptionist directed him to the third floor. When he stepped out, a beautiful blonde receptionist came from behind her desk. She was dressed in a tight, short grey suit, jacket, black stockings and heels.

Smiling and extending her hand, she greeted him in English, "They are expecting you in the conference room, Mr. Hasid."

Her hand felt soft and cool as he took it.

"Down the corridor to the third door on your left," she said, smiling up at him. "Please, if you need anything, anything at all, let me know. I am here to be of service."

He was somewhat surprised she knew his name. The Swiss were usually reserved about their clients. The president of the bank had worked with Quati and him over a number of difficult transactions over the years. It wasn't particularly a problem that this young receptionist new his name, but still, it was disturbing that the bank president had let his name out. He would have to look into that later. They based their business on anonymity and trust and if one of those broke down, well . . . trouble could result. Swiss banks used numbered accounts so their clients could protect their identity, which was the whole point after all. The young lady knowing his name was probably harmless, but you couldn't have this type of thing going on.

All this flashed through his mind as he responded, "Why thank you, young lady. What's your name and where did you learn to speak English so well?" He knew Quati was in a hurry but was unwilling to rush things.

"I learned in high school and more in college. My name's Ingrid and, as I said before, if you need anything, anything at all, please don't hesitate."

"Well, it's been a long time since I've been to Geneva. Perhaps you'd like to have dinner and show me the sights after my meeting." He hadn't noticed a ring and figured she was probably single and looking by the way she was dressed, but you could never tell with European women.

The fact that he was tall, dark and handsome usually made him irresistible, a fact he'd used numerous times over the years in his work. Arab men usually prefer their women conservative and quiet, at least in public, but it was a well-known fact that some rich Arab's from Saudi Arabia, Iran and Iraq went to Europe, Las Vegas and other places to let their hair down.

Her blue eyes looked up at him. "That would be wonderful, I get off at six. If your meeting does not run late, I'd love to have dinner and show you the town." She turned, stretching over her desk and lifting her leg, grabbed a piece of paper, and quickly wrote her number. "If your meeting runs late, here's my number. Feel free to call whenever, I'll be waiting."

"Thank you, Ingrid," he said with a short bow. I hope to be able to call. I never know what the pressures of business may bring, but I thank you. I'll try to see you after the meeting. Hopefully it will not run too late," he said tipping his hat, then he turned and walked down the hall, glancing at the original works of art on the walls that cost a fortune, and opened the door.

Finding Quati, Talbin, and Abdullah gathered around a table, he took a seat at the end, while Quati glared at him.

"It is about time you showed up. I hope you were not distracted on the way in," Quati said.

"Your business is my only interest. My heart and mind are always on your and Allah's affairs."

"I have known you for years and know what you dabble in and what you do not. Never try to fool me! I do not care what you do as long as it does not interfere with my plans. I am outraged at what happened in Greece. We should have put an end to Chad and all we have now done is made him more wary."

"Yes, the whole affair was handled poorly, and Bestin's and our choice of people was careless, but I think it is as Allah wills. The loss of Sa'd and Jettur was unfortunate but I believe it will end up better in the end. Henderson got Luigi out along with some interesting letters. The more I think about this, I think it best to let Chad continue with his work. He will be doing our work for us. We need to keep our people close, though, and ready. In case Chad finds the writings, we must quickly take them before they fall into other hands."

Quati looked sharply at him.

Hasid raised his hand. "I know you believe it a shame that one of the faithful is not bringing the prophet's work to light, but the ways of Allah are strange. We know Allah has plans for the infidel as well as the jihad that will light your path to glory. It may be Allah's will to let Chad do our work for us. Things will be much easier also and we do not have to get Dr. Abu involved."

"The Mullah believes that it is an abomination to have an infidel involved."

"We would never have found the place in Greece if Chad had not shown us the way. Even if we had, we do not know what it means. When we looked at the chamber in Sinai that Chad found, we could not make sense of the inscriptions nor fathom why Chad went to Greece."

"Yes, but we know where this leads now, don't we? Couldn't Abu have figured it out?"

Hasid continued as if not hearing him. "Only after many days and weeks did one of our younger men find the key to the writing. Abu had nothing to do with it. I still do not really understand it myself. This man went to school in America and said he figured it out after looking at one of their children's books. It has something to do with throwing your eyes out of focus and letting each eye see independently. Then the message becomes clear and forms a picture that your mind interprets. Amazing that Mohammad left a message written like that, more than 1300 years ago."

Quati turned to Abdullah. "Your behavior in this and bumbling about has almost cost us our chance to keep this in control. Do you know the price of failure in my organization?"

"I am sorry, Quati, but those men of Bestin's you gave me to work with were inept and I could not control them. They were not our people. Give me men with more discipline next time and I will do your will. It is your own fault for sending these men."

Everyone in the room stiffened at Abdullah's retort. "Next time? You honestly think there is going to be a next time? Sa'd and Jettur were our men and you lost them to a woman, if I have that right and a Jewish one, too. You know the price of failure; it is an early meeting with Allah, and you would do well to remember that. Get out of my sight. Take Talbin with you and wait outside."

When they had left the room, Quati continued. "I tell you, the man is an idiot. I do not know where I came up with him. his loyalty is good but we need to have better brains that will inspire loyalty and above all obedience to my orders. Someone must pay the price of failure, to set the example for others. See to it! Do you hear me! We must not fail in our trust."

"Are you sure, General? He has been a valuable asset to us over the years." For some reason his feelings took off again, roiling like ice in his veins. His feet felt cold and he could feel his blood pressure rise.

"I must send a lesson to some of our people in Lebanon and Syria. They must know to obey my orders exactly and know what the consequences are."

"To hear you is to obey. It will be taken care of this evening. I have a plan in mind. If we are to make an example of this, his failure needs to be made public. Do you agree?"

"I trust you in this of all people. Just take care of it as soon as you are able to arrange it."

"Now, down to other business, my sources tell me that the woman working with Chad, this Julia Apostoli, actually is an agent that works for the Mosad. She is not from Illinois. She is a Jewess and is working with him, and who knows what other help he may have from that group of people."

His feeling rose even higher than before and he felt Quati must be able to see his feelings about Julia. He had found out she was Jewish when he met her in Paris and it didn't matter to him at the time. Did it now? Did he really fall in love with her that summer? How could he have fallen in love with a Jew? "You have known she was Jewish for a long time. Why are you bringing it up now?" He knew the real reason but wanted Quati to state it, so his position was clear when he left.

"Having a Jewish woman in or near our holy sites is an abomination. I agreed to let Chad do our work for us, but having a Jewess involved is too much to ask of the mullahs."

"Sometimes we need to sacrifice for the greater good. If we are to let Chad complete his work, we should not interfere. What harm would really come by letting her continue working with Chad?"

"She's dangerous, I tell you. She took out two of my men in Greece. I think if we take care of her it will be that much easier to find out what Chad is up to. She is Mosad, I do not trust them. I have agreed to let Chad continue his work. Do you hear me?"

"I think the whole bank can hear you by now, and I respectfully disagree. If we remove her from Chad's camp there is no telling what may happen. He may even quit the search or the Mosad may put someone else in. Who knows what may happen. Better to know who your enemy is than be surprised by a new one."

"I do not want an Israeli, let alone a woman, treading on the holy places of Islam, do you not understand? It is a holy abomination to Islam; you act as if you do not know this. I will not have it!"

Why did it have to be Julia, Hasid thought to himself for the hundredth time. It was as if a spark of love still existed inside him and Quati was fanning the flame; he could not bear the thought of seeing her hurt. He didn't know if he could follow Quati's orders and felt like he was treading dangerous ground. "You are right of course, Quati. I will look into it and perhaps we can remove her at some convenient time. I do not think this should be our main priority." Hasid knew that arguing with Quati when he was in this state was useless.

"See that she is taken care of. Abdullah's a fool, Jettur and Sa'd were good men and now they are gone to Paradise. Abdullah blew the operation. He should have gone with Luigi and watched over the whole thing, but, no, he stayed back with Henderson. I was going to send Sa'd and Luigi to follow Chad and that Jewess. Now I will have to find someone else. Don't you fail me, Hasid. We shall then see . . . yes, we shall see."

"I hear you and it will be done as you say. Now onto this other business. I am sure you called the meeting at the bank for a reason. Did they wire the money to our accounts?"

"Yes, they wired twenty million as I said they would. I cannot believe that Henderson and Bestin are such fools. They hate us but give us their money for our revolution. Are they stupid, or do they just want their power?"

"No, they are not stupid. They may be short sighted but want to keep their power the same way we do. They want to keep what they have. They do not foresee that Islam will grow and sweep across the world as our jihad unfolds. They do not care a bit about our revolution, but just want to keep their own nest intact. If they saw the big picture, they would be dangerous," Hasid said thinking and wondering if Quati saw the big picture. Maybe Allah's whole plan was much bigger than all of them. The idealism he had learned from his mother crept back into his mind. He quashed it down, remembering how his father had died. The Israelis had shot his father numerous times as he ran across the street after the Palestinians had bombed the bus. His bullet-ridden body leaked his life's blood out on the pavement as the rain washed it into the gutter. He wished he could kill all the Israelis for what they had done, but Julia was an Israeli. How was he to stop these thoughts? When would this operation end?

"I have made arrangements to transfer half the money into your account at the bank. You will be well taken care of no matter what may come. This is only the first payment for your many years of long and faithful service, Hasid. We will be supplying our Palestinian friends with many arms and much needed ammunition with these funds and the funds from our friends across the globe. Soon . . . very soon, we will be ready to strike at the infidel and strike terror into the hearts of all the unbelievers. Bin Laden and Hussein were fools, thinking the way to strike terror is through a nuclear device or some sort of biological weapon. They and their kind will end up paying a dreadful price and the peoples of the world will cheer when they see them hanging from their toes. No, the way to strike terror into their hearts is to see our children dying in the streets shot by their automatic weapons, our sons burning as they throw stones at tanks. They will not care who started it when they see the innocent children burning and dying for a cause. A glorious way to enter paradise, no?"

"I will contact the Palestinians and arrange for the transfer of the funds. I will also provide them with our contacts so they can get the weapons to start your campaign. It is spring, they will strike during the Jewish Feast of the Booths. We must be patient and wait for the right moment. I know you want this to proceed quickly but the more patient we are the better our support will be." Hasid looked down at his watch. "It is after six. I must go and arrange that other matter we discussed for Abdullah. Look to tomorrow's papers and his failure will become apparent."

"You must bring disgrace upon his family. Failure will not be tolerated, do you understand?"

"Quati, I hear you. I've understood and knew what to do before I came in here. The way has been opened. Do not worry; it will be taken care of as you ordered."

"Tell that banker to come and finish our discussion when you leave. I want the funds transferred before I go back to the east."

"Yes, Quati, I will tell him." Hasid left Quati with his aide and walked out of the room. The receptionist had left for the day but a banker in a three-piece suit and black wing tip shoes stood by his office door at the end of the corridor. Hasid walked up on his way out and said, "President Quati will see the head banker now."

Noting the rain had stopped upon exiting the bank, it looked like it was going to be a fine evening. He walked over to the large black Mercedes where Abdullah and Talbin were waiting. "Drive to my hotel, Abdullah. I want to see you at midnight in my room. We have some things to discuss," he said as he handed him an extra key. "You are free until then, but do not be late and be discreet when entering. I will have other guests. Do you understand?"

"Yes, Hasid, I am to come at midnight and use your key to enter the room."

"Good, now stay out of trouble until then," he said as they dropped him off at his hotel.

Looking down at his Rolex, noting it was 6:45, he made his way up to his room and called Ingrid. She was happy to hear from him, gave her address and arranged for him to pick her up at her apartment at 7:30.

He showered, shaved and changed his suit and clothes. When he arrived at Ingrid's apartment he told the cab driver to wait, while he went up. The apartment block was decently maintained and when he got off the elevator, he noted the hallway was freshly decorated and very clean. Hasid knocked and heard her voice through the door telling him to come in. Carefully opening the door, he heard water running in the bathroom.

"Make yourself comfortable. There is a bar by the tele and ice in the bucket. I will only be a minute. I am almost ready," she said from the open door of the bathroom.

Hasid relaxed when he saw the apartment. It was a small one-bedroom affair with an open floor plan, the closet door standing open. When she came out, Hasid couldn't help but smile. She was dressed in a bright red dress with matching heels and a pearl necklace that the dress showed off to advantage. Her long blonde hair shone and lay on her bare shoulders. He hadn't really been aware at the bank what a striking woman she was, probably because of the business attire but was now having second thoughts about the plans for the evening.

There he was feeling strange again, tense and almost guilty. *Why is this happening to me?* He thought. This was business after all and he worked for Quati. What was getting into him? He berated himself for having any feelings about this type of thing at all. Having emotions was something that only got in the way.

"Boy, you look beautiful. I hope you're ready for a nice dinner?"

"I'd love to show you my city. It is very old and a wonderful place. I know a nice quiet restaurant over by the river where they serve a wonderful steak."

"I had the taxi hold downstairs," he said as he offered his arm.

They took the taxi to a small local bistro, which did in fact serve a wonderful chateau beautechere. After dinner they went to a local jazz club, which had a small dance floor. Hasid had learned to appreciate western jazz while attending school in France and London, even learning to dance in the western style. This woman dancing in front of him would have made a nice addition to his household, but alas, that was not to be. He could not permanently bind himself to an infidel, but an evening of fun and passion was another thing altogether. All the princes from the house of Saud did this all the time. It wasn't the first time for him either, and why was he having these thoughts? It wasn't like him to feel emotions. *Time to get things moving,* he thought as he looked at his Rolex and noted it was after ten.

When the song finished, they made their way back to the table and Hasid glanced down at his watch again and asked, "Would you like to go back to my place for a nightcap?"

"Oh, I'd love to. This place is fun but," she looked up at him as she bent over the table, "the evening is still young, is it not?"

"Yes, it is still young," he said as they made their way out the front door where they hailed a taxi that took them back to his hotel. He glanced at his watch and noted it was 10:45. Time would be tight, he thought, and he would have to move quickly, which he didn't like. Luckily for him, his companion resolved this for him. As they entered the room she walked over and threw her arms around him, planting a kiss on his lips which left no doubt in his mind. Forty minutes later, breathless and sweating, he rolled over and quietly opened his briefcase, reached in for a syringe filled with potassium chloride. She was asleep next to him and he quickly reached over and pushed the needle into her neck. She came awake with a start and then let out a small yell as the drug hit her heart, stopping it immediately. Realization came over her for a second as she looked up into his eyes, mouthing the word "why," as her eyes rolled back in her head.

He got up, took a quick shower and dressed, waiting for Abdullah to show up. When he heard the door open, exactly at 12:00, he greeted Abdullah in the sitting room. "Well, Abdullah, Quati is not exactly happy with your performance, as we know, but I am of a different sort and know you did your best with the men he gave you. Your loyalty is to be commended."

Abdullah looked at Hasid and smiled at the compliment. "I will tell you, I was worried about Quati. He does not always understand but, as Allah wills, is what I say. He is our master, but he scares me sometimes with that look in his eyes."

"Come, I have your reward in the bedroom," Hasid said as he took Abdullah by the arm. He had syringe prepared. The blue color made him cringe ever since his favorite dog was put to sleep when he was a child. They made their way to the bedroom where Hasid had arranged Ingrid. He counted on Abdullah to pause when he saw the girl; Abdullah did not let him down. The Arab man is fascinated when he sees a girl like Ingrid. As Abdullah looked into the dimly lit room Hasid reached up and plunged the syringe into the base of Abdullah's neck. Unfortunately he missed the vein which would only prolong the agony. Abdullah whirled and delivered a punch to Hasid's stomach which doubled him over but he never had a chance for a second punch as the drug hit his heart. It went into a double rhythm and then convulsions. If he had hit a vein the heart would have stopped instantly. It was deadly none-the-less and as Abdullah dropped to the floor and cried out in pain as his heartbeat doubled then doubled again and finally burst.

"You heard Quati and know what the price of failure is, Abdullah. Go meet Allah or the devil," Hasid said as he saw the final look in his eyes.

He stepped back while his stomach churned for some reason. The emotion he was feeling was foreign to him, *why was he feeling things for Abdullah.* He realized it was not for Abdullah, but for the young lady. He had never let emotions get to him and considered himself the man of ice with no emotions whatsoever. He quickly quashed them down with a vision of his father's burning corpse on the streets of Haifa. He then stripped the clothes off Abdullah and pulled him up onto the bed with Ingrid. Arranging them in a pose that would satisfy the police photographers. Taking out his camera he took pictures for Quati and then wiped his fingerprints off everything in the room he may have touched. Making his way to the elevator he got off at the second floor and went down the stairs and out the rear entry.

Walking around the back of the hotel he hailed a taxi a block away which took him to the Hotel Intercontinental on the other side of town. After booking a room he slept until morning.

He was surprised that the morning papers were silent; but filling the front page of the afternoon editions were large photos of the double homicide. They were silent about the cause but Hasid had left Abdullah's passport in his clothes and they now knew he was a Palestinian national. Quati would be pleased when he saw the pictures of him and Ingrid laid out on the bed. The whole Middle East would know the price of failure when working for Quati. After booking an afternoon flight to Beirut Hasid arranged a meeting with a number of Quati's recruits. He needed to reinforce the cost of disobeying Quati. Everyone in this corner of the world had to know not to cross Quati.

As he sat on the jet his thoughts turned to Chad and Julia. One of his agents had placed a transmitter on Chad's car; so, feeling confident that he wouldn't lose them, he dozed off as the plane reached altitude.

❆　❆　❆　❆　❆　❆　❆　❆

Scott, Samuel and Julia sat down to dinner. "Did you notice all the electronic stores in town? They were all in one place, kind of like letting your fingers do the walking," Scott said.

Julia looked puzzled. "I don't think so. I'd think you'd still have to walk to each one, and what do your fingers have to do with it?"

"I meant you don't need a phone book; let your fingers do the walking?"

She shook her head. "Why would you need the phone book? You could just walk to each one?"

"You wouldn't need the phone book necessarily; I was just making a play on words from an old commercial for the yellow pages."

She looked at Scott a moment before answering. "Well, but I don't see what the phone book has to do with it. Yellow pages or white pages or green pages, what's the difference?"

Scott looked her in the eye. "Julia, maybe now would be a good time for that talk you wanted to have. I've noticed certain things over time. The old saying, 'Are we there yet?' every kid and parent in America knows for the country's so big. There are other little things, too. 'Let your fingers do the walking' is an old ad for the yellow pages, which are the commercial telephone book listings. It all adds up to someone who's not who she says she is. There is also the way you handle that 25-caliber auto you carry around. I haven't met any female botanists who can handle a pistol like that. But, even more importantly, you showed your training when you shot those two the other night. Most people would have been a basket case after that and you were as cool as a cucumber. You didn't fall apart and you kept your head." She looked at Scott and wanted to talk, but Scott held up his hand and said, "I have the floor."

She did interrupt, "What do you mean by having the floor?"

"That's just what I mean. Everyone in America knows the saying. It means it's my turn to speak. It goes to show you're not who you say you are. Want to talk about it?"

She thought about her parents and their ordeal in the camps but knew what her controller would say. There was something more at work here; she shouldn't, but she had become attached to these two. They'd been through a lot together in the past months and she couldn't admit it, even to herself, but there was something . . . a growing feeling, or was it an infatuation with Scott that was impossible to dismiss. She felt she had to say something, though didn't know what,

"Scott, I'm sorry. I have been meaning to tell you and wanted to the other night when those guys came at us at the dance. It has been hard. You are right; I didn't grow up in America. I work for an organization that wants to see you succeed at what you're doing. They don't want you to fail, but want you to succeed. There are many powers at work that are trying to stop you and I was to protect you and your people and to help you succeed. It's as simple as that," she said crossing her arms over her chest, with a forced smile on her face.

Scott sat back and looked at her, remembering the tension and the magnetism that came and went whenever she was around. "Not good enough. Who do you work for?"

"I can't tell you, Scott. It's not that I don't want to, but it might jeopardize you and what you're working on if I did."

He suddenly felt he couldn't do this. Julia had become too important to him over the last few months. His anxiety threatened to unbalance his objectivity but he needed to clear this up, to put it behind him. His melancholy was like a thick black shroud that wanted to descend on him, but he had to see this through. If he wasn't dealing with the truth on this, where could he be honest? "There's only one thing I demand from my people and that's honesty. Well, maybe two, a full days work, but if you've got the first the second takes care of itself."

"I haven't lied to you other than about growing up in Illinois. I am a botanist and I think my work and programming skills prove it."

He snapped. "You've lied to me about other things than Illinois! I'm sure your résumé's not real, where you worked before and went to school. I admit your work is first rate, but when I turn in a report with your credentials on it, someone may question your résumé and then my whole report lacks credibility. Don't you see?"

She looked hurt and angry. "I'll redo my résumé and give you the schools I went to before you publish the report, but first we need to finish this business here."

Thinking back to that night where they'd danced in the park, he shook his head and replied with a stiff tone, "The first thing is getting you on a plane out of here. I didn't hire Julia Apostoli; I bet that's not even your real name, is it?"

"Julia is my real name . . . you can't send me away now! Vassilius said there were four men at the monastery. Two of them are dead but I bet the other two are after us now. You could be in extreme danger this very minute. Do you think you can take care of yourselves? These men are dangerous and ruthless!"

His stomach twisted as a leaden feeling crept over his limbs, but he continued, "Julia, come off it. We've fought with the Mujadeen in Afghanistan, traveled the jungles of South America and been attacked by Indians with poisonous arrows and blowguns. We've been through scrapes in Egypt, Japan, and England and dealt with some of the worst and shadiest characters the United States can deal up. Can we take care of ourselves? What do you think? I'm worried about you! Yes, I've seen you in action a couple of times but you can't work for us anymore now that our contract's broken."

"What do you mean our contract's broken?" she asked.

"I meant just what I said. When you signed the contract, the fine print said you confirmed and certified that all the information was true and correct to the best of your knowledge and belief. The contract further said that presenting any false information was a breach of contract and immediate termination would result. Our insurance wouldn't even cover you if you were hurt." He stopped and looked at Samuel. "Granted, we're more likely to die a horrible and painful death with half the terrorists and extremists in the world after us. What have you gotten us into, by the way?"

One of those sullen looks came over her face that only an experienced and mature man has the strength to deal with. "What have I gotten you into, you say? Well, I'm not telling you another thing if I don't work for you anymore and if I'm not on the team. I think you should keep me on, but I don't think I want to work for you or even see you anymore."

Scott shook his head, and then looked into her eyes. "Have it your way then. I guess this is good-bye and good luck to you. I thought there was something more there and we could be honest with each other, but I guess it's not meant to be." He held out his hand.

She didn't take his hand but a pained expression of loss and anger crossed her face. "You haven't paid me yet. I don't think you can get rid of me that easily."

He reached in his wallet, took out half the money and tossed it on the table, then turned to the waiter and said, "check please." After paying the check he and Samuel went up to their rooms.

Julia just sat there.

The next morning Scott and Samuel were at breakfast when Scott looked up at him. "Seen Julia this morning? I think I was a little hard on her last night."

"A little hard. I think you had better have a talk with her."

"I'll go up and check on her. Order me another cup of coffee if the waiter comes around, would you?"

Scott went back upstairs and knocked on Julia's door but didn't get an answer. He tried again with the same result. He made his way back down to the lobby and asked the manager. "Has the lady in room 217 checked out?"

The manager looked at his records. "No sir."

"She works with us and there's no answer at her door. Would you be so kind as to send someone up to check on her?"

"I'd be pleased to, sir. Please meet the maid at the room."

Scott made his way back upstairs where a maid met him and opened the door. When he looked in it was obvious what had happened. The room was in shambles, the bed overturned, clothes scattered, and no sign of Julia.

CHAPTER 32
BATTLE AT METEORA

Packing their gear in a rush, Scott and Samuel hopped in the Fiat and drove recklessly up the twisting mountain road to the monastery. Finding the place in an uproar, Father Nikita rushed up to meet them as they entered. "Father Anthony called and told me you were on the way back. What he did not say was that trouble would be ahead of you or following you. Just before dawn, four men broke into the monastery, holding Miss Apostoli at gunpoint, demanding access to the archive room; Why they wanted to get in there we have no idea."

"Where are they now?" Scott asked.

"They are still in the archive room; they cut the phone lines and took two of our monks hostage. They told us if we get the police involved, they would kill them all. There is nothing we can do! We must to wait, but it burns my heart."

Scott looked over at Samuel and nodded, then turned back to Father Nikita. "Do you have any rope?"

He looked at him for a moment before answering, "I believe we have some in the winch house for bringing up baskets and things. What do you need it for?"

"I've an idea on how we might be able to help. Timing's everything and we'll have to see," Scott said.

The morning sun struggled to break through the building mass of clouds that were piling up to the west, giving a reddish cast to the group as they stood on the summit. Scott turned to the abbot. "Looks like a storm coming. Maybe if luck's with us, it will create a diversion. I would rather wait for nightfall, but they may move as soon as they find what they are looking for and they could hurt someone if we wait. Show me where the window to the room is from up here. We'll try and work out a plan and send someone to get that rope."

"Well, follow me then," Nikita said.

One of the younger monks ran to fetch the rope, while they walked through the courtyard and around the church. There was a large patio perched on the edge of the cliff overlooking the plain, and the drop down to the plain was about six hundred feet. Nikita walked down the steps, leaned over and pointed. "The window to the archive room is about eighty feet down."

Scott looked at Samuel. "We can tie the ropes off on this tree and rappel down the cliff. Got a better plan?"

"That's not much of a plan. We don't know how they're armed or even if they're still in the room."

"Well, if they're not in the room, it won't make much difference, will it?"

"Good point, but I would like to know how they're armed first."

Scott turned to Nikita. "Father, did your men get a good look at them this morning? Did anyone see what they're armed with?"

"It was dark, but they carried pistols and some type gun that was black and square looking with a short barrel. It was ugly and looked like some type of large pistol."

Scott turned to Samuel. "Uzi, I bet!"

"I was afraid of that," Samuel said then turned to Nikita. "Do you have any weapons we could borrow?"

Nikita's eyebrows narrowed. "Weapons? Greek law is very strict." He paused and sighed. "Since the last group broke in, my cousin brought us a couple of pistols. I argued against it, but he was adamant. He gave us two, a 25-caliber auto and a Beretta. You can use them if you must, but I would prefer to avoid bloodshed."

Scott looked at him. "I would prefer that too, Father, but I can't let them kill Julia or your monks. We will use them only as a last resort, but these men are serious and won't hesitate to kill your monks."

Nikita turned to Vasillus. "See that Mr. Chad gets the weapons."

Scott asked Samuel. "Any other ideas?"

"Just what I always wanted to do, go crashing though a window and be turned into a sieve by 9mm slugs."

"Father, here's our plan." Scott leaned over to the monk and described what he wanted him to do. When he was done, he nodded to Samuel and called Vasillus over.

They could hear the distant sounds of thunder echoing off the rocks as the storm, which looked like it was really brewing up, approached.

Julia had fallen asleep as soon as she hit the mattress. The long day and longer night last night had taken its toll and she slept the sleep of the exhausted. She awoke with a start when a hand was quietly placed over her mouth. She felt the razor sharp edge of a knife at her throat and a voice she would never forget spoke, "If you make a sound, it will be the last you ever make. Do you understand?"

Her eyes fluttered open and leaning over her was the man who had kidnapped her and Scott at the dance. Dressed in a grey silk suit, his short-cropped hair belied the cruelty she saw in his eyes.

She nodded her understanding. "I should have left you a little stiffer in that cottage. Is this the way you repay mercy?"

He laughed. "Mercy you say. Is that what you showed those other two men? Your little stunt cost me a bundle, lady. We have chased you halfway across Greece and our employer is very angry. Important people have paid dearly because of your actions." He held up his wrist, which was in a cast. "We are going for a little ride. We shall finish this. Get up and get dressed."

She climbed out of bed. "Turn your head while I get dressed."

"Ha, forget it; you do not have anything I have not seen before. Get dressed now!"

She got up, turned her back to him and pulled her nightgown over her head. She could feel his leer as she bent over and put on her sweater and tugged up her jeans. Reaching down to put on her shoes, she grabbed the twenty-five caliber auto and slipped it into her boot. His breath on her neck and the point of the knife in her back stopped her cold.

"Not so fast. Now slowly slip it out and put it on the bed. If you make a fast move, this blade will sever your spinal cord."

She reached down and started to pull the little gun out with her right hand.

"Use your left hand!" His breath was on her neck, as she felt the point in her back.

"You don't miss a thing, do you?"

"I will not make a second mistake with you."

She reached down with her left hand.

The thin voice cautioned, "Fingers only."

She used her index finger and little finger to grab the gun and tossed it on the bed.

"Now, that is better. Stand against the wall." She backed against the wall as he went to the bed and retrieved the pistol. "This little thing has caused me a lot of trouble." He pulled back the slide, noticed it was loaded, checked the safety and held it up. "Out the door," he said motioning with the gun. "We are going for a ride."

They went out in the hallway where a man was waiting. She smiled at him. "Well if it isn't my old friend Antonio from Suez."

"No talking," the suit said to the feel of the point of the knife in her back.

They made their way down the hall and out into the night air. Antonio roughly shoved her up against another man in the back seat of an old Mercedes and they drove off toward the monastery. When they entered the parking area the driver doused the lights, and they made their way down the stairs then up the heights. They paused only a moment while Antonio picked the lock on the gate. A young monk was lighting lamps for morning vespers and saw them as they were making their way through the courtyard. Antonio jumped forward, pointing an Uzi at him before he could run off.

"Do not move or you will never say another prayer," Luigi said.

"What do you want with me?" the monk asked.

His voice like a cold knife said, "You are going to accompany us! Now move."

They made their way through the courtyard and down to the library, where they found two more monks starting their morning rituals. They herded them together when all of a sudden the lights went on.

A group of monks led by Father Nikita stood at the end of the passageway. Nikita called out, "If you harm them, eternal trouble will haunt your souls. What do you want with us, why have you come here?"

"We are going to do a little research, monk. Keep quiet and all will be well. Do not call the police; you can be sure your young protégés will not be signing any hymns or saying any prayers for you if you do. So keep quiet while we get what we came for."

"What is it you want? The last time you broke in here, you took priceless artifacts from our order. What do you want from us? Why will you not leave us alone. All we want is peace."

"It is none of your business, priest. Do what I say and your men will not be hurt. Remember, no police or—you do not want to find out!"

They pushed and pulled Julia and the three monks down to the archive room, using one of the monk's keys to open the lock. Antonio stood watch in the doorway, while the rest went into the room. Luigi took Julia over to the pile of letters from the time of Father Georges and said, "Now tell me what you know of all this." He pulled out the mirror and letter he'd taken on their previous visit and shoved them at her. "What is the third cave from the top and where is Kofina?"

"You're the one with the letter. How should I know? And what does that mirror have to do with anything?"

"Do not fence with me; you know far more than you are telling," he said, setting the mirror on a little stand by the window.

"We never had a chance to read all that stuff. We're as much in the dark as you are."

"You, monk, over here." He motioned for one of the monks and pulled out the packet of letters. "Translate this for me."

The young monk took the letter he was pointing at. "It is in an old dialect and hard to directly translate. I will do my best," he said as he translated the Greek for the man. They could hear the distant peal of thunder echoing over the plains through the window as dawn opened.

"What does it mean though? Do you know where Kofina is?"

The young monk answered. "I have never heard of Kofina. Perhaps one of the older monks knows something."

"Translate the rest of these for me." He demanded. He stood back and started a tape recorder, then pulled a pad of paper from his jacket.

The monk slowly translated each letter while the other men searched through the room. Forty minutes later when he was done with the letters, the leader said, "Read the first one again. Do not make any mistakes!"

The thunder rumbled closer and Julia could hear the rain splattering against the little window set in the wall. A lightening bolt lit the room and she moved a step toward the window.

"Stop where you are. Do not get any ideas," Luigi said.

He pulled her against the wall and looked out the window. The sky was a mottled green and a flash of lightening hit the mountain next to the window, momentarily blinding him.

Scott and Samuel tied the ropes to the tree at the top of the cliff, trying to judge the distance down to the window in the chamber. They had looped the ropes over their shoulders and through their legs. Scott chastised himself for not asking for gloves as he pushed off and rapelled down the face of the cliff. As he descended he looked left and right for foot or handholds so he could control his descent. Samuel rapelled down after him, bouncing down the cliff toward the window. He planned to enter the window on the opposite side from Scott. The storm had held off until now, but the skies suddenly opened up and the rain came down in torrents as the wind gusted, tossing them sideways as they descended.

Scott misjudged his speed; between the flashes of lightning he could see the light from the window coming up, but he was moving too fast to stop. He had tied the end of the rope around his waist, but without a proper harness, he knew he could break some ribs if he continued his fall. He retained some control with the rope looped around his shoulder but, with the rain blinding him and making the rope slick, he knew he was in trouble. He tried to reach a large rock that jutted out from the cliff, but a large gust blew him away as he reached out, twirling him into space and then slamming him back up against the cliff. As the gust subsided he slipped and swung back and forth, then grabbed a small shrub that was trying to grab a toehold in the rock. His momentum ripped the shrub out of his hand as he slid past, but he had slowed his descent enough to get a toehold onto a small ledge. He looked up at the shrub and window feeling blown.

The window was now above him by twenty feet, which appeared a long way, with the lightning flashing, the rain coming down and the wind buffeting him against the face of the cliff. Vertigo threatened to disorient him as he tried to maintain control while standing on a ledge five hundred feet above the valley floor, with one toe wedged into a crack in the rock.

Samuel was also having a tough time of it, though not as bad as Scott was. He had descended to his planned location and watched the gust push Scott past the outcrop.

Scott looked up and motioned Samuel to stay where he was, since he was in a position above and to the right of the window and Scott wanted to keep him there.

Scott tied a slipknot in a piece of rope, which he fastened around the main one and slowly made his way back up. He put his foot in the loop and, using brute strength and leverage, climbed back up to the small bush he'd grabbed at. A massive lightning bolt hit the spire of rock just above him, knocking him off his hold. He was temporarily blinded by the flash and disoriented by the noise, and it took all his strength to hang onto the rope. Scott shook his head and when his vision cleared, he looked up and saw that Samuel was still in position. Scott continued his climb up to a small ledge, where he paused a moment and massaged his burned hands. Looking up at the window, he calculated that he needed to climb about ten feet higher in order to enter the window. Hopefully their attention was still on the tunnel and the room, not on the window. After he rested a moment, he pulled himself higher with the toe loop and was now in position to repel into the window, when another lighting strike on the spire blinded him and the wind gusted to an unusual extent. He needed slack in the rope, so that when he swung out he would crash through the window feet first allowing him to enter the room with some degree of control. He climbed a little higher because his rope was stuck on a small rock, which caught the rope as he had descended past the bush. Shaking the rain off his head, he climbed up, pulled, and jerked back and forth on the rope, finally getting it to move past the rock. Once the rope came free, gravity rolled him to his right, scraping his face and hands against the cliff, and then swinging him up against Samuel, threatening to knock them both off the cliff.

Samuel reached out and steadied him, whispering, "What are you going to do for an encore? I'm getting tired of hanging around waiting for you!"

Scott smiled. "Do you have anything brilliant to say, or are you just going to hang around all day yourself?"

"You sure ordered up some good weather. I think we have the element of surprise," he said with the water cascading off his face. Samuel was in his element, Scott realized, and was having fun amidst it all.

Scott whispered, "When I get in position, I'll go first, you follow right after. You still have that 25-caliber auto with you?"

"Sure," he said as he patted the pocket of his jacket. "Don't leave home without it. Still have the Beretta?"

Scott reached down and felt behind him where he'd stuck the gun in his waistband and noticed it was empty. He frowned and looked at Samuel. "It must have fallen out when I grabbed at that bush. What are we going to do now?"

"Let me go first; I have the gun."

"No, I need you as backup. It's important that you come in immediately after me with the gun. I'm going to hang upside down and see if I can get a look at how they're positioned in the room. Hold on to my rope for me," Scott said.

Samuel grabbed Scott's rope; he had set a knot so he would only fall as far as the window. Scott then spun around upside down and lowered himself toward the window. When he was even with the window, he had to wipe the rain out of his eyes. Another flash of lighting temporarily blinded him. He waited for his eyes to adjust, then lowered himself the last six inches and peered into the window. Through the dim light, he could make out one man near the corner holding Julia and two others standing by the doorway. Where the fourth man was, he couldn't tell. A gust swung him on his rope and almost smashed his head into a large rock sticking out from the top edge of the window. Samuel pulled up on the rope just in time.

Scott pulled himself the rest of the way up and leaned over to Samuel. "I don't know where the fourth man is. One guy's holding Julia by the corner where the sword was and two are standing by the door. I think if I go through and roll left, I should be able to take the guy holding Julia. That should surprise the two by the door enough that when you come through, you should be able to take them. I can't think of a better plan right now. What about you."

"I didn't think this was that hot of a plan in the first place. We're out gunned, under manned, and the only thing we have going for us is surprise." Another lightning flash punctuated his last remark and Samuel looked up and grinned. "I think maybe we have something else on our side. If we could time our entrance to coincide with a lightening flash that might help."

"How am I going to do that? Would you mind explaining?"

"Luck might have something to do with it, but if you go right when you see a flash, they'll be blinded and the thunder will cover you when you go through the window."

"If that's the best you can come up with, I'd rather be on the other side. I'll wave my hand and signal when I'm ready," he said as he hopped along the face of the cliff. He untied the rope from his waist, which was dangerous with the five hundred foot fall. He couldn't risk being held back or snagged once he got through the window.

When he was in position he held the loose end of his rope, measuring out enough, so when he dropped down, the rope would arrest his fall and swing him feet first through the window. Scott then waited on the weather. The main part of the storm was now passing off to the north and the sky above seemed to be clearing some. It was tiring, holding his feet against the cliff, with nothing holding him but a rope and with a five hundred-foot fall below. He looked up at the sky again as a large dark cloud came racing up from the south, flashing lightning and spitting rain. The front hurtled toward him and the wind came like a small hurricane, plastering him against the cliff, pressing his face against the cold wet stone.

A massive lightning bolt hit the spire just off to his left. Wasting no time, he launched off the cliff, saying a silent prayer that he'd judged it right. The flash blinded him and he hardly noticed as his feet crashed though the glass, accompanied by the most violent clap of thunder he'd ever heard. He rolled to his left and landed on the balls of his feet almost right in front of Antonio, who was holding Julia. Anger boiled in his veins. He lashed out with his foot, kicking Antonio in the shin, hearing the bone crack as Antonio screamed as he fell to the floor. Julia quickly realized what was happening and grabbed Antonio's Uzi from his hands as he writhed on the floor. The two men standing by the door turned toward Scott at Antonio's cry of pain. Scott dashed over and looked down at Antonio, as Samuel came through the window holding the 25-caliber auto, hitting the floor and rolling to the right. Another lightening bolt hit the spire right outside the window, lighting the inside of the room like a strobe light. A violent gust of wind blew in, scattering papers everywhere as Samuel kneeled and let off two snapshots, felling the two men guarding the monks by the door.

A lightning flash revealed Luigi in his grey suit, standing to the side of the window, holding an Uzi at Scott's chest. A smile lit his face as he motioned Scott to move away from Antonio. Scott silently obeyed which opened Julia's line of sight. She quickly pulled the trigger of the Uzi she'd picked up, stitching the man across the middle and forcing him through the broken window to fall five hundred feet to the plain below.

The first to recover was Samuel, who said, "I told you it was a good plan! I just didn't want to hang around out there in the rain." The water dripped off his lank hair and ran into his eyes as he smiled.

Julia rushed over, threw her arms around Scott, and kissed him full on the lips, threatening to break his ribs with the fierceness of her hug. The monks came running down the hall and stood in the entrance watching. Father Nikita stood in the doorway with Vasillus and slowly started clapping as he took in the scene.

CHAPTER 33
THIRD CAVE FROM THE TOP

The ruckus didn't die down for weeks. The citizens of the little village gathered at the tavernas to discuss the happenings over and over again, keeping business brisk. The news media tried unsuccessfully to interview the abbot. Scott found one benefit from all the media attention: he was no longer incognito if he ever had been. He was now able to freely use his credit card and obtain a money order from his secretary.

The afternoon sunshine gave the promise of the hot summer to come, the trees in full bloom even though still early in May. There was a quiet stillness to the day. After sitting up late the night before reviewing all the clues they had assembled so far, they planned to take a look at the old monastery at Kofina. Scott was enjoying a cup of coffee as he and Julia sat waiting for Samuel at the little restaurant on the roadway between the monastery and town. Samuel had gone to Trilaka to bring back the rope and climbing gear Scott had ordered.

Taking another sip of his coffee, he turned to Julia. "Vasillus said the Germans bombed the old monastery to rubble trying to ferret out the partisans during World War II. I thought we were on the right track and hoped we would have found out more. The whole trip seems like a waste . . . except for getting back together with, you, that is."

A smile lit her face. "I don't know what clue we're missing, but I think you're right. We need to look at the old monastery and see what we can find. The trouble is, the monastery was built four hundred years after Mohammed died. I don't see how he could have hidden something there. It doesn't make any sense."

Samuel showed up with the gear an hour and a half before sunset. Scott walked up to him and asked, "How much rope did you bring?"

"Three hundred meters should be more than enough."

"Let's go then. Did you bring flashlights?"

Opening the back of the Fiat, he pointed. "Everything on your list. I even stopped at what passes for the local hardware store and bought some extra batteries."

Julia jumped in the driver's seat. "This car's too small for all this stuff. I'll be glad to get rid of it somewhere along this trip. I've grown to like the old thing and it does keep on going, but it's still way too small."

"Drive up the hill and pull off on that little track we saw earlier. Vasillus said there's a path to the old monastery that winds along the bottom of the ravine," Scott said.

Pulling the car off the road, they bounced down the rutted track and parked between some trees and overgrown old bushes. Unloading their gear, they each took a bundle of rope, Samuel and Scott splitting up the heavier stuff. Once loaded, they hiked down the trail which twisted and turned between old cypress trees that were growing in the tight ravine. A rivulet ran between the stones and soon became a brook where the water flowed over the rocks in its rush and tumble to join the river in town.

Fifteen minutes later, Scott paused and looked at the sketch Vasillus gave him. "Up there, up between those rocks on the left, it should be up there somewhere," he said as he pointed up a steep side ravine.

Samuel looked up at the overgrown trail. "Quite a place for a monastery; inaccessible, remote and private."

Julia, who had been subdued ever since coming back from Thessaloniki, quietly added, "The monks chose these spots for the solitude. They wanted to find a place where they could get away from the world, to get closer to the spirit of God. Vasillus and I talked some, while Father Nikita was meeting with you and the police after you saved me. He is strong and it amazed me that he could throw off the horror of that whole thing so easily and quietly talk about his faith, especially to someone who was raised Jewish and an Israeli, too."

Scott said, "I think he's one of those true holy men. They come along every generation and come in all shapes and sizes. He doesn't think he has a monopoly on it, but hopes the spirit has a monopoly on him. He fervently believes in Christianity and his Orthodox faith, but would gladly talk with anyone. He's one of those men you want to be like and ask yourself, 'What does he have that I don't?' It's refreshing to be around him. He once said to me when we had a quiet moment together, 'Ah, Scott, just for a glimpse of heaven, that's all I ask!' He also reminds me of Father Basil, who said, 'You know, if you don't live it, you don't believe it.' They are two of a kind in some ways."

Samuel was huffing and puffing, for of course he'd taken the heaviest load. He added, "All this jaw cracking about heaven and faith, when what I'd really like is a glimpse of that monastery about now!"

Scott laughed. "Ah, Samuel you're one to warm the heart. Somehow I know the world's the same and nothing ever changes when you're with me. I can always rely on you, for you're solid as a rock. Someday something might break through that armor of yours and then you'll have to choose a different kind of armor."

"Well, I hope it's soft and cuddly and not cold and cranky. You know what the good book says, better to sleep on the roof than inside the house with a cranky woman."

Julia stuttered, "Samuel, why . . . why you're quoting verses now. What has gotten into you?"

"I went to Sunday school. Just picked up a few other things along the way to corrupt my character, that's all. By the way, it looks like we're here," he said as they came to a little clearing at the base of one of the spires. "Look up, see the cave?" He pointed and dropped his load. "Aren't those old ladders and ropes?"

"I think you're right. It matches the description Vasillus gave us," Scott said.

Scott and Julia piled their gear by Samuel's and looked up in the remaining light, trying to plan a route.

"I think we can ascend right here. The rock looks solid from a distance but it's actually full of cracks and holes. Let's move. I'll go first. Samuel, belay me. I shouldn't need more than 100 meters of rope. When I get up, I'll pull up the supplies. Julia next then Samuel bring up the rear. Everyone agreed?"

"No problem, let's go," Julia said as she measured out a rope.

Scott put on his climbing shoes, attached a flashlight with a lanyard to his harness and started up the cliff, which looked smooth from a distance but was full of cracks and crevasses where one could put his hands and feet if careful. It was a more technical climb than the climb down from the top of Meteora, where he'd hung down the cliff. Scott had to find hand and footholds, and place auto-cams in the rock in case he fell. An auto-cam was a spring-loaded device that was placed in a crack. When you pulled on one, the metal jaws expanded, wedging it in the crack and gripping the rock tighter. They were more ecological than pitons and didn't deface the rock. Threading his rope through each auto-cam, he slowly made his way up the cliff. The sun was setting and Samuel was having trouble guiding him to where he could place his holds. A large part of the climb was by feel and he soon made it to the first cave. He pulled himself in, anchored the rope to the remains of an old winch the monks had used, threw down an end and yelled down, "Send the gear up first."

Samuel bundled the extra rope and gear and attached it to the rope Scott lowered. He quickly pulled it up to the cave. Scott threaded the rope through the old winch and lowered an end to Samuel, then pulled him slowly up as he removed the auto-cams from the wall. They lowered the rope and pulled Julia up with no trouble. Standing at the entrance about seventy feet off the valley floor, Scott pulled the rope up. "No one can easily follow us now."

The cave was a narrow grotto with a pair of niches carved into the walls on either side as sleeping platforms for the monks who'd once inhabited it. Old Byzantine paintings on the walls were now faded from years in the moisture and temperature changes inside the cavern. The cave went back about thirty feet and a small altar sat near the end in a little alcove. It was to too dark to climb higher, so they decided to spend the night in the cave.

Julia explored the rear and took picture of a painting of Mary looking at Jesus on the cross that was on the back wall behind the altar. Built into the wall on each side of the painting were two small niches carved from of the rock and built up with mortar. Some of the mortar was coming loose in a couple of the blocks, probably from the shelling that destroyed the church up above. The altar stood alone, carved out of a solid block of white limestone with fluted sides and a flat top.

Scott was startled by the flash. "It's getting dark. Someone might see the flash, so please don't take any more pictures."

"I wasn't thinking, Scott. I'm sorry . . . I must be tired."

He walked to the entrance and looked down. "It's okay. I don't see anyone down there." He couldn't see the road from where he stood; a feeling of being thrown back a thousand years in time crept over him as he looked out over the stone forest. "It's getting late, and the sun gets up early. I don't know if anyone could sleep, but we probably ought to get started at first light. Let's eat something and get some sleep."

"What do you think they did for a bathroom?" Julia asked.

Samuel turned to her. "Probably just went over the edge."

"We'll go in back after we eat; you can then make your own arrangements," Scott said.

"What's for dinner? I'm starved," Samuel asked.

"Look in that blue backpack. Vasillus packed some food for us, said it would save us from having to go to town for supplies."

Samuel went over to the pile of equipment they'd hauled up and pulled out the backpack. "Man after my own heart. Vino Meteora or something like that. Some olives, cheese and sandwiches, which I bet are chicken, which must be the national bird of Greece, and some salad. Excellent choice, my dear Vasillus," he said as he held up the bottle of wine. " I think I could become a monk if this keeps up."

"You a monk! Even if you had a change of heart, I don't think that would be your calling. Maybe a bell ringer or something," Scott said.

The next morning they ate some of the olives, bread and cheese and started their climb. Scott took the lead, then pulled Julia and Samuel up on the rope.

The second cave was much rougher than the first, being only a small hollowed out chamber with four sleeping niches carved out of the rock. After exploring the cave, they continued their climb to the third cave with their anticipation growing about the riddle. They were soon standing in the cave, which was more disappointing than the second. The only difference was the pictures on the walls. The cave was narrow and rough, and a short passage led through the rock and out onto the top of the spire. Walking through the passageway they found the bombed out chapel surrounded by a few stunted cypress trees in a little cleft of the rock.

The remains of the chapel site stood on a small level area on the shoulder of the stone spire. Julia stood in the morning sun gazing, around at the remains of the church and asked, "Why do you think they took the time to bomb this place?"

"Because the partisans had a hideaway up here and used the place as base while making attacks on the German garrisons during the war. Why go to the trouble of sending up troops when you can send in a Messerschmitt and drop a couple of bombs? Can you imagine trying to take this place by climbing up with troops? You could hold off an army with just a few men if you placed them right," Samuel said.

Scott added, "Samuel's parents fought as partisans against the Russians and Nazis during the war. He lost his father to the Russians and his mother escaped and helped fight the Nazi's in Italy after escaping from Poland."

"I'm sorry, Samuel," Julia said, "I know how you must feel; I lost my parents in the camps after the war." She paused then took a deep breath. "I should have told you about Hasid, too. I think he was shocked to see me. I knew him when we were about to go to college in France. I spent a summer in Paris and met him with a bunch of other students and became friends." She looked at Scott's expression. "It's not what you think. I was only his friend; we were not lovers. He may have wanted more, but I was not ready for something like that. I comforted him when he received the news of his father's death and that's the last I ever saw of him until that night in the tent. It's probably twelve years or so since I've seen him."

"I believe you and that's okay, just a small world sometimes. What I really wanted to say is you're one of us now. Maybe you still work for the Mosad, I may not like it, but it's okay. You're one of us; you're part of the team!"

"You don't know how much that means to me," she said, as she started to cry. "I never wanted to deceive you and really believe in your work. The only thing that's been rough . . . well, I guess there were two things. The first was having to report to my superior, so he knew what was going on—he only wanted to arrange protection for us. I was assigned to protect you, but I've found that you don't need much protection. I felt dishonest when I did it as if I were breaking our trust."

"I told you that's fine with me," Scott said.

"The second thing is . . . oh, how do I say it, the . . . spiritual side of the whole thing. What I mean is, I was brought up Jewish, but not very strictly. I mean culturally Jewish, but not religiously, if you know what I mean. We've been to three monasteries and I've met all kinds of monks and even though they're all Orthodox, they seem to really believe in God. I almost became a Christian once a few years after coming to Israel. There was an American evangelist who was going across Israel preaching. He went from town to town with his message. I resented him at first, but I went and listened with some friends one night and talked with him. Two nights later I fell to my knees and thought I needed this Jesus, but didn't know what to do. A couple of months later, I saw Billy Graham on TV saying much the same things and started to cry . . . I had the feeling I was missing something, only I wasn't sure what it was. Do you know what I mean?"

"I've pondered things like that myself," Scott said. "But the scientist in me is always stuck wondering if the Bible is real. Oh, don't get me wrong. I believe Jesus walked the earth and all that, but it's always been hard for me to believe some of the actual stories—the flood, the Garden of Eden and literal six-day creation."

"None of the men talked about that stuff. That's in all the old Jewish books."

"For obvious reasons since we took on this search, I've looked at the story of Abraham, Isaac and Ishmael and the story about Sarah and Hagar. I probably wouldn't have if it wasn't for some of the things Father Basil said to me. Like being destined to do this job."

"Basil seems like one of those true men of God you meet maybe once or twice in your life," Julia said. "But what about Abraham?"

"Maybe you know the story. Sarah was Abraham's wife and an angel promised him that he would have a baby in his old age. He didn't believe the angel because he and his wife were so old. His wife didn't believe the angel either but wanted her husband to have heirs, so she took matters into her own hands like an industrious wife should and sent her slave, Hagar to Abraham. Hagar became pregnant and had a baby boy, which Abraham named Ishmael. Abraham's wife Sarah became jealous of Hagar when she and Abraham had their own son, the son that was promised by the angel, and she made Abraham kick Hagar and her son out of camp. You see, Sarah didn't want her slave's son around competing for her son's inheritance."

"She made her husband kick Ishmael out of camp. What did he think about that?"

"He wasn't too happy about it, but finally agreed to send Hagar and Ishmael away. The story says that the angel appeared to him in a dream and told him they would be all right, so he sent Hagar and Ishmael out into the desert. Hagar ran out of water and sat down crying, waiting to die. The angel then appeared to Hagar and told her not to fear, that God was going to make Ishmael into a great nation and then told her where to find water—so she and her son lived."

Scott paused and looked over at Samuel and Julia. "The Arabs reckon their line back to Abraham through Ishmael who was born from Hagar. The Jews reckon their line back to Abraham but through Isaac, who was born from Sarah. They're actually distant cousins and have much in common. They have a lot more in common than say a Korean and an African or a German and Chinese. What really interested me was that God was going to make both of them into great nations. It baffled me . . . but I digress, back to your other question; something seems to be working at my heart, too. As a scientist, I usually don't believe in that kind of thing because you can't touch it or figure it out. Some of my best friends are astronomers, but they do believe in that type of thing. When I asked them why, they told me to take a look around. 'Look out on the universe,' they would say, 'Then come back, and ask again.' Do you know what I mean?"

Julia looked up at him with the beginnings of a smile on her face. "I know what you mean, even though it's hard to put into words. Sometimes I feel as if I need to make a choice. I can choose to go one way or go the other."

Samuel stood there listening and pondering. "Scott, you're a scientist and all your life you've used logic as a basis for everything you do. Are you going to give that up and start chasing legends and spirits?"

Scott smiled. "You've been my dearest friend for many years and I wouldn't deceive you ever. I'm not going to start chasing spirits; at least I don't think so. Legends are what made us go to Afghanistan in the first place. Don't you remember the legend of the old king's mine and how it was hidden in the mountains of Capri Du Stan, and how the British soldiers from the eighteenth century tried to find it?"

"It's not that type of legend I'm talking about; it's this religious stuff. All legends are probably founded on the truth somewhere but this stuff, it seems hokey to me. You're a scientist! Your life's built on finding the facts and the hypothesis that supports the truth. That's what I'm talking about, nothing more and nothing less. You're not going to start saying the world's six thousand years old now and forget the evidence to support the obvious, are you?"

"No, Samuel, but I will quote the Bible to you! 'In the beginning, God made the heavens and earth. Now the earth was formless and empty, darkness was over the surface of the deep and the spirit of God was hovering over the waters.' This was before there was light; there wasn't even a day back then, as we know it. Somewhere else it says, 'I tell you the truth, a day for the Lord is like a thousand years and a thousand years is like a day.' For God to make the universe, he would have to be outside of time, as we know it."

"But that's not what I mean. I guess I even believe that God made the earth, especially the sunsets, but all that other stuff."

"Look into the heavens, Samuel, look at the galaxies and nebulae, astronomers know more about this than I do; I've talked with them! Every astronomer I've ever met believes in God. They can't help it when they peer through those great telescopes of theirs and see the wonder of the universe looking back at them. Days weren't days back then, not as we know them. Remember God created the galaxies, which are millions of light years away, so he has to be outside of our frame of time; his reference to time must be so different that our feeble minds can't understand it."

"When you put it like that I can almost see what you find fascinating about it. But I think a lot of the fundamentalists and Catholics would have a problem with your line of thinking."

"Maybe they would, Samuel, maybe they would, but the wonder of it is, there aren't any around here right now. I feel . . . feel as if something quiet, peaceful and wonderful is touching me, drawing me toward new insights, helping me understand."

Samuel stretched. "Well, let's explore the rest of this place and see if we can come up with anything. I think we would need a major excavation to find anything up here with all this rubble anyway. Vasillus was right when he said the place probably wasn't worth the trip."

Exploring the area where the church once stood all they found were piles of rubble and the remains of an old winch. Eating a light lunch after searching the area, they sat on the rocks in the sun.

Samuel scratched his head. "I don't get it? I thought we followed every clue. There should be something up here. What did the riddle say again?"

Scott stopped what he was doing and looked at him. "Which riddle?"

"The one from the first chamber."

"'Look in the holy place that Georges held dear.'"

"Well, we're here in Meteora. We've looked at his letters with Vasillus and we've found nothing!"

Julia's stammered, "That's not . . . what it said, it went something like this:

'Follow the second marker to Hellas and near
Go to the holy place that Georges held dear
Your need for Grace will wipe away fear
The lady's reflection will soon make it clear
Long hair is a woman's glory he said
I said that she should then cover her head
She longed for the day when she would be free
To worship a lord on her bended knee
The reflection is the key to marker number two
The woman amongst you will know what to do'

Or something like that. It goes on about the law. I think we're close, but in the wrong place. Remember the mirror from the monastery, property of a lady, I said? She also wrote a poem, what did it say? Something about the third cave from the top, didn't it?"

She paused and put her hands on her hips with a smile. "Well, where's the third cave from the top? Why, the first cave on the way up! If this is the holy place that Georges held dear, then it's somewhere down in that first cave. Remember the altar down there. That could be from the year six or seven hundred, possibly from the time of Georges. This little bombed out church was built way after his time, probably in the year 1400. It's not nearly old enough. The Lady of Ioannia is wrapped up in this somehow. I'm not sure but think we have to search the first cave again, the third cave from the top."

"Well, we're sure not finding anything here. Are you sure you're not just acting out the verse, 'the woman amongst you will know what to do,'" Scott said with a grin.

She didn't even blink but went on, "We have to bring back that mirror. I think that's the key. We should ask Vasillus. Remember the reflection, how it was distorted and curved as if it were heated or something. Actually a very poor mirror for a lady!"

"So you think you have it, huh. Well, maybe you do. You're the woman amongst us, that's for sure. I haven't noticed any others around here, have you Samuel?" Scott said.

"I thought I saw a few sunning themselves on the rocks over there awhile ago," Samuel said as he pointed to the edge of the cliff. "But I haven't seen them in awhile. Want me to go look?"

Scott laughed. "Think you're part of an ancient poem now? Some of this stuff might be going to your head, but I can't think of anything else, so let's give it a try."

Making their way down to the middle cave, they stopped and looked around a minute, but found nothing new. Continuing their descent, they came to the first cave where they'd spent the night. When they entered the chamber, they walked back to the old altar and carefully looked over the two niches in the wall where the stone blocks were loosely mortared.

Scott remarked, "There might be something behind these niches where the blocks are mortared. It's hard to tell."

Turning to Samuel, he said, "I don't understand it but think Julia's idea is worth a shot. Would you go back up to the monastery and ask Vasillus if we could borrow the mirror?"

"Sure, but I think we're at a dead end. From the looks of the rock in this chamber and the rock at the base, there couldn't be much behind there. I think they just added those blocks to square it off. I'll get the mirror from Vasillus and be right back, shouldn't take more than an hour."

Scott held the rope while Samuel descended then pulled it back up. "Call up when you get back and I'll lower the rope."

"Be careful up there," Samuel said as he waved and made his way back up to the car.

❉   ❉   ❉   ❉   ❉   ❉   ❉   ❉

"I do not care, Hasid. I told you. No, I ordered you to keep an eye on them and make sure they followed my orders."

"You kept control over the men; you ordered me to not interfere with your orders. You explicitly ordered me not to change your orders."

"Do not correct me, Hasid. We have lost four men. Bestin is going to be upset that his man Luigi is gone. He did many difficult things for Bestin in the past and I wonder if Bestin is going to follow through on his donation now."

"The infidel's money! He agreed to make a donation to our cause? I counseled you before not to do business with them."

"Business is business, I have told you that in the past. Money has no color, it only stands for power. Working with Bestin and Farrell has reaped wonderful benefits for our organization in the past and will in the future. I have many sources for funds and must use them all if our revolution is to be a success."

"But, General, to be in league with the infidel. They support Israel, too."

"What do I care who else they support. They are interested in Chad and they are on our side in this. They do not want their little nest disrupted. We can trust them on this."

"So you say, but be careful of the viper one holds in the hand."

"I am careful of them. I do not trust them; I just trust their money and their intent on stopping Chad. They want to keep their power. To know one's enemy is to know what he will do next. That is why we can do business with them."

"Momar and Sa'id are now dead. What of their families?"

"Since when did you start caring about things like that?" "General, I believe in our soldiers and what they fight for. I may be rough with them, but I do believe in the quality of a good soldier and the family that supports him."

"I will make a donation to their widows. Will that make you happy?"

"That would be a good start. We now need to plan what to do next about Chad. He is still in Greece and my man tells me that he has taken off into the mountains. I have ordered him to follow him, but we may need to get a team in there quickly. I need your authority to get some men moving now."

"You have it, take whoever you need, move quickly and this time do it your way, I will trust you. Who do you want to take?"

"Bakkar, Mishka Abd and Ali, they are ready to move. I will have them on the first flight and they should be in place by nightfall."

"Good, now move."

❋ ❋ ❋ ❋ ❋ ❋ ❋ ❋

Scott smiled then turned back to where Julia was standing and said, "Alone again. Last time we were alone, we were at a dance and then kidnapped. I hope nothing so drastic happens."

She walked over, put her arms around his neck then pulled his head down and kissed him full on the lips.

"There, I just had to get that over with," she said with a smile, as she drew back. "Now maybe I can keep my mind on my work and look around this cave some more, get some fresh ideas."

Scott stood there dumbfounded, watching as she walked back to the rear of the chamber. His mind was on anything but work. He saw her in a different light, not the light of the dim cave, but a light in his mind's eye, someone precious and wonderful, full of life and overflowing with an effervescent spirit. The feel of her lips still lingered like a burning sensation as he watched her move about the cave with her easy rhythm and grace. He tried to shake off the sensation, stood there lost in thought, when she finally noticed what her handiwork had done.

"Oh, I didn't mean to distract you. I'm sorry, Scott. I have been so distracted and feel close to you, like that time we were at the dance and . . . there's something more. I didn't mean . . . well, yes, I did. It's done and I don't want to take it back! I just had to get that over with." She noticed his wry look. "Don't worry, it's still on my mind, but I can work now. It might be selfish of me but . . . well, I wanted to do that, if that's okay?"

All he could do was shake his head. "I'm on sensory overload. All this talk about God and this search we're on and I'm afraid to voice my thoughts about what I think of you. I feel we're close to finding some answers to this riddle." He walked over to her, wrapped his arms around her and lifted her off her feet. He gave it his best effort. Her long red hair came out of the bun, falling in a golden halo around her shoulders.

Tilting her head back after the kiss, he said, "Enough. We've work to do and then we have to talk!"

He put her down. "Okay, back to work then."

Taking out his knife, he scraped the mortar from around the blocks. "I don't think there's anything here! These blocks are about two feet wide, but the slope of the ceiling and the rest of the cave . . . I just think we are on the wrong track. Samuel's right, they just squared off the end of the original cave. We've run into a dead end, I'm sorry to say."

Looking around the cave for the next hour they poked here and there and soon heard Samuel calling from below, the hour going by a lot quicker than they'd realized.

Scott went to the entrance and saw Samuel standing below with Vasillus.

"Yo, Scott, I brought back a friend," Samuel called up.

"Vasillus, nice of you to come. Remember the place?"

"I've been up there before. I explored around here when I was a kid and once put the old ladders together and got all the way to the top."

"I'll throw down the rope. Put it around your waist; we'll pull you up."

Scott threw down the rope and threaded it through the remains of the old winch, pulling up Vasillus and then with his help, Samuel.

Vasillus looked around the old hermitage and exclaimed, "Looks smaller than I remember."

Samuel laughed. "Well, you're probably a lot bigger now."

"Everything seems the same though. It doesn't appear that anyone's been here in years."

"Did you bring the mirror?" Julia asked.

Vasillus took a bundle wrapped in a cloth, tied with a leather thong out of his pack and handed it to Julia. "I didn't want to risk anything happening to it; it's very valuable. What do you want with it?"

Scott answered, "We thought that it might be part of the clues we're looking for. Something in the message from the first chamber and how to find the second marker. We're not sure we are on the right track." He looked over at Julia. "Take the mirror and look at the mural. See if you can figure anything out."

She walked to the back of the little cavern holding the mirror. She turned around and looked at the mural with the mirror. "I don't see anything. As a matter of fact, it looks worse and almost gives me a headache."

She handed Scott the mirror and he looked at various combinations, getting the same results.

"Try looking cross-eyed at it. Like you taught me," she said.

"That type of pattern's not here," he said. "I think we're looking in the wrong place. Something tells me it has nothing to do with these murals or the niches behind the altar. I just don't get it. Those paintings aren't old enough. Georges may have been here before the paintings were done. The only place something could be is behind those mortared blocks. We'd have to pull them out of the wall and that would ruin the paintings. What do you think, Vasillus?"

"Those paintings are very old and part of my country's heritage. Unless you have a real good reason—I would have to say no. Couldn't you get behind by tunneling in from the side?"

"Sure, if I had mining equipment and about three days." Scott turned and looked at the group. "We wouldn't be able to keep it a secret if we started bringing saws and drills up here and throwing stone down to the valley floor!"

Samuel looked at him. He was tired from hiking up and down the trail and was leaning against the altar as he listened to their conversation. He stretched an arm up and shifted his weight—when the altar slid on the floor.

Their heads snapped around at the sound and they noticed the look of astonishment on Samuel's face.

"What was that?" Scott said.

"Beats me! I was just holding up the altar, taking a little rest while you geniuses were figuring out where the second marker might be. Then the altar moved when I stretched."

Scott strode over to where Samuel was standing. "Well, quit resting and put your back into it. Come on, Vasillus, this won't hurt anything."

"Moving the holy altar! I don't know if we should do that," Vasillus replied.

"Oh, come on. We can always slide it back again," Scott said.

"I suppose you're right, but we Orthodox place a lot of significance on the shape of things. The altar's a sacred object. Promise to put it back?"

"I promise, now push!" Scott said with his voice rising.

The three men pushed on the corner of the altar where Samuel had been leaning and, with a groan and grinding of stone, the heavy altar slid away from its resting place, revealing a dark opening and a spiral stairway descending into the dark depth of the mountain.

Julia stood there with a look of wonder on her face. "I was beginning to lose hope. You astonish me, Scott." She turned to Samuel and laughed. "What would we do without you, Samuel. Trying to hold up the altar!"

They gathered around the opening while Samuel shined his flashlight down.

Scott said, "Everyone bring a flashlight. Samuel, bring some rope in case we need it. Julia, grab the cameras and remember the mirror. Let's go."

As Scott descended the stairs he couldn't get the kiss off his mind. *Why was I so distracted by a kiss?* He thought as he tried concentrate on the spiraling stone steps. He wondered how many feet had trod the stairs over the years. He counted a hundred steps. The shaft never wavering in its construction, width or height. The stairs ended and opened into a small cavern carved from the gut rock of the mountain.

Scott turned to his companions, "Mohammed's second marker."

Julia let out the breath she had been holding and asked, "What makes you think this is the second marker?"

"Look," Scott said as he shined his light at the end of the cave. There, standing covered with dust, was a statue of a bearded man holding two large stone tablets. The statue was carved from a grey granite that wasn't the same as the rock from the mountain. "Meet Moses, law giver and author."

"All I see is an old crude statue, admittedly it looks like it is probably Moses since he's holding two stone tablets—I'll give you that—but what gives you the idea that it's the second marker?"

"I'll show you—it's simple as all things are in the end."

Walking over to the statue, he shined his flashlight on the floor in front of it. Brushing the accumulated dust away, he stood back and pointed. There cut into the rock were these letters written in Arabic:

I brought you out of slavery, I am your God. You shall take no other.

Do not make any idol in the form of any other thing, on heaven or earth or any thing under or in the waters, do not bow down to them for I am a jealous God.

Do not take your God's name in vain, for he is a holy God.

Keep holy the Sabbath, you shall work six days and finish all your work and labor, the seventh day is to be kept holy so that you remember the Lord.

Honor your father and mother, as is fitting in the Lord.

Do not murder or kill, for I your Lord have made all men in our image.

Do not commit adultery, for what the Lord has joined, man must not separate

Do not steal, for I feed the birds and beasts, I will care for you, trust in me.

Do not bear false witness against your neighbor or anyone else.

Do not envy your neighbor's house, neighbor's wife, your neighbor's servants or his cattle or camel or any thing that belongs to your neighbor.

"It looks like a paraphrased version of the Ten Commandments," Julia said.

"Look at the rest," Scott said as he brushed away more of the dirt and debris.

> Solomon knew, and then lost his heart.
> God had given him such a good start
> Wisdom did grow, and was then lost to love
> Look to the mountains, that are covered above
> Make up a new song, with the lute and with lyre
> Sing it to him, of your heart's true desire
> Dancing and singing, of days still to come
> When brothers unite, and bang the new drum
> My people will cry, and then they will know
> That I the Lord have made them just so
> They may choose, why the world is so cruel
> Then they may choose, what is called golden rule
> The brothers and sisters, must soon all unite
> Singing together, in the mist of the night
> Singing a song planned long ago
> I the Lord, say it is so
> I call my daughter up out of Cush
> From the blue river, the banks and the rush
> The river so blue gives birth to new life
> I tell you tis so, it will end all the strife
> When will this day come, only I know
> The heart must be ready, and not just for show
> My servant did look for that day to come
> Bringing the law that beats the big drum
> The law you say, our faults lay so open
> The law is the way to make your hearts broken
> Only one has kept all of the law
> Hearken, dear people, and brace for the fall
> Listen to this, dear brothers and sisters
> The mountain that sighs, and wind that just whispers
> Gold and onyx and spices so dear
> Look to my house, and go without fear
> Bind them up, and tell them the truth
> Some will not listen, but that is forsooth

Danger is around, but I will protect
Watch for the viper, and do not neglect
Love will guide you, oh sleepers, awake
Trust in your savior, and never to shake
Peace is there, for those who will listen
The land will then shine and lay there and glisten.

"A rather rough translation, but I think it's right. Take pictures of everything then let's get moving, I don't want Abu and his men to catch us up here and don't want Luke and Alex to start worrying. The sooner we get back the better."

Samuel who had known Scott for a long time didn't argue. He took the digital camera and started documenting the room.

Julia asked, "Well, what does it all mean, Scott? How do you know there's not more here?"

"I never thought the writings were here as I said before. The trail leads to Ethiopia. That's where the answer will be found. We just didn't know where to look. What the answer is, I don't know. This is just the second marker to the writings. It could lead us or others astray or help guide us to the right spot. We need to go to Ethiopia, as I said. I'm not sure where yet, but this will tell us where once we sift through it all."

"But the first marker was written cryptically and this one's in plain language. Doesn't that strike you as odd?" Julia asked.

"Now that you say it—yes. The woman amongst you will know what to do! What do you suggest?" he said smiling at her.

"I don't know, take the pictures and look around some more?"

"Well,   get   moving   then."
He turned to Samuel. "When you're done, brush the dirt back. I don't want it to look like we were here.

"Julia, take a video so we can review it later. We may have found all there is. I'm kind of disappointed. I think you're right about something more, I just don't know what, but you never know. Maybe we should look at the walls with the mirror or something. Do you have it in your pack?"

"Yes, I'll get it when I'm done taping." Pulling the camera out of her pack, she slapped in a battery pack and proceeded to video the inside of the little cave and statue. She took a long sequence of the writing on the floor and then proceeded to tape the statue and walls. The bright light from the camera played over the lichen encrusted walls. The lichen was mottled green and white and spotted everywhere on the walls, growing well in the moist environment. She was about to put away the camera when she gasped. "Look—look at the wall!"

Scott turned when he heard her shout. "What are you so excited about? Keep your voice down," he whispered with a hiss, but came over to where she was pointing.

She lowered her voice. "Look at the wall where I play the light on it. What do you see?"

"I don't see anything but the rock on the wall. What am I supposed to see?"

Samuel stood behind them as Julia gestured at the wall. He turned and said, "I don't see anything either. What are we looking for?"

Exasperation rose in her voice. "Look at the lichen. Stand back and you'll see it."

"Amazing," Scott said when he noticed. "I can't believe it. Samuel, take pictures of the walls, too. We have to be quick and get out of here."

Julia stood up, put her hands on her hips, and asked, "Is that all you're going to say?"

"What else do you want me to say," Scott said with a half smile.

"I want you to translate what it says, of course," she said.

"Okay, it says this:

> The Horn of Africa, inland and west,
> Follow the river to the mountain that's best.
> Follow the cleft that cleaves through the earth.
> There near to Ghion and the rivers that flow
> Into the dust and then you will know.
> The mountain so high, the river so blue
> The rivers all run to the sea, it is true
> You know that I am the Lord, the I am
> Ghion it runs, reflecting like no other
> On a tall mountain, to the cave of the wonder
> The wind does just blow, through the cave it is known
> The cave of the wind, where my people came home
> Cry of the soul, the Psalmist did know
> The wind raises the call, to all brothers and sisters
> To unite under one, and call all to vespers
> There in the cave a wind blows you hear
> There you will find the writings so dear
> The words of wisdom to fill all your souls
> Take care to share them so that all mankind does grow
> Growing in learning of our Lord that we know.
> Do not forget the key to my ward
> Crusader of Love and soldier of Lord
> To Jerusalem he went and then to abode

To his dearest lady and Hellas some say
On island, their love was lost and then they pray
Her reflection so bright, you know tis the key
To understanding why he is one, two and three
Her love did lead my servant to search
Finding the truth, for all of mankind
The truth of the savior that fills all your mind
They will sing of her wonderful love
Reflection of her hair in sunsets above
Telling this tale of a wonderful maid
A woman so wonderful, songs were just sung
Her hand in his, you know it's begun.

"Look—over there on the left—it looks like a map. Doesn't that look like the horn of Africa, and isn't that the rift valley where it comes up out of Ethiopia and joins the Red Sea?" Scott said.

"See the lake and river," Julia said.

Julia, have you looked at the paintings with the mirror yet?" Scott asked.

"What a dummy. I totally forgot that the mirror reverses the image." She took out the Lady of Ioannina's mirror and played her flashlight over her shoulder as she looked. "This is very strange," she said as she stopped and looked at her companions. "I'd swear it blends the letters into Arabic, Greek and Hebrew. It's almost like a Rosetta stone."

"What's a Rosetta stone?" Vasillus asked.

"It's a large stone found by one of Napoleon's men in Egypt. For years and years, no one could figure out how to read ancient Egyptian hieroglyphics, and the stone unlocked the language. It contained three scripts: Greek, which people could read; Demonic, which they could also read; and ancient Egyptian hieroglyphics. Once they had the other scripts, they could translate the hieroglyphics and created a dictionary of ancient Egyptian. It didn't give all the words, but enough of the structure to figure out the basic mechanics of the language and what the cartouches stood for." She then turned to Scott and handed him the mirror. "You look. Tell me what you think?"

He held the mirror while the others shined their flashlights over the wall. "It just looks blurry to me," he said as he turned back to her. "Maybe the verse is right—the lady will show the way."

She took back the mirror and walked to where she was standing before, then put her flashlight over her shoulder. "Come over here. I still see the same thing. Maybe you need to have the right depth of field or something."

"Let the good father and me have a look, too," Samuel said.

"I'd like a look but please don't call me father, at least not yet. I haven't taken my vows yet and I am just a lowly friar at the monastery. I don't like being called father anyway. Did you know the Bible says not to call anyone father, other than God? So why do we do it? You've got me," Vasillus said.

Scott handed the mirror to Samuel while the others lighted the wall for him. He whistled and exclaimed, "You're right. They were way ahead of their time. I hope we documented this well enough. I wouldn't want this to fall into the wrong hands. Be careful, Vasillus. Some people may still be after us, and not just the Muslim extremists. The camera you're holding contains a dangerous portion of knowledge and it could get somebody hurt."

Vasillus took the mirror and looked at the paintings. He bent his head in prayer when he finished and said, "My dear friends, more than the Muslim extremists are interested in this. I believe this is part of the spiritual war that we've long prepared for."

"What do you mean spiritual war?" Scott asked.

"Our spiritual journey isn't a war against flesh and blood as some ascetics would have us believe, but a war that's taking place in the spiritual realm. Even as we speak the prince of this world stands condemned but not yet vanquished. He is still strong and goes about trying to devour whoever he can. The age we live in is still his. Look around at this country; gay parties and carnivals in Patra. Ladies on the beaches practically naked. I don't mean a man and his wife on holiday, but young single girls dancing naked on the beaches with single men."

Samuel held up his hand. "What beaches are you talking about?"

Vasillus smirked and ignored him. "People don't go to church and, even if they do they do not give it much thought." He paused and looked around the cavern. "The enemy would like to get a hold of this and destroy it for it may weaken his power. You are right, this is dangerous and will get more so. Don't you see? This seems to hint at uniting all people under God. The war requires that we put on His full armor for the fight. It would ease my heart if I knew you were Christians," he said as he handed the mirror back to Scott.

"Another Orthodox monk said much the same thing to me, Vasillus. All I can say is that I'm not ready. I'm a man of science. It's not that I don't believe you. I used to resent it when someone pushed at me. Knowing you and Father Basil has taught me that you really care about me, but enough of that for right now."

"I can read the Greek but it seems to be a verse from the book of Isaiah. I can't read the Hebrew. Can you, Vasillus?"

"Not very well. I took one class and can make out the word Isaiah but that's about it. What about you, Julia? You said you were raised in Israel."

"I can't read ancient Hebrew very well. It wasn't one of my required classes growing up and I didn't get to Israel until I was a teenager. They make young boys take Hebrew, not girls. Might as well be Greek to me."

"The Arabic seems to be a poem. I'll try and translate it. It seems the Greek says the same thing, but I can't say I understand why it changes with the mirror so," Scott said. "We're always looking for the complicated answer; I tend to do it, too."

"No one can figure out God. We try to wrap an infinite God up in our finite minds. But enough of that. What do you make of the verses?"

"See if you agree, but this is how I would translate it:

> I make the great nations, as if from the stars
> long promised before to brothers afar
> When I make a covenant, it always is kept
> I am what I am, and never have slept
> Wake up, oh sleeper, oh why do you drowse
> Look all around you, take stock of the clouds
> The day will soon come, only I Am knows just when
> When the brothers will join and embrace once again
> Isaiah did know of the covenant to come
> Jeremiah too and knows who's the one
> Bringing the covenant, I gave to mankind
> Enlightening them all, even those who are blind
> To learn that at last, an answer to hear
> Look to the East at the mountain so near
> Look north of Medina for the marker so clear
> The Lord said to Moses, some will soon fear
> Mohammad did see, the truth is for real
> Truth that will bind us and will soon heal
> The Lord will surround you, for all the long years
> Wiping away life's dreadful sad tears
> There near the top, been hidden for years
> A cave long and lowly, you must have the ears
> Listen to me, and learn how to pray
> My son he did teach them, on a cold winter's day
> The law was given, if you just look within
> Mankind has known, he is still steeped in sin
> Who is to save us from this long, long cold death
> Look to I Am, Look to I Am, Look to I Am.

Samuel took another roll of film and then switched to the digital camera and said, "I have it, let's go."

Scott stopped before they left and bowed his head. "Thank you for your wisdom." Then turning to Julia with a smile, he said, "That's the first time I ever remember doing that, except when someone was shooting at me."

"You ought to do it more often," she said with a smile.

Vasillus smiled and said, "You did that very well."

They pushed the altar back when they left. Below them inside the small cavern, a remarkable change came over the lichen as it multiplied and spread from the light and powerful flash used by Julia and Samuel, obscuring the map and writing on the wall.

Scott stretched. "Well, I think that was a pretty good day's work. Vasillus, I don't know how to thank you for your help and all your insight. I feel like you've joined our group and want to ask you to come with us to Saudi Arabia, if you'd like. It's most likely going to be dangerous, hot and uncomfortable, but I think your input and insight would be of great help."

"I'll have to think about it," Vasillus said.

They climbed down from the cave, walked up to the car, and then dropped Vasillus off at the monastery on their way back into town.

Chapter 34
Hasid's Raid

Darkness closed on the little village below the rock spires as a group of four men dressed in black moved quietly, descending the trail Scott and his companions had taken earlier. Stopping at the base of the cliff, their leader looked up at the dark cliff, then took a rifle off his back and quickly lined up the sights, firing at the cave. The noise was surprisingly quiet as a thin-grey rope arched upwards reaching toward the cave. Pulling back on the rope, he felt it grow taut as the grapple hook caught. He turned and nodded to his companions then walked up the wall with ease. Looking around the cave, he noticed the old winch and transferred the rope and signaled the others to follow.

Four shadowy shapes soon stood inside the cave.

They fanned out and searched the cave trying to find out what Scott and his companions had been doing up there for so long.

Speaking in Arabic a short stout man said, "There must be something here. I watched them all day—they spent hours in this place and only a short time farther up."

"But why, what did they find, why did they spend so much time here? He spent all day here, there is no point in going farther up," one of the men said.

"Hasid's orders are clear: follow Chad everywhere. Keep an eye on him but let him work. Find out what he is up to and what he has found. Take photographs of everyplace he's been. We might have to climb farther up if we do not find anything here," said the leader.

"It doesn't look like Chad found anything; this place is empty. We should just go back to his hotel and take any information he has with him, then question him."

The leader looked around the cave. "I am not sure. Hasid's orders were to keep an eye on Chad and only stop him if he found anything. We may still need to check out his hotel room, but we are to bring anything we find directly to Hasid. Remember what happened to Abdullah. Hasid and Quati will be in a rage if we fail."

"Yes . . . yes I hear you, Captain; I wish they would deem to tell us what this is all about. Did you ever notice the less they tell us, the more important they think they are. They should tell us the whole story so we know what we are to be working on. Why do they not tell us what this is all about?"

"Because you do not have the need to know, that is why. They expect obedience and that is what they shall get from us, do you understand me! Start looking around—see if we can find out why Chad spent three hours here."

They looked around the cave, at the niches, the altar and the paintings behind it. They looked at the stonework behind the altar but found nothing. No hidden panels, special writing, just the altar, paintings and the sleeping niches.

"There must have been something more than this to keep them here all afternoon," the leader said. "I just don't get it, what could they have found to keep them here?"

"Captain Bakkar, I think I found something. Allah be praised," one of the men, said as he pointed at the floor by the altar.

The tall captain strode over to where he was pointing. Faint scratches showed in the floor where Samuel had pushed the altar aside.

The captain commanded, "All of you—come and move this and we shall see what we have."

The four men pushed on the altar, which moved easily from their combined weight, exposing the staircase.

"It appears that we have found why they spent so much time in here! Abd, stay here and keep watch, the rest of you follow me," Captain Bakkar said.

Bakkar took out a large machine pistol as he descended the stone stairs, while holding his flashlight out in front of him. He soon found that the pistol was a waste of time as he entered the room and found it empty, except for the stone table and crumbled Bible.

Shining their flashlights around the room, the three men stood still then shook their heads.

"Mishka, check the staircase—I want you to look it over carefully for any hidden side passages or cracks. Ali, look closely along the walls, see if you can find anything else. I am going to take pictures of the murals—we will bring them back to Hasid, maybe he will know what they mean. The writing is in Greek, Arabic and Hebrew and only Allah knows what else. That center mural seems strange. I think Chad was studying the pictures."

Searching the rest of the chamber, they filmed and documented the room for their superiors.

Mishka came back down. "The staircase is carved from solid rock, Captain. The only place where a passage could be hidden would be behind those niches next to the altar. I ran my knife down the edge of every stair—they are carved from solid rock. I do not believe there is anything else here, unless . . . unless there is something behind those murals on the wall."

"Look along them, you could be right. We have taken all the pictures we need. So search that area also," Bakkar said.

Mishka carefully examined the pictures and ran his knife along the floor and wall, looking for any hidden joints or cracks, but found nothing except smooth rock. Returning to the center of the chamber he stared at the three pictures on the walls, then looked down and noticed the marks on the floor. "Captain, on the floor. There is some type of mark that may correspond with the murals."

Bakkar looked at the icons inlayed in the floor. "Good work, Mishka." He then looked around the rest of the chamber. "Take another set of pictures of the paintings from each of these marks and when done—destroy them! I do not want anyone else finding this."

"Captain Bakkar, these are ancient paintings, possibly by Mohammad himself. Do you not think it may be wrong to destroy the Prophet's work?" Ali said.

"Whatever gave you the idea that Mohammad painted these murals? They are Orthodox paintings and detestable icons. We do not believe in icons—destroy them I said. General Quati will be pleased."

"I have heard rumors about Chad and why we are here is all, but will do as you command, Captain," Ali said.

They tried scraping the paintings with their knives but found the paint to be surprisingly stubborn to remove.

Captain Bakkar grew frustrated watching them and finally said, "Everyone back out—up the stairs. I will shoot the wall to destroy the paintings. I want you to move back, I do not know if the bullets will ricochet or not—stand clear."

He pulled his machine pistol from his shoulder strap, selected single shot and aimed at the center painting, pulling the trigger once. The bullet penetrated the limestone, knocked off a large flake and embedded in the wall. He carefully shot at the pictures on the left and right, the bullets flaking off large pieces of stone and penetrating the wall. Aiming on a slight angle, the bullet shattered the stone but also ricocheted off the wall before hitting the next wall and falling to the floor, its energy spent.

He yelled, "Back in—shoot straight at the wall, not at an angle. Watch," he said as he fired an automatic burst at the center mural. "If you shoot at an angle, it will ricochet, so shoot straight only. Each of you, take a picture and destroy it."

He backed up the staircase as the three took their machine pistols and opened up on the paintings. It didn't take long to reduce them to dust and after a couple of magazine changes, a yell came from the chamber. Thinking they'd found something, Bakkar raced back down the stairs to find one of his men holding his ankle where a bullet had ricocheted off the wall and grazed the bone.

"Stupid fools, I told you to shoot straight into the wall, not at an angle. Now we are going to have to carry him out of here. Can you walk, Ali?" the leader asked.

"I do not know," he said as he tried to get up. He was not able to put weight on the foot but able to hobble on the other. The wound bled profusely but wasn't life threatening, gouging a narrow furrow in the bone.

"Mishka, help Ali up the stairs. We are done here. We are going to have to check out their rooms and see what else we can find."

They lowered their injured comrade down to the valley floor by using the old winch and moved the altar back, trying to disguise the scratches on the floor. They then took pictures of the cave but didn't destroy the icons. As they descended to the valley floor, a man watched from the trees on the hillside, taking pictures with a night-vision camera.

❋ ❋ ❋ ❋ ❋ ❋ ❋ ❋

Blocks of concrete and burned out cars littered the streets in the area where the abandoned warehouse stood near the outskirts of Beirut. Children had thrown rocks through the windows and broken bottles and trash littered the landscape. A broken down and rusty wire fence surrounded the complex.

Inside, two men were finalizing a plan to spearhead a new order in the Islamic community. The clandestine meeting was being held in the warehouse for security reasons and provided them with a central place for sending out their agents and a pool of ready recruits from the young men without work in the area.

General Quati was in a rage again. "Jihad, I tell you, that is what I will have. I believe the Prophet's writings will bring about the Holy War. The enemies of Islam will fall like leaves before us. We cannot let the infidel gain access to this information. He will give it to the great Satan's press who will twist the true meaning of it. Our Mullahs must have his sacred writings. The Prophet's revelations belong to us, to his people, to me and to no one else, I tell you! It is unthinkable for an infidel to have them."

Slamming his fist on the table, he said, "Jihad, one way or another, I will have my jihad. I believe the revelations will direct me to the proper time to start this holy jihad. We will then bring all those infidel dogs under our wings. Those that are still alive will eat our dust and wash our clothes. We will cover their women so they are not an abomination to our society, except in our homes, of course, where they will dress to please us." Turning to Hasid, he said, "We have lost too many men so far. It was foolish to lose Luigi. Bestin assured me that the man knew his business. Now we have lost Albin, Sa'id and Momar. Chad must be stopped. I gave you the authority this time. Tell me, what is he doing in Greece now?"

"I have sent the new men we discussed. They are there even as we speak," Hasid said, as he walked over to where Quati was standing. "Chad is still at that little village near Meteora and our men are in place. They have sent me information that someone else is interested in what Chad is doing. I am not sure who it could be, but I think from what my men have said that it could be Interpol, Mosad, or possibly CIA. I have assigned one of our men to watch them. If they get too close to Chad, I am going to ask you for more people so we can take them out."

He threw his hat down on the table which raised a cloud of dust that the sun highlighted as it shone through the broken windows. "I do not care. I want action and want it now. I have waited long enough for this jihad and the glorious banner of Islam—the flag of the Prophet must soon fly over all nations. I will lead our heroes to victory against the infidel dogs. Do you understand me and hear me, Hasid?"

"The whole neighborhood can hear you, Quati. Get control of yourself. Our operatives are the best. We will follow Chad and stop him if it is required. Two of my men are going to search his rooms while others are watching what he is doing. My real concern is what these other people want; who they are is what bothers me. I half expected the Mosad to show up, but they seem quiet, I do not know why. They are formidable enemies, praise Allah. The two we caught in Sinai last November were superb soldiers; they died well. I would love to have an agent inside the Mosad working for us so I knew what they were planning and thinking. I do not agree with you about Chad. I think we should let him keep working—stay close, yes, and when he finds what he is looking for, tighten the noose. If we snuff him out now, we may never know what he has found or what to do if we have to take up the trail. Abu is good, but not as good as Chad. He could not figure out the first chamber, remember. If we take Chad out . . . ?" He raised his palms and eyebrows.

"Get rid of Chad and that Jewess, I say. I do not have forever. I am still not sure of your loyalty to my cause. Are you sure I can trust you?"

"General, my father was gunned down by the Israelis. How can you not be sure of me?"

"Chad and that woman is why. You were not honest with me when this started and did not tell me of your past."

Hasid stood a moment while a string of thoughts raced through his mind, from the time at the café in Paris, to playing with Chad as a child. Taking a deep breath he said, "Give the order and I will personally do it. She may be a Jew and if that is what it takes for you to know that I am loyal to you, so be it."

"Enough, you are right—let Chad work, but keep an eye on that Jew." Hasid noticed a look of pain cross Quati's face. "Are you all right, General?"

"No, I am not all right! The doctors have told me this pain will not go away and I will have to live with it. I do not have the time. My great and holy jihad must start soon." He calmed himself with a visible effort and looked at Hasid. "You speak with some wisdom, if I can believe you. Perhaps it is better to let Chad keep working for a while, but keep a close eye on him. If I were to bring forth the light of the Prophet's writings, just think how that would help our cause! You are wise, Hasid. I must remember, a wise man has many wise counselors, as the prophet has written. I must control my emotions and listen to my counselors. Let it be as you say, keep an eye on those others. Too many cooks spoil the broth. Is that not what the Prophet has said?"

Hasid nodded. "You learn well, General. I will keep an eye on these others and our man will follow Chad and his companions to see where they lead."

A look of pain crossed Quati's face. "Islam, Hasid, my banner must fly. I do not have forever. I will listen today, but if you fail and the infidel gains the Prophet's writings before we do, you will pay. Do you understand me?"

He bowed to the general. "To hear you is to obey, my General, and to understand you is to learn wisdom, my leader!"

Slamming his fist in his palm, he said, "Make sure I am kept aware of Chad's movements. I may also assign others to watch them. You have served me well in the past and I believe you will serve me well in the future. Just be sure of your priorities and loyalty. I have learned it pays to be careful and wise."

"Well said, but if you assign others, we may get in each other's way. I counsel patience, or at least let me know who you are sending so I may keep track of things. This is what I do best and why you hired me."

Quati walked to the window. "I will think about this, now go. I have other matters to attend to—the doctor is coming to change my medicine."

He bowed. "As you wish, Quati."

Making his way out of the small room and down to his waiting car, he paused and looked at the black Mercedes 300, which looked like a polished stone amidst the gravel. Gazing back at the building he noticed a group of boys as they came around the edge of the building, rolling a hoop through the trash, while an old man went from can to can looking under the rubble for something to eat or sell.

He looked up at the rust streaked sides of the building and wondered if Islam wasn't becoming like this building. Saudi Arabia and Kuwait were shining and gleaming examples, but the rest seemed to be crumbling. They did not have the glut of oil money from the west to feed off and from Morocco on the west to Indonesia and the Philippines on the east, Islam seemed to be like this building. All of their ideals were tribally centered and not centered on the growth of the individual.

Getting in the car he looked back. Yes, faith must come first! He had known this since a child, but he'd seen with his own eyes the horror of what mankind could do. This saddened him for some reason he couldn't understand as he thought of it. Old newspapers blew around the courtyard of the warehouse, swirling them around and around, trapped by the shape of the building. Was this what his faith had become? Like a sirocco that went around and round and never went anywhere? This worked well two hundred years ago, but something was missing and he didn't know what. His people had to grow to bring enlightenment to man. Had to grow to make them one with Allah, but the faith seemed to be following the ways of the dictators like Quati and the charismatic leaders like Osama Bin Laden, who appealed to the bored young men of Saudi Arabia who were out of work, since ninety percent of the jobs in the country were done by immigrants. A great leader, but Bin Laden seemed to have fallen on folly. Well, perhaps these writings would lead them to a new path. Could he really kill Julia and Chad if Quati was to order it? He told himself yes when he told Quati to give the order, but could he. His feelings were so strange it was as if he didn't know himself anymore. Allah had given him a path to follow and he intended to follow it to the end. *You never knew where it would lead, did you though,* he thought as he told the driver to leave.

The old man watching the dust from the car went to the side of the building and pulled up some old boards and pieces of moldy carpet where he retrieved an object from under the rubble, which he quickly tucked it into his robe. The children continued to play with their hoop, while the papers continued to swirl around and around in the courtyard, going nowhere.

Scott drove up to the monastery the next morning to say good-bye to Vasillus and Father Nikita and take one last look at the beautiful place before heading to Athens. When they arrived at the parking area, they were surprised to see Vasillus, Father Nikita and a number of the other monks waiting outside. Father Nikita strode over as they got out of their car. "Mr. Chad, Samuel and Ms. Julia, how good of you to come. We've something for you as our way of saying thanks for your help."

Scott extended his hand. "You've helped us immensely. No thanks are necessary. Though, we wouldn't mind a basket of your fruit and cheese."

"I want you to take my car instead of that little old Fiat you keep driving around. I don't even see how the three of you fit inside the thing," he said as he pointed to a BMW 328i parked in the parking lot. "It has a lot of power and I hardly ever drive it. I would feel much better if you were in a safer car. Just leave it at the airport and we will pick it up later."

Scott smiled, "I don't know what to say, Father. You give charity a whole new meaning. I'd always thought of charity as helping the poor, but you show it in a completely new way by finding ways to help people.

Father Nikita laughed then slapped Scott's shoulder as they walked toward the car. "My boy, we are going to make a philosopher out of you if you keep this up. Now transfer your stuff and get going," he said as he showed Scott over to the car and opened the trunk.

Scott noticed two baskets inside and looked at Nikita to say something. Nikita just winked and Scott said, "Thank you again, Father." Scott transferred their packs and Julia's clothes to the BMW, while Samuel and Julia were talking with Vasillus saying their good byes.

Julia reached up, gave Father Nikita a kiss on the cheek then Samuel shook his hand vigorously. When all was said, they hopped in Nikita's car and made their way down the twisty mountain road and through the little village. Scott drove with Julia in front while Samuel sprawled out in back, snoozing already. Passing through Kardista, they came upon a little church with a huge stork nest on top, where a large stork was feeding its young. Julia let out a little yelp of surprise at the sight, which woke Samuel from his nap, momentarily.

❋   ❋   ❋   ❋   ❋   ❋   ❋   ❋

Tel Aviv

Benjamin limped down the hallway, his mind in a turmoil, the green color on the walls sickening him. Turning into the office, the two men sitting rose as he walked in. Motioning for them to sit he started, "I think Chad is going to need help. Quati has so far held off, only God knows why, but we cannot rely on him acting this way forever. He does not have that long and he will want to move quickly on this as it develops."

The middle-aged man looked at Eli. "What does he mean he can't wait long?"

"He is sick."

"We all know he's sick. What's the rush now?"

"No, I mean he is sick and dying. Our operatives have seen the medical reports and we have talked with the doctors. He has a certain type of cancer. It will not kill him right away, but it is incurable. We fear he will become more irrational as time goes on also."

Benjamin interjected, "You do not really need to know all that. I need to get you in place to help Chad if he needs it. Help him in some way—so he does not know it is us."

"You know your business better than I do. What do you want me to do?"

"I want you to pack and be ready to move. We will let you know when. It will probably be somewhere warm, but we are not yet certain."

"Do you have any idea when?"

"Be ready to go at a moment's notice. Now leave, I have important matters to discuss with Eli."

After the man walked out Benjamin turned to Eli. "Do you really think it wise to give it to them?" He said as he pulled a slip of paper out of his jacket and tossed it onto the table in front of Eli.

"I think it will help—I do not want Quati to get it though. We are taking a big chance. He has shadowed them and it now appears that he has put Hasid in charge and I would love to get my hands on him."

"We should not let our emotions get in the way, old friend, but I know what you mean. Quati has spied on them and ransacked their rooms more than once. Yes, we are taking a chance but worth it in the end."

"When did we not take chances? Seems that is how we came to be where we are today."

"I know, but this is different. If we do nothing we are safe, but if we move on this the payoff may be large but we may also be helping Quati."

"Remember the saying, 'The only thing necessary for evil to triumph is for good men to do nothing.'"

"You are calling us good men then. I wish I had your faith."

❋ ❋ ❋ ❋ ❋ ❋ ❋ ❋

The hotel in Beirut had seen better days, but Hasid threw his thoughts aside as he entered Quati's room. He stopped when he entered and stood facing Quati where he sat behind his desk.

"Where are they now?" Quati asked.

"Headed toward Athens. I have a car tailing them."

"Make sure you do not lose them. I would rather you killed them than lost them."

"He has reservations at the Olympia in Athens. I do not think we will lose him." *Just yet at any rate,* he thought to himself.

"What do you think he will do next and have you analyzed the data from the second cave?"

"Our men are working on it. It is difficult to understand and is not like the first chamber. I have given copies of the photographs to Dr. Abu as you ordered."

"Good, but you only answered part of my question. Where do you think Chad will go next?"

"I think he will head back to Sinai, check up on his team before he makes another move. This will give us time to analyze the data and give us some breathing room."

"Just make sure you do not lose him."

"Do you have any information on the other people following Chad? My men have not seen them since Meteora. Have your sources uncovered anything?"

"Mosad is all I know. I told you so."

"It is good to know one's enemy."

"Get over to Athens and keep an eye on things, then report back to me."

"Yes, General."

CHAPTER 35
BACK TO EGYPT

They made their way to the Athens airport and secured three seats to Cairo on the 10:30 A.M. flight. They decided to stay at the airport and wait. They dropped the car off in the long-term parking lot, then called Father Nikita to let him know where to pick it up.

The flight was on time and when they disembarked in Cairo, they rented a blue Chevy Suburban for a two-week period. They didn't notice a small black Opel with three men inside following about three cars back as they made their way out of the city. Every couple of miles it would fall back and a white van would take its place. The men working for Hasid weren't taking any chances and were using three vehicles. One would speed ahead while the other two took turns shadowing them. The third vehicle was an old black battered Mercedes that used to be a taxi with the sign and logo removed. The Mercedes had gone ahead and was waiting to take over the tail position as the others passed. Once out of Cairo, Scott took highway 33 across the eastern desert where he could increase his speed. This stretch of road, between Cairo and Suez, is one of the few modern roads in Egypt and they made the eighty-mile trip in just over an hour.

Scott was looking at the bone-dry sand of the eastern desert as they crested a rise and saw Suez laid out before them. It was easy to envision the large waves from the Red Sea becoming gentle rollers as they drifted up the gulf to expend their energy on the sandy shore, trying in vain to reach the Mediterranean. The canal had changed all that, but the old mud-wattle huts that were scattered here and there must have looked the same as they had around a thousand years ago when the Bedouin traders and others trafficked in this area. The Gulf of Suez narrowed and the waves still washed up on the shore as they had for thousands of years, but now great ships plied the gulf, taking their cargo to ports in Europe and from Europe to places throughout the world. After crossing the gulf at Suez, they made their way south along the eastern shore headed toward their base camp.

The traffic thinned out after leaving Suez when Julia turned to her companions and said, "Don't look now, but I think we've picked up a tail!"

Scott and Samuel turned at her words and she snapped, "I said, don't look now! That's the third time that black Mercedes has passed us since we left Cairo. He's stopping somewhere up ahead, getting off the road and then letting another car keep on our tail. It's a common shadowing technique. I must be getting rusty since I've only noticed one other car, a black Opel which is two cars back. They're probably using three or more vehicles to tail us. If they were good, we'd never have noticed. The problem is what to do about it, and why are they shadowing us?"

"It seems they got wind of what we were up to since I booked the airline flight. They couldn't catch up with us in Athens but got someone in place in Cairo." Scott paused and laughed. "It probably means trouble. I would think they knew we were headed toward our base camp so why not wait at our camp for us. What do you think?"

"If I wanted to stop someone, I'd set up something around Umn Bugma or farther south. We'd better be prepared to do something. What, I don't know, depends on what they have in mind," Samuel said.

"The most important thing is our lives," Scott said. "Maybe we can hide some of the film if they stop us, but I don't want any heroics. We don't have anything other than the tire iron in back to defend ourselves with, so play it cool. See if you can hide the film and data from the laptop. Samuel, take one of the floppy disks and make copies of the picture files and other data. Julia, hide the pictures wherever you can and keep your eyes open. Now that we're out of Suez, it can be a very lonely and desolate road down to our camp in spots."

❈ ❈ ❈ ❈ ❈ ❈ ❈ ❈

Hasid had used the group of men he'd hired once before. He hired them specifically to shadow Chad. His orders to them were very specific: stop Chad and take all of his information, computers, pictures, and notebooks. No harm was to come to them. They were to only take information related to the chamber, nothing else. Their leader, a tough young Palestinian soldier called Yasuf, had been raised in a refugee camp in the Gaza Strip and had seen any number of his childhood friends blow themselves up in suicide attacks. His loathing for anything to do with Israel knew no bounds and his dedication to the cause was without question. Hasid debated telling him that the woman traveling with Chad was an Israeli, since that might have incited and confused him, making it difficult to control him. He was paying Yasuf and his men a substantial sum for this job and had gone so far as to show him the news clippings of Abdullah, lying dead and naked with the western whore.

Hasid had warned Yasuf in no uncertain terms that this would be the price of failure. This more than anything reinforced his conviction to follow his orders explicitly. Nearing the little seaside town of Abu Zanima, Yasuf radioed ahead to where he'd stationed a large tanker truck on a little gravel side road. As soon as the Mercedes passed, his plan was for the truck to pull out and block the road.

The little town of Abu Zanima was right on the gulf and was a pleasant place where rich Egyptians took a break from the winter and sometimes during the summer, when they wanted a beach vacation with their families.

Scott rounded a bend after leaving Abu Zanima and the black Mercedes passed them on a straight section of road and disappeared around the next bend. As Scott rounded the bend, a large tanker truck pulled off a gravel side road in front of him, ponderously turned into the road, and stopped. The black Opel and a white van quickly closed the distance behind, screeched to a stop, and turned sideways in the road, blocking the rear. Three men jumped out carrying assault rifles and the truck effectively blocked any escape down the highway. Scott glanced at the little gravel road, hit the accelerator and spun the Suburban up the steep embankment. The gravel track crested the hill, twisted and turned as it climbed along the steep banks of the wadi and wound back into the interior. The Suburban drifted around the corners going at a tremendous pace and raising a cloud of thick dust in their wake. Julia looked back around one of the bends and could see the Opel and van following them into the hills. Cresting a hill, she saw the Mercedes also following in the distance.

Scott looked back in the mirror, around one tight corner. "They moved the truck, and the Mercedes is now behind us! All three are on our tail and who knows where this road, if you call it a road, leads," he yelled as they bottomed out their shocks bouncing up the wadi. "We're north of the limits of our survey, so we're heading into the desert of Tih. I don't recall any roads up here. Any ideas, I could use one or two about now. We've only got a couple of minutes lead on them!"

Samuel pointed out the window. "See the mountain range on our right. St. Catherine's is just on the other side of it. If you managed to get over that, we'd find the road down to the camp. They would probably just follow us into camp, but . . ."

There was a loud bang as the left-front tire blew, immediately shredding and almost forcing Scott to lose control. Julia rolled down her window and dropped a diskette and pack of negatives into a bush by the side of the road while Scott pulled around a large boulder off to the side of the gravel track. The Opel passed them in the dust but the driver of the van noticed and pulled up next to the Suburban, two men hopping out and covering them with their rifles. The driver spoke into a hand-held radio, and the Opel turned around. Five men stood there pointing their Kalashnikovs at them.

Yasuf glared at them. "Everyone out of the car, now! Against that rock, put your hands up and keep them up, move now." He fired a burst from the rifle into the air for emphasis.

Scott and his companions quickly did as he ordered, putting their arms against the large granite boulder. One of Yasuf's men came over and expertly frisked them, lingering a little longer on Julia than necessary. He held up two packets of pictures that Samuel had stuffed down his pants and two others that Julia had stashed in her pockets. Another of his men quickly and expertly went through the car, pulling out their backpacks, laptop computer and notebooks. They laid everything in a pile beside the white van and then pulled out the spare tire and jack, looking under the seats and though the glove box.

Yasuf asked his men, "Is that everything?"

A tall lanky man snapped to attention at his voice. "Yes, Yasuf, we have found everything. Unless they had time to sew it into the upholstery?"

Yasuf snapped, "No names, idiot. Pack everything, pictures, notes, computers and cameras and we shall leave. We are soldiers and have our orders."

One of the men pulled out the mirror from the pile, whose stones glittered in the sun, and asked, "What about their money and this?"

Yasuf snarled. "Leave it, we have our orders, no looting—we are professionals."

After quickly throwing everything into the van, Yasuf walked over to Scott and said, "We are being gentle with you, infidel. Do not expect this kindness the next time we meet. Kindness is not one of my faults, but I have my orders and I am a soldier and obey them." He took his rifle and shot out the other front tire of the Suburban, jumped in the van, and left them standing in the desert sun without any water or way out.

When the dust finally settled, Scott said, "Everyone okay? I'm getting burned at these guys. Don't they ever give up? Next time I'll dress for one of these parties. How about you, Samuel?"

"I think dressing for one of these parties would be fun. I think I'll dress up as a commando."

Julia just shook her head. "What are you two talking about? We were just robbed of everything we worked so hard to get, except . . ." She walked down the slope to where she'd dropped the negatives and floppy disk Samuel had prepared. "Except for this!" she said as she held up the disk and negatives. "I also have this," she said as she reached in the car and under the seat and pulled out two strips of negatives.

"Amazing girl," Scott said. "I always knew there was more about you than met the eye." He stopped and looked around. "The problem is, how are we going to get out of here? We must have driven eight miles from the highway and the nearest town is another ten once we get back to the coast. For some reason, I don't think anyone in town is going to carry 235X16 radials for the Suburban. What do you think, Samuel, you're the mechanical genius?"

Samuel looked at the holes in the tires. "The left-front's shredded—you must have hit a sharp rock or something—and the right-front has a nice round hole in it from the rifle. We have the spare but we still only have three tires. It might be better to drive it on the two flat ones and see how far we get. Let's see if there's anything in back." Samuel rummaged through the back and came up with a first-aid kit, but nothing else.

"So you're saying we're out of luck?" Julia said as she put her hands on her hips.

"Lady luck never deserts us. We're not out of luck, just out of ideas. Let's try it on the two flats and see how far we get. We can always change the spare for one of them. We'll take it real slow, it's bound to beat walking."

Scott looked at him. "Did you see the gravel road on the way up here? Two flat tires and we'll be plowing gravel all the way down. Some of those sections are steep, too."

"I didn't say it would work. I said let's try it, unless you want to start walking out."

Scott sighed. "Everybody hop in. Let's give it a try."

They climbed in the Suburban and Scott slowly turned it around and proceeded down the hill at slightly better than a walking pace. "At this rate we should be back to the main road in about an hour or so," he added while his hands tightly gripped the wheel.

The difficult part was when the rubber shredded and started flopping around, banging the fender. It finally tore loose, and they proceeded on the rims only. This gave a somewhat better feeling of control as they dug into the gravel when he turned and gave some purchase, instead of just waffling back and forth, as the flat rubber had done. The hard part was when they descended some of the steeper and rockier grades, where the car tended to drastically under-steer and slide on the rock, threatening to take them straight down into the wadi. He kept their speed down and would stop and back up whenever the front slid out too much. They could have walked down these steep stretches quicker, but the car's air-conditioning kept them cool and Scott kept it turned on high since they had plenty of gas. When they finally made it back to the highway, he pulled over and they jacked up the car put the spare on the left front wheel, since the rims just slid on the asphalt pavement. He could control the car better, albeit slowly, until they came to the little seaside town of Umm Bugma.

Scott pulled into the only gas station in town and the attendant came out and smiled a toothless grin.

"Where's your tire?" he asked Scott.

Scott shook his head. "We left it back in the hills. Do you have another?"

The attendant looked at him. "Probably not that size. But you bent your rim, too. I have to try and bend out the rim or you have to get a new one. I'll look and see what we have."

They all bought a cold Coke, which was a wonderful thing about the new Egypt. They stood there enjoying the cold drink when the attendant came back. "No 235X16, but I do have a pair of used 200X16's, which I can put on the rims. They will get you to where you're going and I could order the tire for you if you want to come back next week. I have the old steel wheels for the things, too. I cannot fix yours, you bent it up to much."

"You've got a deal. Let's see the tires," Scott said.

He showed Scott the wheels and tires, which really weren't very bad, being part of a set that was changed. They still had some tread, though worn at the edges from improper alignment. Scott haggled with him for a moment and agreed on a price for both. They walked over to the little restaurant and ordered a late lunch while he changed the tires.

"It doesn't drive too bad, pulls a little to the right. I'm sure it'll get us to camp." He increased the pressure on the accelerator and they were soon turning off toward St. Catherine's. They took the cut-off and went directly south to the camp. As Scott neared the last turn, he leaned on the horn announcing their arrival, rounded the corner and found Luke and Alex running down the hill toward them.

They stood in the hot sunshine. They were back at camp, and had lost most everything they'd gone to find, everything except a few prints, some negatives, one computer disk and the mirror. Scott had written down his translation of the poems, but they took his notes also.

Scott walked up to Luke and Alex. "Glad to see you." He noticed a large crate over by the command tent and nodded. "When did that come?"

"It came yesterday," Alex said.

"Mabel said you ordered it the other day—didn't say why," Luke added.

"How did it go?" Alex said.

"Did you find anything more about the chamber?" Luke asked.

"Whoa, one at a time," Scott said. "First things first; how are you two doing, any trouble with the survey?"

"We're on schedule, if that's what you mean. Actually we're almost done, well . . . there's always more to do, but essentially—we're done," Luke said.

"Good, because troubles have been following us ever since we left. I was concerned about you two," Scott said as they walked up to the command tent.

CHAPTER 36
ABU'S ORDERS

Cairo stood sweltering under the late spring sunshine. The exhaust from its myriad vehicles blended with the unmoving desert air into a noxious brown soup. Hasid's limousine pulled up to the Palms Hotel and the attendant scurried to open the door. Tipping the man, he then nodded to the doorman, the air-conditioning feeling great after the heat of the street. The concierge hurried to hand him his key when he saw him and he went straight to the elevator. Walking into the suite, Hasid found to his satisfaction that Dr. Abu was waiting along with Yasuf and his men.

"Good, I am glad someone can follow orders for a change. Show me what you have."

Yasuf put the laptop, photos, disks and notes on the table. "That is all they had. We followed your orders exactly and did not harm them. We looted nothing from them. We left them with their money and an old ancient mirror."

Dr. Abu stammered, "I do not understand why you let him go. Chad is an infidel westerner who wants nothing more than to steal our national treasures. He perverted the Saudis into developing their oil fields, and what he did in Afghanistan is a disgrace. What mirror did you say? Are you sure you got everything?"

Hasid raised his hand and locked eyes with Abu. "We agreed that we were not going to harm them. Chad may have a role to play in this before it is all over. Take the data, analyze it and give me your report. That is what you are being paid to do. Do you understand me, Doctor?"

He looked shaken, but slowly straightened his back and turned to Yasuf. "What mirror are you talking about? You said something about a mirror."

"It was an old silver mirror studded with emeralds. It was not even a very good mirror for the glass was old and distorted. It had nothing to do with my orders, so I left it with them. Those were my orders."

"You are an idiot then. They probably got it in Greece and it has something to do with what they found there. All these pictures are distorted like the ones from Sinai, but different somehow."

He turned and looked at Hasid. "You and Quati have probably let some evidence slip through your hands. Where do you think Chad is going next, have you figured that out?"

"You forget your manners and who you work for." His eyes took on a steely appearance as he looked at the doctor. "If you mention Quati in that tone again, you will find yourself cataloging penguins next, if there is a next time."

Abu looked at the men in the room. "I am most sorry, Hasid. It is Chad. The man has no scruples, no religion and Allah knows he is an infidel. Why is he on this trail? It should be me. I am a learned man and have devoted my life to Allah since I was a boy." Taking a deep breath, he tried to calm himself then added, "But as Allah wills it is written."

"You would do well to remember that, Abu. Study the material and give me a report immediately, do you understand? I want answers now. If you do not have something for me by the end of the week, I will have to discuss your performance with Quati." He paused and looked at the Palestinians. "Yasuf, you and your men may go. I want to talk with the doctor alone. Make sure you report in tomorrow morning. We may need to move."

Yasuf and his men took their leave while Abu walked over to the table and took out Scott's notebook and looked through it. He leafed through the pages. "This is meaningless rubbish. It is written in some sort of code."

"What do you mean by code?"

"Just what I said. Chad writes in his own code and he is the only one who can understand it. You might be able to get a code breaker to crack it. I do not know. It would not be easy though."

"Show me what you mean," Hasid demanded.

"See, look here," Abu said, as he pointed to a page in the book. "It is gibberish. It is not written in any language I have ever seen, not Latin, Greek, English, Arabic or any other language I know. It is some type of shorthand notation he has probably used since college to write quickly and keep his research secret."

"Leave the book with me and work on the disk and film. See if that will help. I have the tape Yasuf and his men took."

"Why did you let them destroy the chamber? If Mohammad built it why destroy the work of the Prophet?"

"We have no control over it and it's in Greece. We don't know if Moham-mad built it. He sent messages there to one of his friends from St. Catherine's and we don't want one of his holy sites in a place like Meteora."

Abu shrugged. "It is not that important . . . just, well, we may have needed to go back."

"Do you think we could go back after what happened at the monastery? Forget it, Greece is closed to us."

"I will look at the data, but I believe that mirror is important. Yasuf should have taken everything, I tell you—that was stupid!"

Hasid calmly cracked his knuckles. "You forget to whom you are talking again, my good Doctor. Do not use that tone again, or you will find yourself in a hotel room with your picture in the paper the next morning. Your job is to work on the data and let me know what you find."

"Yes . . . yes, Hasid, I understand and will get you a preliminary report tomorrow afternoon."

"Make sure you do. I need to give Quati a report tomorrow as well and I would like to speak highly of you and your research."

Hasid went down to the nightclub after Abu left. Nursing a drink, he watched the lithe, redheaded belly dancer do her act. His mind wandered and he thought of Julia as a slow rage started growing in him—to think of her with Chad. Why do I care was the question he kept asking himself. Imagine the two of them falling in love—what if she danced for Scott like this. His hand slammed down on the table as he ordered another drink. Meeting the dancer after the show, he couldn't remember much and was still bleary eyed the next morning when General Quati called wanting an update.

❋   ❋   ❋   ❋   ❋   ❋   ❋   ❋

Quati's room at the Palms was more opulent than Hasid's. The peach-colored carpet was thick and a golden light came through the windows. "Where are they now? You said you were keeping track of them."

"Chad is south of his camp. I think he is going to Saudi Arabia. Abu is on his way to Jebel-en-Lawz, which is where he believes the final marker is."

"Can we be sure we are not on a . . . how do they say it, a wild goose chase?"

"I have two helicopters standing by to comb the area should Chad slip our grasp. We can always go back to his camp and interrogate his workers. I have kept that as a backup plan."

"Make sure you do not lose him. This is too important."

"We are doing everything we can. I console patience."

Quati's hand came slamming down on his desk. "Do not tell me to be patient. I will tell you what to do and you would do well to remember it. Now get out of my sight and only come back when you have something positive to tell me about Chad."

❈ ❈ ❈ ❈ ❈ ❈ ❈ ❈

The small restaurant in Joliet had closed early and was mostly empty—the only sound coming from the agitated men in the rear room. "I don't care, Farrell. Time's running out. We've come up empty handed while doing things your way. Now we are going to do it my way. Do you hear me?"

"Everyone in the place can hear you. You forget, Bestin, we did it your way last time when you hired those thugs out of Sicily. I let you bring Luigi and his men over. It cost me a pretty penny too and what did it get us—nothing! Where is Chad now, that's our problem. It's not doing us any good to sit here and bicker."

Henderson got out of his chair and paced the room. "Stop it, both of you! I think Farrell's right. Lower your voice and calm down. Remember what your doctor said about getting yourself worked up and losing your temper." He patted his chest. "We must work together on this. The latest word is that Quati had his men following Chad. We think he's going into Saudi Arabia, but we haven't heard anything since."

"You could have been more help," Bestin said.

The bishop stroked his cross before he spoke. "I still believe that the best trap is laced honey. Maybe we just used the wrong bait."

Henderson shook his head. "What kind of bait do you want us to use?"

Farrell looked at the two of them with a smile on his face. "The right kind of course. A bait Chad can't resist. What's the man's weakness? For many men it's women, for others power. For Chad, the offer of a tremendous new project, something loaded with diamonds or gold. Something no one has ever done before. We need to set the right project in front of him and he will then come to us, something that will distract him from this little adventure of his. Contact his office and request his services, something a mineralogical surveyor can't resist, something with adventure, riches and prestige. Now think—who can we get to offer him a new project? One where he'll stop what he's doing—something so big that he'll come out in the open so we can deal with him."

The Bishop looked up and smiled. "I think you've got it wrong. I don't think he'll come out for riches, power or prestige. He's been donating his time to countries that are impoverished and helping them develop resources that benefit their people. He's very careful who he's worked for in the last five years and has only taken one job in Saudi Arabia, working for the Saudis where the downtrodden masses didn't directly benefit from his work."

Farrell turned to him. "I wonder . . . I wonder . . . it's dangerous—but in the end we both want the same thing. Maybe we should ask Quati for help, and ask him to join forces with us."

Henderson's mouth dropped. "What do you mean, ask Quati to help?

Join forces with the infidel himself. He calls us the Great Satan. I think he's Satan personified. Are you nuts?"

Bestin stroked his cross again. "Here we go again, you two, pipe down. Farrell's got a good idea in some ways. I sent Luigi over to help and he worked with some of Quati's men. It didn't work out, but that was underestimating Chad, not because of Quati."

"I know Chad. At least I used to. Bestin's right. Chad won't stop what he's doing for fame and fortune, but maybe if we dangle a noble cause in front of him that'll catch his attention. How about a survey for some African government, a survey that will benefit the impoverished people and bring prosperity where it doesn't exist? Something that will appeal to his higher instincts. Keep Quati on a back burner if this doesn't work, but we have to find out where Chad is and get our people moving so we can keep track of him. We can't afford to lose him. I say we try and entice him out with something like that first and see what happens. Then we'll ask Quati for a couple of his men."

They nodded their agreement after listening. They'd come to trust Henderson's judgment over the years and this new idea appealed to them.

Bestin answered after a nod from Farrell. "I think anything's better than getting deeper into bed with Quati, except for Chad being successful, that is. I agree with you, Frank. But first, we need someone over there who can move fast when we find out where Chad is and where he's going! Second and even more important, we have to get someone in the government of one of the African countries to offer him a real project. It needs to be someone who will entice him to come out in the open, stop the chase he's on, and get right to work on their job. Some project that promises to feed the poor, develop the resources of the country, something that will appeal to Chad's sense of honor. The job he's doing in Sinai's finished; his assistants can finish it up."

The Reverend Farrell's face lit up with a cold narrow smile. "I have just the men to send over. They're brothers born in Jamaica of Libyan parents. They speak English, Arabic and Italian fluently. They moved to New York when they were teenagers. Their father worked on the docks and they joined a gang in the inner city and learned the ropes the hard way. I met them on one of my crusades through the state and they answered the call and have proven very useful. My theology's been well impressed on them and they're totally trustworthy to our cause. I've used them a couple of times on very delicate matters and I'm sure I could present this in such a way that they would be motivated to use all their talents for our cause."

Bestin scratched his neck and cleared his throat. "Have I worked with them before? What are their names?"

"You've never worked with them and you're probably glad. They're hard, tough, and totally dedicated to our cause. The older brother, Shula Williams, is twenty-six; Mulama is two years younger. He's the dangerous one, though they're both dangerous when focused on their beliefs and our cause."

Henderson stretched and cracked his knuckles. "What makes them so good?"

Farrell looked at the diamond ring on his finger. "Growing up in the Bronx and having to fight their way to the top. They each killed numerous times. When they heard my message and offer of forgiveness, they responded deeply. I learned about them after my crusade in the northeast. They scared my staff at our local center when they came in and the director of the center called me. When I met them, I could see why. Shula weighs 260 pounds while his younger brother weighs 245, and they're all muscle. What's frightening about them is the look in their eyes. You can tell they've killed before. They fought and clawed their way to the top of the gangs in the inner city. That's what's truly frightening."

"A bunch of thugs like Luigi. We need someone trained, someone we can control, too," Henderson said.

"After joining my organization, I took them under my wing and moved them to our farm in Ohio. I hired a martial arts instructor to round out their training. They wanted nothing to do with it at first until I explained that our faith had enemies and needed its soldiers, too. I explained that the Crusades were never over until the Lord's and our enemies were stamped out. They were both enthusiastic and once during one of our little problems, Shula broke a man's neck with his bare hands and came to me full of remorse afterwards. I explained that the Lord works in mysterious ways and that as long as he came to me and continued to work through me, he would be absolved of any sin. He loves to come to me weekly now for absolution and confession. I offer up my prayer for forgiveness and blessing on him and he looks up at me and smiles this big smile."

Bestin grunted. "That all sounds well and good. A couple of big strong men, but we need brains and real training, not just some Kung-fu boys to run around in the desert."

Farrell raised his palm. "That's what I've been trying to tell you. They each went back to school and received degrees: Shula in accounting and Mulama in chemical engineering. I arranged for them to train with some special operations groups who were ex-Marines—they trained them in special warfare, counter intelligence, electronic warfare, covert operations and hand-to-hand combat. Not your typical converts, I don't think, but I think they'll do nicely."

"Why didn't you use them before, Farrell? Why did you let us use Luigi and those other men if you had these so-called super agents?" Henderson said.

Farrell calmly answered, "They were on an operation for our group in Central America. There's a cult down there that needed to be taken care of. We can't let these cults just spring up all over, you know."

Bestin said, "We'll give it a try your way. I'll contact some friends I have in the Ethiopian government and see if we can get them to make an offer and contact Chad's office. Lord knows how much this is going to cost us. I think Bestin should contact Quati to at least open the door. We are probably going to need a couple of his men—wait before saying yes, but open the door. Two heads are better than one and he has Hasid working for him. He's smart and knew Chad when they were kids, if it's the same man. My sources tell me that he changed after the death of his father and Quati trusts him, he's one of his top lieutenants now; I say call him."

Farrell asked, "Is it safe to do business with him?"

"No, I dare say not. He's known far and wide as a dangerous man in Quati's organization. He's intelligent and ruthless, but I believe he is trustworthy and honest to a certain extent. He has a type of honor that is Middle Eastern, but noble. You ask if he is safe to do business with. I ask you if you're safe to do business with for you are a dangerous adversary. I say Hasid is safe enough if we are on the same side, though."

"What about Ethiopia? Can we trust the government there?" Farrell asked.

Henderson shrugged. "Africa wins."

"What the heck does that mean?" Bestin asked.

"Africa wins! It means that no matter what power, what money, Africa's like a pit that swallows everything and always will. It has a will of its own. Africa wins—is a saying like Murphy's Law, but more pessimistic. Hunger for Africa sends ten million dollars of food. Some local politician steals it then sells it to Australia or Europe and puts the money in his Swiss bank account—Africa wins. World Relief sends a ship full of antibiotics to Uganda. The President steals the shipment, sells it to hospitals all over the world and puts the money in his bank account—Africa wins! AIDS vaccines are shipped over then disappear—Africa wins! Great white hunters pay $50,000 to shoot an elephant. The local villages are supposed to get the money and the meat. All they see is more dust, because—Africa wins! Do you get the picture?"

Fingering his cross he said, "All right, I'll let you know tomorrow morning if I can get hold of the Ethiopian ambassador and get the arrangements going. If I'm successful, we'll put your plan in motion. Let's conference tomorrow at eleven. I have to get back to the Cathedral, some of my parishioners are doing a fund raiser tonight and I need to be there."

The three made their way out of the restaurant to their waiting cars. Farrell motioned Henderson over after the Bishop left. "Addis Ababa can be a rough place. It's one of the oldest Christian countries in the world, one of the poorest places and one of the most backward. The Catholics have always wanted a toehold there and the Ethiopian church has fought having them there for almost a thousand years. This could be more difficult than we imagine, but I don't see that we have any choice. We may need that back-up plan. This is too important to all of us. We have to find Chad and stop him. The alternative, using Quati, may be our last resort, and I don't like last resorts."

❄ ❄ ❄ ❄ ❄ ❄ ❄ ❄

Quati was subdued for once as he stood in the backroom of the barracks after meeting with his doctor. Turning to Hasid, he asked, "Have you heard anything yet?"

Hasid stood dressed in a grey suit obviously tailored by a professional, his shoes shined and not a hair was out of place. Looking Quati in the eye he nodded. "No, General, the helicopters did not see a thing. We believe Chad has gone over to the mountain, but have not found any evidence yet. Doctor Abu and his crew should be on the mountain about now, so we will soon receive reports, hopefully this afternoon or sooner. They may even find something, Allah willing, even if we do not find Chad."

"Hasid, I am tired . . . tired to the bone. Please keep your eye on this. Nothing would please me more than to bring the Prophet's sacred writings to our Mullahs and protect our faith. Abu is good, but I do not have faith in him for some reason. He is a sincere believer, but he does not have the zeal for the faith that is required. I cannot stand the thought of that infidel Chad handling the Prophet's sacred writings before I do. When you find him, he should be eliminated, painfully and without remorse. Put and end to him, do you hear me, Hasid? I am tired of this. Perhaps it would be better to let it all just lie."

Hasid paced the room. "General, we have been over this before. Chad must be allowed a free rein, so we can keep an eye on him and use him. You said it yourself, Abu is capable but something is missing, something he just does not see or comprehend. He might not be able to follow the trail of the Prophet. He was not able to decipher the writings from the first chamber until we heard of that book that the children read. We must give Chad a free rein. You said you were sending someone to keep an eye on things. What have you done so far?"

"I have done nothing other than send out helicopters. Do not question or countermand my orders, Hasid. I know . . . I know." He held up his hand. "We have talked about this. I changed my mind. The only thing I have done is allow the helicopters to search for Chad. It was of no help. You have lost Chad and do not know where he is!"

"It does not matter where he is. I know where he is going next, so who cares."

A look of excitement grew on Quati's face, his lethargy and pain seemed to vanish. "You know where he is going? Why did you not say something?" He leaned forward in his chair. "Where is he going next?"

Hasid leaned forward on the general's desk. "Ethiopia, to the capital. I have spoken with Abu and looked at all of Chad's notes. All trails lead there."

"How could you read his notes? It was my understanding they were in some sort of code."

"It is not so much his notes, but what his sketches and maps show. He drew a map of Lalibela and the capital, Addis Ababa. That is where we think he is headed. The verses from the second chamber bear this out also. The land of Cush is mentioned and . . . Abu agrees."

"Do not let him get away. If he finds the Prophet's writings first . . . if he, an infidel, finds the sacred writings that were meant for me, I will . . . I will squash him like the infidel dog he is." Quati stood, obviously in some pain. "And Hasid, you must not fail me in this. I wanted to put an end to this the last time we had a chance with Yasuf, but you said . . . no. I may have you pay for that mistake. Do not fail me in your trust. Now get out of here, I need to think."

Hasid nodded and took his leave. When he was in the hallway, he met the doctor who'd been treating Quati. "Is there any hope?"

The doctor knew Hasid well. "The pain grows worse. I have given him pain medication that should help, but it may cloud his thinking at times. I advised him to give some thought to succession, but he does not yet realize the truth."

"Do the best you can. Please keep me advised. The pain medication seems to make him tired and . . . irrational."

"The pain will grow worse. It may go into remission at times, or may not. The medication can also make him depressed or manic at times. You may not notice with him, since he's depressed and manic anyway, but it will make it worse, as Allah wills."

"Thank you, Doctor. You have done your best."

Hasid made a mental note to talk with the doctor again and left the building to his waiting car.

CHAPTER 37

RED SEA

Scott turned to Luke and Alex once they were all in the command tent. "I know everyone's tired but I don't know how long we have. I don't think we have long. Pack up everything. Let's move people."

"Where are we going?" Luke asked.

"To the fabled land of Cush. The land of sun, sand and bullets." He laughed and grabbed his shoulder. "Come on, we don't have much time before someone shows up here. They let us get away too easy."

Samuel frowned. "Too easy! If you call that easy, I'd hate to see what a hard time was."

Scott paused and looked at Luke and Alex. "That's not what I mean. What I meant was they didn't really question us. They let us go. There are more than Yasuf and Abu involved in this and more than the Islamic extremists, too. Remember the Italians when we left, the pair that followed us in Suez. I'm sure they weren't working for the Islamics. I want us out of here right away."

Luke turned, lifted a crate and said, "You're the boss. I've worked for you for two summers and you haven't been wrong yet. Come on, Alex, get a move on," he said as he walked away and helped Alex load a box into the back of the pickup truck.

Julia walked over to Scott. "I have the disks of the survey. I'd like to make copies of them so all our work won't be lost. Do I have time to do it now with the laptop or should we wait until we stop tonight?"

"What makes you think we're going to stop? I'd like to make copies, too, but I've a feeling we have to get out soon. No telling what resources they might bring up. They might be after us in something a lot faster than this old truck and overloaded Suburban. Make copies when we get on the road and make a couple. We'll find somewhere to hide them along the way and keep a set with us. I want you to encrypt them so no one else can read them, know how to do that?"

They finished tying the loads on the roof of the Suburban and made their way down to the coast highway, proceeding south along the Gulf to the tip of the peninsula. Taking a small rocky trail, they drove inland following a trail along a steep-sided wadi with scrubby thorn bushes growing along its banks. After a mile of twists and turns between the boulders, they came to a small open area where the shrubs were taller and pulled the trucks underneath.

"I want us to rest here tonight," Scott said. "We should be safe unless they have planes or copters with infrared. We're well screened and the turn off's rocky and gravely." He yawned and stretched, then looked at Luke and Alex. "We all need some rest after last night and we have to decide what to do next. Part of me wants to send you two back to the States, but I don't know how safe it would be to send you up to Suez to get a flight. It's probably better to make your way into Israel and book a flight out of Tel Aviv."

Alex looked at Scott with a hurt look on his face. "I think we could be of some help as back up if you get in trouble. I don't even want to stay here as back-up and think we should come with you to help all the way, but you're the boss. I know you need someone you can call if you run into trouble."

Scott sighed. "I know how you feel, Alex. It's just that I know your father. You're young and I feel responsible for both you and Luke, and I don't think this is what you signed up for."

A gleam was in his eye when he answered, "No, you're right. I didn't sign up to be hung or shot at by terrorists. What I did sign up for was to be bit by snakes, burnt by the sun, fall off a mountain and die of thirst when the car broke down in the middle of the desert. I'm not a kid anymore and my father, even though he's your friend, wouldn't want you to treat me like one either. I know if you called him, he'd say it was my decision—that I'm a man now and need to make my own decisions. He didn't like it when I joined the Marines, but was proud of me after I came out of basic training—said it made a man out of me. So no matter what you decide, I'm with you, but I'm not going back to the States. After seeing and hearing what that group has done, I want to see this through to the end. There's something more important at stake than just Luke or me or you or anyone for that matter and I can't explain it any better than that."

"Well said, Alex. I knew I chose well when you signed up."

Luke was standing listening to them. Scott turned to him. "Do you feel the same way?"

"Alex and I talked about this, and, well, yes, I feel the same. Maybe even more so. As you know, I was raised in a strict Christian family, Plymouth Brethren, almost modern day Pilgrims, some might say . . . but what I mean is, I think we're supposed to make a choice, to go ahead on this project no matter what or choose to take the easy road and fail in the test. It doesn't mean we're all going to be safe or everything will turn out the way we think. I believe

God's plan for me is far better than anything I could figure out for myself. I don't know if you understand or see since you're not a Christian, Scott, but I respect you immensely nonetheless."

Scott straightened his shoulders. "Luke, I know I've never professed to believe in Christianity. It always offended me as a scientist. I thought Darwin knew it all, that the stories in Genesis were just stories made up for the ignorant. I still see things in a scientific way, but ever since I've been on this quest, something has been tugging at my beliefs."

"Probably the wind of the spirit," Luke said.

"Julia was raised Jewish, Samuel Catholic, and I was raised believing in mankind. I've found that none of us really measures up, that there is something bigger out there. The faith I've seen in men like you, Father Basil, Vasillus, and his Abbot Father Nikita astounds me. You all seem different from what I thought of as religion. I always related faith to religion—but they seem to just believe in something . . . something that is more spiritual than religious. What little religion I was exposed to as a child seemed all about rules. Do this, don't do that; if you do this you will burn and rot in hell. I swear they tried to scare me into contributing to their church and I could see right through it.

"No matter how hard I tried, I couldn't see through those three. I can't see through your faith either, Luke. I agree, there's something at stake here that requires that I make a choice, to see this through until the end. I don't know what it is for sure but if I were to put a name on it, I'd say God wants me to finish this. I just can't make that decision right now. I believe that I have to do this, to finish it to the end. I know God's real, but I don't feel I can give myself up to him. Am I making myself clear?"

Julia looked over at Scott after his talk, a look of disappointment slowly forming on her face. "I thought you were going to say yes. Seems to me that there is probably more freedom in that choice. You make it seem like slavery. I've felt that something was calling me too . . . and I do agree with you about organized religion and rules . . . but the faith and freedom that Vasillus shows is something different. Father Basil's desire . . . what did he say, 'it would ease my heart to know that you were Christians,' was a desire not to convert you but a desire to show his love for us. I think it's a decision that is before us now."

"I know, Julia, I really do, but I can't right now. I look at it this way, if he's real and God, he will know what and when I will decide anyway, for he's much bigger than me and as I said before probably knows everything, for he's beyond time."

"You may be right, but there may not be another time."

"Very dramatic and you may be right, but . . ."

"Aside from all that, I say we finish this. We can't quit, we have to finish it. I think Basil's right and that something would come of that choice, but you're the boss."

Samuel stood and scratched his chin. "Well, I know I'm not a quitter, I say we see this through. We have never given up on anything before. I've worked beside you for years and I'm not about to quit now. As far as converting me, well, I was raised Catholic and then learned that it was okay to check in now and then. Well, I probably chose more the then than now, but most good Catholics like their whisky, too. I'm not much for speeches and am with you all the way on this."

Scott stood there amazed at the group of people around him. "I don't know what I did to deserve all of you, but a man couldn't ask for better companions. Something's going on and a time long awaited is approaching. I've been reading the Bible some and the Koran and believe that God's creation of the great nations is at hand. Will they be joined as brothers and sisters or will they be at each other's throat, that's the question. Enough for now, we need some sleep and to figure out how we're going to get into Ethiopia."

Scott led Julia away from the others as they were getting ready to make camp. They were both silent for a while and turned to each other and started to speak at the same time. "I'm sorry, I . . ."

"No, I'm sorry, go ahead," she responded.

"You first."

She looked up at him. "I was proud of the way you spoke to Luke back there. I know what you mean, no one in my family was ever comfortable talking about religion when I was growing up."

"Well, I wasn't actually talking about religion but being lead by his spirit. I think there's a difference."

"We did a lot of ritual things growing up, but now and then they talked about King David and how he was led by the spirit."

"When David wrote his psalms or songs, he said a contrite spirit and quiet heart is what God wanted, not a religion based on robes, washing a cup, throwing incense around. I don't think religion ever saved anyone! I read something in Matthew where it says, 'you go over land and across the seas to make just one convert. When you do, you make him twice as much a son of hell as you are yourself.' I think he was talking about religion there, too. Jesus said the Sabbath was made for man, not man for the Sabbath. I'm not sure what it all means. He spoke in parables, some of which are easy to understand and others difficult. Some even have double or triple meanings."

"Well, I do know one thing," she said taking his hand. "I think God has sent you into my life."

They stood holding hands and looked into each others eyes and a bond formed that has been a great mystery to men for all ages.

Scott continued to look in her eyes as a great sense of peace and a clarity of mind came over him that he'd never experienced before.

"I have never felt this way before. But I still feel I should have listened more to that evangelist when I was a kid," she said.

"I know . . . I know. I didn't listen either. I have always believed that mankind and science were the answer. Mankind must spread throughout the universe, must evolve and spread his wings and become like gods themselves. Little did I know that each has his time and season, if we only have the ears to hear and wisdom to understand."

"I know what you mean, but you know I'm feeling something else that I've never quite felt before."

Scott looked into her eyes. "What is it?" Then he saw it in her eyes and pulled her close and couldn't stop his emotions. "I know, I feel it, too. Something has happened to my love for you. I think I fell in love with you the moment I saw you, that first day you walked into camp. That time in the tent when you were so angry."

"Forget that time in the tent—that wasn't me." She laughed.

"I don't want to forget that or any other time. Don't say that wasn't you, I wouldn't want to change you a bit. Most women are offended by the male-ness of their counterparts, because it upsets all their primness and neatness. Most men are offended by a woman's need to nurture, to be held, to feel close and be reassured, but they compliment each other—when they truly love each other."

Julia rested her head against his shoulder and then looked up in his eyes as he bent his lips to hers. The kiss was different from the quick kiss in the cave at Meteora. It lasted longer, was much more tender, but most of all there was a natural peace to it that asked nothing more from the moment.

Julia broke it off and said, "I think we ought to be getting back. The others may be worried about us."

"You're right, let's head back and get some rest, even though I'm not tired now. I know we need sleep if we're going to be of much use tomorrow."

Scott awoke feeling more refreshed than he could remember the next morning. He set up the phone with the laptop and went online. He then opened up the pictures they'd taken in the cave in Meteora. "This is interesting, Julia. There might be more to the pictures than we first thought." He beckoned her over. "Look at this. Tell me what you see?"

She leaned over in the car to get a better view of the screen. "It looks like a man sitting on top of a tree with another tree leaning over him. Just appears to be an old Byzantine painting. That's all, other than the Greek letter-ing underneath."

"Now, look close at it. What do you see now?"

A puzzled expression grew on her face. "I see a man in the picture. He seems to be reading a book or scroll. What am I supposed to see?"

"Well, first of all, remember it's written in Hebrew and Arabic and the writing goes from right to left, then kind of step back and take a big look at the picture. See it now?"

She frowned and leaned back, shaking her head. "I don't read Arabic. My Hebrew's not very good; I didn't have to learn it for my batmitsvah!"

"Okay, not fair. It says, 'The Way of the Truth lies in Cush—The Negus knew the way!' It doesn't make sense to me, but when I read the next line, 'The Wisdom of the Wise King and his Queen will guide your way,' I wonder what that means?" Scott said.

"I suppose it means to look further! The text at the bottom's in Greek, but if you translate the letters at the top it's in Arabic. We missed it all the time! We should look at the text at the bottom with the mirror from the lady. I have it in my pack. I'll get it from the back. Thank God Yasuf didn't take it."

She rummaged around in back and drew out the mirror wrapped in a fleece sweater. "Take a look at that bottom line again with this!"

He took the mirror and said, "Let's see, the main text still says,

> I make the great nations, as if from the stars
> Long promised before to brothers afar
> When I make a covenant, it always is kept
> I am what I am and never have slept
> Wake up, oh sleepers, why do you drowse
> Look all around you and take stock of the clouds
> The day will soon come, only I am known just when
> When the brothers will join, and embrace once again
> Isaiah did know of the covenant to come
> Jeremiah too and knows whose the one
> Bringing the covenant, I gave to Mankind
> Enlightening them all, who are not so blind.

He turned the laptop around and held the mirror up to read the reversed text and through the distorted wavelength. "I think you're right. The Greek lettering changes, too. I don't know how we missed it in the cave. I'd translate it like this:

> Look to the land, where spices are near
> The mine of the king, whose wisdom is clear
> He took a bride, from here some may say
> My wisdom will grow, and all will soon pray

Will pray just like brothers, sprung from the same seed
Knowing the Lords, one, two and three
Giving his love to all who believe
The law was given, for light does not deceive
Onyx and Gold, the land is so high
His mine was not fabled, so look to the sky
The sign that you're near, will speak in your heart
Jeremiah and Isaiah, will give you a start
Knowing what wisdom is, and what is the law
Takes some discernment, not known by us all
Remember his wisdom, and look to his words
There you will find it, and soon save the world.

"I'm starting to feel as if we're on a scavenger hunt. Remember that old man in the Plaka district—the note and map he gave us?"

She smiled and winked. "How could I forget that night?"

He turned and smiled at her entendre, then sat in the Suburban staring at the pictures, feeling perplexed. "I'm not sure what these verses mean. I've slept on it though and have decided we go on to Ethiopia. The two chambers have been clear so far, so I'm going to follow the clear path. There's that reference to the wise king and his queen from the land of spices." He stopped and cracked his knuckles. "Who that is, I don't know. Wasn't Solomon called the Wise King—but didn't he have a bunch of wives?"

A frown grew on her face. "I don't know that much about it. You'd need to talk to a rabbi or biblical scholar, but from what I remember, he had a lot of wives and even more concubines. Which wife they mean, if they mean Solomon at all, I have no idea."

Samuel walked up scratching his head. "Lots of wives and concubines. I thought monogamy was the rule for the Jews?"

"It's the rule today, but during the time of the Patriarchs they lived much as their neighbors did. Muslim law allows four wives, but how harmonious the household is would be anyone's guess," she said with a laugh.

He stopped and looked down the wadi.

"What's your plan then?" Julia asked.

"The way is clear. We have to get across the gulf or down the gulf to Ethiopia. I say we cross tonight, then make our way south. Luke and Alex can stay here as backup. I'll call them at seven every night. So they'll have to keep the phone on at that time."

Julia looked at him dumbfounded. "That's your plan? Let me get this straight, we're going to sneak across the gulf into Egypt, a foreign country I might add, under cover of darkness without the proper papers. Then we're going to find transportation south through the Sudan if I remember right. Get into Ethiopia and find this lost chamber. Do I have this right so far? Now, let's see, if we get in trouble, you're going to try to call Luke or Alex who will get in touch with one of your friends from the Saudi royal family to bring in the cavalry, right? Oh, and don't forget Dr. Abu and whatever troops he has working for him chasing us around. Do I have this plan right?"

Scott laughed. "It's probably more complicated than that. You forgot the snakes, scorpions and roving patrols of border guards." He looked at her again and smiled. "But, yes, that's the plan! I haven't had time to think of a better one and we need to get moving."

A smile spread out on her face. "Sounds fun to me, not like anyone's given us a nice relaxing time lately anyway. Are you sure Luke and Alex will be safe waiting here?"

He frowned. "I'm not sure, but I think they'll be safer than with us. We have to take the chance. We need someone for backup and we only have one boat." He turned and looked at Alex. "Keep the phone on at seven every night as I said and I'll call if we need you."

He paused and called everyone over. "Now gather around." He took out a large-scale map of the area. "Here's where we are now," he said, using his pencil as a pointer. "We're going to cross near the end of the wadi at dusk, it shouldn't take too long with the electric motor, and we should have enough battery to get there if the current's not too strong. I want to land by this headland. We should be able to stash the boat and make our way up to the road. My best guess we should be able to find some transportation with what money we have."

Julia looked over at Scott. "What if we can't find any transportation?"

"There's a pretty big town about thirty miles south, Turghada, which is a dive center for the islands and reefs offshore. We should be able to rent a car there."

Samuel spoke up. "The moon should be out and the forecast's for high pressure the next couple of days."

They all looked up as they heard the unmistakable sound of a pair of helicopters approaching from the southwest.

Samuel was the first to move. "Quick, throw the tarps and branches over the trucks and get under them. Quick, move now!"

They grabbed the tarps out of the pickup and threw them over the vehicles, then tossed small branches and handfuls of sand over the tarps to conceal the vehicles. The sound from the helicopters was echoing off the rocks as they crawled under the tarps. The thump-thump-thump of the approaching copters grew louder as a pair of them crested the rise to their west, just as Julia crawled under the tarp by Scott. The helicopters followed the wadi and trail down toward the sea, flying right over their position. Julia peeked out from under their shelter and saw one stop and hover downstream from their bivouac. It rotated around, headed back toward them, and was almost on top of their position when the pilot spun around and altered course, quickly following the other helicopter down toward the gulf. One turned south down the coast while the other headed north. The first one came back north, flying low and slow along the coastline and continued heading north toward Elat. They didn't hear anything else that afternoon and continued with their preparations, getting the boat ready, but leaving the tarps and branches next to the vehicles should they hear anything again.

As twilight closed in, Scott assembled the team together. "Alex and Luke, I hate to leave you, but it's our best plan. I want you to drive us down to the coast and once we're gone, get back up here and wait. If all goes well, we'll be back in a week or so."

Loading the back of the pickup full of the gear, they drove back down the wadi to the coast. The sun was setting as they came upon the coast road. Turning north once back on the road, they passed the turnoff to Ras Moham-med, then followed a small gravel track surrounded by low rocky hills mostly devoid of vegetation. Scott told Alex to pull over just past a small rock out-crop that looked like a lonely sentinel on the shore. Lonely rollers washed and stirred the azure waters from some far away storm in the Indian Ocean.

Scott turned to Alex. "Remember to monitor the phone and be ready to move. I think you and Luke should take turns sleeping and keep your heads down."

Lifting the inflatable boat from the back of the truck, Samuel pulled the tag to the inflation valve and watched it inflate. Attaching an electric motor and battery pack, he then threw in their gear as Scott and Julia grabbed a few more items from the truck.

Alex walked down to the shore. "Be careful, I haven't . . . said much but I know I speak for Luke too . . . when I say, we really think a lot of you and don't know what we'd do without you. So please be careful."

Scott looked at the tall lean young man and smiled. "You've come to mean a lot to us, almost as if you're family. Take care and monitor the phone!" he said as he shook hands, then turned with Julia and walked down to where Samuel was waiting.

They pulled the boat into the warm gulf waters and waved to Luke and Alex who were becoming difficult to see in the twilight. It was slack tide and the current weak. Scott and Samuel took a paddle while Julia held the tiller of the small electric motor. They quickly became a small speck bobbing on the swells.

Five hours later, just about when Scott's arms were about to give out, Julia whispered, "I see a light ahead."

Scott's expression was hard to read in the darkness, but his answer clear enough. "We should be almost there, at least my arms hope so. It might be a fishing boat, a shepherd or just someone camped on the shore. The road's back from the coast at least six miles. The land between's full of rocky hills. It won't be any picnic getting across them to the road and then up to the slopes."

They rolled into the shore between some gentle breakers, finding a deserted beach by a rocky headland where they could stash the boat. Scott held up his hand when they were all assembled. "The light we saw is just around those rocks. I think we should check it out before making for the road. Best to know what's around us."

They all nodded and followed Scott's lead as they scrambled over the rocky shoulder of the little headland. Scott was surprised when he peered around the rock and saw a blue forty-five foot Hatteras anchored in the cove.

He held up his hand and stopped Samuel. "Go quietly here. I'll go first in case there's trouble."

He left Julia and Samuel crouched in between some large boulders while he quietly made his way around the headland and looked into the little cove. The smell of cooking came to him off the gentle northerly breeze and he saw a man and boy on the beach raking coals on a hearth they'd made from rocks, on which they were roasting their morning catch. Scott crept back to where they waited and raised his finger to his lips. "There's a nice dive or fishing boat in the cove. An old fisherman and probably his son or helper are on the beach, cooking up some breakfast. I think it will be safe to go down there, but we're taking a chance."

Julia whispered, "I'm tired of all this sneaking around. I didn't like your plan in the first place. I say let's take the chance, if you two agree."

"I agree with her, Scott. I say let's try it. Most people are hospitable to strangers in this part of the world. We've just run into a streak of bad luck lately with good ole Dr. Abu and his friends."

"Okay, but I'll go first. Wait until I call you, if it seems okay," Scott said.

The morning sun was now in the sky and the azure blue of the waters and waves glistened in the light.

Scott strode around the boulder, hopped down onto the beach and called out a greeting in Arabic to the fisherman and boy. They both stopped what they were doing and stepped back from the fire when they saw the tall stranger approach.

He walked up to the weathered old man and said in Arabic, "Good morning. Do you have enough to share with some starved travelers?"

The old fisherman stared into his eyes, and then answered in English. "We believe in sharing with travelers in this part of the world and practicing hospitality, as told in the Koran, but you speak of travelers and there is only one of you?"

Scott looked into his grey eyes. The man's face was wrinkled by many years in the sun and salt of the seas. "My companions and I have had a rough time of it lately and we're cautious until we know more of you. It is not wise to descend upon people, all at once, until you know more of them. My name's Scott Chad. I'm a surveyor working for the Egyptian government on a job across the Gulf in Sinai."

"I am Mishma Abubakar, at your service, sir. This is my son, Adbeel. If your companions are not too many, we would be glad for them to join us. I know how you feel for we ourselves have journeyed far and do not take kindly to some of the people that are here about."

Scott made a snap decision based on looking at Mishma's eyes and seeing the truth in them. It wasn't easy to lie to Scott, since he practiced telling the truth.

"There are three of us, another man and a woman. We would be pleased to join you and hear your tale." Scott whistled and Samuel and Julia came around the boulder to join the three on the sandy beach.

Samuel walked up and bowed to Mishma and to his son Adbeel, and Julia came up, lowered her eyes, and curtsied. Mishma looked them up and down and turned to Scott. "You did say that one of your companions was a woman, but did not say she was tall and beautiful with golden hair. We have an old prophesy that when the princess with the golden hair comes among us, the lost and sundered brothers shall join again in harmony and the great nations will be like one as Allah ordained long ago. This area was not always known as Sinai, you know! It used to be called Havilah and Shur and my son and I are descended, son to son from Abraham. We reckon our lineage through Ishmael and his son Mishma. Since we reckon our line back to Abraham, we remember what the Lord promised his descendants. The Arabs and Jews are people of the book, even though there has been enmity between us for many a generation. Still, we are all people of the book and worship the one true God."

Julia blushed as she listened, taking in his words.

Scott smiled. "Well, we are pleased to meet you, Mishma. What are your plans after here?"

Mishma laughed. "Well, I can tell you are not Bedouin. We are on our way south, fishing and looking for a new place to call home. Ever since the House of Saud took an interest in this area, we have been moved from one place to another. My wife was stoned by the Saud's security forces on a false charge. The village we lived in accused her of blasphemy and the House of

Saud turned the village against her. Our people are from ancient Havilah and Shur. This is the real Sinai," he said with a sweep of his arms. "By Allah, I will see the House of Saud fall one day! Enough, we are on our way to the south. How may we assist you?"

Scott looked him up and down. "We're on our way to Ethiopia. There are factions from Egypt, Saudi Arabia and others that are interested in seeing our venture fail. If you would agree to take us as passengers, we may be able to make it worth your while?"

Mishma looked at Scott. "I don't know what you mean by worth our while—but I do believe in our prophesies, the golden haired princess, and I would not wish to see harm come to her. We also value beauty when it is tempered by a reverent heart." He looked at Julia and asked. "Tell me child, are you of the book or one of the heathen?"

Julia stared at Mishma then defiantly lifted her head and answered, "I was raised Jewish. Yes, I am of the book, but my heart has now turned and I believe my heart belongs to another, to the one whose sandals I am not fit to untie."

"Ho, that is a good tale," Mishma said. "One that is worthy of the truth, but that doesn't change the prophecy. Do not look so startled, I know of whom you speak, you speak of the Lamb of God, that is clear. Muslims know and respect the Christ as a great Prophet, but some among us believe he was something much more, if we are willing to search the ancient writings and scriptures."

"Do not misunderstand me. You are amongst friends here. We believe in the Christ also. We believe that his Prophet Mohammad will lead us one day into the truth of the Messiah, to the way of truth and grace. We are considered heretics to have this belief, of course, but have you heard of the Satanic Verses? Rushdie wrote a book about certain verses in the Koran and one of the ayatollahs set a bounty on his head, last I heard. But I digress, Mohammad was illiterate, we now know, and could not write down his revelations. His trusted scribe wrote them down for him and others read them back so he knew they were the truth and not some fabrication. We believe the Koran was divinely inspired, too, but man is fallible while the divine is infallible."

"Mishma, I hate to interrupt but we have to decide on our next course of action. We'd love to come with you as far as the Horn of Africa if you would agree to take us. I would also love to hear your story, but a group of men has been chasing us and if they caught us here, our mission would fail and they would take great pleasure in that. There is some danger to what we are asking, and time is of the essence. We should depart, or go our separate ways."

"My friend, we are not easy to lie to. We are men of the truth and are able to discern when we meet someone who speaks the truth. I am not afraid of danger since they stoned my wife." He stopped and looked at his son and smiled. "Enough! We will take you. When time is short, use what time we have to Allah's advantage. Come, let us go." Mishma said, waving them toward his boat.

Samuel yelled. "Hold on, we have something for you," as he ran across the beach. He pulled the tarp, brushed the sand off their little boat, and dragged it over to Mishma. "I don't see any reason to leave this here. Can you use it?"

Adbeel came over, helped Samuel drag the boat to the shore of the cove, and looked it over. His eyes lit up as he looked at it and Mishma noticed his interest. "You are too generous. I do not think we should leave it here. Come, let us hoist it onto the davits."

They waded out to his boat and climbed the ladder to the craft. It was a forty-eight foot light-blue fiberglass boat that reminded Scott of a Cape Hatteras he had had his eye on when he lived near Washington. He'd always wanted a 46' Hatteras with twin diesels and dreamed of living on Chesapeake Bay. They climbed aboard, pulled the dinghy around the rear and attached it to the davits. When all was ready, Mishma signaled his son to hoist the anchor and started the engines. They came to life with a quiet burble and he deftly swung the boat around.

They headed out into the Gulf and Mishma called out, "Adbeel, let out the line. We will troll a line during the daytime, in case someone's watching and put on more power whenever it looks safe."

"Make yourselves at home," Mishma said, as he got comfortable in the captain's chair. "Adbeel, when you're done with the lines show our guests around. The lady may have the forward cabin and the men may share the salon. See to their comfort."

Scott was worried about Luke and Alex waiting on the far shore but decided that picking them up during the daytime would not be a good idea. He pulled out his satellite phone and showed it to Mishma. "I'd like to call some-one who's waiting for us. Do you mind?"

Mishma simply shrugged.

Scott quickly dialed the phone, let it ring, and ring and ring, and then hung up. He tried again, but there was still no answer.

Adbeel came back from setting the lines so that it looked like they were fishing and said, "Come, I will show you our boat."

It was obvious he took great pride in the craft which was beautifully maintained, and Scott was surprised to see that in fact it was a Cape Hatteras 48 when they went below. He would have never guessed from the look outside with the fishing gear attached, but inside the salon, cabins and appointments showed the beauty of the craft. Adbeel showed them the salon, his and his father's cabin, the heads and the rest of the craft. They were amazed at the opulence. It looked like just a dingy blue fishing boat from a distance, but below was all teak and polished cherry with granite counter-tops. Adbeel showed Julia the forward cabin and told her to make herself at home then showed Scott and Samuel how to convert the salon into bunks. He obviously took special pride in the engine room with the twin-turbo diesels. His face beamed as he pointed out the engines and he lovingly patted the starboard plant as he showed them how to check the oil, hydraulic pressure and electrical generator.

Chapter 38
Farrell's Boys in Africa

Hasid looked at the pair as they walked up thinking. *I hope they're better than Luigi. Farrell's report was promising, but they're still infidels.* Walking across the dusty floor of the warehouse in Cairo, he extended his hand. "You must be Shula and you must be Mulama," he said.

"Farrell said you knew Chad when you were kids?"

"That was years ago in Illinois. We spent a few years together in the same school and neighborhood."

"How old were you then?" Shula asked.

"About fifteen."

"The formative years. I would think you know his tactics."

"He's smart and it's hard to tell what to expect out of him."

"Is he tough though?" Mulama asked.

"Not in the sense you're thinking, but tenacious and cunning are more the words I would use. His partner is tough and the Israeli with him is smart, too."

"Reports are she is a woman agent trained by the Mosad, do you know her too?"

"I know of her," Hasid said not wanting to disclose too much to these two for some reason.

"Farrell said you had a car rented for us and knew of a place to get our supplies. Is everything ready?"

"We can leave as soon as you're rested."

"We can leave now then," Shula said.

"You just landed after a twelve hour flight. It's a long way down the Red Sea and to the Horn of Africa."

"We're ready. We just need to procure some items we couldn't have brought through customs."

"As I said, all is in readiness. The car is loaded and ready to go," Hasid said, pointing to the car parked in the old warehouse.

"Let's go then," Shula said walking over to the car.

The bright red orb of the sun was rising over the desert as they left Cairo and headed east. The air-conditioner was set on full blast and outside was the Sahara.

The heat blasted Hasid as he pulled over four hours later to fill up the car at what passed for a filling station.

Shula pulled out a cell phone and called Farrell, who sounded distant on the phone. "I told you I'd call you when I had things in place. Your job's to obey orders, get yourselves in place and wait for my call! What do you think of Hasid? Can we trust him?"

"He seems smart and in control, if that's what you mean. I haven't known him long enough to form any other opinion. What about the Ethiopian survey. Is that arranged for Chad yet?"

"I am not sure yet, but there's no point in interrupting me when I'm doing important work. I will call you when I have information you need to know. Remember this job you're doing is important, but the Lord has work for me, too. The fields are ripe and the harvest is great. You're to be my winnowing fork and I need you sharp and rested so you are ready and in place for the harvest. Don't underestimate Chad or the others with him. They're dangerous to our plan and probably in league with the evil one. Keep your mind sharp and rested and keep an eye on Mulama. Make sure he doesn't go astray with some infidel woman while he's with you. As soon as I know something, I'll page you or call on the cell. Wait to contact me on our schedule, do you understand me?"

"Yes, Reverend, I understand. We will do as you say. I'll contact you every other night at eleven o'clock your time. Is there anything else?"

Farrell sighed, "No, just be careful and keep yourselves clean!"

Continuing south, they following the coast route to Port Sudan and had no trouble crossing the border with Hasid with them. Farrell had arranged their passports and documents and the border guard was surly, but consulted a list in his shack and came back with a smile to Hasid, handing them their passports, then waved them through without checking the car.

Two nights later they stopped at a roadside stand and Shula called Farrell while Hasid and Mulama went inside.

Farrell came on the phone. "I spoke with the Ethiopian minister and he's trying to contact Chad to arrange a survey. They've contacted his office in Illinois and are trying to locate him. We didn't get much information out of his office, but hopefully they will know how or where to contact him and he'll respond to our offer. Once I find out where he is, I will let you know. Go to Addis Ababa as planned and wait."

"Don't you think we should wait closer to the border, what if he doesn't fly in but comes in by car or boat?"

Farrell sighed. "The government is going to let us know the moment he crosses the border. Don't worry, we'll find out where he is. They won't stop him, one of their men is on our payroll, and we'll know when he comes in and how he's traveling."

"Are you . . . sure? Some of these people down here don't seem too trustworthy. Hasid is good and I will admit he did pretty well at the border in Sudan, but he's not a Christian. Can we trust him?"

"Just follow your orders, Shula! Bestin and Henderson are paying good money for this and you need to be my instruments down there. Be sharp, do you understand me?"

"Yes Reverend, we understand. We'll check into the hotel in Addis Ababa and wait for your call. Is there anything else?"

"No, just call every other day like we planned. Good bye, Shula, and good work so far."

They entered Ethiopia the next day and took the highway to Addis Ababa after clearing the border. Booking a room in a medium priced hotel, Hasid took a suite on the top floor while Shula and Mulama shared a room downstairs. The city was much larger than they had expected and Mulama looked around with delight as he saw the young women walking to their jobs.

❊ ❊ ❊ ❊ ❊ ❊ ❊ ❊

Julia and Scott sat on the front deck as they made their way south. They hadn't seen any pursuit or helicopters and were now past the tip of Sinai and into the Red Sea proper. Mishma came up carrying a tray of food. "This is Injera. It's a flat, sourdough pancake which you will see a lot of in Ethiopia. It is inexpensive and made from one of the local grains they call T'ef. I do not know what you would call it, but try it. It is very good." He smiled as he handed them the dish and pointed to another. "This is a lamb stew that Adbeel made. Use the Injera to pick up the meat or vegetable and dip it in the sauce."

Scott said between mouthfuls, "I agree. It's a lot better than Aunt Jemima is and probably healthier. The sauce in the lamb stew's wonderful, but hot." He fanned his mouth and dipped another piece in the dish.

"The sauce is made from, Berbere, which is a blend of spices that give Ethiopian food its distinctive flavor. They use it in everything. Another of their popular dishes you will see is Wot, which they seem to have at every meal. It is made with a hot spicy pepper sauce that they mix with vegetables, meat and chicken."

Mishma added, "Be careful of the drink. They drink a wine called T'ej, which they make from honey and be especially careful of the local beer, which they call T'ella. Both are much stronger than what you are probably used to."

When they'd finished and cleaned up, they joined Mishma in the cockpit. He turned to Scott. "I would like to get cleaned up and get some rest. These old bones are not what they used to be. Do you feel comfortable taking a watch?"

"No problem. I almost bought one of these when I was in Washington," Scott said, patting the hatch.

"She's a good boat. I will take first watch in the morning. Keep heading south and turn the radar on now and then to see if anything is in front of you," he paused and raised an eyebrow, "or behind you! Every half hour is usually enough."

Samuel came up on deck. "Quite the fellow, I like his son Adbeel, too. He gave me a tour of the boat and he's really proud of her. I'm bushed," he said as he turned and winked. "I'm going to bed too. Mishma said he'd wake me to take a watch before dawn, so I'd better get some sleep." He looked around at the dark horizon. "I don't think we're going to run into anything I'd find too exciting anyway."

"You know, Samuel, I want to thank you for being with me through all of this. I don't mean to get sappy and know you hate it, but I just wanted to let you know."

"You don't have to say it," Samuel said.

"I got hold of Luke and Alex. They turned the phone off to conserve the batteries. The interesting thing is they say Mabel called and the Ethiopian government's requesting that we do a survey for them. Mabel said they want us to start right away and want us to chart whatever gold or platinum deposits we can find. It's a huge job and they're saying they want our team for the project. The plan's full of ideas to raise their people out of poverty and they want us to give them a proposal to survey a large interior section of the country like we did for Saudi Arabia." His eyebrows rose and he looked Samuel in the eye. "I think it's an amazing coincidence and asked Luke to call Rusta to find out if he'd recommended us. I have an odd feeling about this. Sounds too good to be true."

Samuel laughed. "We're headed to Ethiopia and all of a sudden they want to meet with us to provide them a survey. Why couldn't it have been Japan or Canada or something? You know, Scott, our work's always come to us by happenstance and word of mouth. But every time we've been offered a job it's always . . . always the most inconvenient of times and most inconvenient of places. I agree with you," he said as he headed down the companionway.

Scott sat at the helm and set the autopilot, switched on the radar transmit button and let it sweep a couple of times. The only thing showing was the western coast about seven miles off. He glanced at all the gauges and kept the throttle low to conserve fuel, then leaned back in the captain's chair. "Ah, this is the life, I'll tell you. There were times I could turn it all in and just cruise around in a boat. I've always wanted a sailboat but never seem to have found the time to get one. I rented one for a week once in the British Virgin Islands and it was one of the best times I ever had."

Julia perched on the captain's chair and Scott put his arm around her, pulling her close. He looked at the way the wind blew her hair back and she nestled her head on his shoulder and said, "Scott, you know this could be our last adventure! I'm not sure why I'm saying this . . . but after what we've been through, I know you wouldn't stop for anything, and neither would I. Now this offer of a survey in Ethiopia, I'm kind of afraid about it."

He pulled her tighter in response. "We don't have to answer the call you know. We can just sneak into the country and get about our business."

She turned her head and looked up at him. "Africa wins! Didn't you say? It makes me afraid. The funny thing is, I've never really been afraid before! I think it is because I have grown close to you and am not sure if I'm afraid for myself, or afraid of losing you, or afraid of . . . oh I don't know . . . what. Now that I've found you I'm concerned."

"I've felt the same. I've always cared for Samuel and my employees, but I've felt the same tightening type of fear myself. A fear of your getting hurt and not being able to stand it. I've seen Samuel get hurt before and have even laughed about it. One time he took a bullet in the butt and I rolled with laughter, even though it wasn't something to laugh about. I thought it was so funny, I knew he wasn't going to die of course and knew it hurt a lot, but it was funny. I just couldn't bear to see you get hurt. Maybe you should stay with Mishma!"

"You better stop that thinking right now and get used to thick and thin mister."

Scott turned and winked. "What do you mean by thick and thin, young lady?"

She backed away. "I mean where you go, I go! I've been talking about my fear of you getting hurt. I want . . . no, I need to be there. I need to know you're safe."

"Isn't that my job, to keep you safe?"

"Well, we'll keep each other safe, watch each other's back. Is that how you say it? Remember we've also got Samuel, and I've a feeling he's a lot tougher than he lets on."

"Samuel's quite the man. He's tough, sweet, smart, stupid . . . you name it, he's it. What I most admire about him is that he's honest to the core. Not that he can't superbly lie his way out of a jam, but I mean honest in a real sense. He'd never cheat anyone, always tells the truth, and always fights for what he believes in."

She laughed at her thought. "I thought his second home was in a bar somewhere?"

"He puts on his tough guy act around other people when he doesn't know them well. Sure, he's seen his share of bars and been in his share of fights. He was never one to back away from one. Whenever we had time off in Illinois, he's was off working with kids in various ways. One summer he coached a Little League team to a championship season. A bunch of twelve-year olds, with Samuel out there coaching them. Getting their dads to coach bases, finding someone to keep score and getting the kids to behave. They went 14–2 for the season and came in first in their division."

They sat quietly as the darkness grew deeper over the sea. Scott switched the radar to transmit every now and then as the boat slid south though the warm waters. She turned around while Scott was checking the radar and gave a little gasp. "Look at that!"

The wake was creating a phosphorescent trail behind them that slowly faded to nothingness in the distance. "Oh, how beautiful," she said as she looked up at Scott piloting the craft. "This is one of those moments I wish would never end. Sometimes life's so unfair. Get up at six, shower and go to your job. Have a long day doing the same old thing day in and day out. Come home, watch TV, or read the paper and then go to bed and do the same thing the next day. I wonder though, if you had beauty like this everyday, it might fade. We should take it as a gift. But it does beat nine to five."

He looked down at her. "I've had that choice a number of times. It's probably exciting for some people, but not for me. I've always been the kind of guy who wanted to know what was around the next corner." He looked at her. "Did you know that Scott means to wander?" At that moment, a shooting star shot across their bow and seemed to disappear into the sea in front of them.

She nestled her head into his arm. "Wander like a star, wander like a vagabond, wander like the wind in the trees, but just wander back to me."

They sat in the darkness just drinking in the night as the craft continued south. The next day they pulled into Port Sudan, refueled the boat, stocked up on provisions, then headed for Massawa on the Eritrean coast. They were hugging the western shoreline and navigation became more difficult as they avoided the little islands and reefs that dotted the region.

Julia looked at a mountain that Scott pointed out far off in the interior and turned to him. "Looking at the Red Sea on a map it always seemed so small, just a little crack with some blue in it dividing Egypt from Saudi Arabia. I had no idea it was this big!"

"Africa's huge, the only place bigger is Asia. The whole of the United States could fit inside the Sahara desert with room to spare, and that's only part of Africa. Ethiopia's the size of France and Spain put together, but it doesn't look like it to most people when they look at a map. I haven't scaled the chart, but the Red Sea must be a thousand miles long. The coast of Eritrea alone is four hundred miles long. When we dock at Massawa, we'll try to get transportation to Asmara and then on to . . . well, I'm not sure. I think we should go to Axum. Some people say the cradle of Christianity is there, while others say that's where Islam really took off. They had a great king named Lalibela, who constructed eleven churches, hewn right out of the local cliffs and rocks. They're still there today and some people consider them the eighth wonder of the world. There's also the tale of the Arc of the Covenant and the Ten Commandments. The arc supposedly rests in Axum, too! Quite the land of contrasts, high mountains, deserts, plains, antelope and elephants."

Later that day, Mishma took over the helm from Scott. He turned to Scott once he was seated at the wheel. "We should reach Massawa by tomorrow morning." He paused and laughed. "I have grown to like you, even if you are kind of a rascal. I have also heard you talk and I sense your fears. My son and I have discussed this and we would deem to help you on this quest you are on. Are you sure you would not like us to accompany you?"

"That's very kind of you, Mishma! But I believe it will be a dangerous journey and if something were to happen to you or your son, I wouldn't be able to forgive myself. You could do something though. We need to rent a car or truck to arrange some type of transportation once we get into port. I'm afraid to use a credit card or my identification because the people who want to stop us are able to get into the computers that track the world's finances. If there's some way I could pay you and you rented the car, it might keep them off our trail. I haven't told you all, my secretary received a call from the Ethiopian government, which is offering us a large survey of the interior region. We think it's a ruse, designed to lure us out in the open. It seems too coincidental to us. The longer we can keep under cover, the better."

Scott paused and looked at Mishma. "It might help if you could work on your boat and hang around for a week or two. If we're not back in two weeks then you can leave. We may need to get out in a hurry and it would be nice to know you're there, if we're moving fast."

A look of concern crossed Mishma's face. "If you got a cash advance and then paid me they'd know you were in Eritrea. That won't work!"

"You're right. I was going to have my secretary wire you the money, to pay you back for your time, fuel and to rent the car. That still leaves a computer trail, but it's the best I can come up with. Think about it. Do you have a bank or know a bank in the area?"

Mishma's face brightened. "Sure, I have a bank and a credit card. I could not run this boat without it. The tourists I take out on dive trips all pay by credit card. I will give you the routing information. I do not have to think about it. We will help, but . . . I was coming down here anyway. We do not really want to take your money." He shrugged. "But funds are short and anything you can spare would be appreciated, these days." He looked over at his son, who nodded to him, then back to Scott. "We will stay in port for two weeks. The bottom needs scraping and the diesels should be looked over. There is also some good fishing in the area and maybe we could secure a charter or two, take some tourists out to the reefs."

"That's settled then. I'll have Mabel wire twenty thousand dollars to your account." Scott paused and said, "No, let's make it thirty. You give ten back to me in cash and you'll not consider the trip wasted." He looked Mishma in the eye again. "I mean it, keep your eyes open. The people who have been after us are not to be trifled with."

"My friend, as I said before. We can take care of ourselves." Mishma pulled up the cockpit seat, lifted a false bottom and two well-oiled Uzi's, strapped to the bulkhead, shown out. "Adbeel and I have been in scrapes before. We know how to watch out."

"When we get to Massawa, we need to rent a car. I'm planning on heading right to Addis Ababa if everything goes right. I have a feeling that things are coming together quickly and that time's running short, so we have to move quick," Scott said.

"Where do you propose to look, my friend?" Mishma asked.

"I'm going to Addis Ababa, I don't think it would be safe to tell you more. No . . . no," Scott said and raised his hands when he saw the look on Mishma's face. "It's not that I don't trust you, but these men who are after us . . . well, it would be better if you don't know anything more. The less you know, the less trouble you could be in. These men don't mind murder or torture and I don't think they'll stop at much of anything. Trust me on this, you don't want to know and don't need to know. I'll tell you what—when the wire arrives, why don't you get a cell phone, call my secretary Mabel and give her your number, then I can contact you if we have to. Is that fine with you?"

"That is no problem. I can tell when great things are in the offing. When they are, we must rise up to meet the needs of the times. I trust you and understand. You never know what portion a person may play. It is our place to play out the portion as Allah wills. May your God and Allah protect you."

The next morning the sleepy little town of Massawa, Eritrea appeared on the horizon. They docked at one of the local fishing docks and cleared customs easily. No one even asked questions or reviewed their passports. Julia wore a chador so she wouldn't arouse suspicion and stick out as a western woman. Mishma rented a Land Rover for their use and once they'd said their goodbyes, they loaded up the vehicle and proceeded south on the main highway toward Asmera and then Adigrat. Asmera was a large town filled with rich and poor alike, the poor were poverty stricken while the rich drove Mercedes, BMW's and other vehicles around the dusty city. The poor lived on the outskirts of the town, in little tin-covered shacks and hacked out an existence that was Africa.

"Africa wins," Scott said, as they made their way though the city. "I'll never forget how Africa seems to bring out the best and worst in people. It's one of the most blessed continents and one of the harshest at the same time. The problem is what man's done to man here during the centuries. First slavery, then colonization. Tribalism is the worst of all and the pure unadulterated racism. If you're not one of their tribe, you're scum and they don't care. Africa wins."

Crossing the border into Ethiopia, they made their way to the little town of Adigrat where they booked two rooms for the night and looked forward to sleeping in a bed that didn't move for the first time in awhile.

They went out for an early dinner and stopped at a little restaurant serving local cuisine.

Scott ordered the Injera made from T'ef with some of the local beef stew loaded with Berbere. Samuel ordered a steak and beer while Julia opted for a salad.

Relaxing after supper, they strolled back toward the hotel. It was early evening and Scott cautioned them. "We want to get an early start in the morning. I want to take the eastern road, in case someone's watching, and then cut over on the back roads to Axum." He noticed the look Samuel wore. "I know. I told Mishma we were heading to the capital. It's not that I don't trust him, but sometimes disinformation is the best offense. If someone comes to talk with Mishma, all he can say is we're headed toward the capital."

"But you lied to him. Don't you think he knows that?" Julia said.

"Yeah, he does, remember he asked to join us. He's probably figured out that we're not going to Addis Ababa."

He looked around at the town. The sun would set in about and hour and he turned to his companions. "I'd like to explore the town and some of these old Coptic churches." He pointed across the square at an old church carved from the rock of the cliff behind it.

"Can we stop and look in a couple of the shops on the way back to the hotel?" Julia asked.

Scott looked up and down the street, not seeing or sensing anyone taking an interest in them, and said, "Looks safe to me." He turned to Samuel. "But I don't think stopping in one of the local watering holes would be a good idea."

Samuel shrugged, feigning indifference as they walked up a short hill. "Now, what kind of watering hole did you think I'd find here?"

"I think you could find any type of watering hole you wanted. It's not a teetotaler country."

They came to a small shop that looked like a combination jewelry store and a knickknack shop rolled into one. Julia hooked her arms through Scott's and Samuel's and asked, "How about here, gentlemen?"

Samuel glanced at Scott who said, "Don't see why not—let's see what they have!"

They were greeted by one of the tallest and thinnest men any of them had ever seen when they walked in the shop. The owner wore a long white caftan, with grey stripes and must have stood seven feet. He was willow thin with long arms and long thin fingers. His dark complexion blended well with his white eyes and teeth that gleamed when he smiled. He greeted them in English. "Welcome to my establishment. How may I be of assistance?"

Julia looked up and answered, "We saw your shop and were interested as we walked by." She looked around at the glass cases full of jewelry, with art wares stacked here and there everywhere on the floor. The shop was filled with carved wood, woven baskets, and silver and gold jewelry in the glass cases. Boxes and paintings were stacked here, there and everywhere, as were decorated flutes, drums, old spears and odd assortments of various and sundry goods.

"Seems you have a little bit of everything here," Scott said. "Do you have any antique pistols or sextants?"

The shopkeeper scratched his head. "I have an old pair of Turkish pistols and an old French one from the 1700's, somewhere around here. Aside from that, the only other things I have along those lines are some rather primitive percussion pistols that were used in the last century. Sextants . . . let me see," he said as he rummaged through the shop. "I had an old astrolabe of Turkish or Arabian origin here somewhere . . . I am just not sure where I put it. Ah, here it is." He leaned over an old barrel full of knickknacks and pulled up an old wood box, blew the dust off of it and set it on the counter. "It is a beautiful piece. I got it from an Arab trader who had sailed his Dhow across the Indian Ocean. He was down on his luck, needed money for some sort of problem he was having with his crew. I actually think it was a woman problem. You know these sailors." He opened the box and a beautiful, brass astrolabe shown forth only slightly tarnished by time. He handed it to Scott who held it up and looked it over.

Scott smiled when he saw it. "Beautiful. I'd like to see the old pistols, too. How much for the astrolabe?"

The shopkeeper winced and looked at Scott somewhat amazed, but quickly recovered, "Nine hundred dollars for the astrolabe. As you can see, it is a wonderful antique . . . and I would be giving it away for that price, I can assure you."

Julia looked at the astrolabe Scott was holding and shook her head.

Scott put a finger to his lips, as the shopkeeper turned and started rummaging through a cabinet behind the cluttered counter. The setting sun was coming through the windows, which were incrusted by old paint, while the fan tried to stir the dust motes in the air, to no avail.

"Here they are," the shopkeeper said. "Here is the French one. As you can see it is a very fine piece." He produced a box with a green velvet lining. Nestled inside was a beautiful French target pistol, with a powder flask and bullet mold. The checkering on the stock was crisp and the bluing expertly done. The shopkeeper pulled out another box, this time of stiff cardboard, inside of which were two old percussion pistols wrapped in towels. They were ornately carved and inlaid with brass and silver wire and were obviously of Turkish or Arabic origin.

Scott looked at the old percussion pair first, then the French target pistol. "How much for the pistols?"

The shopkeeper sensing a profit on the day's work, quickly answered, "Three thousand for the percussion pair and another three for the French."

Scott looked at the old percussion pair again and said, "I'll give you two thousand for the lot, including the astrolabe."

"What are you trying to do—drive me to the poor house? My mother would turn in her grave if I was to give these away for that? I have seven children to feed and a wife who takes every penny I earn. I could not possibly part with them for less than five."

"Twenty-five hundred, and that's robbing me," Scott said.

"Sir, I can see you are a man of fine discernment. The French pistol alone would bring five thousand in London. I will tell you what. You may have the lot for four thousand and I am giving them to you at that price."

Scott shook his head and looked at the tall man. "Twenty seven hundred and that's all I have."

The shopkeeper acted as if he would pull his hair out. "Sir! You are trying to rob me. Look around, do you see this shop? I am a poor businessman trying to make a living. Would you deny me the right to a profit? Thirty-five hundred."

This went on and on for another ten minutes with Scott giving a little and the shopkeeper giving a little. Scott went so far, as to walk out of the shop, saying he was sorry, when the merchant came out and dragged him back in.

"Three it is. You cannot tell a soul about this. If you did my reputation would be ruined." He then wrapped up the pistols and astrolabe and took Scott's credit card and ran it through. He turned to Scott and bowed. "It has been a pleasure doing business with you, Mr. Chad."

They made their way out onto the street when Julia asked, "Why did you drive such a hard bargain with the poor man?"

"I didn't drive a hard bargain! I could have gotten them for two thousand if I wanted, but it wasn't worth the time. I like the French pistol and astrolabe. The Turkish pair's only so-so. I wanted to use the credit card to throw them off. They obviously now know we're in Ethiopia. Whoever is behind this is no fool. I want them to think we're headed to Addis Ababa. Adrigrat's on the main road to the capital and, hopefully, they'll think we're going there. We have to move fast. They'll be looking here and Addis Ababa for us, if the plan works. Sometimes misinformation's the best defense."

Samuel asked, "You're speaking in riddles again. Where are we headed anyway?"

"I spoke with Julia about this on the boat, Axum. Ethiopia's an old Christian country and, hopefully, we'll find some answers to what we're looking for there. We need to be careful tonight. We'll get out of here at first light and head toward the capital, then cut across country toward Axum."

They went to bed early and immediately after breakfast loaded the car and made their way out of town toward the capital. They drove south though the little village of Idga Hamus, following a dirt track to the west toward the village of Hawzen. The road was rough and partially washed out, but their Land Rover was able to negotiate the worst stretches when they put it in four-wheel drive. They spent most of the morning and part of the afternoon following the rutted track and pulled into the town of Adwa, just off the main highway. It was the middle of the afternoon as they made their way onto the highway and filled the Rover up with gas at a little wayside station at Adi Abum. Axum was a few miles down the road and the highway was paved, at least by African standards, and they were soon in the ancient town where the great Axumite kingdom flourished and Christianity first took firm roots in Ethiopia.

Their eyes were wide open as they pulled into the African town. "This is amazing," Julia said. "I had no idea things like this existed in Africa!"

They traveled down the main road passing a conglomeration of buildings distinctly African. Along the roadside, gaudily painted stands selling fruits and vegetables stood next to thousand-year-old churches, carved out of the sides of the cliffs. Great rocks towered over them as they made their way through the town.

Passing a complex of building surrounded by large trees, Julia shouted out, "Look at that old church. Reminds me of Meteora."

"Except it's not on a mountain," Samuel added.

Scott looked to where they pointed. "I bet it's St. Mary's of Zion. Supposedly the two stone tablets the Ten Commandments are written on are inside there."

"Oh, come on, the Ten Commandments. What do you mean?" Samuel said.

"You shouldn't sleep so much. Julia and I talked about this on the boat too. Didn't you ever go to Sunday school? The Ten Commandments that were written by God on top of the mountain and given to Moses. You remember the statue. The tablets God wrote and gave to Moses after bringing the Jews out of Egypt. Those Ten Commandments."

Samuel asked, "How would they get here? Why aren't they in Israel?"

Scott pulled the Rover over to a little parking area by the church, shut off the engine and parked the car under a massive Eucalyptus tree. He beckoned for Julia and Samuel to get out, then walked under the giant tree and raised his hands. "I've researched on line and read up on this trying to find the answers. Ancient Ethiopian and Hebrew legends say that Queen Makeda was actually the Queen of Sheba, who had her palace here in Axum. The Arabs say this queen was actually Queen Bilkis from Sabea which is on the southern Arabian Peninsula, close to today's Yemen.

"I had no idea Ethiopia had such a history. Is it really the land of Cush?" Julia said.

"They believe their land was settled by Ethiopic, one of Noah's descendants. It was Ethiopic's son Aksumai who founded the capital here at Axum. They reckon their dynasty back to that long distant time, almost 97 generations ago. They say this dynasty stood intact until modern times with the last king, Halie Selassie, early in this century."

"The city's obviously ancient. The Greeks and Romans knew it well and called the whole area Cush. It was the main center for the gold dust, spices and ivory trade out of the center of Africa. The city also traded across the Red Sea with Arabia and there are numerous Arabic writings and inscriptions on the buildings and old ruins in the area. If you look around, a large part of the population's of mixed Arabic and African descent."

Julia asked, "But how do you know the Ten Commandments are here? I grew up in Israel and never heard a thing about this?"

"I'm not sure. They won't let anyone in to see them. No one in Israel claims to have them. It's interesting that Hitler sent some troops down to try and find them during World War II. The monk's and priests took everything out of St. Mary's and hid them up in the mountains to keep it all out of Hitler's hands."

"Would they give us a tour of the monastery?" Samuel asked.

Scott shrugged. "Wouldn't hurt to ask. We're here. Let's see!"

"Do you think they'll let women in? I'm tired of all these old chauvinists and their thinking that women are inferior and only men can go in and see their holy of holies."

"Well, if they don't allow women, we won't go either, okay?"

She looked somewhat mollified. "As long as we stick together." She frowned and paused. "But I guess I don't want to deprive you men."

Battlements surrounded the flat roofed monastery and there were huge Eucalyptus trees scattered around the complex, with small shrines and churches under them. The leaves were blowing and dancing in the afternoon breeze and the sun was peeking through the large cumulus clouds that were scuttling overhead as they walked up. They entered the main entrance through a portico and walked up to a little gift shop.

A tall Ethiopian priest stood behind the counter. His quick and quizzical eyes quickly sized up Samuel, Scott and Julia. He greeted them in Aramaic, the official language of Ethiopia, which is descended from Hebrew and Arabic and is close to the language spoken in Jesus' time. Scott answered in English, "I'm sorry I don't speak Aramaic."

"I thought you were probably Americans, or at least Europeans, but we greet everyone with, 'God be with you. May I help you?' in our own language, for that is the language of our Lord and Savior. How may we help you?"

Scott took the lead even though he could sense that Julia wanted to speak up. "We've come from St. Catherine's monastery in the Sinai and Father Basil, the abbot, sends his greetings. We were wondering if we could have a tour of your monastery."

The tall priest looked them over and frowned, which only caused Julia to fidget more, "Ordinarily no, not on Tuesday's. We are closed. May I ask your names though?"

Scott felt a feeling of dread and concern wash over him and wondered if someone had already gotten to these quiet monks. The look on the priest's face was one of quiet and honest peace, so he swallowed his anxiety and took a chance. "My name's Chad. This is Julia Apostoli, my biologist, and Samuel Rogowski, a technical engineer who works with me. I'm a surveyor and scientist, working for the Egyptian government and was recently asked by your government to complete a survey for your country, too. My main work's mineral surveying and ecological preservation so countries can safely develop their resources."

The priest dismissed the final part with a wave of his hand. "We've heard of you, Mr. Chad. My name is Bejitou. I am head abbot at St. Mary's. Word has come down to us from Father Basil. Even though we are from different orders, we are closer to the Greek Orthodox than many other branches of our faith. We consider ours to be the cradle of our religion and, of course, Father Basil considers his to be the cradle as well."

He raised both his palms. "But that doesn't concern you. In matters of faith and your mission, we are united with Basil. We know of your mission and what it may portend to His will being done, and, therefore, Father Basil and I are in agreement. I digress—I do not mind giving you a tour but do not believe it would be beneficial in what you are looking for." He then glanced at Julia. "Our order normally forbids women entrance into the monastery." He noticed the frigid glance Julia wore, "ut in this case, we will make exception. You must understand, Ms. Apostoli, no woman has entered the monastery in more than a hundred years. I do not agree with this tradition, but old traditions are not changed easily. Some in my order may well be upset, but most will see reason, after they hear of our conversations with Father Basil."

Julia visibly calmed herself after hearing this, nodded and said, "Why, thank you, Father Bejitou. You are most gracious."

Scott felt his anxiety rising. "You've spoken with Father Basil? How did he ever know we'd come here?"

"Father Basil, as I said, told me of your quest. It is a matter of understanding and the mind cannot understand certain things until it is ready. Sometimes my mind is not ready." He laughed and smiled. "But I know our Lord came for all men. Will men listen though, that is the question!"

Scott laughed. "Well, at least that hasn't changed. Both you and Basil speak in riddles."

"How can I explain it? The spirit wills and I follow. When our Lord spoke with Nicodemus he said, 'Do not be surprised that you must be born again.' He then said, 'The wind blows where it will, you can hear its sound, but no one can tell where it has come from or where it is going to. So it is of everyone who is born of the spirit.'"

"Riddles and parables. I'm sorry, Bejitou, but you've got me there. No one has ever explained that one to me. Father Basil tried, but I'm not sure if I understand it."

"It does not matter. Basil and I do not really understand either. It is all too big for us and we live in awe of his plan. Come, I will show you our monastery. I need to meet with a few of the priests first, to explain it, as I said, but I am sure it will be okay. I am only worried about one of them anyway."

They followed him down a long brick corridor where he paused and spoke to a young monk, who took over his duties at the gift shop. They came out of the corridor into a walled courtyard, the center of which was bare dirt with a little shrine on the left. Bejitou motioned for them to remain while he went in a side door of the monastery. He didn't keep them long and when he reappeared, another priest who was even taller accompanied him.

"This is Father Aquius. He is assistant abbot of St. Mary's. He wanted to see you and verify for himself that you are the people Basil told us of."

Aquius walked up and offered his hand, bowed politely, if coldly to Julia, and asked Scott, "Mr. Chad, Father Bejitou's told me of you and we have both spoken with Father Basil. My only concern is that you and your companions are the people Father Basil spoke of. Is there anything you can tell me to calm my concerns and prove you are in fact, Mr. Chad?"

Scott looked at the tall Ethiopian. "I can show you my passport and the passports of my companions if that's what you mean?"

Aquius coldly answered, "Documents do not interest me. The heart and the soul are my concerns!"

"Well, I'm not sure how to answer then. I'm not sure what type of assurances you're looking for. I can tell you this, ever since finding the markers, people have tried to stop us and kill us at every turn. Normally, I wouldn't have continued, but somehow after meeting Basil, Nikita and his monk Vasillus in Meteora . . . I have felt called, if you will, to see this through to the end. I don't really consider myself a Christian—well, I considered myself a Christian, but I have come to learn it really means something more—something spiritual. I went to church and my parents had me baptized, but something was always missing. I know from talking with Vasillus and Father Basil that I am supposed to make a choice and turn myself over to God, but I can't seem to bring myself to do it. I don't know what I'm waiting for, but I've always considered myself as my own man—in charge of my own destiny, but I do think that the wind's blowing into my heart and encouraging me to follow this through."

"Passports are of no use. At least you are honest. We had your description anyway and have spoken with Father Basil and Vasillus in Greece. We may seem like archaic monks stuck in the middle of nowhere, but you have heard of the Communion of the Saints. It is real!" A small smile lit his face, "The Internet also helps!" He turned to Bejitou and said, "I concur, anywhere but the Holy of Holies." He turned back to Scott, "We have not allowed anyone but our order to enter there, in more than two thousand years, and I do not believe this situation changes that."

"I agree, Aquius. Will you accompany us? You are in agreement on the woman being allowed then?"

"I have no objection, even though it offends me. I am sure it is just my old traditions rebelling, but I must also remember our Lord's fight against traditions and how we always wash the cup on the outside but neglect the inner. It is difficult for an old man to change."

"Good, then, let us start," Bejitou said as he motioned them into the monastery.

They walked into the monastery and were immediately overwhelmed by the beauty and art. The walls were painted in Coptic designs and the columns embossed and layered with gold leaf. The artwork on the walls told the story of Genesis, from Adam to Jacob, and was very detailed and beautifully done.

Scott looked to Bejitou and asked, "Do you mind if we take pictures? It may help in our research."

Bejitou winced and visibly controlled himself. "Normally, that is never allowed, but if you promise not to publish them." He looked to Aquius, who nodded. "We will allow it. Do you agree this is for your research only, Mr. Chad, and not to publish any pictures?"

Scott nodded. "I agree. I don't normally publish anyway. All my work's normally owned by whoever hires me, but since I'm working for myself, I agree."

Bejitou lifted his hand. "Go ahead. We see no problem then."

Samuel used the video camera while Julia took shots with the digital. Scott liked using the Nikon and took color negatives on four hundred ASA film.

They finished documenting the incredible artwork and then continued outside taking pictures of the chapel that housed the Ark. It was heavily fortified and a priest stood at the door acting as guardian.

Aquius nodded toward the monk. "He never leaves the grounds and there is always a priest or monk on duty. The young monks believe it a great honor to guard the chapel."

The chapel had a small dome and was painted green around the windows. Even though small and not impressive, Scott felt a sense of awe and power creep over him as he stood before it in the afternoon sun.

When they'd finished their tour, Father Bejitou walked out to the entrance with them. Scott and his companions turned and thanked Bejitou as they walked to the parking lot.

Bejitou paused, laid his hands on Scott's shoulders, and whispered something in his ear while Julia and Samuel stood by the car.

CHAPTER 39
PLASTIC TRAILS'

Walking into the restaurant in Joliet, Henderson looked with disdain at the crushed blue velvet chairs as he pulled one out and sat next to Bishop Bestin. "We finally found them. You were right, at least in part, it's Ethiopia."

"I told you, Henderson, that once the Ethiopian Government requested Chad take the survey he'd jump at the chance. Didn't cost as much as we thought. They actually want him to do a survey. Someone's heard of his talents."

"Who cares? When Farrell's boys and Hasid get a hold of him, he won't be in any shape to do the survey. Do you have any idea on the next move?"

"We'll have a better idea of what to do next when Farrell gets here," he said as he fingered his cross.

"Farrell can be most persuasive. I've seen him in action—leave it to him. Now down to business. How did you find where he is?"

"His company made a wire transfer to some boat captain in Eritrea. We have some local people looking for the captain now. I don't know how much luck we'll have, but we have to try. I want to get Farrell's boys and Hasid on his trail—I think Chad's headed for the capital."

"Did you ever think Chad may have set this up to send us on a wild goose chase?"

"It's possible—but I don't think so," Henderson said. "We have the data from the first chamber and have the same information that Abu has. We know what was found in the second and third chambers and everything points to Ethiopia. It's a big country though."

He continued fingering his cross. "What did Abu figure out from the third chamber, and why are you so sure the answer's in Ethiopia?"

Pulling a folded sheet of paper from his coat, he handed it to the bishop. "I've jotted down what I thought were the most important parts of what Chad found carved in the floor in front of the statue of Moses."

I called my daughter up out of **Cush**
Hiding in the river, the banks and the rush
The river so blue, gives birth to new life
I tell you it's so, it will end all the strife
The hearer who listens, a **wise man understands**
The spirit will gleam, of wisdom's demands
Carved from the rock, and do not look back
Onyx and Spices, and loves long track

Looking at the paper he asked, "What's the bold type supposed to mean?"

"I just highlighted my thoughts. You're a learned man and went to a seminary—see if you don't agree. 'Cush and the river so blue,' now that has to be Ethiopia and the Blue Nile river. Then, 'The wise man understands.' Well, you're wise. Where in Ethiopia are Churches carved from the rock?"

"I don't know that much about Ethiopia, the church has tried to get an inroad into there for years. You tell me?"

"Lalibella, Bishop. That's where we ought to look."

Farrell interrupted holding up his hand as he walked into the room, "I heard that Henderson, I've decided . . ."

"Hold on, we're in this together—tell us what you think," Henderson said.

"Lalibella's full of rock churches, you're right, and it could be where Chad's heading. I just don't want Shula chasing shadows here and there all over the country. I want him right on Chad's trail. We'll find someone else to check out Lalibella—if they find Chad, we can send Shula and Mulama over there. Hasid is with them, so Quati knows what's going on, too."

Henderson asked, "Who are you going to send?"

Farrell shook his head. "I don't know, but we'll find someone. We . . ."

"We need to get this over with, is what we need!" Bestin snapped.

As they walked back to their car under the trees, Julia asked, "What did Father Bejitou whisper to you?"

Scott smiled at her and put his finger to his lips. "What's the old saying—loose lips sink ships!"

A quizzical expression crossed her face. "I don't get it, 'loose lips sink ships.' Why would he say something like that?"

Scott laughed. "That's not what he said. It's an old expression from World War II. We use it when we don't think it's a good idea to tell a secret." He looked at her face and a feeling of anxiety rose in his gut.

"I'll tell you, mister, it's mighty hot out here and I'm not in the mood for any of your shenanigans. We've been through a lot together and if you don't trust me with your little secret, I think I'll just pack up my bags and go my own way!"

Scott stopped in his tracks. "Okay I'll tell you! But you're spoiling it. Father Bejitou told me that he believed that we were meant for each other and that you could be the one to fulfill the prophecy."

"Prophecy?"

"He believes in some of the same prophecies that our friend Mishma does. Something about a tall golden haired princess that will come forth and bring the people together. How or why or what people, he doesn't know. He told me to love you deeply and care for you greatly. There—are you satisfied now?'

She blushed. "I'm sorry—but this is all too much."

"His words were meant for me and I do mean to take care of you, if you really want to know. I think I fell in love with you that first day we met and mean to love you deeply too—." Scott looked over to where Samuel was standing with a grin on his face. "You stay out of this, Samuel. Don't give me that—all this is mush and I'm a diabetic look."

He turned back to Julia. "Yes, I love you—but your mistrust and flash temper make it difficult. Take things a little slower and mellower and it will all work."

"I'm sorry, Scott. I don't know what's come over me. First, I was afraid they wouldn't let me into the monastery and then that whispering in your ear and—oh, I don't know—let's just get going, all right?"

Samuel drove while Scott sat in front giving directions. "We need to find this cave of the winds. Bejitou didn't know where it was. I shared the verses from the chamber with him about the rock churches and he thought Lalibella, but wasn't sure. I'm not sure if we should go there or . . .'"

"Why don't you just follow the map!" Julia said.

"I forgot the map—I keep concentrating on the verses."

"You're a surveyor and you forget the map? Some surveyor you are. I would have thought you'd been pouring over it," Samuel said.

"You forget what we've been through during the last week or so."

"I haven't forgotten, it's just not like you to not follow the map."

"Pull the laptop out of my pack, would you, Julia."

"Pull over there by that group of trees. We'll stop and check it out," Scott said to Samuel.

Julia set up the laptop and they gathered around to look at the picture they'd taken with the digital camera in the cave.

"See this big lake? It has to be Lake Tana. It's the only big lake around,"

Scott said. "Doesn't that look like a mountain to the southwest of the lake with the squiggly line drawn under it? Probably the Nile River. Get out the map of Ethiopia. Maybe we can correlate the two."

"Did the verses mean anything to Bejitou?" Samuel asked as he unfolded the map.

"The only thing he knew was the ancient name for Mt. Sencai was Roha. The Blue Nile goes right under Sencai as it winds through a steep gorge according to the map here."

"Well, from looking at the map—it makes sense. There's the mountain and that squiggly line must be the river. Simple, you said. All things are in the end. Why complicate them!" Julia said.

"We'll try it and see—any objections?" Scott asked.

Samuel shrugged and Julia nodded.

"We'll drive down to Lake Tana then take the road toward the Sudan. Not a great place to visit these days, but that should throw off anyone trying to track us."

After passing Gonder, they descended a steep grade and laid out before them, in the vale of the upland countryside was Lake Tana. Their first glimpse was breathtaking as they descended from the upland plateau. Their eyes were delighted as the scene unfolded. The lake was 1,400 square miles and more than sixty streams fed it, one of which was considered the source of the Blue Nile. The far shoreline was lost in the humidity and mist. Studding the surface were more than thirty islands with old monasteries built on their craggy cliffs and shores. Cumulus clouds floated across the deep blue sky as a cool wind from the heights caressed the waters, stirring the surface into waves and casting the sun's rays into the air like glinting diamonds.

Situated at an elevation of 6,000 feet, the water looked cool and inviting after the heat of the afternoon. Small reed boats plied the costal areas and larger fishing boats and very large ferries sailed on the waters. Stopping at a small roadside stand near the shore, they stretched their legs and bought a soda pop from the vendor.

The next morning they followed the main road toward Addis Ababa, which climbed above six thousand feet while the mountains stood a mile above them as they made their way up the grade. Taking a rough gravel road after Dangla, they headed west toward the Sudan.

Scott turned south after ten kilometers following a very rough dirt road. Hidden behind a bush was a small faded blue plaque for the village of Debra Zei.

They had to unload and push the Land Rover over the rougher sections that were washed out from the spring rains. Late in the afternoon, they crested apocrypha

a hill and could see the sun shining through the clouds onto the summit of a tall mountain off to the west.

"That's Sencai or Roha," Scott said as he pointed, "Where I'm hoping to find the cave of the winds."

"How are we going to get there?" Samuel asked.

"If our map's right, there is a little village up ahead called Debra Zei. I saw the sign behind a bush back at the turn off, and Bejitou said there's an old monastery on the slopes of the mountain. He went there once when he was a little boy, but didn't remember much more than that."

"Well, let's get going," Samuel added.

They stretched their legs and piled back in the Rover. An hour later they came upon the little hamlet of Debra Zei. The village was small, even by Ethiopian standards.

"It's amazing it's even on the map," Scott said as they pulled to a stop in the dusty center of a collection of mud and thatch huts with conical roofs. A large number of children, followed by a few dogs and goats, surrounded the Rover when they stopped. Julia opened her pack and took out a handful of suckers she'd secreted away, handing them out to the delighted and noisy children, then shooed them away.

The village was perched on the side of the mountain, overlooking a deep valley to the south. Winding below in the distance was the Blue Nile, which cut a deep gorge through the colored and banded stone of the mountains. The late afternoon sun lit up the canyon walls exposing the striated rock, highlighting the layers of brown, red, orange and black as birds wheeled in the air and sang in the trees. The blue water glinted far below as if hurrying on its way to the distant sea.

"Sure know how to pick a spot," Julia said. "Why don't they put this in their guide books? People would come from miles around to just gaze on this."

"We should have gone to the Blue Nile falls; all the guide books talk about the falls but forget to mention what the rest of the country's like. We're close to the Sudan and this is Africa, don't forget," Scott said.

CHAPTER 40
CAVE OF THE WINDS

A very tall, thin man dressed in a long brown robe with leaves embroidered on the collar approached. He was the first adult they'd seen and his long limbs and way of walking made him look like a heron as he strode toward them. He walked up, bowed to Scott and said in excellent English, "My name is Halie. I am head elder of our village. Strangers do not often come here. How may I help you?"

Scott bowed in return. "You speak English very well, Halie. My name's Scott Chad, and with me are Samuel Rogowski and Julia Apostoli. We came to find an old monastery on the mountain. Father Bejitou, Abbot of St. Mary's in Axum, told me of it and said they may have information that's important to some research my friends and I are doing. That is, if the monastery still exists and it's still inhabited."

"Well, yes, it still exists, but things are not what they were, or shall I say are not what they used to be. The young leave for the cities and the rain falls or does not fall and nothing is what it was. My father fought the Italians before the great war and told me many stories of the bravery of those times. The monastery was used to nurse many of our warriors back to health in those days. The Italians never came to it even though they used their airplanes to scour the countryside looking for our men. You seem honest. Are you Orthodox?"

"Orthodox, no, I can't say we are, but for the first time in my life, I'd be proud to tell you that I've been reading the Bible. I haven't really gotten all the Orthodox, Catholic and Protestant stuff straightened out. It seems that something's calling me . . . well, I don't want to bore you."

"You are not boring me young man. My name is Father Halie, and I am the abbot of the monastery. If you have come for information about the monastery, you have come to the right place. I am not much of a judge, but I am also head elder for the village. They say I am too soft, but I believe I am a good judge of honest character. Follow, and be our guest. We will walk to the monastery and you may rest for the night, then we will see how we may help you."

They got their packs from the car and Scott started to lock it when Halie raised his hand. "No need to lock it. There is no thievery in the village. It will be safe. Your lady friend has hired many young watchdogs with her gift of sweets. This has earned her the respect of everyone in the village."

They followed down a narrow path and then up the side of the gorge, the path tending to rise more than it fell. After walking an hour, Halie stopped by a little stream that tumbled and bubbled from the heights and cupped his hands in a little pool of water, drinking deeply. "I never get tired of drinking from the mountain, the springs are so cool and refreshing. Come drink and refresh yourselves. The water is good."

Julia bent down, tasted the water, and then drank deeply. She stopped and spilled out her canteen and refilled it from the spring. "If I didn't know better, I'd say the water was treated with something. I've never tasted anything so good."

Scott and Samuel followed, drank their fill then refilled their canteens. They followed Halie up the steep and winding path, feeling energized and refreshed. Halie explained, "The spring is about halfway between the village and the monastery, but it speeds travelers on their way and makes the last part much easier. I look forward to it on my way up and on my way back down, especially when it is hot like today. I do not think the weather will hold. Rains are expected soon and when it rains the spring can be a torrent and you have to take care crossing it."

They walked for another hour and the last rays of the sun were lighting the top of the mountain, when they rounded a rocky shoulder and there, set into a cliff on a small plateau, was the monastery. It was not large or pretentious, but was incredible because of the way the whole structure appeared to be carved out of the living rock. Two fluted pillars stood in front, sculpted out of the rock wall of the cliff. They were lovingly polished by the stonemasons who'd created the church as if it were a living thing. The lintel above the door was decorated with African scenes of antelope, tigers, lions, and set in the exact center was a deeply cut cross, flared on each end. The entrance was through two thick large doors that were set deeply into the rock and stood open. Constructed from a deep-red, very hard African wood, the doors were strapped with iron bands and studded with large rivets.

"Welcome to the Monastery of the Promise," Halie said. "It is here where we look for the coming of our Lord and Master. It is here where we pray for the saints, and it is here where we give all travelers sanctuary, at least those who call on the name of the Lord. During World War II, some Nazis' wandered into the area with our warriors hot on their trail. How they had managed to wander into our valley, no one ever found out. The Nazi's had heard of people taking sanctuary in our churches and knocked on our door demanding sanctuary. The abbot led them into the little courtyard here," Halie said as he showed them through the large doors and into a small courtyard. They looked up at the roof that was lovingly carved from the gut rock of the cliff like the rest of the church and had skylights that let in the late afternoon sunlight. "The abbot stopped and asked in what name they declared the right to sanctuary."

"I bet they said the name of the Fuhrer or something," Julia said.

"Exactly! They said, 'In the name of Adolph Hitler, we declare Sanctuary.' The abbot nodded, and went out the side door, locking the Nazi's inside. He showed the Ethiopian warriors up to the sky lights, where they rained arrows down on the Nazis. To my knowledge it was the only blood ever spilled on this ground and, even though ashamed, the abbot was proud of his people."

They followed him into the beautiful church and were amazed at the way the masons had cut and shaped the church from the rock of the mountainside. The floor was smooth and placed here and there were windows along the face of the cliff, which looked out on the river flowing below. The ceiling was decorated with intricate carvings following the Coptic motif, and various rooms and chambers opened up along the central passageway.

Halie showed them to a pair of rooms off to one side of a passage, the windows overlooking the gorge below. "These will be your rooms while you are with us. You may visit anywhere in the church or grounds, except behind the altar or one of the monk's rooms, without their permission. We do not have many monks here, only a dozen or so, and they usually come to us as small boys." Halie paused and shrugged. "Their parents may have too many children to feed and we look for men with a special aptitude for learning and a love for the Lord. Please make yourselves at home and join us for dinner in an hour."

They unpacked and found a basin of water in each of the rooms where they were able to clean up. Julia changed into a long black skirt and brown blouse and Samuel and Scott changed into a pair of khaki trousers.

Halie knocked on their door forty-five minutes later and showed them to the common dining room, where they joined the other monks for supper. The meal consisted of a goat meat and potato stew, spiced with some of the hot Ethiopian spices. The monks passed bowls of fruit and a local wine around and a reader read from the Bible in Aramaic while they ate.

When the meal was over, the reader put the Bible away and Halie led the assembled monks in a prayer. The group broke up and Halie came back to them. "Simple life, good food and wonderful people. I would be pleased for you to meet one of my young apprentices. Evanie, would you come over please." A tall but tough looking young monk approached the group and bowed as he approached. "This is Evanie. He also speaks English and has lived here ever since he was a young boy. He studied in England and received a bachelor's degree in agriculture. I thought we would lose him to the outside world, but

. . . well. I will let him tell you his story. I have assigned him to be your guide while you are in our care and to keep you safe. The trails may be dangerous and I would not feel comfortable if something happened while you were here. Evanie is most knowledgeable and runs the satellite communications and computer for us, to keep us connected with what is going on in the world."

Halie bowed and left the room and Evanie extended his hand to Scott. "I'm pleased to meet you. We don't get many outsiders here and it's nice to speak English again. Sometimes I think we need a little earthquake to wake up some of our people to what's going on in the world. Please follow me and I'll show you around a bit before bed? We tend to go to bed early and get up early. Vespers is at ten and morning matins at five." He saw the look on Samuel's face and said, "I know—I know, six hours sleep, doesn't sound like enough, heh? We make it sound very pious, but I'll let you in on a little secret. We tend to take a nap around two in the afternoon, and some of the older monks sometimes miss morning prayers. But come, you'll enjoy this!"

Showing them through the carved passageway of the church, he led them to a little chamber on the south side. Opening the doors, he took a candle then lit two others in the wall. They stood in a round room about forty feet in diameter and fifty feet high. The whole room was carved out of the living rock of the mountain. "This is our vespers chamber—we meet in here for vespers and to sing to our creator."

Samuel asked, "It looks like granite, the stonework's incredible—the highlights in the rock. I wonder how they did it?"

"We have some old books that tell of it—but it's almost legend now. A number of masons in the third century wanted to build a church here. Why here—I see the look on your faces. A number of the old Jewish patriarchs, prophets and stuff are wrapped up in this place. I never put that much stock in it, but someone felt the church needed to be built on the mountainside, to prepare the way for a day—a day they say was long foretold."

"The rock's like black granite. I see blues and a sheen of green and white in the rock."

"Beautiful, isn't it? Wait until you see it in the morning when the sun shines in."

Julia yawned. "Incredible, Evanie. It must have taken years and years to carve this from the mountain."

"It appears that you have all been up for days and days. I'm forgetting myself, you've been traveling all day. Why don't I show you back to your rooms?"

They followed Evanie back through the twisting passageways to their rooms where they said goodnight. The next morning Evanie showed them the gardens and orchards, then showed them the library and explained how they catalogued their volumes. Evanie was explaining about some of their old manuscripts when a monk, who if possible was even taller and thinner than Halie, came up and whispered something in Evanie's ear.

Evanie turned to Scott and asked, "Were you expecting anyone to come and meet you here?"

A look of concern passed over Scott's face as he looked at Julia and Samuel, then turned to Evanie. "No, we weren't expecting anyone. As a matter of fact, no one to our knowledge knows we're here."

"Two men just left the village and are on the trail headed toward the monastery. One of the village elders called after these men started asking suspicious questions of the children and were rather rough with one of the older ones."

"I'm sorry, Evanie, I had no idea anyone would follow us here, or at least I was hoping no one could. I think we should leave, so you can honestly say we aren't here when they come and ask for us. There have been many people trying to stop us and we don't know who it is this time."

Samuel added, "Evanie, these are bad men who are trying to stop us from bringing knowledge to the world. These men haven't hesitated to kill and kill quickly to get their way. We've had run-ins with some of them a couple of times and have had to fight our way out. I agree with Scott. We don't want them coming up and destroying your monastery or your peace."

"I don't like running from men like these anymore than I can see you do. You're acting out of noble intent while we're merely hiding here from evil. I don't like the choice, but I cannot let them destroy or damage the monastery. I'm taking you to a safe place and we'll then consult with Halie. It will be a few hours until they get here and probably longer if they don't drink from the spring. It's hot and a long climb . . . and I wish they could just get lost on the way."

Evanie led them to a small cave in the hills. They had to walk around a large boulder that hid the entrance, then duck under an overhanging rock to get in. Once inside, they felt the cool air and were sheltered from the midday heat. There were two benches carved into the walls and the rest of the cave was rough and unadorned.

Evanie turned to Scott before he left. "Please stay put until I talk with Halie. I will return as soon as I can."

Once Evanie left, Scott sat on one of the benches next to Julia, took his canteen out and drank some of the precious water then passed it to Samuel and Julia. "Who do you think it is this time?" Scott said.

"I'm not sure, but I would bet it's the extremists working with Abu again," Samuel said. "What do you think, Julia?"

"Could be, or I wouldn't be surprised if it was those Italians who tried to get to us in Suez, maybe all of them together. I thought they might start working together, particularly as we got closer to the end."

Evanie showed back up later that afternoon and brought them food and drink. "There's probably nothing until morning. They're still on the mountainside and probably won't get here until after sunset, but more likely tomorrow morning. We think it best that you spend the night in the cave. They just might travel in the dark. It would be dangerous if you didn't know the pathway, but we don't know these men."

"Thank for your kindness, Evanie. You've no idea what this means to us," Julia said.

Evanie handed them the supplies he'd brought. "Eat up. It's good fruit from the monastery and the drink's very good, for I helped brew it myself."

CHAPTER 41
LIVING WATER

Mulama and Shula met Hasid in his room. "I'm going to coordinate things from here. Once you find Chad's trail, call me on the satellite phone. We do not know where he has gone and I have men looking in Lalibella, as well as here in the capital. Use whatever means you find necessary to find him."

"We'll find him—do not worry," Mulama said.

"Make sure that you do, and call me immediately when you do. I'll bring the men we have in Lalibella with me—Chad will not escape this time."

"Our orders are to call Farrell every other night at seven. We must keep in contact with him. I don't think our cell phones will work outside of the capital area," Shula added.

"Use the satellite phone to contact him. It will work anywhere, as long as you get a satellite lock. Where are you going to start?"

"I think we'll go north toward Axum. I asked around last night and don't think he's come to Addis yet, if he ever planned to."

"Well, may your God go with you and keep in touch. This is important to both our faiths."

Working their way up the trail after leaving the village, Shula thought back on events—Chad's trail had been difficult to follow, but not impossible if you knew where to apply the right pressure. It wasn't easy for a white man to hide in Africa. For a black man it was simple, if you knew where to go—but not for a white man. Chad had used his credit card and shown his passport at the border. Working with Hasid had its benefits. He seemed to have many contacts and was able to open doors in the Sudan that would have been very difficult if he had not been with them. He was a tough customer and even gave Shula the shivers. Something drove the man and he was afraid to ask.

Farrell thought Chad might head toward the capital, but they could not find any sign of him—so they worked their way back north toward Axum and found themselves lucky after talking with a gas station attendant. The difficult part had been at Lake Tana. The search of the lake area had delayed them but finally luck was with them when they talked with owners of one of the little restaurants by the lake, who had described Samuel. After leaving the lake area, they headed back south, but lost his trail.

They were a half day behind him and stopped to stretch and, out of pure luck, a shepherd boy had seen a car with three white people take the road toward the Sudan. Driving past the turnoff to the village, they drove thirty miles to the river near the border then came back and found an old man watching a goat beside the road. Jogging the old man's memory with his knife, Mulama was able to persuade him to share where he had seen Chad turn off toward the monastery.

Following the road, they could see where Chad had pushed the Land Rover through one of the washouts. Negotiating it easily with their Jeep, they pulled up and parked next to the Land Rover in the village.

As they walked around the shoulder of the mountain after leaving the village, they didn't notice nor care about the beauty that unfolded before them.

Shula said, "You didn't have to be so rough with that girl."

A look of hatred crossed Mulama's face. "If I had left it up to you, we'd still be there tomorrow morning wondering where they'd gone."

"Farrell will be upset if he finds out you roughed her up."

"Who's going to tell him—just mind your own business and I'll mind mine. If something needs doing, you can rely on me."

Mulama smiled as he thought of the young girl in the village. The look of fear on her face as he had grabbed her around the neck and squeezed had given him an intense feeling of pleasure.

Shula turned to him. "I'm going to call Hasid and tell him we found Chad's truck and bring him up to date. He may be able to help. We don't need the Ethiopian police on our trail. I know it's getting harder for you to have a good time, but you've got to get control of yourself, brother."

"Speak for yourself—I think you've forgotten how to have fun. I'm going to have some more fun when we catch Chad and that woman he has with him. I don't like the thought of Hasid around either. He gives me the creeps with his pious ways and 'as Allah wills' stuff—why do you have to call him, we can handle things." Noticing the look his brother gave him he added, "You may be right. Perhaps we could use the help, but once we dispose of Chad and that Polish guy, we'll have some fun with that Jewess."

Rounding a corner in the trail, they passed a small waterfall coming down the hillside.

Shula stopped and wanted to rest, but the look on Mulama's face changed his mind as he frowned and motioned that they go on. Taking a quick drink from their canteens that they carried along with their Uzi's and knives, they trudged up the mountainside as the heat built and the sun beat down. A half hour later, the trail took a sharp turn as it followed the switchbacks. Shula stopped under the boughs of a large tree growing out of the rock, set down his pack and sat under the branches of the tree. Taking out his canteen, he took a long swig and leaned back. Mulama was so hot he didn't disagree as he tossed his pack to the ground, slumped down and took out the satellite phone and tossed it to Shula.

Hasid answered on the third ring. "Did you find them?"

"Not yet, but we're on his trail."

"Are you sure it's Chad?"

"Yes, we found his car and have talked with people who have seen him. He's on the side of mountain just past a monastery near the village of Debra Zei."

"I am going to send some men to help you. You're in charge, but use them well. They are good men."

"I will call as soon as we've found him."

"Good work so far, Shula. Keep it up," Hasid said, then severed the connection.

Shula put the phone back then looked over at his younger brother, the sun blazing in the cloudless sky and the shade of the tree feeling wonderful. Bees were buzzing around sounding to his ears as if singing a song. "I can't remember when I felt so tired. It must be a hundred and ten degrees—how far did that girl say the monastery was?"

Mulama leaned back against the tree. "I don't know. She said it was a couple hours walk along the trail and that the water would refresh us. She must have been talking about that little stream we passed. She probably wanted to poison us with some dirty water so we'd catch dysentery." He yawned and stretched. "I know what you mean about being tired. I could take a nap. These bees seem to be singing me to sleep right now. Listen to them buzz." He stretched his legs out under the tree and propped his head on his pack and before he knew it, he and his brother were fast asleep.

They woke late in the evening, with the last glow of the setting sun lighting up the western sky, covered with mosquito bites. Shula was itching all over and Mulama took some lotion from his pack and rubbed it onto the bites on his back, arms and face, then handed the bottle to Shula.

Shula scratched and looked at his brother. "I hope we don't catch malaria."

"Malaria supposedly doesn't exist at elevations over two thousand meters. I'd think we're above that here. It's cooling off now—let's move."

"In the dark? Are you crazy? This seems as good a place as any to camp for the night. Why take a chance of falling off the cliff in the dark. If we're going to fall, I'd prefer to do it during the day—when I could see."

"I agree, but this spot seems unhealthy. Let's move up the trail a bit as long as there's some light left and see if we can find a better place."

Shula shrugged and they picked up their packs after drinking some of their water and made their way up the switchbacks in the quickly fading light. The twilight was very quick in the tropics and before they'd hiked twenty minutes, they were stumbling up the trail in utterly complete darkness. Rounding a bend, they *felt* more than saw a level spot in the trail and took off their packs, stretching out on the grass. After their long nap, they weren't able to sleep—the night noises keeping them awake long into the night. Mulama finally dozed off sometime during the middle of the night, waking once and finding his brother Shula sitting awake. Turning back over, he fell back into a dreamless sleep and when he awoke found Shula asleep at his side. Reaching over he shook him and was surprised to find that he felt warm to the touch. He felt his own forehead and arms and thought he might have a touch of fever also, or was it was just sunburn from the day before.

Shula shook the sleep out of his eyes and sighed. "I hardly slept, and I feel terrible after not sleeping all night. What about you?"

"I don't feel well either. I wonder if we caught a bug from the water or from those bites, when we napped under that tree. We ought to get going and find this monastery and see if Chad and his group are there. Farrell won't be too pleased if we don't deliver. He was put out when he called us to do this operation and was upset with Bestin. Those other guys had failed. Farrell doesn't take too kindly to failure, so let's go."

They hoisted their packs and started up the trail. An hour and half later, they came around the bend and saw the little church. Two monks were outside, pulling at weeds.

They walked up to the monks and asked, "Hello! We're traveling these parts looking for some friends who may be working on a project near here. Have you seen two white men and a woman with red hair in this area?"

Halie and Evanie looked up as they approached and listened to them, feigning incomprehension. Halie turned to the pair and answered in Ahramaic, which neither Shula nor Mulama understood.

Shula shook his head, switched to French and asked again, "Hello, we're traveling these parts looking for some friends who may be working on a project near here. Have you seen two white men and a woman with red hair in this area?"

This time Evanie answered in Aharmaic, showing a look of bewilderment on his face.

Mulama then tried Italian and German on the two monks, with the same result.

Shula was getting tired of this and his fever and general disposition started to show. He reached in his pack, pulled out a picture of Chad and showed it to Halie and Evanie. By gestures alone, he tried to make them realize that this was one of the men they were looking for.

Halie and Evanie looked at the picture, shrugged and shook their heads no.

Shula motioned for his brother to step away from the two monks and spoke quietly to him. "I think it's odd that they only speak their native tongue. Monks train and study for years, at least learning Latin and Greek. I think they know where Chad is and are just playing dumb."

They hadn't walked far enough and Halie could make out what they were saying, gesturing to Evanie to follow a plan they'd worked out before. When Shula and Mulama turned toward them, they bowed and motioned they should come into the monastery.

Shula shrugged and nodded toward Mulama who agreed. It was hot standing with the sun blazing down. There wasn't a breeze and the cool interior looked inviting. They followed Evanie through the large doors and stopped in the courtyard. The air was cool and refreshing and Evanie bowed to them and motioned for them to wait while he went inside. Once inside, a silent bolt was thrown in the door, the outside door was quickly shut, and the outer bolt thrown.

They pounded and pushed against the stout wood doors to no avail. Mulama waved his brother back, pulled out his Uzi, aimed at the door and squeezed the trigger. The gunfire echoed in the enclosed place and he emptied a whole clip into the door, which easily absorbed the 9mm full-metal-jacket rounds. The door was six inches thick and bound with iron, it was one of the hardest woods in Africa and even though the shells disfigured the wood, they did little real damage. A high-powered rifle may have eventually worn down the door. The Nazi's had also tried and failed. After emptying the clip on the outer door, he reloaded and tried the inner door with the same result.

Evanie had climbed up to the skylights and stood watching them. When Mulama finished his clip, he shouted down, "Had enough yet? That's not a way to show us welcome!"

Shula looked up at Evanie as Mulama quickly put another clip in his Uzi and fired a burst at him. Evanie simply ducked and the full-metal-jacket rounds ricocheted around the chamber. Shula shouted, "Stop it, idiot. Do you want to kill us both?"

Mulama lowered his weapon and yelled up, "Feigning ignorance to travelers and locking them up is no way to show hospitality where we come from."

"You didn't come to seek hospitality, but violence. We know of you and how you treated the young girl in the village. The only way you're leaving is without your weapons and with a pledge to go back to where you came from."

Shula looked over at his brother and nodded. "If we leave our weapons and give you our word, will you let us go?"

Evanie laughed. "See that little door in the bottom of the big one?" They looked over and noticed a small square door about three inches tall and six inches wide in the bottom of the door leading to the inner courts. "Yes, that's the one. Open it. Go ahead, pull on the knob then place your weapons in there."

They placed their Uzi's inside the little door, and then Mulama yelled up. "Now what, monk? We're defenseless. Will you let us go now?"

"Empty your packs on the floor, so I can see what else you have. I can't have you terrorizing the villagers on the way back."

"You ask too much, monk," Shula said.

"You ask way too much, monk. If I ever see you again, you'll pay for this," Mulama added, as he emptied his pack on the floor and spread out the contents. The satellite phone sat in a small steel box amidst the pile of clothes. Mulama looked at it out of the corner of his eye then quickly looked away.

Evanie called down from the window. "Put the knives and the things with long wires and wood handles in the door. Then strip—show us your clothes."

Shula and Mulama looked at each other and a look of comprehension passed between them. Taking off their clothes, they threw them in piles on the floor. They bent over and picked up the knives and garroting wires, placing them inside the little door and noticed the Uzi's were gone.

Evanie looked down and said, "Now get dressed, and open the small door again."

They quickly dressed then opened the small door and found a tray with fruit and juice.

"We could have sent you to your maker, but we'll let you out in a couple of hours. You don't know what this costs us nor will you ever understand our history and hospitality. You come armed and threatening our village, then ask for hospitality. You deserve death, but we show you grace. You can't understand us for you have been given over to a reprobate mind."

CHAPTER 42
THE FINAL CHAMBER

Evanie showed up at the little cave a bit after noon. "Two of them are locked in the courtyard. We took these from them." He handed Scott and Samuel the Uzi's and clips, along with the garroting wires and knives Shula and Mulama had carried.

Samuel looked at them. "These guys are pros. Did they have anything else with them—what did they look like?"

"No, they only had the guns and a phone inside a steel case."

"You should have taken the phone," Samuel said. "Trouble's going to come of it, I bet."

"Not right away, we still have them locked up, but the abbot is a compassionate man and will probably turn them loose or over to the police. The men are very tall and muscular, part black and part white. I forget your word for it. They're not black men like us, but still men of color. One of them called the other his brother and they speak English well—without an accent. They also speak French, Italian and German," he said and chuckled. "They spoke among themselves, thinking we were stupid and didn't understand. They talked amongst themselves and I overheard them talking about someone named Farrell who hired them to find you. Does the name mean anything to you?"

Samuel looked at Scott who said, "Could be. One of the groups chasing us had a list of names and Farrell was one of the names on the list. I found it hard to understand at first, since he works with a group of Christian men who take great pride in their faith."

"Well, these two say they are Christians, too, and were rather put out when they couldn't open the door and shot up the place with those things, trying to shoot through the doors."

"You did well, Evanie. These things probably didn't hurt the doors, but I wouldn't want them pointed at me!" Samuel said.

"I'm proud of you for bringing these, Evanie, but I don't think it's too smart for us to take them with us. What's the penalty for carrying weapons in Ethiopia without the proper papers?" Scott asked.

"Death."

"Death, for everyone, no first time offenders, or something?" Samuel asked.

"No, just death. They do not tolerate weapons violations. The only weapons in this country are with the army, police and big game hunters, and we don't have many of those in Ethiopia. They could possibly let you off since you're a foreigner, but your embassy would have to get involved and there would be political implications. I came to warn you that we're moving the villagers out and over the mountain until this whole thing settles down to keep them safe. We don't know what else we can do, since Halie won't let us kill them. We sent an e-mail to Addis, but it will be a day or two before any help comes."

Scott looked at his friends, "I'd feel better if you could keep them locked up until we are away, but I don't want your people hurt. Give the weapons back to Halie, we don't want to take them and break your laws. Would you ask Halie if he has any objection to us searching the side of the mountain? We're looking for a small cave, much like this one, though I think it's higher up and overlooks the river."

"I'll ask. Eat the food I've brought and I'll be back in an hour and let you know."

"I don't know how to thank you, you've been so kind," Julia said as she walked over and took the basket. She then reached up and gave him a small kiss on the cheek. "We'll wait for you here."

Opening the basket, they found it full of fruit, bread and a goat's milk cheese. Included in the basket was a small bottle of wine. Julia pulled out a note, "Evanie left a note, 'The wine's made from grapes on the mountain that grow by the little spring you passed on the way up. It's very good but potent—enjoy.'"

Taking the small bottle, Samuel poured them each a small cupful, then took a sip. "That's wonderful. If the world knew what they fermented out here on this mountain, civilization would beat a path to their door."

Scott smiled after tasting the wine. "I don't think they want civilization beating at their door. It's probably the same wine they use for their communion ceremonies. What's the verse . . . you've kept the best wine till last!" he said raising his small glass in a toast.

Julia tasted the wine and added, "It's better than the stuff they ferment on the Kibbutz, which is very good. They're selling it in Europe now, actually competing with some of the French brands. I'd say it's better." She finished her glass.

After eating they lay back in the cool shade of the cave and for lack of a better option dozed off. Scott would have said that the wine put him to sleep, whereas Samuel would have said that he'd been sent a dream. Whatever it was, they all experienced the same thing. The next thing they knew, Evanie was shaking them awake.

"I told you it was a heady wine. Put you to sleep, huh?"

Scott looked up at him bleary eyed. "Well, I never, we only had half a glass each. I know you said it was strong, but . . . well, I haven't drunk any wine in a long time, and it tasted good, almost as good as the water from the spring on the way up."

"It's from vines that grow on the banks of the spring, just a little farther up the mountainside, but enough of that. Halie said he would only keep them for a couple of hours more. He thought it would be a good idea if you started moving now and not wait. The sooner you're gone, the better."

Julia looked over at Evanie. "We've come through a lot in the past couple of months and this is one of the few places we've been able to relax, even for a moment. Thank you very much for all your help. Do you have any idea where we should look for this cave?"

"I'll do even better. Halie's given me permission to accompany you. I've brought provisions. If you'll help me split them up, we can get going."

Samuel and Scott looked at each other and nodded after getting a smile of assent from Julia.

"That's too much to ask, but we think it would be wonderful," she said.

Splitting up the provisions they each filled their packs. Evanie then led them along a disused trail that headed farther up the mountainside toward the summit of Sencai.

Shula and Mulama flinched when they heard the little door open about four that afternoon. Mulama looked inside and found a meal of fruit, some sort of flat bread and water on a small tray. He shrugged, pulled out the tray out and took it over to his brother, where they sat and ate, finding no point in starving themselves.

"When do you think they'll let us out?" Mulama asked.

"When they're good and ready," Shula snapped.

Mulama laughed. "The great warrior giving up?"

His brother shrugged. "Wait to fight another day. Our time will come, you'll see."

An hour later, the front door opened and the two looked up to see Halie standing there, holding one of their Uzi's that Evanie brought back.

"Okay, you can get up and get going. Do not try anything stupid in the village, we've moved the people, and your little stunt with the girl has not gone unnoticed. We have phoned the police in Addis and you may find them in the village. I do not know why we are giving you this chance. Something in me says you are not all bad, but I have not seen it anywhere in you. Perhaps the Lord's trying to tell me something. I do not know. Now go." He motioned with the Uzi.

A quick glance between the brothers and a look of understanding passed between them, as they got slowly to their feet. They moved slowly and Shula wiped the perspiration from his forehead as he got up. They had worked day after day in the hot Louisiana sun and, while it wasn't the same heat as Africa, they were in amazingly good shape. Mulama walked out the entrance, past where Halie stood holding the Uzi, while Shula shuffled slowly behind. This separated Halie's attention and required that he watch both directions at the same time.

Mulama was five feet past the entrance when he stumbled, which was the sign for his brother to move. Halie had never seen anyone move so fast. In a fraction of a second, Shula was holding the Uzi. He tripped Halie to the ground, threw the safety off and pointed the Uzi at his head.

"Tell me now, where are Chad and his companions? Where did you hide them?"

"I do not have them in hiding anywhere. They left this morning, after you showed up and I have no idea where they have gone."

Shula smiled and tested the Uzi. He held the muzzle by Halie's head and fired a three round burst into the ground about six inches from his head. The impact of the bullets peppered his face with sharp bits of rock and sand and the muzzle blast ruptured his left eardrum. Beads of blood slowly grew on his face from where the sand blasted up and blood trickled out of his left ear. He raised his hand to feel the damage to his face, but his cheek felt numb. A feeling of thankfulness crept over him as he looked up at Shula.

"Enough, stupid old man. If you don't tell us where Chad is, I'll do more than visit some of your peasants in the village. We'll start by hanging a few of your monks out here by the main gate and see how you feel about that."

Mulama rushed back into the monastery's main gate, tried the inner door and found it now open. He dashed through and found two of the younger monks hiding around a corner. He grabbed them by their robes, dragging them through the inner courtyard to the square in front of the main entrance.

One of the monks was about sixteen while the other nineteen and they'd never experienced anything as quick and dangerous as Mulama. He dragged them to where Shula was holding the gun by Halie's head and said, "Kill the young one first. Listen, old man, we're not going to give up. Chad's up to something very dangerous to our and your faith, something so dangerous that your little flock and church mean nothing at all. Did he tell you that?"

Halie sat up. "I do not know what you are talking about, but I am able to sense the spirit of things and the spirit of our Lord is not in your words."

Mulama rasped at Shula. "You're wasting your time with this old man. Chad's gone off into the hills. I don't think he's in the monastery. The old monk is assisting Chad in some way. Even now, he's playing a dangerous game and wasting our time as we speak. Can't you see it in his eyes? He knows where Chad is and he's wasting our time so Chad gets away. I don't think he'd talk even if you shot him. I'll do something better. Give me the gun."

Shula held Halie down with his foot and tossed the Uzi to Mulama who dragged the youngest monk over, then bent down to Halie and said, "One last time, old man. I don't have time for this. Where did Chad go? If you don't tell me, I'll start shooting off pieces from the younger one here. First his foot, then his knee, so that he walks with a limp the rest of his life, then maybe his elbow. It might just blow his arm off. You never know with this solid-ball ammunition, it's a high velocity nine millimeter round and has a tendency to create a great amount of shock damage."

Halie turned his head in the dirt and looked at Mulama, then at the young monk they were holding and saw no fear in his eyes, just plain faith and courage. He slowly answered, "By their fruit you shall know them." Halie looked back at the young monk, "Jules, put on his armor."

Mulama smiled, reached down, pointed the Uzi at the young monk's foot, and pulled the trigger. The report was deafening and young Jules screamed when he saw the round hole in the top of his foot and the blood bubbling out, carrying away bits of sand from where the bullet had gone through his foot and sandal into the ground.

Halie shook his head, bowed and slowly said, "All right, may God forgive you and me. The monk you met earlier has taken them around the western side of the mountain. I truly don't know where. Mr. Chad said he was looking for a cave of some sort that he hoped would uphold the faith."

Mulama looked at the old man and snapped, "Twice stupid fool. Uphold the faith. Chad's not even a Christian. What would he know about upholding the faith? The faithful fight to keep the faith pure and holy and you've been helping an unbeliever. Come, Shula, leave them—let's go."

Walking out into the clearing, they heard the beat of the rotors before they saw it. The helicopter came low in over the trees, flaring out and raising a cloud of dust as it settled to the earth like some huge insect.

Three men jumped out carrying packs and rifles, while Hasid stood in the doorway looking at Shula. He turned and spoke with the pilot then climbed down. The craft lifted off, turned and headed back.

Walking up, Hasid extended his hand. "Good work Shula, I've brought more men. What have you found out?"

"Chad took off over the side of the mountain. We were just about to follow."

"I asked that you keep me posted on your movements. Why didn't you call?"

"The monks were a little trouble and we had to persuade them to give us the information."

"What's done is done—as Allah wills. Lead on, time is wasting," he said as he tossed a rifle to Mulama.

Walking up the trail that hugged the top of the gorge above the river, they climbed over the rocks to the final marker.

Evanie lead the party higher up the mountain to an area where he once played as a child, heading toward a cave that wasn't much more than a crack that went back into the mountain and had a small fissure near the top, where the wind whistled down. He'd always liked going there, even though he was afraid of snakes. He used to toss rocks into the cave before venturing in to drive out any snakes. The cave was perched on a ledge above the gorge where one could stand and view the river as it bent its way around the foot of the mountain.

Leaving the trail, they started clambering up the rocks that had tumbled down from above. Thorny bushes littered the mountainside and the red rock gave it a surreal look in the late afternoon sunlight.

Scott looked over at Julia and could tell she was glad the sun was fading, for the afternoon heat had been intense—as only in Africa. He laughed at the thought of some of those old movies where the actors were always cool, finely dressed and in command of themselves. They couldn't have been filmed in Africa, for it was hot, dusty and the sun was so intense, it was like being slapped.

"Africa wins," Scott said to himself. What could it mean, other than a beautiful land wonderfully blessed and cursed under a merciless sun. He thought of the animals that graced the plain, from the elephant and giraffe, to the antelope and how they said man had developed here first, and then fanned out across the globe. His belief in science was challenged as he thought of it but the evidence was hard to dismiss. Did it really matter? If God wanted to create his Adam and Eve and wanted to dabble in other forms of creation for millions of years, who was he to second-guess God? The fact that God made the universe was obvious. He was coming to grips with something much stronger than anything he'd ever felt or believed before.

Evanie motioned for the group to stop when he reached a shelf of red rock that jutted out from the mountainside and overlooked the river gorge below. "This is it. I used to throw rocks in there and hide as a child when we played on the mountain." He gestured behind him at a small crack in the wall of the mountain. "I know it's not much to look at, and maybe it's not what you're looking for, but it's the only place I could think of that fit your description, cave of the winds and overlooking the river."

Scott wiped the sweat from his brow and stood trying to catch his breath. He reached over and gave Julia a hand as she climbed over the last rocks up to the ledge. They stood a moment, breathing deeply while taking in the sight of the glistening blue river wending its way through the steep gorge below.

"The Blue Nile, what a long journey it must make before finally finding its way to the sea," Scott said. "The river Ghion and we're looking to the west." A gust of wind blew down the slope and a whispering sigh escaped from the cave, as they looked out at the sun across the gorge.

Scott turned at the sound. "This is it. The land of onyx and spices, the window on the west, the Ghion River and the mountain that whispers. Now what does it all mean?" he said as he walked toward the entrance.

Taking out their flashlights, they squeezed into the cave. The first thing Scott noticed was a large asp wiggling away on the floor to the rear of the cave. Holding up his hand for his companions to stop he said, "I just saw Cleopatra's end wiggle to the back of the cave. You were right to throw rocks in here, Evanie."

Evanie stuttered, "Cleopatra's end . . . what do you mean by . . . that?"

"Don't you remember your African history, how Cleopatra chose to be bitten by an asp instead of being taken by Caesar's troops?"

Julia grabbed Scott's arm. "Did you . . . see anymore? Is . . . is it safe to go in?"

"Safe, I dare say not. But they're shy and know we're here. Just don't stick your hands into any cracks along the floor or walls without pushing a stick in first," Scott said.

They shined their lights nervously around the cave as the wind came whistling across the vent in the rock above, creating a moaning sound that reverberated in the confined space. The cave was eighteen feet deep by twelve feet wide, by Scott's measurements. The walls were generally smooth, with a few rocks sticking out here and there. The vent was a small oval hole eighteen inches in diameter, which wended its way up through the rock to an outlet above. When they shined their lights up, they could see about ten feet, then the chimney turned and they could see no farther. The floor was of rough rock. Drifts of sand lay here and there and a small pile of old bones and litter lay in one corner. Aside from that, the cave was bare and unadorned.

Scott looked at the pile of bones and debris and pushed at it with his boot, scattering the contents across the floor. He shined a flashlight along the edges of the cave and came back to where his companions were standing. "Any of you have an idea?"

"You're nuts," Julia said. "I know that look by now and you're not going to get away with it. Come on, out with it."

"Samuel knows, don't you old buddy?"

Samuel stood scratching his head and then a look of comprehension dawned on him. "Of course, where'd the snake go? There's a crack along the floor and wall, but it is too tight, isn't it? He either went up the chimney, which isn't likely because snakes don't climb rock that well, or we're missing something somewhere. Where'd the snake go, indeed!"

Evanie asked, "What are you taking about? Where'd the snake go? We probably chased him out when we came in."

"So, you think he just slithered by all four of us as we waltzed in? Just slithered on by while we were standing there with flashlights and we didn't see a four-foot asp? Come on, Evanie, we're missing something. Sometimes the eyes can be deceived. Let's look around."

He handed Julia his flashlight and motioned for her and Samuel to shine their lights on the wall, while he felt along it with his hands. He moved methodically over the surface and did the same with the other walls, working his hands over each of the rocks protruding from the walls.

"I don't know. I have to admit, I'm stumped. Where did the asp go? I don't feel any obvious cracks and the walls seem natural enough. There's a crack at the floor and the wall, but it's tight. The snake didn't get out that way. It's getting late, the sun's going to set in a couple of hours and I'm tired. I say we set up camp outside, take a rest and think some more about it. I don't think we'll sleep well inside after seeing the snake," Scott said as he leaned against one of the small stone projections that protruded from the wall of the cave.

Two things happened at once. First, the sound of the wind in the chimney doubled and a loud groan issued from the vent. Then the part of the floor they were standing on dropped out from under them as if they were on an elevator.

Julia screamed and grabbed Scott's shoulder as the floor sank, carrying them down into the mountain. It seemed to take hours but was probably no more than a minute when the floor stopped and they looked up and saw they'd only descended about thirty feet. Lying before them was a tunnel seven feet high and five wide that led into the mountain.

Scott looked at his companions and smiled. "Where the snake went?"

"Couldn't you come up with anything better than that?" Samuel said.

"If you gave me some more time maybe. It's the best I can come up with on the spur of the moment. I thought it would cheer up the lady and Evanie."

Julia jabbed him in the ribs and said, "Cheer up the lady, right. If you think I'm cheered up by the thought of a four foot asp down here, you're sadly mistaken."

Evanie stood there looking perplexed and finally asked, "Do you three always act this way?"

"Please forgive us, Evanie, we jest sometimes when things of import are upon us. It's just our way of keeping up our courage when things look tough. I'd like to know where the asp went, too. I don't fancy finding him here in the dark, but I have a feeling it's not as bad as we think. We'll keep an eye out for him."

Scott led the way down the tunnel, which took a ninety-degree turn to the left and then started to climb. After a hundred yards they came to a fork in the tunnel with a smooth four-foot wall separating the two shafts. Carved deeply into the rock in Arabic, Greek and Hebrew was the following:

I will praise the Lord who instructs me

Yes even in the darkness my heart instructs me

I will set the Lord always in front of me

and I will not be shaken.

"Even in the darkness, you said Scott, but it could also mean night," Evanie said.

"You're right, Evanie, and it could also mean before me instead of in front of me. I translated it literally using the Arabic meaning. What do you think it means?"

"That the Lord is the fount of all wisdom. He instructs us day and night and is always with us, guiding us, and it is He who gives us strength and protects us."

"I guess you're right if you say so, but why place this here at the parting of ways? I take it as a warning and a guide to look for some instructions; some things are easier than they seem and we make it more complicated."

"Why don't we try the other tunnel first and see where it leads?" Samuel said.

"It probably leads to where the asp went. I bet this inscription is meant to be our guide, but lead on, Samuel."

"Let's try the left branch first," Samuel said.

They followed him down the tunnel for about fifty yards. He was walking very slowly, feeling his way with his toe, when the floor gave way right in front of him. They watched in horror as the thin sheets of rock fell fifty feet, shattering on sharp knives of stone waiting for anyone careless enough to blunder along the tunnel.

Across the chasm the tunnel continued.

Samuel looked back at his companions. "Wrong turn. Let's try the right hand one."

Carefully making their way back to the fork, they followed the right-hand tunnel, going even slower. Samuel shined his light along the floor and walls and gingerly placed one toe at a time, feeling the floor. A hundred paces from the fork, they came upon an inscription, caved in the floor in Arabic and Hebrew that said:

Blessed is the man who does not walk in the counsel of the wicked
Or stand in the way of sinners
Or sit in the seat of mockers
But finds his delight in prayer to the Lord.

"Down now! On your stomachs!" Scott screamed as he threw Julia and Samuel to the floor. Evanie needed no urging and was instantly on the flat of his stomach. They hadn't acted a moment too soon—the ceiling fell from its seven-foot height to only two. Tapering down to nothing farther along the passage, they would have been crushed by the weight if they had passed the warning. Left with barely enough room to wiggle back, the farther back they wiggled, the higher the ceiling rose until they were finally able to stand again.

"Didn't give us a lot of time to figure that out," Samuel said.

"One of us probably stepped on something past the inscription at some point and triggered the trap," Scott said.

Walking back to the fork they stood looking at the inscription.

Scott asked Evanie, "What does it mean to you to praise the Lord, Evanie?"

"To give him thanks and . . . give him his due and things like that, I suppose."

"What do you think it means to praise the Lord, Julia?" Scott asked.

"We always gave gifts to the poor when we praised the Lord, as a gesture of thankfulness. I guess I agree with Evanie."

"I always thought it meant to pray and give him thanks," Scott said.

"What about you, Samuel, what do you think it means to praise the Lord?"

"Why are you asking me, the only praising I ever did was sing in the bars whenever I got safely back into port. Silly sailor songs, songs of drunken sailors or just songs of thanks. What do I know, I was too busy having fun and singing my heart out to give it much thought."

Scott turned to Evanie. "Believe it or not, I think Samuel's onto something. You know better than I do, Evanie, but doesn't it say, 'Make up a new song to the Lord, sing to him your praises'?"

Evanie laughed. "That's what we do most of the day. I don't know what I was thinking. What do you think it means here though?"

"I don't know—sing and see!"

They stood around looking at each other, feeling embarrassed, trying to think of something to sing and praise the Lord about. Being in a dark tunnel and almost falling into a pit of sharp stones or having the ceiling fall on your head didn't help either.

Scott tried first. "My eye is on the sparrow," but his voice faltered off.

Evanie started an Ethiopian hymn then his voice trailed off.

Julia and Samuel stood feeling uncomfortable, with their small flashlights creating a circle of light around them.

Julia started an old Jewish hymn which none of the others had ever heard of. Scott was surprised at the beauty of her voice, but her voice soon fell to a whisper.

They stood their with blank stares on their faces, until Samuel of all people finally piped up and sang,

> A sailor's glad when he comes home
> he sings his thanks to the Lord
> A sailor's glad to see his lass
> on land and raise his glass to the Lord
> Amazing grace is what we say
> how sweet the sound it tis
> to save a wretch like me this day
> I know that I am his
> Was blinded then
> But now I see
> I raise my glass to the Lord
> I once was lost but now am found
> My port is safe for me.

Scott looked at the amazing sound coming out of Samuel's wizened and unshaven lips. He smiled and laughed then said, "Turn off all the flashlights except mine." He then slapped Samuel on the back and joined in the song.

> A sailor's glad when he comes home
> he sings his thanks to the Lord
> A sailor's glad to see his lass
> on land and raise his glass to the Lord
> Amazing grace is what we say
> how sweet the sound it tis
> to save a wretch like me this day
> I know that I am his
> Was blinded then

> But now I see
> I raise my glass to the Lord
> I once was lost but now am found
> My port is safe for me
> Amazing grace how sweet the sound
> to save a wretch like me
> I once was lost but now am found
> was blind but now I see
> Twas grace that saved me
> through the years.

When they came to the last verse, Scott walked up to the wall, turned his flashlight off and pushed on the writing where it said, *I will put the Lord always in front of me.*

In the pitch-black darkness that can only be truly experienced underground, the only sound they heard was their own breathing and hearts beating. Nothing happened that they could tell. Scott listened, felt along the wall and noticed nothing.

"Turn on your flashlight, Julia. I don't know what else to do," Scott said.

She turned her flashlight on and the welcome light seemed blinding after the darkness. They looked at the space between the tunnels and didn't notice anything until Julia let out a gasp, "Look there on the top, where it's written in Greek, between the letters, was that hole there before?"

Julia noticed that a small flake of stone or mortar, the same color as the wall had fallen off between two of the letters for "Darkness", the Greek word was SKOTOS when translated, and the "T" had been replaced by a small hole.

Scott turned on his flashlight and shined the beam into the small hole, shrugged and turned to Samuel. "Let me see your knife."

Scott probed the hole with Samuel's knife to no effect. He pushed and turned the knife, doing everything he could think of but deface the rock.

"I could swear there's some clue here that I'm missing."

Julia was starting to feel anxious. "Maybe you have to say a password to get the door to open."

"Sorry, but that's only in the books and movies. I know what you mean, though. The flake fell off when we sang. I think it's a key or something. I just wish I had the key."

Samuel was standing feeling nervous. It was cool in the cave and he put his hands in his pockets fingering the contents, as was his habit whenever he felt anxious. He was flipping over the coins in his left pocket and fingering something in his right when he exclaimed. "A key you say? No, it couldn't be!"

"What on earth are you talking about, Samuel?" Scott asked, "Come on, out with it!"

"Remember the amulet I found back in Corfu at the old castle? The one that rather looked like a cross? We thought some old knight might have carried it at one time. Well, I was feeling nervous and fingering the stuff in my pockets. I said if I re-buried it, some kid would come along and take it and, well . . . here it is. I was thinking . . . maybe this would work as a key."

Scott took the amulet from Samuel and turned it over in his palm. It was a pretty thing made of silver with what appeared to be gold lettering. "I looked at this before, but the inscription didn't mean anything to me then. It says, 'Yes, even in the darkness my heart will instruct me.' This just gets better all the time."

He inserted the end of the amulet in the hole between the letters. It went in and fit perfectly. He pushed until he felt it stop and tried turning it to the right, but it felt stuck. He then turned it left and they all heard the snap. A crack appeared in the wall between the two tunnels, the space suddenly transforming itself, as a door appeared, where none was before. Scott gave a little shove and the wall moved on a hidden hinge, revealing a small chamber with an altar in the middle. Lying on top of the altar was a small octagonal cylinder, carved out of acacia wood, lying on an embroidered cloth and a golden cross-studded with emeralds.

The room was adorned with Byzantine artwork and paintings depicting the crucifixion of Christ and his ascension into heaven. The paintings were also of Christ's transfiguration on the mountain and of him greeting the little children.

The only writing was by the picture with the children, which said:

Let the little children come to me and do not hinder them, for the kingdom of God belongs to such as these. I tell you the truth, anyone who will not receive the kingdom of God like a little child will never enter it.

Their flashlights lit up the room. Scott went over and picked up the cylinder, marveling at the workmanship. He pulled on the lid, and inside he found a scroll neatly written in Arabic. The cylinder was lined with gold. Peering inside and marveling at the way the gold was wrapped around the inside, he then noticed a small notch in the bottom. On the outside of the cylinder was a small silver pick with a hook on one end, which could be slid out of the carved wood. He pulled out the silver pick, inserted it into the cylinder, caught the notch on the bottom, and pulled on the golden lining, which slid smoothly out of the wood. Neatly wrapped inside, was another scroll nestled up against the lining.

Scott stuttered for the first time Julia had ever heard, "I ... th, think, I ... mean I think we're at the end. I think this is what this has been all about." Carefully laying out the second scroll on the altar, he unrolled the first one written in Arabic.

Quickly scanning the words, he caught his breath. "We're in bigger trouble than I thought. Now I know why everyone's been after us. They must have had some sort of inkling about this. Julia, take pictures of this while I look at the second manuscript."

She grabbed her camera and snapped off a roll of film and then just to be careful, reloaded her camera and took a few more pictures, then took pictures of the altar and chamber.

Scott turned to his companions. "The second scroll's written in Hebrew. Look at this, Evanie. Can you translate it for us?" He handed the second scroll to Evanie who quickly read the Hebrew, his face becoming pale as he read.

"This is the most amazing find since the Dead Sea Scrolls. Imagine an original scroll written by Isaiah. If this is true and all the evidence as I see says it is, you're right, we are in bigger trouble than you imagine. This is what those two were trying to prevent you from finding."

"What do you mean, we're in big trouble? How could we be in more trouble than we are already?" Julia asked.

Scott answered first. "These two manuscripts could bring a new light to the Bible and Koran, changing the beliefs and faith of millions of people across the globe. Not everyone will accept this, of course, but Christians, Jews and Muslims all over the world may have a new course to steer by. When these manuscripts are read and accepted, it could mean a change of heart and peace for a large portion of the planet. They were written to bring the dawn to a new age of love and enlightenment for millions and millions of people."

Samuel scratched his head and said, "I don't get it. What do they say?"

"They say that God's sacrifice has been completed for once and for all. His Son died for all men and is the answer. Simple clear and concise. Without a lot of theology."

"Who wrote the one written in Arabic and what's on it?" Samuel asked.

"Mohammad dictated it to his scribe when he was at St. Catherine's in 622. It tells of a revelation from the Archangel Gabriel. It says that his people needed law to live by. They needed to live under the yoke of the law—that the law was the schoolmaster that would lead them to grace—a grace freely given by Allah to all who would believe. A grace that will come to them not by following the law but will be a free gift from Allah."

"Mohammad wrote something that's not in the Koran?" Julia asked.

Evanie answered, "Of course Mohammad said a lot more that's not in the Koran. The satanic verses were taken out of the Koran if you read Rushdie's book, where Satan appeared masquerading as an Angel of light. They tell a story of how Satan deceived Mohammad and gave him new revelations, if you believe the book. Gabriel corrected this deception and the verses Satan or Lucifer gave Mohammad were taken out of the Koran. The apostle Paul says it's not surprising that Satan's servants masquerade as servants of righteousness, for even Satan himself masquerades as an Angel of light. Lucifer, the great deceiver, the light bearer, was thrown out of heaven and he's going to do all in his power to stop us from bringing these to light. We're in big trouble and have to get out of here."

Scott looked to Evanie. "The second scroll's written by Isaiah's scribe and tells of how the sons of Ishmael, who the Arabs reckon their lines from, are Isaac's nephews and are going to be joined back to the family when Mohammad's revelation is found. Isaiah said that Ishmael's sons will suffer and will be given a law to serve under. They must learn to serve under the yoke of the law until they realize their need for grace. Only when their sin is fully ripe can they truly know the grace of Allah and his Messiah. Isaiah says the time will be right when his daughter is called out of Cush, that's Ethiopia, right where we are now."

"Isaiah himself?" Samuel asked.

Evanie chuckled even though he felt an inner fear and awe. "Yes, Samuel, Isaiah himself. Some legends say that Mohammad came here himself. Legend says that he came and spoke with the Negus of Ethiopia after he left St. Catherine's. It's told that the Negus wouldn't let the Muslims practice their religion in the country until Mohammad told him about Mary."

Samuel asked, "What do you mean by Mary?"

Evanie smiled. "There are some verses, from the Koran, I recall . . . at any rate two messengers came to see the Negus. One was named Jafar, who recited to the Negus some verses which go something like this:

> Mention in the book of Mary
> She left her people and went
> to a place far to the east
> she separated from them with a veil
> the spirit was sent to her
> and the spirit hovered over her
> A man came from this
> in whom was no fault
> Mary then said, I shall take refuge in
> the forever merciful
> I shall fear God
> He then answered and told her,

I am only a messenger
And come from the Lord
to answer your prayer
He sends you a son most pure
She answered, how may I have a son
No man has ever touched me,
Never have I been with a man
The angel answered, even so the Lord has said
This is easy for the Lord and he shall give you a sign
A sign for all men
Goodness and Mercy shall flow to all of us from him
It has been decreed.

"When the Negus heard this, our legends tell us that his tears were so copious that they soaked his beard and ran down to his sandals and finally made a puddle on the floor."

"It almost sounds like Isaiah, doesn't it?" Scott asked.

Evanie raised and eyebrow, "Isaiah? Oh, I guess. What are you thinking, 'For unto us a son is born, unto us a son is given? And the government shall be upon his shoulders.'"

"I don't know, Evanie. Something like that, I guess I have to study my Bible better so that this all fits together. I know one thing, the whole thing is a lot bigger than I imagined."

I feel so puny and honored at the same time, I don't know what to say. I must thank the Lord right now," Evanie said as he fell to his knees. They all did likewise, even though they felt awkward. Evanie bowed his head and prayed:

"Lord to have been an instrument of your service and to have been given the wisdom to make the right choice. Oh how wise and wonderful you are. No one can ever encompass the wisdom of the Lord. We have argued for centuries about how you choose and if we choose and you have shown that all is meaningless, for you are Lord. You have created man in your image, but as man is to the earth, you are to the universe. I thank you, Lord, for you are an amazing God."

Scott said, "Thank you, Evanie. I'm not ready to do that—something tells me I should be, but I thank you nonetheless."

Scott turned to Julia. "Please take pictures of the rest of this. We have to get going and get somewhere safe and decide what to do."

She quickly finished photographing the rest of the scroll and chamber then changed the film.

Chapter 43
Escape

Walking out of chamber, Samuel asked, "How do you close the door? Are we going to just leave the gold cross on the altar?"

He needn't have asked. Julia walked out and stepped on the paving stone outside the chamber and the door started to close on its own.

"Everyone out," Scott said as they quickly scrambled out the door. Scott was last and had to turn sideways to fit through the rapidly closing door.

When they stood between the two tunnels again, they caught their breath and shined their flashlights on the wall. The wall looked the same, except for the small slot between the letters for SKOTOS, where the "T" had been.

"Well, that answers that," Scott said. "The cross can lie there. I feel better about leaving it for some reason. It was very beautiful, but I think it's best that it stay on the altar. Seems to belong there."

Samuel shrugged. "It would have brought a pretty penny in one of London's antique markets. But I think you're right. Let's go."

They followed the twists and turns to where the floor had dropped out from under them. Scott noticed small handholds cut in the wall that the builders must have made when they designed the place. They were able to clamber up to the little cave of the winds where the wind was still singing its song as the breeze played across the opening on top. They retraced their steps into the sunlight and stood on the little shelf overlooking the river. To their surprise, the sun was still shining, but dark clouds seemed to be massing to the east. They'd only been inside for an hour. The heat still hit them like a slap in the face after the cool of the cave, but the breeze, sunlight and freedom from the tight space were welcome.

They stood on the shelf for a moment collecting their thoughts. Scott stood thinking of a way or even if he should bring this great find out to the world.

Samuel cried out and a second later Scott heard the crack of a high-velocity rifle off to their east along the mountainside. It was an amazing shot— amazing they'd hit Samuel from a distance of three hundred yards and uphill.

The high-velocity round hit Samuel in the shoulder, spinning him around and knocking him into the dirt where he now lay on his side. Scott pushed Julia to the ground and saw Evanie lying in the dirt also. Looking up, he noticed two men carefully jogging up the trail toward them. If they had stayed in the cave one minute longer, they'd have been trapped. Why they'd shot from that distance and not waited until they were closer, Scott didn't know or care. Crawling over to Samuel, he checked the wound and saw that the round had passed cleanly through his bicep, luckily missing arteries and bone. Evanie waved and caught his attention, motioning for him to follow. Quickly grabbing Samuel, he pulled him over the ledge.

Scott half-carried Samuel down the twisting and rocky trail, trying to keep up with Evanie. Samuel shook himself and turned to Scott. "I'm okay for now. It's just a flesh wound."

"You're tougher than you look. I thought I lost you there for a moment."

"Take more than that to stop me. Just stay in front of me in case I get going too fast."

Hurrying after Evanie, they stumbled and almost fell down the steep slope as he led them on an old trail he'd used as a child to negotiate the mountainside that led down to the river.

❋ ❋ ❋ ❋ ❋ ❋ ❋ ❋

Hasid snarled at Mulama, "What did you do that for? We could have sneaked up and captured them, now we'll have to trail them over the mountainside, and Chad's aware of us—he might lay a trap. That was a stupid thing to do."

Mulama spat. "You're wrong. I slowed them down. If I had killed him, it wouldn't have accomplished the same thing. Chad would have left and been moving fast. I wanted him to know we're after them, then terror will fill their hearts and make them do stupid things."

"You forget that Chad and his sidekick have been in battles before. I don't think giving them notice that we're on their trail was such a good idea," Hasid said.

"What's done is done—maybe you're right, Hasid, but sneaking up on him could have also put us under fire. The monks took our Uzi's so we don't know how he's armed," Mulama said.

"Yes, what's done is done—see that you don't do something stupid again."

Hasid was angry after trudging up the mountainside. He was about ready to shoot Mulama himself, but was afraid that he might still need him if he was going to be successful. "No shooting unless I say so. We want to take them alive. Do you understand me?"

Climbing to the shelf in front of the cave, they noticed a blood trail leading down the slope where Scott and his companions had clambered over the edge. Hasid turned and noticed the cave and walked inside, while Shula and the other men waited outside. He saw the shaft to the lower level, but it was difficult to see in the diminishing light as the thunderstorm approached. Walking back out, he collected his thoughts and appraised the men standing with Shula and Mulama. The four men he'd brought on the helicopter were rough and rugged men, used to climbing hills and mountains. Their leader was tall and wiry and carried himself on the balls of his feet like a trained fighter, which Shula and his brother instantly recognized and respected.

"There's nowhere to go around here and the storm's coming up fast," Shula said as the first large raindrop splattered against his face. He pointed at the cave and tilted his head.

"May as well. Hopefully it will blow over. It's going to wash away the blood trail no matter what. That's too bad. It would have given us something easy to follow—it was still a stupid thing to do," Hasid said.

The sky opened up and the rain came in torrents, driving them quickly into the small cave. Gathering around and shaking from the chill, they listened to the rain, then the cave gave a loud sigh as a gust of wind blew across the shaft.

Shula asked of Hasid, "Did they tell you what Chad was doing here?"

"Quati has given me his orders and what I know is for me to know and not to share if Farrell has not told you; just follow your orders."

"You're a cold one, Hasid, that's for sure," Mulama said.

"Hold your tongue, Mulama," Shula said.

"Our orders were to stop Chad and bring any papers and research back to Farrell and Bestin. They feel this is important to their faith. I gather it has to do with something they don't want public. Maybe Chad found it here and that's why he was looking in here. Maybe he found something back at that old monastery," Mulama said.

"The monastery looked deserted when we landed there. Did you two have anything to do with that?" Hasid asked.

"We needed information and the monks wouldn't talk, so I had to loosen their tongues. I don't think Chad found anything there or else he wouldn't have come all this way. I think what Chad was looking for and our employers want was here. Bestin thought Chad was close. When the storm blows over we should finish the job and kill him."

Hasid looked Mulama in the eye. "If you say anything about killing Chad again, I will kill you. I have had enough of your stupid antics. Does anyone have a flashlight? We should explore this area while we're here. I don't want to waste this time!"

Frank, one of the three men Hasid brought, threw his pack on the floor then pulled out a mag-light. "This ought to do," he said as he turned it on and looked down the shaft. "We may as well explore this first. Maybe Chad was skunked. Wouldn't that be nice? We can find whatever it is he was looking for and save ourselves a lot of trouble."

Guido, a short-wiry man, dug another light from his pack and shined it down the shaft at the floor below. He could see the tunnel leading off into the mountain.

Shula nodded to Mulama to stay with Frank and watch their backs. He started down the shaft with Hasid and Guido. Once at the bottom, they followed the trail to where it forked.

Mulama, Frank and Tony remained just inside the cave watching the storm. Mulama sat back against the wall watching the lightning whipping the mountainside outside.

Deciding to explore the left passage first, they stopped short of where the floor fell away.

Guido chuckled when he looked down. "Pity we didn't find them down there. I wouldn't want to take that fall myself."

Shula just smiled, while Hasid felt nervous.

Backtracking to the junction, they followed the right tunnel to where the ceiling descended and could go no farther. Shula pointed to the drag marks on the floor where Chad and his companions had crawled back when the ceiling fell. "Looks like they triggered a trap of some sort. Be careful. There may be others." They came back to the fork in the tunnel, shining their flashlights on the wall with the inscription.

Guido shrugged, not being able to read the inscriptions.

Shula noticed the missing letter and asked, "D you have a knife?"

Guido lent him his knife, after a nod from Hasid, which Shula inserted in the slot where the letter "T" had been, trying to get the catch to turn.

"I'd swear they got in here somehow," Shula said.

Hasid snarled. "We're wasting time in here. Chad's getting away. We're going to have to go after him. Forget the storm. Let's go!"

Terror-filled screams came to their ears from above, startling them into action.

"Quick," Shula snapped as the three men raced back down the tunnel to where the shaft led to the surface.

Shula cupped his hands and yelled, "Mulama, what happened?"

All they could hear was moaning.

Shula climbed the cut rock face, as Guido shined his light in front of him so he could better see the handholds.

"Be careful, Shula, Chad may have come back," Guido advised.

He briefly looked down, nodded, then continued. When he got to the top, he quickly peered into the little cave and saw Frank, Tony and his brother lying on the floor.

Mulama lay on the ground holding his hand to his neck. His neck was swollen and was turning an ugly bluish black color that was running up the side of his face too. Shula stood, looked around but found the cave empty. He dashed over and grabbed a flashlight, shining it around the cave and noticed a long tail disappear into a crack in the floor, near where the wind whistled down the chimney. He spun and noticed a large asp slithering its way toward the entrance. The rain had stopped and the large snake was quickly getting away. Shula faster still, darted after, drew out Guido's knife and threw it, pinning the snake to the ground. The snake writhed and wrapped its length around the knife, coil upon coil, trying to free itself from the cold spike.

Hasid quickly took in the scene as his head appeared at the top of the ledge. Before he could utter a word, Shula said, "Asps! They should have been more careful. Quick, Hasid, see if we can help them—watch out, there's more than one snake about. I saw one make its way into that crack where the wind's coming from. Have Guido watch it."

The asp had sunk its fangs high into Mulama's shoulder, next to his neck as he was leaning against the wall.

Shula quickly cross cut the bite area and sucked out the venom, spitting it on the floor, while Hasid did the same for Tony. Frank was gone, the snake bit him in the thigh, the fangs directly striking a vein. Tony's wrist was swelling where the asp had sunk its fangs. Hasid put a tourniquet around his arm and lanced the wound, drawing off most of the poison.

Shula couldn't isolate the wound on Mulama's shoulder. The proximity to his neck and interior organs only increased the rate at which the poison was spreading throughout his body. His face contorted in pain, and spasms wracked his body as his breathing became ragged and his eyes glazed over. Shula looked at his brother, whispered something in his ear as he drew out his knife. He bent his brother's head down and drove the knife between the vertebrae of his neck, killing him instantly.

Hasid watched as he lowered Mulama to the floor. "Why did you do *that?*"

"He didn't have a chance. I loved my brother and didn't want to see him suffer. I know he would have done the same for me!"

"Strange family you have," Hasid said.

Tony looked on in horror as Shula came over to check his wound. His eyes wandered back and forth from Shula's dark visage to Hasid's. Shula turned to Hasid. "I think he'll make it but we can't take him with us. If he moves too soon, the poison will move up his arm into his body. He has to keep the tourniquet tight and loosen it a little bit every half hour. Guido, you're going to have to stay and keep a watch over him in case he falls asleep. I suggest you move outside for the night, too."

Hasid looked at Shula. "You're amazing. Where did Bestin and Farrell find you?"

"Farrell saved us years ago and brought us to his church. We considered Farrell's church our only family."

Hasid looked quickly at Guido. "You okay with staying here?"

Guido nodded, lifted Tony off the floor and grabbed his pack. When they made their way outside, Shula pulled his knife from the asp, which had finally quit coiling around the blade. Shula quickly slashed off its head. It writhed once more then lay still. He picked up the four-foot body and tossed it to Guido. "Makes good eating. Good luck to you."

Shula and Hasid made their way to the shelf where they'd last seen Chad and looked down at the river below. The sky was getting dark and the towering thunderclouds off to the west dimmed the remaining light. Shula took his binoculars out and scanned the mountainside looking for any sign of their prey. He stood so long that Hasid thought he was daydreaming, when all of a sudden he pointed. "There, down near the river. I see them. Let's go." He pulled up his rifle, then looked at Hasid.

Hasid quickly apprised the situation and said, "Don't kill Chad."

Shula took careful aim and squeezed off a shot.

CHAPTER 44
JOINING FORCES

It appeared as if a golden light shone from the windows as Bestin and Henderson sat in Farrell's study, listening to him talk with Quati on his secure phone. The study shined with chrome and leather and occupied a small part of the home on the sprawling estate.

"Quati, this is important. I know we haven't seen eye to eye on a lot of things, and I'm sorry about that little deal with the press in Iraq."

Quati answered from his own palace, where he walked in the courtyard as evening closed in. The heat of the day had dissipated and the cool water from the courtyard fountain seemed to fill the air with humidity. The inner areas were air-conditioned for his wives, but the men stayed in the courtyard, where the fountain showered the air and the water trickled down the rock walls into the pool below, the evaporation lowering the temperature and providing a cool and comfortable place to relax at the end of the day.

"Farrell, sometimes I think you are no better than the Jews. You are trying to kill your own people. What are you doing? Tell me that—?"

Farrell started, "General . . ."

"Listen, Farrell, we have to stop Chad—do anything in our power—he is to close, I tell you, too close," Bestin interjected.

"I'm sorry, General, I was interrupted," Farrell said while giving the bishop a glare. "Chad's not one of our people, he's an infidel, not a man of the book. He's never gone to church to my knowledge and, therefore, he's an infidel. We're on the same side in this, General. If they find the writings and bring them out, it could change everything. Just think of it, General, Imans sitting around with Rabbis talking peace and drinking tea!"

Quati spat. "Farrell, do not tell me what holy Islam requires or tell me we are on the same side. You have no idea of the politics of Islam, may Allah be praised. Perhaps you do make a small point though. We do not want our sacred writings falling into the hands of unbelievers and waved to the masses, who have no way of interpreting the true intent of the Prophet. I will give you this much credit, we may agree on that at least."

"We must stop Chad now and pool our resources. I agree that if we find the writings first, we'll gladly give you Mohammad's, and if your people find them first you will deliver any Hebrew manuscripts to us; agreed?"

"Yes, I agree, but on one condition. You will not interfere with my people once I put them in motion. When they capture Chad and his group, I, and I alone, will be the one to decide what to do with Chad and his people. I get Chad."

"General, you agreed we could have the old Jewish texts," Farrell interjected.

"Do not quibble with me, Farrell. I told you that you could have them. I am talking about Chad and his group. He has done things to my people that deserve more than just taking away what he has stolen. Yes, much more! I have plans for him and that Jewess with him."

"Fine, General. I want to send someone over to see if we can lure Chad out into the open."

"Who did you have in mind, Farrell?"

"You've met Frank Henderson before haven't you, General?"

"Yes—yes, get to the point Farrell. I do not have all day and this tires me."

"Get with it, General, we have contributed to your cause and your training camps for years, even though we do not like everything you have done with the men or money. We did not like that stunt you pulled over here either. If we were to let it out that you had a hand in that, a few aircraft carriers might be parked off the beach near your lovely country."

"Why you, pompous ass, you dare threaten General Quati, why . . . I will deal with you."

"General, you misunderstand me. I don't threaten you. I'm only pointing out that we need to use honey on this—not a hammer."

"That is better, Farrell. Remember to speak with respect or we will get nowhere. Give me your best ideas of where he may be and let me know if you have anyone else working on this."

Farrell filled him in on the latest news he had about Shula, Mulama, Hasid and the other people he had sent over. "The last we've heard they were south of Lake Tana and headed into the hill country, possibly west to the Sudan. As soon as I get any confirmation from Shula, I'll let you know—but that's where I would start."

"Yes, Farrell, I agree, but you can also contribute something to the training camps for all my expenses and the trouble I am going to."

"No, problem General, you'll have a wire transfer right away to your Geneva account, as usual. Call me and I'll advise you on any new developments."

"Fine, Farrell, make sure you do the wire transfer," Quati said and slammed down the phone. He then turned to Dr. Abu who was seated on a couch in the courtyard.

Quati was in a rage. "What do you mean, you have lost them in Ethiopia? If we do not find them first, those stupid Christians will and then where will we be? I am tired of this incompetence, Abu. I tell you, tired of it."

"General, Ethiopia is a predominantly Christian country and is very backward and poor. It is mountainous and the infrastructure is unbelievably primitive. The great Arabian Desert is like civilization compared with some of the areas in Ethiopia. Give it time and relax."

Quati screamed, "Do not tell me how to think or feel. If I have told you once, I have told you numerous times; I do not care about Farrell, Chad or anyone else who does not help us fly Islam's banner across the capital of that Great Satan empire, the United States. I want Islam's banner to fly at Westminster, Bonn, Washington, Chicago and especially Los Angeles. The sooner Islam's flag flies over Tokyo the better. This is about Islam and the great awakening of its people. We have people in place all over the world. If Allah is with us, who can be against us?"

Abu cringed. "Your will is for me to obey."

"Get Hasid on the phone—quickly, do you hear me? Listen and obey and you might learn something, Abu. Hasid is far more cunning than you."

CHAPTER 45
WHITE WATER

Quickly checking Samuel's condition, Scott stripped off his shirt, ripping it in strips and pushing one into the entry and one into the exit wounds as Samuel scrunched his face. Binding the rest of the shirt around his shoulder, he then fashioned a crude sling. Scrambling and stumbling down the path, Evanie led them on. Suddenly, lightning flashed on the mountainside off to their left as they descended. The clap and crash of thunder instantly followed, almost deafening them.

"We have to get out of the storm," Julia yelled as the rain came pouring down.

Scott yelled back, "The storm's going to protect us from them. If we can't see them, they can't see us. We have to chance it and keep moving."

Julia's long hair was plastered over her face and neck. She looked at Samuel being held up by Scott and asked, "How are you doing? Can you make it down the slope?"

He nodded and shrugged off Scott's shoulder. "Keep going. I don't want them to catch us now."

Scott nodded and they continued down the mountainside, following switchbacks as the trail descended the gorge. The rain lashed them even harder the lower they went and they were soon dodging small rivulets and waterfalls. At one switchback, they came upon a ravine where the water was moving in a torrent, but Evanie calmly led them around a large boulder, where it overhung the ravine, and stepped from rock to rock to the other side. He would have been washed down and over the edge if he'd made a misstep. They could hear the water roaring all along the ravine from the quick cloudburst as they crossed over.

The storm blew itself out and ran off to the west to flash and crash against the mountain. The light was fading as they came to the riverbank and they finally stopped and rested on a rock ledge fifteen feet above the river, which was running swiftly through the confined channel, racing to find its way to quieter water.

"The river runs fast until it gets to the Sudan. Once it crosses the border, it runs out onto the plain and begins its journey north. There's a road and bridge across it, just past Jebel Mongasho, that will take us north and around the backside of Lake Tana. I was hoping to make for that road. We can use it to skirt the border." Evanie paused and looked at the group. "I don't think we want to go to the Sudan."

Scott replied. "I agree. Let's stay out of the Sudan. Al Queda has training camps there and I hear the leader's none too friendly toward Christians and westerners."

Scott turned back to where Julia and Samuel were resting. She turned to Scott when the rock exploded into fragments at her feet. They heard a crack from a high-powered rifle echoing down from above.

"Sorry, Samuel," Scott said as he threw him over the bank. Before Julia could protest, he grabbed her hand and leapt to the water below. The water was cold and when she came up for air, she saw Evanie holding their packs, leaping in after them. Scott held onto her arm and let the current take them downstream.

"What about Samuel?" she said as she twisted and turned in Scott's grasp.

"Right behind you."

"We're old swimming buddies. We were on the swim team in college. I'm sorry about that, but just had to act quickly."

"Aren't there alligators or crocodiles or something in this river?" Julia said.

Evanie floated over. "Not on this stretch. It's too fast. If we come to some flat areas where the banks aren't so steep, maybe. But they don't like fast-moving water."

The last rays of the sun glinted on the water when it peeked out from under the storm, which was still crashing away out to the west. Its dying rays were golden on the mountainside, but the cool water was taking its toll on their body heat.

Evanie grabbed a large log floating in the river, which he dragged over to Samuel and helped him up. He slowly paddled the log to where Julia and Scott were floating. "Hypothermia's a possibility, hard to imagine after the heat of the day, but we can't stay in the water all night. We ought to look for a place to pull out before it gets dark. What do you think, Scott?"

"We can go on for awhile still." He looked back up the river. "I'd like to put more distance between us. We need to find somewhere to give Samuel a better rest. How far does the trail go? Does it follow the river the whole way?" Scott asked.

"It turns inland a mile west of where we jumped. I'm not sure how far we've come, but they'd have lots of trouble following along the river after the trail turns. The trail goes high over a ridge on the slopes of the mountain, and then heads back near the river, and then it goes up and over another ridge. It's about thirty miles of rough going to where it stops at a little fishing village along the bank. We could get out there and spend the night. The village is about six miles or so from here down the river. They can't follow the river. It's too rough and the trail's a long way, especially in the dark. There's no way they could make it until sometime tomorrow morning."

"What's past the village and how far to the road?" Julia asked.

"The Didesa River joins the Blue Nile just past the village. The river's swift where they join and will be faster still, after the storm. The road I was talking about is still . . . I'd guess . . . about thirty miles farther downstream. The current's quick though. Say ten hours or so past the village."

"Let's stop at the village and see if we can find a boat or make a raft. We don't need hypothermia. Any ideas on when we get to the road?" Scott asked.

"Get some sort of transportation and make our way north," Evanie suggested.

"Well, keep thinking. I'd like to find a way to call Halie and see if he can get our car to us." Scott said.

"Maybe if we can find someplace where they have a phone," Evanie answered.

Samuel added, "I agree with Scott. Let's find that village. We've been in tougher spots than this and pulled through."

They grew quiet as they floated along, sometimes moving quickly and other times slowly and quietly as the current took them along. The rock walls of the canyon rose higher and higher, and then slowly sank until they saw the spot Evanie mentioned along the right-hand bank.

Samuel kicked while Evanie used his arms to pull the log toward the bank. They soon felt the bottom and dragged themselves out.

Scott turned to Julia and said, "Look in our packs. See if you can find a flashlight and something to make a fire. We need something warm to drink and eat."

Julia got Samuel comfortable while Scott and Evanie explored the village. His wound stopped bleeding and looked better after being in the water. They found that the village hadn't been lived in for some time. The huts were in disrepair and even the refuse piles weren't attracting flies anymore, a sure sign that it wasn't recently occupied. They found old wood crates, empty plastic milk, pop and water bottles. Scott looked at the pile of refuse and saw broken Coca-Cola bottles and a broken radio.

They found nothing usable along the shore, but one broken down canoe with a big hole in the bottom. Scott looked at Evanie. "Not much here to make a raft out of. We might be able to use one of the walls from those huts and make something out of it, but if we hit any big rapids? No way we'd make it strong enough to make it through."

"Let's keep looking. Julia's got a fire going," Evanie replied. A small glow showed against the vegetation and a tendril of smoke slowly rose from the glowing ember by the riverbank where they'd left Julia and Samuel.

"It's dark, I'm chilled, let's get back and maybe Julia's got some tea ready. We have to conserve our supplies and stretch them out. No telling how long until we get more. That was quick thinking back there to grab the packs, by the way," Scott said.

Julia had water boiling for tea, had changed Samuel's bandage and cleaned the wound. She looked up when Scott returned. "I'm concerned about the size of the exit wound and his ability to use his arm. I made a sling from one of my t-shirts, but he has to take it easy."

Scott looked at Samuel's arm again. "I think he'll be okay. He's pretty tough, but I'd like to get him to a doctor as soon as we can."

They gathered around and warmed themselves by the cheery blaze. Luckily, they'd kept their tea bags dry in zip lock bags. Julia poured the boiling water into cups and brewed the tea as they sat staring at the fire, absorbing its warmth.

Scott, squatting by the fire, broke the silence. "We didn't find any boats and I'm sure we'll see someone on that trail by morning, so we can't stay here. We think we can make a raft, but there's not much to work with and I'm afraid if we come to any rough rapids it's likely to fall apart. We'll take the side of one of the huts and reinforce it with what we can. I don't see what other choice we have."

After drinking tea and eating some granola bars, Scott and Evanie went back to the village and started dismantling one of the huts. Julia came over and held the flashlight while they dragged the wall down to the riverbank. After wrestling the wall down to the bank, they took whatever rope, vines and wire they could find to reinforce it. Julia looked around with her flashlight and came back carrying an armful of empty plastic milk and pop bottles.

"Wire or tie these to the raft," she said as she deposited them at their feet.

When she came back, she was dragging a large plastic tarp. "You said you found a canoe with a hole in the bottom?"

"Over by the bank in the reeds," Evanie said.

"Drag it out and pull this over it, maybe it will be large enough to seal the hole."

Scott looked at her. "You might have something there. Let's give it a try. It would be much safer than the raft."

They walked over and pulled the canoe up and out of the reeds onto the bank. It was twelve feet long and had been well made at one time. Scott stretched the tarp out beside the canoe and said, "It's about two feet short."

Julia came up with another arm full of bottles and said. "Turn it on an angle, use the diagonal and see if that works. We only need to get it up and over the front and back."

Scott nodded, then turned the tarp and found it was just long enough to cover the bow and stern.

She showed them how to wrap it over the sides and tie it. "We may have to bail it some," she said as she cut one of the plastic jugs with a handle and threw it in the canoe. "Look around for something to use as a paddle."

"I don't think we'll be safe in a twelve-foot canoe. If we come to any rapids, we might be in big trouble," Scott said.

"You're right. We'll take the raft, too! We can tie our packs to the raft and pull it behind us. It will lighten the load on the canoe and one or two of us can always ride on the raft, if needed," Julia said. All this took much more time because of the dark and need to share the one flashlight remaining to them.

She went to see how Samuel was doing while they scrounged around looking for anything to use as a paddle. Scott came back carrying some boards he'd taken off the walls of one of the huts. He rummaged in his pack and pulled out a knife, while the others started tying their gear to the raft. Julia lashed bottles to the side of the raft and a few to the side of the canoe.

Samuel's shoulder was stiffening up and he tried to help as best he could with his arm in a sling. "Why are you tying them to the canoe?"

"I thought if we lashed them to the sides they might help keep us afloat and the canoe upright if we hit any rapids," Julia answered.

Scott held up two of the boards he'd taken from the huts, which he'd whittled away to the shape of a crude paddle. He handed one to Julia. "Watch out for splinters. You may want to wrap your hand in a shirt or cut it up and tie it around the board."

"Should work," she said as she hefted it and then set it in the canoe.

"Let's get going. Evanie would you put out the fire?"

They dragged the loaded canoe down to the river and then pulled the raft down. Scott and Evanie tied the two together with a pair of ropes they'd scrounged up, and then scrambled aboard. They were surprised at how well the tarp kept out the water when they hopped in the canoe. A small amount seeped in, but they were able to keep up with it by bailing. The canoe sat low in the water, but the bottles lashed to the side buoyed it.

Drifting and paddling their way downstream, in the starlit night, they passed a small village and Scott asked, "Should we stop and ask for help?"

"I don't think so. It's just a small fishing village and we're near the border of the Sudan. No telling which way these people lean. There may even be Sudanese troops training here with only the river for access. They couldn't help anyway. Maybe they could give us some food, but they're poor."

A little dog set to yapping as they passed but soon quieted down as they floated downstream. The banks rose and at one point hundred foot high cliffs overlooked the gorge. Scott was looking up at the cliffs when he heard Samuel cry out, "Whoa, rapids ahead."

He could see the white water and a huge rock, looking like a sentinel, lying athwart the river, causing the main current to huddle and gather for a leap. They grabbed their paddles, aiming for the center of the current. Straining and paddling as hard as they could, the raft surged ahead and swung them around as it was caught up in the swifter current to the side. The huge rock loomed large and black with boulders scattered at its feet. It was worn smooth at the water line and shrugged the river to the side like some brooding presence.

The current dragged them toward a gap between two of the boulders, and the raft dragged them through. The canoe banged into the side of one of the boulders and threatened to tip, but the buoyancy of the bottles kept it upright. A large wave crashed over them, swamping and filling the canoe and floating their packs, while Evanie and Samuel bailed as fast as they could. Bouncing up and down, they raced through the neck and then traded places as the raft was caught in an eddy. Scott and Julia tried to paddle against the current, but the eddy pulled the heavy raft into the back flow below the rock sentinel. The canoe was pulled into the eddy and spun around with the raft, then spit out below, bucking into a maelstrom of white water. All they could do was hold on as the canoe and the raft kept trading places. Another boulder divided the current and the canoe went to one side and the raft the other. The rock halted them both and the water washed over the canoe in waves.

"Cut the rope," Scott yelled.

Julia sliced the rope with her knife and the raft took off downstream.

"That's probably the last we'll see of our packs," Samuel said.

"Maybe so, Samuel, but at least we're not banging against that rock any more," Scott replied.

The canoe behaved much better without the raft in tow. They had a wild ride between the tall cliffs and the river finally grew placid and quiet a mile downstream.

Scott looked up from bailing. "Everyone okay?"

The group merely nodded and grunted as they breathed a sigh of relief. The cliffs lining the river had disappeared into the distance and low earthen banks, with long grass growing on both sides taking their place. They glided into the placid section and Scott saw a low hump in the river.

"River cows up ahead," Evanie said. "Be careful and steer clear of them. They can be dangerous."

"River cows? What are they?" Julia asked.

"Hippos. They're not the placid things everyone thinks they are. Their jaws can cut a man in half and they've been known to turn over boats and do just that. Steer clear of them. If there's a cow with babies, they're even more dangerous," Evanie explained.

They drifted with the current and when they came abreast of the herd, they held their paddles still. They were almost past when one of the large beasts made a lunge at the canoe. Scott pushed at it with the paddle, which only seemed to enrage the animal; the hippo took the paddle in its mouth and snapped down, breaking it in half like a toothpick. The beast's lunge swamped the canoe, while Scott sat holding the splintered and broken end of what had once been his paddle. The hippo made another lunge, opening its jaws wide as it surged at the canoe, its fetid breath enveloping them as it exhaled. Scott reached, out jamming the broken paddle into its soft palate and the beast reared back and bellowed as the water swamped them again.

Scott's thrust with the broken paddle must have discouraged the beast, for it backed away as they drifted down the current, quickly trying to bail the canoe. Julia furiously paddled and Scott grabbed one of the loose boards, helping as best he could. The rock walls rose on the river again, giving them some protection from the hippos, which only lived along stretches where they could easily exit the banks.

They felt safe at first as they entered the steep chasm after the encounter with the hippo herd, until Samuel yelled, "Rapids ahead!"

They braced themselves for another encounter with the wild river. A large spiked boulder acted as sentinel in the center of the stream, splitting the current to the right and left.

Samuel cried out, "Head for the left channel!"

They frantically paddled to the left channel and barely missed the rock. The current grabbed them and deposited them into a long chute of white water that rocked, bucked and swamped them. The rapids spilled them out between steep rocky walls where the water slowed. When they looked back, they saw a twenty-foot waterfall on the right-hand channel that they would have plunged over if Samuel hadn't yelled his warning.

"Out of the frying pan and into the fire," Samuel said with a laugh. "The road's ahead!" He pointed to a rock bridge spanning the river. The rock walls descended, but the bridge was still fifty feet above the river on sheer rock walls.

Scott stared up at the structure. "How did they build the thing out here without access to the river banks to put up the abutments? It's amazing enough that they built a road out here. I would have placed the road at a ford in the river or at least somewhere that had easy access to the banks."

"The Italians built it during the thirties for access to the mines farther south. They carved rock like butter and built bridges wherever they wanted," Evanie said.

The current swept them under the bridge, and a hundred yards farther downstream they noticed a small beach along the right hand bank.

"Yo, over there," Scott said and pointed. "That's where the engineers accessed the river to put up their abutments."

They paddled and steered for the little beach and dragged the canoe out of the current onto shore. Climbing out, they stood and took stock of the situation. They'd lost all but Julia's pack, the small field pack Scott carried, where they'd stashed their film, the acacia wood cylinder and Scott's notebooks.

Scott pointed to the stairway cut in the rock embankment. "They brought their material and equipment down this way. There was probably a hoist on top at one time. I now see why they chose this spot. It's narrow. The bridge didn't have to be too long and the height avoided the flood plain. I'd bet this river rises ten to twenty feet or more during the rainy season, and you want to build the bridge deck above the flood plain to keep it from being washed out. There's good solid rock to anchor the abutments and that's why it's lasted seventy years."

Julia yelled out, "Look the raft! Quick, try to grab it."

They turned to where she was pointing and saw the raft with their packs bobbing along in the current. It was near the middle of the stream and Evanie and Scott quickly jumped back in the canoe, pushed out from shore and tried to grab it before it passed.

When they reached the raft, Evanie grabbed the rope and Scott tried to paddle the canoe back to the beach. They were drifting past the beach and headed downstream so Scott was paddling against the current. He could tell it was a losing battle, for every three strokes, he was taken downstream at least one.

"Evanie, it's not going to work," Scott said. "Grab the packs from the raft and throw them in the canoe. Evanie jumped over to the raft, cut loose the packs, but instead of throwing them into the canoe, he dove off and swam toward the little beach.

Scott cut the raft loose and paddled as hard as he could toward the beach, but still couldn't advance against the current. The best he could do was hold against the current. He was fighting a losing battle and gave up when he saw Evanie wade onto the shore with their packs. He threw the paddle in the water and jumped, swimming toward shore and found it much harder than he thought. He'd seen Evanie swim with the three packs in tow and he'd made it easily, but for every stroke he made, the current pulled him downstream half a stroke. He was tiring quickly and he stroked and stroked losing strength. He looked up, noticed the current taking him downstream, and lowered his head for another effort, when he felt something strike his head. Evanie had thrown a rope that he'd pieced together from the pieces holding the packs to the raft. Scott grabbed at it, but it slipped out of his grasp. Evanie pulled it back, as the river swept Scott farther downstream. Evanie threw it again, but it went wide.

Scott was nearing the end of his strength and lowered his head for another effort. He turned his head and could see a wild stretch of white water downstream as the river entered another set of rapids. Evanie coiled the rope and threw it, sailing it out and landing it across Scott's back. He twisted and grabbed, but felt it slip through his fingers. The rope kept sliding through his grasp and he was about to give up, when his fingers closed around one of the knots and held tight, as Evanie and Julia quickly pulled. All he could do when he felt the sandy bottom was fall to his knees in the water and gasp for air.

"That smoking I did years ago didn't do me any good. I thought my body was back in shape after quitting, but I couldn't keep up with you Evanie," he said between gasps.

"The current sets faster where you jumped in than where I was. I was closer to the bank and the current's slow there. That boulder over there," he said, pointing to a large rock in the bank, "kicks the current into the middle of the stream. That's the current you had to fight against."

They climbed the stairway and lay in the grass by the side of the road, sleeping in fits and turns. Scott took first watch and the remnant of the night passed. The morning sun rising over the mountain greeted them cheerfully. Walking out on the road, which was nothing more than a small gravel track, they strolled out onto the bridge. It was magnificently engineered and the gravel road seemed insignificant in view of the beautiful workmanship of the seventy-year-old bridge.

"The town of Guba's about ten miles north and there's a much better road that leads off to the east toward Injibara and then Lake Tana." Evanie pointed as he explained. "This road continues north for another sixty miles, following along the border, and eventually ends at paved road that runs off to the east toward Asmera. That's a very good road from there to the Red Sea, but I don't know if you want to go that way or through Eritrea again?"

"I'm not sure myself," Scott said. "The first thing I want to do is to get Samuel some medical attention. I'm afraid our extremist friends may have good connections in the Sudan. As I said, Al Queda trains there, so I'm sure we don't want to go anywhere near there. I believe we have to get this information to Jerusalem, if I read the signs correctly. What's the fastest way to get north? I'd think the way we came in would be the best, but who knows. I say let's try to find a phone, call Halie and see if we can get our car back. What do you think, Evanie?"

"The closest phone would be in Guba. The only thing to do is start along the road, but we should boil some water and fill our canteens so we don't dehydrate first."

"Samuel needs to drink plenty of fluids to make up for the blood loss," Julia said.

Back down at the river, they made a fire and boiled water for tea, ate and filled their canteens, then started the walk along the road in the building heat. There wasn't a cloud in the sky and the dusty road followed the shoulder of Sencai to the north paralleling the river. They'd trudged along the road for an hour, when they heard the unmistakable sound of a truck coming up the long grade they had just climbed. Scrambling to the side of the road, they lay in the weeds and hid amongst the rocks as best they could as the vehicle approached. Scott peered between two large rocks and around the bend came an old faded blue Volkswagen microbus. Driving the beat up vehicle was a craggy faced, bearded man with long blond hair wearing a battered hat. He had a pipe sticking out of his mouth and was intent on the road in front of him.

Scott said a small prayer, made an instant decision, and jumped out onto the road waving at the driver. The old bus came to a halt and the man cautiously opened the door and stepped down. Walking up to Scott, he turned his head and held out his hand. "Howdy! Name's Taylor. What can I do for you?"

"We need a ride to Guba to use the phone. One of my companions has been shot and we need a doctor."

"Been shot, you say? Not good. Are you in some sort of trouble?"

"We're not running from the police or government, if that's your question. Just your typical tourists being attacked by bad guys. Came down the river from out east," Scott said.

"It's your lucky day then, my friend. I'm going to Guba and then on to Lake Tana. Been prospecting these hills and need to take my stake into Gonder. Let me see your friend. I was a medical corpsman during the Korean War and know something about gunshot wounds."

"Come on out. I think we've found a friend," Scott yelled across the road.

When Taylor saw Julia, he whistled, then tipped his hat. "Sorry, m'am, just haven't seen a beautiful woman since I can't remember. Let me take a look at your friend though."

He examined Samuel's shoulder while they rested in the shade of one of the boulders lining the road. He took off the bandage, then went back to his bus and brought out a first-aid kit. After cleaning the wound, he reapplied the bandage, then turned to Scott. "The river's cleaned the wound out as well as

I, or anyone else could have. My only concern is infection. The river's fairly clean . . . the wounds closed up and the bullet didn't hit any bone or major organs. When we get to Guba you can find a phone if that's what you want, but I'm going to Gonder. We can find a pharmacy there and get some penicillin, which we should probably pump him up with. It's up to you."

Scott looked to his group and they nodded their assent. He then reached over, offered his hand to Taylor, and said, "There might be some danger in having us with you. You've been helpful and I don't want to bring trouble to you. We'd love to get all the way to Gonder. We're headed north toward Eritrea and there are some troublesome characters after us. If they catch up with us, there's no telling what might happen."

Taylor just smiled and opened the door of his bus, reaching inside and pulling out a Winchester Model 70 in 30–06 with a 3x9 scope attached. He handed the rifle to Scott, reached back in, and pulled out a pair of 45 caliber automatics. "I think we could handle some trouble with these."

"Don't you need a permit from the government for these?" Scott asked.

"Permit, well. This is Africa. I had one once when I registered as a guide. Problem is you have to bribe your way to the top and wait a year whenever you renew it. Then they revoke it and start the bribery process all over again. Whenever I'm stopped, a little grease takes care of everything. Come on, let's get going. We haven't got all day and it gets mighty hot out here around noon."

They piled in his bus and took off down the road, grinding the gears of the old bus every now and then. The overloaded bus was filled with prospecting gear, a couple of jerry cans of gasoline and water and four passengers. The forty-horsepower motor struggled up the grades, but Taylor was an expert at negotiating the steep terrain and grades. He didn't stop when they reached Guba and continued north, avoiding the improved road that headed east toward Lake Tana. Scott glanced at Taylor when they crossed the road.

Taylor noticed his look. "If you're being followed the most logical place to look would be down that road. If we head north, toward Shek Hasan and Shenhedi, we can catch the paved road that runs over to the north side of the lake, and then it's only five miles further to Gonder. Less chance of being followed that way."

They bumped along the west side of Mount Beleya as they gained elevation. The scenery changed and became more wooded as they passed through a village near the crest on the road. The red and grey rocks of the ten thousand foot peak stood out in stark contrast to the lower slopes. When they reached Shenhedi, they turned east toward Lake Tana and the road was even paved in spots, at least by African standards. Following the river valley, the road wound back and forth uphill, the old bus struggling to the crest. Once over the divide, they saw Lake Tana below and glided down the grade, skirting the north side of the lake, coming upon the main road to Gonder. Stopping at the first pharmacy, Taylor came out a moment later with a small package.

"Penicillin. Give him two tablets now and one every four hours. It will keep any infection down."

Julia felt Samuel's shoulder and forehead to see if he was running a fever, but he seemed cool to her touch.

Taylor continued north, passing through Gonder and Scott turned to him and said, "I thought you were going to Gonder?"

"Seems as if you folks could use a friend and some help. I thought I'd take you to Asmera or even Mitsiwa, where you can catch a boat and move up the gulf. You might even be able to catch a plane in Asmera. If they're looking in Ethiopia, it might be best if you're not in Ethiopia, get my drift?"

"Friend indeed, why you doing this?" Scott asked.

"As I said, I was a medical corpsman during the Korean War—but that implies that I'm an American. I came out here prospecting because I liked the countryside and the solitude, but most of all because I became friends with some of the monks in the monasteries after the war. Took a trip through Europe when I got out. It was beautiful, but something was missing."

"Traveled all around, kind of like a vagabond?" Julia asked.

"Kind of, but I studied history and read about the reformation, the crusades and the inquisition. I'd always thought Europe would be a hot bed for religion. You know, Notre Dame Cathedral and all that. Well, when I was in Korea, I became a Christian, not that most men didn't when they were in the trenches with mortars and bullets flying over their heads. 'Aren't any atheists in the fox hole,' they'd say?"

"Amen, brother," Evanie added.

"Well, I found Europe mostly devoid of what I'd call faith. I don't like to call it religion. Europe was full of nude billboards, pornographic television, and it seemed as if most people were chasing after their own appetites. It didn't sit well with me. I then went to Greece and found things much the same, except the peasants didn't necessarily subscribe to this new-age appetite and actually went to church and believed, trying to put their faith into their feet, so to speak."

"You know, Taylor, that's refreshing to hear. I have been struggling with this whole thing. I can't call myself a Christian, but feel as if someone was calling me to the question so I know what you mean. Did you feel as if someone was calling you?"

"Calling me, I don't know. When you're in a foxhole and people are shooting at you, who knows? I think the Lord's calling everyone, calling them all the time. Do we listen though? Hah, that's the question!"

"Father Halie believes the same thing," Evanie said.

"At any rate, I came to Ethiopia by way of Egypt, and saw what the Islamic clerics were preaching . . . it's all works! They talk of their faith, but you have to work your way to paradise. It didn't fit with what I believed. How could a poor cripple work his way to heaven? How could the mentally ill or the disabled work their way to heaven? I knew a kid who had Down's syndrome; he went to a church and was one of the most spiritual people I'd ever met. Works were out. This kid brought so much joy to me that once I got over his handicap, I found that it was just an expression of the spirit working in his life."

"That's beautiful, Taylor," Julia said.

"Where was I . . . Ethiopia. The country seemed like the last bastion of untainted Christianity. I didn't really care for all the Orthodox stuff—each to their own, though—but they have a deep true belief and practice charity. Amazing people. I met a monk in Axum named Friar Bejitou, who taught me a lot when I first came here."

"Bejitou, he's head Abbot of St. Mary's in Axum now," Scott interjected.

"Abbot, well I'll be . . . Abbot of St. Mary's. What's the world coming to?"

"We met him on our way up here. Bejitou and his assistant Aquius were helpful."

"Maybe we can stop and see them. So . . . where was I? I've been in Ethiopia ever since. Missed the states some and even went back once or twice, but it was too tame for me. I love the wilderness. Don't need the money. Have a house by Lake Tana that I go too now and then. Don't really know why I keep it. Place to relax during the hottest part of the year, I guess, but I'm always back in the wilderness looking for that one big find. I guess I'm like that widow looking for the lost coin. Found enough gold and other stuff to retire in splendor back in the states, but keep it in a bank in this country."

"Aren't you afraid of losing it in an Ethiopian bank?" Julia interrupted.

"Don't care all that much. I have some stashed away in the classical kind of bank. Most of it goes to an orphanage in Axum that Bejitou administers for me. Got to keep it invested like a good steward, they say."

Continuing their drive, they pulled into Axum near dusk.

CHAPTER 46
TROUBLE NORTH OF AXUM

Hasid and Shula plodded along the trail over the mountain. It was dangerous in the dark, but as dawn broke they came upon the abandoned village where Chad and his companions had spent part of the night. Their campfire was still warm but old, and all signs of them gone.

Shula looked out at the river, figuring Chad had gone down stream. Kneeling in the dust by the river, he read the signs in the dirt from dragging something heavy into the water. He wanted to head back to their car so they could conduct a proper search. He felt disappointed at losing them after sprinting down the hill and taking a wild shot at where they sat above the river.

"I think we should follow them. Make a raft or just float along the river," Hasid said.

"I don't swim that well and there are crocodiles."

"Chad will have to deal with them as well."

"We would do better to go back and get that helicopter. Can't you call it in here with the satellite phone?"

"I'll try," Hasid said as he opened up the case.

Aligning the antenna, he set up the phone but could not get a signal. "I think it's broken."

"Does your cell phone work?" Shula asked.

Hasid took out the phone, noticed it still had a half battery, but no signal. He tried to place a call, but it wouldn't work. "No, there aren't any cell towers out here last time I looked."

"Head back to the car then. We'll get the helicopter and follow Chad that way."

Hasid looked thoughtful. He needed Shula out here in the wilderness, but would he need him once back in civilization (if that was what one might call Ethiopia). "Yes, let's head back to the village and get the car. I'll then call the helicopter back. We can then decide the best course of action. I think we need someone on the ground directly on his tail."

They found an Ethiopian police car parked next to their vehicle and two officers questioning the villagers.

One burst from Shula's Uzi sent the men flying into the bush. He calmly walked over, reached into the police car and shot out the radio. He then shot the tires with a few well-placed shots.

"Okay, Hasid, which car?" Shula asked as they looked at Shula's Jeep and Scott's Land Rover.

"Let's take the Jeep. It's in better shape. I'll fix the Rover so no one can follow." He pulled off the distributor cap, then let the air out of two of the tires.

Making their way down the main highway, they spent the night in Gonder at one of the local hotels. Hasid called the helicopter pilot, telling him to pick him up the following morning.

"I don't know how these people can live like this. It's almost as if they enjoyed filth and squalor," Hasid said with a grunt.

"It's a hot place, they're short of water and the country's poor. Their civil war with Eritrea didn't help. At one time Ethiopia was one of the richest countries in Africa, but decades of misuse by the Germans and Italians, then their own people, bled the country dry. They're just now starting to look forward to a brighter future."

"I've called the helicopter pilot. He's going to pick me up tomorrow morning. I want you to try to pick up Chad's trail on the ground. Head over near the western border and see what you can find."

"What are you going to be doing?" Shula asked with a sneer.

"Do you really think talking to me that way will help? I know you're tough, Shula. I saw how you helped your brother when the snake bit him. You're a man I can admire, but this is bigger than us all."

"I just wanted to know what you were going to do."

"Take this cell phone—I know they don't work well outside of the city, but we'll be able to contact each other when we're near a cell tower and keep each other apprised. We need to cover both areas. I also need to get to Asmera. I have other traps laid."

Shula nodded. "The man in the gas station may have had word of them already."

"Why didn't you say so in the first place? What did he say?"

"He saw five westerners and one of them a redheaded woman, which is rare around here. It's hard to hide Ms. Apostoli in this country, unless she went around with her head covered like an Arab."

"Did he say which way they went?"

"He wasn't sure, but thought they went toward Axum. At least they started that way. I think that makes the most sense. If they found what they came for, they'd be trying to get out."

"We ought to go after him now instead of spending the night in this flea-infested dump."

"I still have to report to Farrell, and don't forget we have a border to cross. I can't take the guns with me in the Jeep. What are we going to do if I catch up with Chad on the other side of the border and don't have anything except stones and knives to throw at him?"

"You're right, of course. We've also been at it all day and all night trying to track them down. I'm tired, wake me at dawn."

Hasid lay on his cot and pulled the mosquito netting over his head. The room wasn't as bad as he'd let on. There was a small ceiling fan and the bed was equipped with mosquito netting. There was a communal bath in the hall with actual running water. They didn't have hot water, but at least the water was warm. He was afraid to drink the stuff, and even afraid to brush his teeth after getting sick in Morocco a couple of years ago. His last thought as he dozed off brought a smile to his face: the big tough Hasid was afraid to brush his teeth. *What would Quati think?*

The next morning the helicopter picked up Hasid, who took the weapons. Shula headed off at a fast pace for Axum in the Jeep. The road between Gonder and Axum was in the high country and the two hundred fifty mile trip took most of day. The road was a two lane, somewhat paved country road, so it was hard to average more than thirty miles an hour. It was near dusk when he pulled into Axum. He stopped at a roadside stand to ask around and see what he could find out.

Chapter 47
Micro Tunes

The microbus pulled into Axum in the afternoon, the old bus chugging and blowing smoke as it had all day. They'd only stopped once to check the oil and add a quart.

When they pulled into St. Mary's, they stopped and talked with Taylor's old friend, Father Bejitou.

"It's good to see you again, Mr. Chad and Ms. Apostoli. Taylor, how good to see you, too. I see you're keeping better company than the last time we met."

"It's just good to see you, Bejitou. It's been many long years since that young monk and I caroused around the town together."

"Don't spread that carousing part around—I have fond memories of our times together though." He paused and looked Taylor in the eyes. "Take good care of these people. I believe what they are doing is important to the Lord's work. How are you keeping these days; what have you been up to?"

"Fairly well. I find it strange the way the Lord works things out though. I'm out minding my own business and Mr. Chad and his group drop into my lap in the middle of nowhere. I then discover that they know you and are working on something important to the faith. What do you call it, communion of the saints?"

"Don't call me a saint. Save that for Bejitou," Scott said.

"You misunderstand him, Scott. Once part of the spirit, we are all considered saints in his kingdom," Bejitou said.

"I like the sound of that, but I'm still struggling with the whole idea. Something keeps holding me back. I will tell you that our trip was a success, but I'm afraid we're in even bigger trouble."

"People have been asking about you in town and word is out that some woman is asking for you in Asmera. They say she's even offered a reward to find you."

"A woman looking for Scott? What type of woman, father?" Julia asked.

"A blonde western woman has been asking questions around the market in Asmera. Rumor has it that she's offered a reward for information about him."

"Are you hiding something from me?" Julia asked Scott.

"I've no idea what this is all about."

Bejitou turned and spoke to them all, "I think you should be careful and move on right away if your venture is to be a success. The border is usually open to Ethiopians and Eritreans and is not a problem to cross, but rumor has it they are stopping cars and checking papers. I do not know if you will have a problem or not. Maybe you can find a way to cross without using the road. Be careful."

Scott walked with Bejitou and paused a moment while the others went back to the bus. After shaking hands, Scott came running up to his companions.

Finding a gas station and hotel on the outskirts of town, they filled the bus with gasoline along with the jerry cans and stocked up on water and supplies, then slept the sleep of the truly weary. The next morning they started toward Asmera in Eritrea.

There were three ways to cross the border: the main western road to Asmera, the road from Adigrat to Asmera and a small dirt road between the two which followed a dry wash between the two mountain ranges. Leaving Axum, they followed the road to Adigrat, then took the dirt road to Dekemehare and were able to cross the deserted border as Taylor had guessed. They couldn't even tell when they'd left Ethiopia and entered Eritrea.

Getting back on the main road to Asmera, they found a group of hotels on the outskirts and booked separate rooms. The hotel was a small African affair without the standard plumbing and air-conditioning that would appeal to most westerners.

When they first arrived, Julia looked at Taylor and raised an eyebrow.

"We'll be less conspicuous here than if we booked a room downtown."

"Suits me fine," Samuel said.

"Good, Samuel, for that's all we're going to get," Scott said.

They met as the sun set and walked down the street to a local establishment for supper, then strolled back to their rooms. As they approached their hotel, Scott caught sight of a small man running quickly off.

When they entered their rooms he motioned for them to gather around. "Okay, change of plan. I think they're on to us and we have to keep moving. Taylor and Julia get the bus and meet Samuel and me around the corner. We'll bring the bags."

CHAPTER 48
FLIGHT TO THE RED SEA

Taylor and Julia were waiting in the microbus around the corner of the hotel as Scott and Samuel came running up. Driving the sixty miles to Mitsiwa, dawn was breaking as they saw the Red Sea glimmering ahead. Not stopping in town, they headed directly to the harbor where Scott went to the port office, requested use of the radio and called Mishma.

Adbeel answered immediately. "Yes, Scott, we're in the harbor. We did some work on the diesels and my father had some business to attend to."

"Are you available for another charter, Adbeel?"

"We would be pleased to, if you promise us some fun and excitement. We are bored in this port."

"Probably more excitement than you'd want. Where are you?"

"We are moored to a buoy in the center of the harbor on the north side. I will come in the dinghy for you."

"That would be fine, my friend," Scott said. "We'll be ready, but tell your father to make ready to leave right away. We may have someone on our tails."

"It pleases me to hear from you again, Scott. How was your trip?"

"I will tell you when we see you."

"We're ready for some fun after rotting in this port."

"We'll see how much fun you can stomach, Adbeel, we'll see."

Making their way down to the dinghy dock, they unloaded the bus and waited for Adbeel. Taylor shuffled his feet and said, "Well, I guess this is good bye. I was kind of getting used to all this. Seems the more I think about it, maybe hanging out and prospecting in Ethiopia was fine for awhile, but maybe it's time to do something now."

Scott looked at him with a smile. "You're saying you'd like to come with us?"

Taylor looked sheepish. "I didn't realize until now, but . . . yes, that's what I'm saying. I didn't know my own mind. If you'll have me, that is?"

"We'd love to, but I warn you, it's going to get dangerous. We're not out of this yet."

"That's why I'm coming. I've been bored stiff, too. Something your young friend there with the boat said about fun and excitement stirred the same thing in me."

"Well, get your stuff. Here he comes."

Taylor unloaded the van and left the key, so whoever came along wouldn't have too much trouble taking it. When Adbeel brought the Zodiac alongside they loaded their gear, but had to make two trips to get all their equipment on board.

Scott climbed up on deck of the Cape Hatteras and took his hat off to Mishma and Adbeel. "I've missed you, my friends. Seems like we're fated to be together on this. I don't want you getting hurt, though."

Mishma smiled and drew Scott into an embrace, kissing him on each cheek. Mishma's scruffy beard scratched him, even though Scott was quite scruffy also. Mishma smiled then turned to Scott. "Tell me, were you successful?"

"More successful than I could have imagined. We ought to get underway though—some unsavory characters are on our trail and the more distance we put between us, the better I'll sleep tonight."

Mishma went into action, casting off the lines while Adbeel cranked up the large diesels, spun the boat around and motored their way out of the harbor. The navigation grew tricky once out of the harbor. The sea's coral reef system was extensive and dangerous in this area. You needed skill and a good chart to thread your way through the numerous islands and reef systems in this part of the Red Sea. Many a ship had holed its bottom on a hidden coral head and Mishma, even after sailing these waters for years, still consulted his charts as he headed north.

"To get to Sinai, we must stop for fuel at Port Sudan or Jiddah in Saudi Arabia," Adbeel said.

Taylor smiled. "I know Port Sudan. That wouldn't be my vote. The government's big trouble. Ever since that Umar Hasan Ahmed al-Bashir took power, things have gone from bad to much worse. From what Scott said, Saudi Arabia could be a bigger problem. Quati probably has a lot of the Saudis on his side."

Scott added, "The National Congress Party and Islamic Front are both big trouble in the Sudan. The Christians in the south are aligned with the animists, and they tend to get together to fight against the Islamics in the north. The country's been torn by civil war for years and there's no sign of it coming to an end. The last elections were in 2000 and, guess what, al-Bashir was elected again. Seems nobody wanted to vote and al-Bashir was the only candidate!"

Samuel looked up. "No kidding, no one turned up to vote?"

"That's right. If you voted against al-Bashir, you might not wake up the next morning," Adbeel said.

Julia looked over. "We stopped there on the way down and didn't have any problems."

"Yes, but we didn't have Quati hot on our tails then. He's well known in the Arab world, gives money to Al Queda and supports the suicide bombers. For my money, I'd vote for Saudi Arabia," Scott said.

"Well, we don't have to worry about it today, do we?" Julia asked.

Mishma turned. "No, not today. We have enough extra fuel to get past Sudan. We might possibly make it to Egypt, which would be best. Maybe we can get to Marsa Alam or even Ras Banas on the western coast. But we must go slowly to conserve fuel."

Scott interjected. "Our hope's in stealth and speed, but it wouldn't do us much good to go drifting around the Red Sea without fuel."

Mishma sighed. "We will hug the coast and islands, particularly during the day. At night, we must go farther out to miss any of the reefs along the shore. Who knows what Quati might send after us. Our hope is in stealth, probably more than speed."

That day was uneventful and Adbeel kept the boat on a northwesterly heading, cruising along at eight knots. It didn't seem like a lot, ten miles an hour, but they covered two hundred and forty miles that day, and it added up.

That evening Scott and Julia sat on deck, watching the sunset over the desert. "How did it get the name Red Sea? I've never seen anything bluer in my life!"

The inky sky was punctuated by stars and, except for an occasional tanker heading to or from the Gulf of Suez, they were alone. The Milky Way slowly wheeled overhead as they sat on deck, the sound of the engines lulling them as they pushed them along. Scott imagined they were riding on the back of a great whale while the earth slowly turned below them, as he watched the panoply of lights overhead.

CHAPTER 49

GUNBOAT

Shula followed Scott's trail to Asmera. It was slow and tedious, stopping at every gas station, store or hotel on the way, but once in Asmera, he figured Chad was headed to the port of Mitsiwa. Driving up to the port office, he checked with customs for any word of Scott or his party. The little man running the port office remembered Mishma and Adbeel, having dealt with them on and off in the past, and when some Bakeesh had changed hands he offered up what information he knew.

Hasid met him at the port after talking with him on the cell phone.

"We need to get a fast boat and go after them. They could be going to Egypt or Saudi Arabia, hopefully not Israel," Hasid said.

"Why do you say hopefully not Israel?"

"I've dealt with the Mosad before and don't want to again, if I don't have to. They have excellent soldiers and make wonderful enemies, but enemies I do not need right now."

"I'll see if Farrell or Henderson can get us a fast boat."

Shula called Farrell to explain the situation. "We think Chad's on a boat headed north, Reverend. Mulama's dead—bit by a snake."

"I'm sorry about Mulama, but why didn't you catch Chad?"

"The operation didn't go as planned. We hit one of them, the Polish guy—wounded him in the shoulder. It should have slowed them, but . . ."

"Did you get any of the information, what did Chad find?"

"He found a cave. That's where Mulama was bit by a snake, but we weren't able to get inside. Chad had left when we got there. We think he got in, but can't be sure. We can always go back and force our way in, but thought it better to trail Chad."

Farrell snapped into the phone, "Exactly what happened."

"We came up on the mountainside and winged that Polish friend of his as I said. Chad and his companions ran down the cliff and jumped in the river, all during a blinding thunderstorm. I searched the cave, found an old tunnel and saw where Chad had probably accessed a secret door of some sort."

"Why couldn't you get in?"

"I couldn't find a way to open the door without blasting the rock, and we didn't have any demolition equipment anyway."

"Maybe Chad didn't get in either. Perhaps you should go back and not follow Chad."

"He sure cleared out in a hurry and didn't seem to want to get back. I think he's headed up the Red Sea, possibly for Israel. I believe we should go after him."

"I don't know, Shula. I'm sorry about your brother; he was a good brother of the faith. Maybe you're right. I'll consult with Bestin and Henderson. Keep near this phone; I'll get back to you as soon as I can. It could take awhile; it's the middle of the night here."

"Thank you for your concern about Mulama. We'll wait and see what transpires." He hung up the phone and said to Hasid, "He wants me to stay by the phone. He's going to see if he can find us a decent boat. Let's look around the harbor while we're waiting and see what we can find."

Hasid left Shula by the port office and walked the harbor. The sun came out after a short storm and hit him like a slap. He didn't see how anyone could live here. Looking over the harbor, the only craft that appeared acceptable and fast enough was a Sudanese patrol boat moored alongside an old rusting and listing tramp steamer. The steamer was a piece of junk, but the patrol boat looked in good enough shape. It looked menacing and fast. Mounted on the bow was a machine gun with a metal shroud. The steel boat was painted grey and the craft looked deadly and capable.

Standing by the port master's office, Shula waited for Farrell's call. He was bored and hot when Hasid strolled back up, wiping the sweat from his brow.

"Find anything?"

"Something that would work. It's a Sudanese patrol boat. I'm going to call Quati to see if we can use it."

"Maybe Farrell can do something. I'll ask him, too, when he calls again."

The phone rang in the port master's office as they waited. The port master called, "If your name's Shula, it's for you—make it quick."

"Shula here, Reverend. I need you to call up someone in the Sudan and see if we can use one of their patrol boats that's in the harbor here. It's the only boat in the harbor capable of following Chad."

"I'll get on it but it's the middle of the night here. I'll call when I find out something."

Hasid pulled out his cell phone and punched the speed dial.

"This had better be good, Hasid," Quati said.

"I need you to call al-Bashir and see if we can borrow his patrol boat that is in the harbor of Mitsiwa. I need it to follow Chad."

"You're asking a lot. Al-Bashir's a pig. I'll call him and let you know."

Shula and Hasid stood waiting, watching the docks. About an hour later, the portmaster called again, "Hey, Shula, or whatever your name is, got another call."

"It's the middle of the night over here, but Bestin has a call in to al-Bashir to see if he can help. Henderson called a friend in Saudi Arabia. Bashir's closer though and it will probably take a day or so to get a boat down to you to help."

"There's already one of his boats in the harbor here. I told you that when I called before."

"I'm sorry, as I said it's the middle of the night. I'll let you know as soon as we find out something concrete. I called Quati, too, and his aide says he's not around; he's off on business somewhere."

Shula quietly said, "Quati's down here, as if you didn't know."

"Henderson and Bestin sometimes do things on their own and don't tell me. Quati could be of some help. Hasid has been helping you and he has many connections of his own. Quati can be of more help. As I said, I have a call into him."

"Yeah, but his forces are a thousand miles away. I don't know what help he could be."

"Hold on a moment—Bestin's on the other line," Farrell said as he leaned back in his chair and put Shula on hold. "Farrell here, morning Bestin. Al-Bashir says he'll help. That's good news. Yes, I know he's a beast, and all he wants is money. Hold on, Bestin, get a grip. Enough about al-Bashir. How can he help?"

"It seems he wants more money for those damn training camps. The man's a complete beast, and I don't like dealing with him," Bestin said.

"I agree the man's a beast, but how can he help? There's a patrol boat in the harbor. We need it."

"Farrell, you don't understand, he's a complete and utter beast. Those camps he's running are training men to do despicable acts throughout the world. I don't think we should . . ."

"Stop it—this is too important. Will he give us the boat?"

"Have it your way then. Let it be on your conscience, not mine . . ."

"Bestin, if I have to ask you one more time!"

"Yes—it appears Quati has talked with him, too. He has a boat right in the harbor where your gentle friend Shula is . . . right in Mitsiwa. He said we could use it as long as we donate to his bloody cause. Listen, Farrell, I don't . . ."

"When can we get it?"

"Now. I said, it's parked ... docked or whatever, in the harbor in Mitsiwa. A man named Jetur's captain. Shula and Hasid are to ask for him and he will arrange everything else. I tell you, al-Bashir's bad business," but Bestin found himself talking into a dead phone.

Farrell quickly switched over to Shula's line and said, "Ask for a guy named Jetur. He's captain of that patrol boat of al-Bashir's. It's out in the harbor down there somewhere. The captain is being notified to help you. Don't mess this up, Shula!" Farrell said with an edge and severed the connection.

Shula stood there holding the phone before putting it down. "Good bye and a good day to you, too. It was so nice to talk with you, Reverend." Shula turned to Hasid. "Seems the good Bishop has connections in high places. At least we don't have to try and take over a boat. That beast al-Bashir has agreed to lend us the nice patrol boat you found. We're to find a fellow named Jetur— he's been instructed to help us."

"Good, things are looking up—let's go find this Jetur."

They walked along the waterfront stopping at the cafes. At one portside restaurant, they asked for Jetur and the portly manager said, "Jetur, yes, I know of him. What's it to you?"

Shula looked at him with contempt. "Al-Bashir sent us to talk with him. If you know what's good for you, you'll tell us where to find him."

"Kind sirs, my mistake, please wait here in the cool shade. May I get you something cool to drink while you wait?"

"No, just get Jetur," Shula snapped and gave him a cold look.

The man waddled past Shula, who watched as he talked with one of the ladies sitting in the shade inside the seedy building. He saw her make her way to the stairs and then heard some shouting and cursing. Apparently, Jetur didn't like being interrupted.

A few minutes later a medium sized man with a mixed Arabic and African cast walked out to greet them, speaking in fractured English. "What do you want, something about al-Bashir sending you."

"Are you done yet?" Shula said with a calm demeanor.

"I do not know who you are or what your game is, but you may quit wasting my time. I am one of al-Bashir's captains."

"If you value your hide, and take the time to call your master, you'll find out who we are and quit wasting our time."

"You are crazy if you think I am going to call al-Bashir."

"I think it would be wise of you to make the call, or else you're going to be cleaning latrines in the southern part of the Sudan," Shula said.

"This better be for real or there is going to be hell to play!"

"To pay, to pay, not to play, my friend. We're the ones who are going to play if you don't get moving," Shula added.

Something in the tone of Shula's voice and the look in his eyes finally broke through Jetur's demeanor. He gathered himself, bowed and said, "Okay, gentlemen, come with me and we'll contact al-Bashir and then see what he has to say."

They walked with Jetur back to his tender, rowed out to the patrol boat and climbed aboard, where he picked up the radiotelephone and spoke with the operator in Port Sudan who relayed his call to Khartoum. He was instantly put through to al-Bashir and his visage slowly changed as he looked Shula and Hasid up and down, then he put down the phone.

"Okay, I guess we are going on a trip. We may leave as soon as I get my crew together."

Hasid asked, "How many men do you have?"

"Six, plus me."

Hasid looked at Shula. "Do we need them or is it better to get moving now?"

"I don't think we need them. Let's go." He looked over at Jetur. "Are you fueled up and ready to go?"

"Tanks are full. We have an eight hundred mile range." He was obviously proud of the boat and took good care of it no matter what his portside habits were.

"Forget your men, we don't need them. Time's more important. Let's go now," Shula commanded.

"I need my men. I cannot leave them here."

Shula had enough. "Call al-Bashir again and waste some more of our time. First, we take almost an hour to get you out of that brothel, then you waste more of our time trying to verify your orders. Follow your orders or not, maybe we'll just take the boat and be on our way. The only thing from stopping me right now is maybe you know something about this boat that I don't."

Shula's lecture had the desired effect. Jetur went to the helm, fired up the engines and signaled Hasid to cast off the bowline while he cast off the stern. Expertly backing the boat away from the steamer, he quickly spun the boat around, pointing the bow at the entrance to the harbor and gunned the motors out to the main channel.

"Have to be careful here. There are reefs on all sides. Most of the coral's dead in the harbor—killed by the filth everyone and the town pumps into the sea—but the coral is hard enough to rip the bottom out of the boat."

He slowly advanced the throttles as he negotiated the channel, then headed the craft north.

Hasid and Shula looked around the boat and checked the supplies. It was loaded with fresh fruit, but more important to them was the armament on board. There were high-powered rifles, grenade launchers and the 7.62 mm machine gun on the front deck. It looked menacing from a distance and Hasid checked the action and feed mechanism when they were away from the harbor and headed north. He turned to Shula and said, "Thing's a piece of junk. We ought to throw it overboard, maybe we'll go faster.

"Don't your men ever oil this thing? It's rusted and the action's dangerous," Hasid said to Jetur.

"They oil it all the time, but the salt air gets into everything. It was made for the desert and modified to fit the boat. I am told that a true marine gun would be made differently, able to withstand the corrosion."

"Maybe you're right. I just hate to see good equipment going to waste," Hasid said.

Hasid fired off a few rounds into the sea to get a feel for the piece. It jammed after twenty rounds and it took him five minutes to clear it.

"Thing's just about worthless. It's so badly corroded from the salt air, it's a wonder it even works. Let's check out the other guns."

Jetur put the craft on autopilot and they went below, looking at the rifles and other armament in the locker. The Kalashnikovs were in good shape. There were a couple of Uzis and rocket propelled grenades, or RPG's. Hasid brought an RPG on deck, fired it off, and saw it splash harmlessly in the sea. The round sank and about five seconds later the surface welled up and froth exploded.

"They need to hit something to explode," Jetur explained.

Hasid asked, "They don't go off when they hit the water?"

"They need to hit something solid. They are a land weapon. They work well against a boat though. I know, I have tried. They will explode when they hit the water if you shoot them high into the air like a mortar, but it is difficult to hit something that way."

Shula looked at the helm and saw they were going at ten knots. "How fast will this thing go, Jetur? We have to catch someone that has maybe a day's lead on us?"

"She will do twenty knots or possibly a little more, but she drinks her gas very fast then."

"What's the range at twenty knots?"

We have enough fuel at ten knots to make it all the way to the canal: at twenty knots we would not make it halfway. We would need to stop at Port Sudan and fill the tanks."

Shula pushed the throttles forward to the stops. "Head for Port Sudan then."

Jetur eased the throttles back. "You cannot run them at full speed; you will burn up the engines. You may only do that for a short time or the engines will overheat. Relax, I will pilot the boat."

After filling the tanks at Port Sudan, they continued north scanning the horizon for any craft. They stopped and checked out a few of the small craft they saw plying the sea, fisherman mostly and occasionally a dive boat taking tourists out to the splendid reefs. The trip became hot and boring. The only excitement was when they pulled alongside one of the dive or fishing boats. A number of large tankers and occasionally a cruise ship used the sea in their passage up to Suez. The Red Sea was a major thoroughfare and was always somewhat busy, but a big place nonetheless.

The trip north was beautiful. The wonderful days were followed by even more beautiful nights and their worry about fueling the boat was unfounded. They refueled and picked up supplies without incident at Jiddah in Saudi Arabia. Continuing their journey up the Red Sea, they had wonderful weather the next couple of days.

The next morning they were nearing the Sinai Peninsula when Mishma yelled, "Someone is coming up fast behind us!"

Everyone turned in the cockpit and looked where he was pointing. "Looks like a patrol boat. I don't think we'll be able to outrun them," Scott said.

"Put on some speed to give us more time," Samuel added.

"There is not much we can do against an armed patrol boat. They have a machine gun on their deck. I will not let them have my boat without a fight though," Mishma answered as he pushed the throttles forward.

The Cape Hatteras surged ahead to eighteen, then nineteen knots, occasionally reading over twenty as they surfed down one of the following swells that surged north. The patrol boat slowly gained as the morning waned. There was nowhere to run to, except to keep heading into the Gulf of Aquaba.

Hasid spotted the yacht ahead and exclaimed, "That's it—I know it . . . it must be Chad. They've increased their speed. Looks like they've seen us. Get the binoculars, Shula." His emotions took a twist as he thought of catching up with them. Chad and Julia, what would he say? They had given him a good run, but now was the pay off time. Quati would want this to end now. Could he do it? He had to do it or he was no longer living the faith.

Running back to the cockpit, Shula grabbed the binoculars out of the cabin. The 7x50 binoculars were great for night vision, but the seven power lenses showed little detail at that distance. They still showed enough for Hasid to make out Scott standing on the stern of the cruiser. "That's Chad all right. Tell Jetur to push the throttles all the way forward."

Shula relayed Hasid's orders to Jetur, who complained, "If I overheat her, I might burn up the engines. I have to monitor the temperature and if she starts to run in the red, I will have no choice but to slow down."

"I don't care if you burn it up, do as I order," Hasid said.

Pushing the throttles forward to their stops, the boat surged ahead until it hit twenty-four knots. Jetur glared at Hasid, but carefully watched the temperature gauges.

The distance between the craft slowly decreased as the morning went on. When they were a quarter mile apart, Shula ran up to the bow and opened up with the 7.62 mm machine gun.

Everyone hit the deck as the shells smacked into the cockpit of the beautiful craft. Scott and Adbeel slithered through the hatch to where Taylor was coming up to find out what was going on. Samuel charged past Taylor and dove into the cockpit, jerking open the seat, then reached in and pulled out Mishma's guns, handing one to Scott and taking the other himself. Taylor dashed back in the cabin to get his rifles.

"Keep your head down, Taylor," Adbeel yelled without really having to.

Julia was on the floor of the rear cabin, going through their packs, looking for something. She looked up for a moment and quickly ducked again as a round came splintering through the beautiful woodwork over her head.

Scott yelled at her as he looked down from the cockpit. "Keep you head down!"

"Here, take this!" she yelled back and tossed him a wrapped package.

He grabbed the package and turned just as Taylor came up the stairs from the cabin. He was dragging his rifle case with the 30–30 Winchester and an old but beautiful model 70 in 30–06. "Time to liven things up," Taylor said to Scott as they crawled back to the back rail.

Mishma kept their speed up as best he could. They were still a quarter of a mile ahead of the patrol boat, which explained the inaccuracy of the machine gun fire. Bullets whizzed overhead or splashed in the water all around them from the intense fire. Taylor kept his head down, pulling out the model 70 with the 3x9 scope, then rested it on the cockpit rail. The scope amplified the motion of the boat as he looked it, making it extremely difficult to get off an accurate shot. The view kept bouncing up and down with the swells. The waves were running at about six feet and though not unduly rough, they were close together. Taylor did the best he could trying to judge the shot, but when he squeezed the trigger, he could see the shot splash the water near the waterline of the boat.

"I'm amazed they can hit us at all," he said as he jacked another round into the chamber. "I know I'm a better shot than that."

"You've got to lead it more," Scott said.

"Just like on the ole Missouri," they heard Samuel say as he let off a burst with Mishma's Uzi.

"Any more advice?" Taylor asked.

"Keep your head down," they all said at the same time.

He squinted through the scope and squeezed off another round as the boat steadied. He wasn't sure if he'd hit anything this time, no splash and the large man working the machine gun didn't flinch or move.

Scott turned and saw Mishma down on the deck with blood oozing out of his shirt, his eyes looked glazed and his breath ragged.

"Julia, get Mishma below and see if you can do anything for him!" Scott yelled.

She and Adbeel grabbed Mishma around the arms and dragged him down the cabin stairs to the cabin sole. Hoisting him onto the settee, she pulled off his shirt and inspected the wound. "I think he'll be fine. Looks like it went through his side, might have nicked a rib, which probably hurts like the dickens. Our biggest concern is to keep him from going in to shock."

"Are you sure?" Adbeel asked.

"I'm not sure of anything right now, but I think so. Find me a blanket while I wrap up his side. We have to keep that other boat away and I think you're going to be needed at the wheel."

"Go, son, I will be fine. The lady is right, save the boat," Mishma said.

They both were surprised at the strength of his voice. Julia quickly finished bandaging him up and wrapped him in a blanket.

Scott grabbed the lever action and started pounding away at the patrol boat, not sure if he was hitting anything. It didn't have a scope and he pretty much just aimed at the boat, which filled the sights from that distance.

He emptied the lever action and was about to ask Taylor if he had any more shells when a large explosion—then a geyser of water—rocked the boat, laying it over at a forty degree angle and literally moving it sideways in the water about ten feet. A fountain of spray shot fifty feet in the air, soaking them as it fell.

"What the heck was that? I didn't see anything on that boat that could do that," Samuel asked.

A twin-rail of geysers appeared on the water racing toward them and going on each side of the craft as the high-pitched scream from the jet came to their ears.

"You had to ask, didn't you, Samuel? This might be a good time to think about being somewhere else, other than on this boat," Julia said from the interior hatch.

"You could be right," Scott said. "But look, they seem confused!"

Two jets turned together and joined up with two more and started to come in again, but this time they dove on the Sudanese patrol boat. Two large geysers of water rocked the boat where the first pair dropped their bombs. The second pair of jets opened up with their cannons, strafing the patrol boat, disintegrating a large black man who was manning the bow mounted machine gun. The 20mm cannon rounds vaporized Shula into a red mist mixed with bits of torn plywood from the patrol boat.

The four jets pulled up in a power turn and started to turn in for another run. Running right at Mishma's boat, the lead jet fired off a rocket, which leapt off the rail trailing a cloud of white smoke.

Scott stood rooted in horror as the rocket sped toward the craft. Adbeel spun the boat as the rocket approached. The explosion was deafening as the rocket impacted a wave in front of the boat, blowing a hole in the bow of the beautiful craft.

The second plane fired at the patrol boat again. The rocket's heat-seeking head found the signature from the overheated engines and impacted amidships, blowing the craft in two.

The other pair of jets turned in to finish the job when they exploded before their eyes.

"Who did that? Did you shoot at them, Taylor?" Samuel asked.

"Not me, I kept my head down. I was thinking of playing with the sharks after seeing what those cannons did to that man on the boat. I've never seen anything like that in my life. I think we're sinking, though, and it looks like someone's still alive on what's left of the other boat."

"I didn't want to see it happen to this boat either, but I think you're right. We're down at the bow," Adbeel said.

Mishma limped up from below with a blanket around him. "We have an oil pressure problem, and water is coming in the bow. You have to drop her speed and we have to get something to patch her up, quick."

Adbeel hurried over to the throttles and pulled them back, quickly checking the gauges. "I forgot I had them wide open in the all the excitement. I quit watching the gauges. Both engines are in the red. We have to run them slower until they cool down."

"What got those two jets?" Julia asked.

"Look up there." Scott pointed at the remaining two, which were headed north on their afterburners. They heard them crack through the sound barrier as they accelerated and saw four F-14's in hot pursuit. One of the F-14's shot two missiles off its rail. The smoke trails were easily visible as they fell off the wings and accelerated to Mach 4 in pursuit of the two remaining Migs. The Migs jettisoned flares and chaff, twisting and turning in an effort to evade the missiles.

One of the pilots dove under full power toward the sea, at the last moment pulling up to evade the missile that had locked on him. The missile dove after the Mig and looped into the turn, but caught the top of a wave and exploded into the sea, raising a huge column of water and foam.

The other pilot stood the craft on its tail in a power climb, trying to evade the missile, which just followed it up and higher up, following its hot exhaust. The warhead exploded when it was about six feet away, slicing into the jet, which added its fuel load to the expanding ball of gas and titanium parts.

The remaining jet stayed low to the waves on its afterburner, heading north as the Israeli jets trailed it.

CHAPTER 50
TO ELAT

"Whoa, that was close," Adbeel said as he took his place back at the wheel. His father slowly hobbled up the companionway, nodded to him and looked back at the remains of the patrol boat, which was drifting on the swells and still miraculously afloat.

The machine gun lay in shambles on the forward section of the deck. Its cabin was in wreckage and a man clung to the remains of the craft, staring at the aft section as it sank below the waves.

Hasid climbed to the top of what remained of the cabin, finally standing and staring at Scott in the other boat a hundred yards off. He swayed back and forth from the shock of the attack, but lifted his rifle and started shooting again.

Scott and his companions scattered down the stairs and dove below the cockpit combing. "Why doesn't he give it up? Can't we call for more air support?" Samuel asked.

"We didn't call for it in the first place, as I recall," Scott said, then turned to Taylor. "Have any ammo left?"

"A couple of rounds in the model 70, but I can't seem to hit anything with these waves tossing the boat around. Slow the boat a moment, Adbeel. Let me see if I can get a shot off."

"That boat is going to sink in a moment anyway. It probably does not matter. But keep your head down," Mishma added.

Adbeel pulled the throttles back to an idle while Taylor crept to the rear railing. Taking careful aim, he slowly squeezed the trigger. The model 70 barked in his grip and Hasid lurched. "Don't know if I hit him or scared him," Taylor said.

Taylor tried again but thought he shot low. What was left of the patrol boat started spinning on the swells and settling deeper into the waves. "Maybe I hit something this time."

Samuel tossed the empty Uzi on the deck as Taylor fired his last round at the patrol boat.

The remains of the patrol boat spun around again on the swells and Hasid lifted his rifle and fired off two more quick shots. Taylor lurched as one of the shots hit him high in the shoulder. The force of the round spun him around and dropped him to the deck. Julia screamed when she saw blood appear on Samuel's leg as he staggered back from the force of the second high-velocity round.

Scott rushed over to Samuel. "Are you okay?" he asked as he bent down and looked at his leg.

"It's just a scratch. Check on Taylor. I'll be fine," Samuel said as he held his hand around the wound that thankfully went through the muscle on the side of his thigh.

Scott slid across the cockpit to where Julia was bent over Taylor. She turned to him and said, "I think he's going to be okay. It didn't hit any bones."

Taylor nodded. "Take care of that guy, we'll be okay."

Scott walked over to where Adbeel stood by the wheel. "Steer over by him. We have to end this."

His words weren't necessary as the patrol boat finally succumbed and sank below the waves. Hasid popped up and struggled, but quickly weakened in the heavy swells.

Taking in the situation at a glance Scott, stood on the rail and looked down as Hasid slipped beneath the waves.

"He can't swim!" Scott said.

Hasid came to the surface, his arms flailing and a weak shout escaped his lips.

Scott shook his head and thought, *I just ought to let him drown.* But another, stronger thought hit him and he gathered his courage and leapt from the rail with his arms stretched above his head. Arching over, he held his legs straight and broke the surface cleanly, going so deep he felt the pressure on his lungs.

Turning and looking he saw no sign of Hasid then struck hard toward the surface. He came out chest high and expelled the breath he'd been holding, then scanned the area for Hasid.

Mishma's boat had drifted past and he could see where the missile hit the craft in the bow, blowing a hole in the craft at the water level. Adbeel steered slowly around to where Scott tread water.

Looking back along the wake he could see no sign of Hasid but struck out in a crawl to where he thought the patrol boat had gone under. Stroking with all his strength, the water churned behind him. The salt stung his scrapes as he powered ahead. Judging what he thought was the spot, he paused and tread water, taking in deep draughts of air to feed his tired muscles.

Why, oh God am I doing this? The thought went unfinished as he flipped over, his feet-pointing straight toward heaven, and dove deeply below the waves. Shafts of light from the sun's rays went deeply into the clear sea, but he could see no sign of Hasid.

Peering through the clear water, he scanned the area then finally, deep in the bluish green depths, striated by the sun's rays, he saw a faint movement far below. His lungs ached from lack of air and he didn't think he could make it, but he turned and dove deeper still. There—below and to the right, he saw Hasid's form spinning weakly in the current like a piece of flotsam or jetsam discarded and thrown overboard. His lungs ached from lack of air but he took one last effort, grabbed Hasid's wrist, and struck toward the surface far above. Kicking with what remained of his strength, his vision darkened as his oxygen-depleted muscles screamed in protest. Hasid's unconscious form slowed him and he almost gave up and let him go, but held on.

You can do it—have courage, he told himself through the screaming of his lungs and muscles. He thought he was going to lose but gave one more kick and his head broke the surface as he inhaled a great draft of air that never tasted so sweet in all his life. Gasping and moaning as he bobbed on the surface, he pulled Hasid's head above the waves. He sighed as Hasid lay limp like some dead thing in his arms. *He's dead, I was too late.*

Grabbing him in a bear hug he squeezed with all his might, his mind going back to the day at the pool. Placing his mouth over Hasid's, he blew, then squeezed again. Suddenly Hasid coughed and a great gout of seawater spewed from his lips as his lungs took in the air. Scott tread water with one hand and held him by the shirt with the other as Hasid took in breath after breath.

"Why did you save me?" Hasid gasped.

"That's the second time I've saved you. I don't know why."

"I wouldn't have saved you."

"That's the difference between you and me," he said as Adbeel pulled the craft alongside.

Pulling Scott and Hasid to the deck, Samuel threw a towel around Scott then hobbled over and stood over Hasid.

Julia rushed up, threw her arms around Scott and stared at Hasid, clenching her teeth.

Hasid sat rigidly on the deck and shook the water off his head, then glared at Julia and Scott. "I don't know why you saved me. I was ordered to kill both of you."

"Would you have really done it?" Julia asked.

"I was the one on the machine gun. I had my orders. It's bothered me ever since this whole thing began—but, yes, I think I would have to save the faith."

"You talk of your faith but it has become twisted in you ever since your father's death. We were good friends once and I thought I knew you. Your faith was quiet and full of love at one time. But now what has it become?" Scott said.

"Yes. When we were friends in Paris, your faith was something you were proud of, something that your mother taught you—a thing filled with care and compassion for others. What have you become, Hasid?"

A look of anguish crossed his face as he took in the words of the only two people who were ever his friends. *Friends,* he thought. *They're right, I don't have any. Everyone is a comrade and Quati is nothing but a tyrant.* "This is bigger than friendship. This has to do with the future of Islam. The tribes need this to bring their faith together. Our friendship means nothing now. What did you find? I must know before I die."

"Who said anything about dying," Scott said.

"I would not let you live if I were in your place."

Letting out a sigh, Scott said, "We found Mohammad's final revelation. It's not what you think—it's something for the scholars to study. It will not help you in your war of terror. It is about peace, love, and light. The wind blows and you don't know where it comes from or where it is going, so it is with everyone born of the spirit. I pray, dear Lord, for this spirit to accompany me."

"What are you talking about?" Hasid asked.

"Something I've been putting off for too long."

A smile lit Julia's face as she heard the words, and tears coursed down her cheeks. "Yes, may the wind blow in my heart also. I give myself freely to you, oh God. Yes, freely given, so that you may guide me in all your wisdom."

Samuel sat up. "To think you finally made the choice. I've been waiting to hear you say it. And it's about time, too!"

"Who are you to talk, Samuel? Since when did you ever make a choice?"

"I made the choice years ago. I just don't advertise it. I kind of keep it quiet and to myself."

"What are all of you talking about?" Hasid asked.

"The choice—the one and only important choice," Scott said.

"What choice?"

"The choice everyone is given, to choose light or dark."

"I still don't understand. What do you mean?" Hasid said.

"Allah did send his son. I have just been too blind to see it, but it's true. The choice is to believe in him or not. That's what this is all about."

"This is about the lost writings."

"No! It's about each of us making a choice. Do we choose to walk in the light or dark—I choose the light."

"But what about the writings?"

"They are safe and will stay that way, until the right time comes to disclose them."

"What do you mean they're safe? Don't you have them?"

"No, I left them somewhere to keep them safe."

"Fool—Quati will not rest and will flay your hide to find out where you hid them."

"Perhaps, but they will still remain safe, for I don't really know where they are now. That was another choice I had to make."

"I hate to interrupt, but we have another choice to make," Adbeel said. "We're sinking."

Mishma came up, his arm in a sling, dragging a large sheet of canvas. "We have to get this tarp over the bow to slow the water. If we cannot slow it, the pump will not be able to keep up."

"Tell us what to do," Scott said, jumping to his feet.

"Someone has to go over the side and tie the canvas over the hole in the bow. The water pressure should hold it on. But it needs to be tied on so it stays in place once we start moving again."

Scott grabbed the canvas and went to the front of the craft, followed by Hasid and Julia. Scott quickly cut lengths of rope and tied them to the eyelets in the canvas tarp.

"I'll go in the water and put it over the hole in the bow. Hold it here and tie it when I throw you the ropes, Hasid."

Hasid nodded as Scott jumped off the rail.

The tarp was difficult to get into position and flapped around in the current as he struggled with it. He was finally able to plaster part of it over the hole in the bow, but his foot became tangled in the ropes. The water pressure held the tarp over the hole but he could not free himself to tie the rope. Struggling to the surface, he cried out, "My foot's tangled in the rope."

Wasting no time, Hasid tied a rope to the rail and slid over, using one hand to hold onto the rope. Reaching Scott, he dove under but couldn't free Scott's foot using one hand. He grabbed the loose end of one of the ropes and tossed it on deck to Adbeel, who quickly pulled it under the bow to the other side and tied it off to the rail.

Diving under again, he struggled with the rope holding Scott's ankle. He let go of the rope he was holding and started to drift away but Scott pulled him back. "You can't swim, what are you doing?"

Shaking off Scott's grip, he took a lungful of air and went down again. This time he could free the rope that tangled Scott's foot and pulled it loose.

Adbeel ran the rope through the anchor windlass and tied it off as well. Scott swam back and pulled on the aft rope then dove under the boat while Hasid pressed in on the canvass patch with his feet while holding onto the coping. The rope twisted and curved catching him in the back. Scott tugged on it from the opposite side and tossed the end to Adbeel who pulled up on it.

"Everyone set?" Adbeel yelled.

Scott said, "Okay on this side."

"Set over here," Hasid said. The rope pressed him against the canvas tarp and into the hole the missile had made. The addition of his mass stopped the water.

Mishma called up from below. "Water's stopped coming in. I think we have it."

Adbeel tied the rope off tight then ran back and started the engine.

Julia looked over and helped Scott to the deck, then ran over to help Hasid.

The craft surged ahead as Adbeel advanced the throttles. The bow wave went over Hasid's head. His body's mass keeping the canvass centered over the hole.

Julia cried out, "Hasid's stuck. The rope's around his back!"

She almost fell overboard as Adbeel stopped the craft.

Scott dove off the bow and cut the rope holding Hasid.

"Why are you doing this?" Hasid said.

"I'm not going to let you die that way."

"It's finished—I have no reason to live."

"That's between you and Allah, but I'm not going to let you do it that way."

"You saved me twice now. It was my turn to save you."

"You don't have to do it that way," Scott said as they climbed back on the deck.

He then tied off the tarp and Adbeel advanced the throttles again.

Mishma stuck his head up thru the hatch and said to Adbeel. "Leaks a little, ut I think she'll make it. Take it easy though."

Sitting on the deck as they made their way north, Scott didn't notice Hasid reach behind him until it was too late. He pulled a razor-sharp knife out of his belt and threw his arm around Julia's throat. "If you don't tell me where the writings are, I'll slit her throat."

"I told you I don't know where they are now. Why are you doing this?"

"Ever since my father died I have to fight back—I have to fight to kill the pain."

"Forgiveness is a better way to kill the pain. It brings more relief. I know I had to forgive myself."

"You have no idea of pain."

"Yes, I do. I had to forgive myself for all my mistakes. I had to choose and the shroud has lifted that kept me blind. You don't have to do this, you can make the right choice."

"No—there is no choice but to keep up the fight. Where did you put the sacred writings?"

Scott felt the package Julia had tossed him earlier and a plan came to mind. He needed time to think if he was going to save Julia.

"Search the boat if you want. You won't find them here."

A wild look came to Hasid's eyes as he saw Scott's hand on the package. "What's in the package? Open it up."

Scott reached down, grabbed the package and slowly opened it.

Hasid held Julia roughly at his side and peered forward to get a better look when Scott jumped to his feet, bringing out one of the old percussion pistols. He pointed at Hasid and pulled the trigger.

Nothing happened. Scott forgot to pull the hammer all the way back and left it on half cock. Hasid watched as Scott held out the pistol. His rage was such that he pushed Julia away and charged Scott, slamming him backwards and knocking the pistol from his hands, which went sliding across the cockpit floor.

Hasid pulled back his arm and hammered Scott in the face with a right jab.

The blow stunned him. He saw lights and thought he was going to lose.

Hasid then lifted Scott and threw him against the cockpit seat, wrenching it off its mounting and splitting the woodwork.

Scott shook his head and felt his back as he slowly got up. Hassid stood on the balls of his feet and delivered a sharp punch to Scott's stomach.

A gust of wind blew out of Scott's lungs and his legs went to jelly as he fell back to the rear of the cockpit.

Hasid smiled and pulled back his arm to hammer Scott once again. He never had the chance as he was lifted off his feet and thrown against the cabin bulkhead with such force that it broke from the impact.

Samuel stood there with his knees bent and his arms out. He held his palms up as if begging Hasid to try and hurt his friend some more. He just stood there and grinned.

Hasid slowly shook off the blow, reached down and grabbed the knife where it had fallen on the cockpit floor. Samuel eyed the blade but watched

Hasid's eyes as he slowly advanced. Quick as lightning Hasid lunged, cutting Samuel across his right arm.

Samuel didn't even flinch but spun on the balls of his feet and threw a kick that smashed Hasid back into the bulkhead. He tried to follow with a jab but Hasid was too quick.

Hasid dodged to the back of the cockpit grabbed Scott's head by his hair and laid the knife across his throat. "Where is the material you found in the cave? Give it to me and I'll let him live."

Scott held up his hand. "Don't give him anything. He's in league with the devil and doesn't even know it."

"I'll cut him and cut him deep. You say I'm in league with the evil one. All of you are helping the evil one with his plan to usurp the prophet. You're trying to bring writings to light that an infidel has no idea how to interpret. You will distort the prophet's holy truth. The one true faith requires our protection and only by our protection is it kept safe. Enough of this talk, where have you hidden them?"

"Don't give him anything, Samuel, no matter what he does."

"I don't need him nor any of you," Hasid said as he reared back to slash Scott across the throat.

A cloud of blue white smoke blew across the rear of the craft and a deafening explosion stunned their ears as hole appeared in Hasid's chest. He dropped the knife and looked down at his chest in disbelief. As he teetered on the edge of the boat he saw Julia standing with one of Scott's old pistols, its muzzle still smoking, and he fell off and the water closed over him.

Julia looked at the group. "That's about enough of that. Let's see if we can get this boat someplace a little safer and drier," she said as she stuffed the pistol in her belt.

"Farrell, you blew it and all your little schemes came to naught," Frank Henderson said as they sat in the restaurant. "I had faith in you and trusted those two men you sent. You called them Christians. What have we become, I wonder."

"Oh, shut up, Frank," Bestin said. "We've all got problems because of this. We tried the best we could and have to make the best of it now. Let's see what kind of damage control we can do."

Farrell interjected, "I expected more out of your men, too, Bestin. Only two of them back alive and one of them has to spend time in an Ethiopian prison. Not a well thought out plan if you ask me. What about sending a small expedition back to look in the cave where Hasid said that Chad found the scroll."

"I agree with Bestin. Let's find a way to do some damage control and get on with things. Maybe, just maybe, we should see what the scroll has to say. Find some way to come to grip with the changes it may bring," Henderson said.

"Are you nuts, Henderson? How are we to agree with something that Mohammad wrote. Don't you believe that the devil himself gave him his revelation?"

"Oh, Farrell, get off your high horse for a moment, would you. I don't know what to believe, but I know that God is bigger than all of us and he proved it this time. We're just too stupid to see it, so get off it," Henderson said.

"Henderson, you're a sap is what you are." Farrell spat out.

The Bishop looked at Farrell's face and for some reason a softening of his heart came over him. "I think I'll help him plan that wedding," Bestin said.

"Both of you now, is it. Well, I'm going to have to find some new believers in the cause because you're not part of it any more. You've proved that today. I'll go blow that wall and we'll find out what's really inside that place. Just you wait and see," he said to the two departing backs.

News Flash CNN:

Undisclosed sources reported an air strike in the Gulf of Aquaba today. Sources indicate that two Israeli jets shot down three Migs belonging to General Quati's air force at an undisclosed location near the Gulf of Aquaba. Reports indicated that Quati's air force was strafing an unarmed fishing boat in Israeli waters. The Israelis have not commented about the incident nor has General Quati's staff.

Other sources reported that portions of a severely damaged Sudanese patrol boat were found adrift near the same area. It was not readily apparent if the two incidents were related. Calls and requests for information to General Al-Bashir in the Sudan have gone unanswered.

❄ ❄ ❄ ❄ ❄ ❄ ❄ ❄

The boat was running on fumes and they had poured the last can into the tanks to feed the big diesels. Adbeel kept the boat under eight knots in order to conserve fuel, but the big diesels still drank it at a prodigious rate. They had to run at high speed when fleeing the patrol boat and Adbeel was worried they might not make it to Elat. His father was doing much better after Taylor and Julia had worked on him, but he still needed a doctor and possibly a hospital.

Adbeel was at the helm when Taylor cried out, "Land ho. Elat up ahead. We made it."

The customs officer impounded the boat when they docked. Taylor's guns were still on board and it would have been ironic to be thrown in jail after what they had been through. They did allow Scott and Julia ashore, where she made a quick phone call. Thirty minutes later a man showed up in a large limousine and spoke with the customs officer, who immediately cleared the boat and all the passengers without another look. The large Mercedes limousine pulled up to the dock and Julia helped Mishma down the gangway and out to the waiting car. When she walked up, the man tipped his hat to her and said, "Well done, Miss Apostoli, well done indeed."

"Mr. Rabin, how nice of you to show up and offer to help us. I'd like to introduce my companions, Scott Chad and Samuel Rogowski. They have been working with me for the last few months."

"Mr. Chad, you have no idea how much we appreciate your honesty and willingness to finish this task you set yourself on."

Scott looked quizzically at him and extended his hand. "How much do you know about what we've been doing?"

"Don't worry, your affairs are your own. We know you found out that Julia was working for us and I'm sorry. She's an excellent botanist and biologist. I hope she's done and excellent job for you." He paused and looked at her. "Even though she hasn't followed orders or reported in for some time."

Samuel stood there in his quiet stoic way without saying anything.

"And you, Samuel, you're to be commended, too, for none of this would have been possible without your devotion to Mr. Chad and willingness to sacrifice all for the benefit of the truth and your own beliefs. You've passed the test with honors."

"What test are you talking about, Mr. Rabin?"

"Why, the test of faith of course. The whole thing has been a test of all our faith. From beginning to end. Even a test of faith for a man like Quati. His faith was only in himself and preserving what he had. The man did not trust Allah, only his own power."

"Parables again," Samuel said shaking his head. "Can't anyone ever speak plainly."

Rabin laughed, "Only when we're talking to ourselves, I fear, or maybe to our spouses. We tend to weary with long explanations. Come now, we've booked you a room in the King David in Jerusalem. You must all be tired and we've a doctor waiting to take care of your friend."

They piled in the car which whisked them north to Jerusalem. They were put up in adjoining suites when they got to the King David Hotel. Samuel relaxed and took a long hot bath and then took a nap, of course.

Scott went to talk with Julia and knocked on her door, but there was no answer. He walked downstairs and waited in the lobby. An hour later she came walking in and he could tell she was upset.

"What's wrong, Julia? You look like you've had a rough time of it. Was it that Rabin guy? What did he say to you?"

"No, it wasn't Rabin. It was the old man. Benjamin's his name only that won't help, for he's invisible. He's a monster that Benjamin. I quit, I tell you—I quit, and he threatened me."

"You quit, why?"

"Because I don't believe in what they do anymore and I don't trust the old man."

"I thought they sent you out to protect me."

"They did, it's not that. He wants me to keep working for him and go on another assignment right away. No rest for the weary and I was thinking . . . oh, I don't know what I was thinking," she said as she looked at him with her tear-streaked eyes.

"I'm glad you quit, Julia. For we're a team now. I could not go anywhere without your support. You're on the team, for now and forever."

She perked up at his words. "What do you mean, for now and forever?"

Scott looked at her. "I mean you're on the payroll. You've been from the start, and you have the job permanently if you want it. You pass the test."

"I don't know if I want it now! I think I've had about enough of your ego, too, enough to last for a long . . . long, very long time," she said and started to walk away.

He walked across the polished marble floor of the lobby and grabbed her elbow. "Oh, Julia, I'm only teasing. What I meant by forever . . ." he dropped to his knee and took the box out of his pocket.

❋   ❋   ❋   ❋   ❋   ❋   ❋   ❋

Scott and his companions stood at the dais in the hotel conference room in front of the assembled reporters. The room was packed and religious leaders, ambassadors, and reporters filled the room. Scott walked up to the podium. "Dear assembled guests. We have recently completed work in the Sinai area which promises untold new wealth to Egypt. This mineral wealth will help her people enter the next century with hope and promise for her children. Of more import, our work took us to new horizons both physically and spiritually.

I wish to let Ms. Apostoli tell you of these things. Her parents were Jewish refugees and being brought up in Israel by her aunt and uncle gives her a special insight into our recent incursion into Ethiopia. Or should I say the fabled land of Cush. Her faith and commitment to helping us achieve our ends is what made our quest a success. It is my pleasure to give her the honor of explaining our recent finds. Ms. Apostoli, would you please explain to our guests what we found?" Scott bowed to Julia, who stood there in shock.

She was wearing a long brown dress for the occasion, but the red in her face was plain for all to see. She stepped forward and grabbed the edges of the podium. "Thank you, Mr. Chad. Dear assembled guests, the people of Israel have longed for peace for thousands of years. We have recently uncovered something new. It is as old as the story of Adam and Eve or Abraham, Isaac and Ishmael. But it's really the Lord's plan to see all his creation united in love. . . ."

The room went into an uproar after she finished. Scott strode up to help her field the thousand questions that were shouted out. A smile came to his face as Father Basil raised his hand from a back row.

"But where are they," Julia asked. "When did you ever have time to hide them?"

"Remember the eucalyptus trees? A friend is keeping them safe."

A look of comprehension dawned on her. "I get ten guesses and the first nine don't count."

"You've got it, but you only get three guesses."

News Flash CNN:

Scott Chad, mineralogical surveyor, geologist and explorer who has completed numerous projects and provided invaluable development information for Saudi Arabia, Egypt and many Caribbean nations, held a press conference in Jerusalem about his recent survey of the Sinai Peninsula. Attending the conference with him was Mr. Samuel Rogowski, engineer and Ms. Julia Apostoli, botanist for his expedition, and his two interns.

Of import, Mr. Chad turned the press conference over to Ms. Apostoli, a Jewish national. The conference was attended not only by scientists but by a number of the world's religious leaders, including representatives from the Roman Catholic Church; Greek Orthodox Church, who sent a representative from the Patriarch of Constantinople; Ethiopian Orthodox Church; Church of England; Southern Baptist Convention; Episcopal Church in America; Assembly of God; and head clerics and Ayatollahs from Iran, Afghanistan and Saudi Arabia. Also attending were leaders from the Evangelical Association of non-denominational reformed churches, magazine publishers, *Time* Magazine, and others.

To those who will believe!

.

Postscript

The story grew in the telling from the original story that told the tale about the ancient search for the lost manuscripts of Isaiah and the Prophet Mohammad, but became so much more throughout the long years. The author takes full responsibility for all its faults and the way it took on a life of its own.

For such readers who would like delve deeper and desire further information should look to the Holy Bible and Koran. Further information and studies may be found in the Gilgamesh Epic and some of the phantasmagorical studies of the ancient religions of the near east, particularly some of the religious practices of the Canninite tribes that inhabited the region of Palestine and Israel may be of interest to them.

The author lives in the Midwest with his wife and three sons. He has worked as a land surveyor and engineer and traveled extensively in Greece and other areas of the world. A deep love of the written word and good story well told are his passion.

Contact T.S. Ferguson
or order more copies of this book at

TATE PUBLISHING, LLC

127 East Trade Center Terrace
Mustang, Oklahoma 73064

(888) 361 - 9473

Tate Publishing, LLC

www.tatepublishing.com